MW00646972

Glory Boys

Alaric Bond

Glory Boys
Copyright © 2023 by Alaric Bond
Published by Old Salt Press LLC

Paperback: ISBN: 978-1-943404-45-2
E.book: ISBN: 978-1-943404-46-9

The cover artwork shows a detail from *In and Out* by Jim Rae. *"Two MTBs inbound and three Minesweeping Trawlers outbound."* Jim Rae served in both the Merchant and Royal Navy. Further examples of his work can be seen at Fidra Fine Art: www.fidrafineart.co.uk

Publisher's Note: This is a work of historical fiction. Certain characters and their actions may have been inspired by historical individuals and events. The characters in the novel, however, represent the work of the author's imagination. Any resemblance to actual persons, living or dead, is entirely coincidental. Published by Old Salt Press. Old Salt Press, LLC is based in Jersey City, New Jersey with an affiliate in New Zealand. For more information about Old Salt Press titles go to www.oldsaltpress.com

Thanks are due to Fred, Joan, Antoine, George, Tony, and Rick for their support, Tessa for copy editing and Kitty for keeping me sane. Also, Bernard at the Military Wireless Museum. (www.qsl.net/g4bxd)

For Bob and Regan

Other novels by Alaric Bond

The Fighting Sail series

His Majesty's Ship

The Jackass Frigate

True Colours

Cut and Run

The Patriot's Fate

The Torrid Zone

The Scent of Corruption

HMS Prometheus

The Blackstrap Station

Honour Bound

Sealed Orders

Sea Trials

Lone Escort

The Seeds of War

On the Barbary Coast

and

Turn a Blind Eye

The Guinea Boat

The Coastal Forces series

Hellfire Corner

Contents

Glory Boys

Chapter One

"I'm afraid your appointment as Flotilla Senior Officer has not been confirmed."

Harris blinked once but said nothing as the base captain's words had yet to fully register.

"In fact, your flotilla's being disbanded." Brooks was sorting papers on his desk and giving much of his attention to them. It was a cold January morning and the windows of the office dripped with condensation, despite the efforts of a two-bar electric fire. "It was never official, and you know as well as I do eight boats are needed to make a serviceable unit; you've been running below that for much of the time."

Harris finally stirred himself into action. "We're not the only ones, sir," he said. "There's been talk about new boats in the offing, but few have materialised."

"Indeed, so redeploying your lot elsewhere makes sense." Finally Brooks looked up and did appear slightly awkward. "And you must admit, Bob, several of your COs have been active for much of the war; they're due a break. We're sending them up to *St Christopher*'s to pass on what they've learned."

"Training?" Harris shook his head. "I suppose you mean the older ones: Barton and Shaw. The schoolroom's not the place for them, they're active officers!"

"And have been for too long." Now there was a slight edge to Brooks' tone.

"But those that remain, can they stay with me?" Until then Harris had not fully appreciated how much the young men he commanded truly meant. All were volunteers, of course, and inclined to bend what rules they didn't break, but of late they'd been working as a team. "Within a different flotilla, I mean?"

"I'm afraid not. No senior officer would appreciate what would be seen as a separate unit working within his command. Chapman and Collins will be detailed to other flotillas based here at *Wasp*, while Potter's moving to *Beehive*. When *194* comes back from the yard she'll be transferred to Johnston's lot."

"Johnston!"

"Believe me, Bob, it's for the best."

"But his flotilla's younger than mine, as are most of its commanding officers!"

"In which case they'll be a darn sight fresher so less in need of a rest. Besides, Johnston was senior officer in a previous flotilla – and both positions were confirmed."

"And what about *194*?" Harris was fighting to keep the frustration from his voice. "Is she still my boat?"

The base captain gave a brief smile. "Yes, Bob, she's still your boat, and this is in no way a demotion. You did well as a temporary SO and will probably be appointed again. And there *are* new boats – better boats – coming; as soon as a new flotilla can be formed, I'll do my best to see you lead it. Think of this as a chance to take a step back – a breather, if you like."

"I've just had two weeks' leave." Harris' expression was now quite fixed.

"After a pretty severe bump on the head as I recall."

"Which has healed perfectly."

"I'm glad to hear it." Brooks sighed. "Look, I don't want to argue with you, Bob. To tell the truth, we're hellishly busy; 1942 has all the makings of our hardest year yet, and it's only just started. I have to make the best use I can of the men and materiel at my disposal."

A row was also the last thing Harris wanted. He tried a different tack. "I can see changes may be needed, sir, but why put me under Johnston? Damn it, we're the same rank!"

"I'm aware of that, Bob, though he was promoted before you."

Harris shook his head. "Only by a few months!"

"Maybe, but they matter, though I accept it makes things a little awkward. My guess is you'll end up his deputy and might lead the flotilla on some ops."

"But Johnston's a wavy type, a reservist." Harris had nothing against RNVR officers, but any weapon that might strengthen his argument was worth considering. "As are all his COs; he speaks their language." He sighed. "Maybe that's where I went wrong?"

Now Brooks leant forward in his chair. "I wouldn't say you went wrong, Bob. Your flotilla was one of the most successful on the base. But you have to admit, the RNVR has produced some excellent officers."

Harris scratched at his head. It was his first day back at HMS *Wasp*, the Coastal Forces base that had been his home for several months, and this was not the interview he expected. "Oh, the wavy boys are fine – most of them," he said, "Though Johnston's different, and not someone I care to serve under."

"A little gauche, perhaps," Brooks allowed. "A barrister before the war, I gather."

"That figures," Harris grunted. "He certainly has the manner though that hardly qualifies him to command a gunboat, let alone lead an entire flotilla."

"Bob you're starting to sound like a regular salt horse. And it's an attitude that has to change."

"Maybe so but come on; we're both straight stripers." He tried to catch Brooks' eye. "You know the score. While Johnston was defending drunks or filing divorce papers, you and I were training to be professional Naval officers; that must make a difference."

"Not as much as you think. We might have prepared for war but, when one came along, a Navy full of career officers could hardly manage on its own; volunteers have been essential for some while. And don't assume because a man's experience is elsewhere, he knows nothing about leadership."

Brooks was quite correct. Harris knew that, just as he knew he was speaking out of turn. Normally it would never have done to bring up the age-old rivalry between the regular Navy and the Royal Naval Volunteer Reserve, especially when there were many reservists he actively admired.

"You only have to look at your own number one." Brooks had obviously been reading his mind. "A year or so ago Anderson was nothing but a geography teacher, yet now he's one of the best first lieutenants on the base."

Brooks was right there as well, although, after the dullest Christmas leave ever, Harris had been looking forward to knocking his flotilla into shape. Instead, he must go back to being a regular gunboat captain and serving under a man he did not respect.

"*194*'s due back any time, or so I understand." Now Brooks was obviously keen to move on; as base captain, this must be one of several interviews on his list that morning, each one affecting men's lives – and careers – just as much. Yet Harris was not in the habit of giving up without a fight.

"I'm sorry, sir, but I still don't understand why this is happening; was it to do with that last operation?"

Brooks shook his head. "Not at all, Bob, that was deemed a success. We didn't get the German cruiser, though that was a lot to ask. But our torpedo boys accounted for a destroyer which would have been impossible without the very able support of your flotilla."

Harris' shoulders dropped. "Still, if we'd sunk the *Seydlitz*, or even hit her..."

Now the base captain's face broke into a smile. "You'd probably have gained a full stripe," he agreed. "And I know it might not seem fair, but few things are right now. Take my advice, Bob, stick it out."

"I don't see I have any choice."

"Perhaps not," Brooks agreed, "though if something else comes along, you'll be the first I call."

Harris perked up. "I'd appreciate that, sir."

"Fine, get *194* back to Dover, settle the new members of her crew in, and bring her up to scratch. Then we'll see what can be done..."

* * *

The house that sheltered them over Christmas had been unoccupied since the previous summer and the scent of damp and drains was very evident. There was a naked bulb hanging in the living room that flickered and numerous draughts the archaic wood stove could not hope to counter. Much of the wallpaper was mouldy or peeling and they never got used to the constant patter of mice running about the loft. Yet now, as they prepared to leave,

Anderson realised just how perfect it had been.

"Have you cleaned out the fire?" Eve was in the kitchen but, even with the door closed, he could hear her perfectly.

"Doing it now."

Anderson bent down and worked the flue, bringing up a small cloud of soot that made him cough. The thing always produced more ash than heat and he had never been able to light it without filling the room with smoke. But as he brushed out the remaining embers and removed two partly consumed logs, his sorrow only grew.

The door creaked and he looked up as Eve entered.

"I dare say we can borrow this place again, or one like it," she said. "Most of the street's empty. I reckon the landlord was glad to see it used."

"He may even let us have it for nothing," Anderson agreed. "Unless we can find something better..."

She smiled. "It's been fine, really."

"More than fine." He stood up and held her lightly. "You're still set on walking to the station on your own?"

"Oh yes; I hate long goodbyes, especially public ones." She touched his bruised nose lightly. As war wounds went, the injury was hardly significant, though both knew it might have been so much worse. "I really think it's healing, Ian."

He smiled. "About time too; I must look a sight. Sorry if it spoiled your enjoyment."

"Not a bit."

For a moment they were together then Eve drew away and made for the kitchen once more while he returned to the fire. Her Y Section training was due to be stepped up in the New Year so they probably wouldn't meet again until the next long leave. Which might not be for some while; it could even be judged fortunate that *194* was damaged so close to Christmas. The thirteen days together had been wonderful and, despite being no more than a mile from Dover, sometimes they forgot there was even a war.

But the evenings were already growing lighter, and the recent terrible weather could not last for ever. In no time *194* must resume her nighttime patrols and Anderson would take up his old post as second in command of a gunboat; one that regularly pitched her frail hull and inadequate armament against the might of Hitler's Kriegsmarine.

The previous autumn was busy enough and had accounted for his last boat as well as several decent men; there was no telling what the coming months would bring, and the thought of returning to the Channel's dark waters made him shiver slightly.

"Ian, are you alright?"

Anderson hadn't heard her return and felt guilty at being caught so.

"Fine, just a bit cold," he said, standing quickly and brushing the dust from his arms; the last thing he wanted was to introduce Eve to his private demons.

"When do you expect the boat to be ready?"

"By the end of the week, or so they say; she was badly beaten up and we've had Christmas..."

"So, you won't be back on patrol again for a few days?"

"Or even longer, a lot depends on the weather."

"Shame I have to go back now, we could have spent the rest of the day together and maybe met up one evening. But you know how it is..." She collected her bag and, after checking the contents, buckled it up.

"Of course, and you should qualify before long."

"February, if all goes according to plan." Now the bag was on her shoulder; soon she would be gone and suddenly Anderson felt foolishly keen to delay her.

"You've no idea where your first posting will be?"

"None, but the South Coast's most likely." She smiled. "With a bit of luck, I'll get Abbots Cliff and be able to hear what you lot really get up to!"

That was another thought entirely, and one they had discussed on several occasions. Eve was keen on the idea although Anderson remained unsure if having her at the nearby Y Station would be such a good move. Her job would be to monitor enemy communications, although she could listen in to British boats as well as German, and there were aspects of his work he would rather keep to himself. However, Anderson was also a realist and knew any such doubts must be treated like his personal fears and remain secret. And there was some consolation in these being the only things he kept from her.

"Right, I'd better be off," she said. "Send Billy my love."

Eve's brother, Bill Newman, was a mechanic aboard Anderson's boat. "That might not be easy," he said, and they both

6

laughed, before drawing close once more. Yet this was not the time for a lengthy embrace, to delay would make a mockery of the intimacy they had enjoyed, and within a minute she was gone.

Anderson considered the closed door for a moment, then turned back to the room. There was a pile of scrap wood next to the stove that might prove useful to the next resident, or he could light another fire and settle with one of the many books that had lain untouched since before Christmas. He was not due at the base until later; there were still several hours of relative peace and, though now alone, he wanted to savour every moment of it.

All too soon they would be back at sea and meeting the enemy in a particularly brutal form of combat. During his brief time in Coastal Forces, Anderson had seen and survived much and counted himself blessed in coming out with little more than a bruised nose. But some of his shipmates had not been so fortunate and he couldn't help wondering exactly how long his own luck would last.

* * *

Murder had not been on Reg Gibson's mind; carrying a gun was one thing, using it a completely different matter. But when the time came – when that darned postmaster resisted and, rather than simply unlocking the cash drawer, began to shout – he hadn't hesitated.

And the crack of a single shot did make things easier. One of the weekday shoppers that made up his audience even followed the old man's example and crumbled to the floor. No one tried to intervene, though, leaving him free to slip outside and into a world so profoundly normal it seemed remarkable.

But once there, and sheltered by the damp street's anonymity, things became more complicated. The sudden act of violence had hardly affected him; Gibson was highly trained; the light calibre pistol now sitting warm in his pocket was no more than a toy when compared with what the government paid him to use. And killing was no novelty; in the course of his work he must have accounted for a dozen lives – maybe more; even at close quarters it could be difficult to tell. There had been no doubt with the postmaster, however, and the look on the old boy's face stayed with him until a more important matter pushed it to one side.

7

Gibson spent the previous evening in a seedy club where the prices hardly matched the entertainment and was relying on a reasonable haul from the Post Office to pay for his digs. The bill waiting at Sunny Meadows would not be high, but there was little in his pockets other than small change. It would hardly be the first time a sailor left a landlady wanting, yet the loose end concerned Gibson far more than any regret about ending another's life.

His mind ran on while he did his best to merge with the other pedestrians. There was a main line station close by, and the Dover train was due at four. He still had the travel warrant and would be able to draw two weeks' pay on arriving at *Wasp*, his new base. With luck he would be there, back in funds, and safely installed behind an armed picket by the time the local rozzers woke up. And this was wartime; civilians were dying every day, no one would worry for long over one less postmaster.

And then he remembered his luggage. An old brown overcoat currently covered his number two uniform; only the most observant would put him down for the Navy. And he was reasonably non-descript in himself; Gibson's hair had been closely cropped throughout a lifetime spent in orphanages and reformatories, yet in a world where service cuts had become the norm, it hardly stood out. And neither did his partially broken nose – a souvenir of his short time in gaol. But the duffel bag left in the small back room contained far more than a spare set of togs and his razor; there was enough to identify him for sure and even the wartime police were not that stupid.

So, what was he to do? The landlady was an elderly widow with a son serving aboard a cruiser. Apart from Gibson, there were no other tenants, and she might take pity on him – another sailor. He'd go back and tell her the truth, or at least the bit about having no money, and see if she couldn't be won round. When it came to manipulating women, Gibson was a master, and an old bird shouldn't be any different. Once he drew his pay he could post a ten bob note on. And he would do so – Gibson was not without scruples and privately regarded himself as an honourable man.

Yet he was also no fool; it was possible the landlady might not fall for his soft words, in which case he would take an alternative course. The warm gun was still in his pocket and he may as well be hung for a sheep as a lamb. But one thing Gibson knew for sure, when the Dover train left at four, he would be on it.

Chapter Two

"Harris? Bob Harris?"

He was making for *Wasp*'s officers' mess when Lieutenant Commander Johnston accosted him.

"It *is* Bob, isn't it?"

"If you wish." Harris paused and cautiously accepted the proffered hand. Like the majority of RNVR officers, Johnston had the annoying habit of leaving the top right-hand button of his jacket undone. The effect might appear rakish, but to Harris' ordered mind it made what should have been a smart uniform scruffy.

"Glad we've run into each other, much to discuss." Johnston released his grip and took a fresh hold on Harris' shoulder before steering him towards the nearby bar. "Fancy a snifter?"

"It's a little early, I was going to get some lunch..."

"Then we can eat together, but maybe sink a gin or two beforehand, what? Pink, is it?"

"Scotch." Harris' reply was automatic; he rarely drank during the day and never spirits, but the bonhomie was infectious.

"Scotch it is." Johnston caught the steward's eye, adding, "And a large Gordon's for me with double bitters."

Harris looked about for a table but his new senior officer was more at home at the otherwise empty bar and leant against it with elaborate casualness.

"It's one of the advantages of a Dover posting," he said. "Nine out of ten of the natives have moved out, yet they're still allocating booze as if it were a full population. This must be the only place in Blighty where a man can drink like an American!"

Harris sniffed at the Scotch; it was blended and rougher than his usual malt.

"I say, would you like some soda in that?"

He closed his eyes at the suggestion. "Just a splash of water, thank you."

Johnston passed a china jug across. "So, when's your boat

due back, old boy?"

"They're saying Friday and I should have a full crew by then." Harris added the smallest dash of water then swirled his glass. He had no objection to being called Bob, certainly by close friends, but 'old boy' from a younger man went beyond the pale.

"In that case I expect you'll be ready for working up exercises at the weekend," Johnston continued.

"The weekend might be pushing it a bit – we still have to victual and take on ordnance. Is there anything scheduled?"

"Not yet, but that doesn't bother my lot – you'll find we push things quite a bit." Johnston took a healthy gulp of his drink. "Currently I've seven boats on the active list," he said on coming up for air. "Eight, when *194* joins; I like to see at least three of them out every evening and there are regular daytime drills, whatever the circumstances."

Harris took a more discreet sip at his Scotch. "That's quite a commitment," he said.

"It's why we have such a favourable strike rate; six E's damaged and an R sunk," he added a smug smile. "We don't bother counting anything else."

It was a reasonable record but no more; Harris' previous flotilla had actually done better although this was not the time to say so. From what he knew of Johnston the man was almost pathologically competitive; a hint of escalation on his part was likely to provoke some absurd drinking game.

"I gather you won't be going out tonight?" he said instead.

Johnston, in the process of raising his glass for a second dose, lowered it. "Why should you think that, old boy? No, I'll be there, don't you worry. It's only a small job – watching over a couple of minelayers while they lay a few eggs – but there's another newbie to break in. Know Happy Hopgood, do you?"

Harris shook his head.

"Came down from *St Christopher*'s while you were on leave. Reasonable enough fellow but even the best training base leaves a few rough edges." Johnston smiled. "Best way to smooth them off is a couple of meetings with Jerry. I dare say you'll be a darn sight easier when your time comes."

Harris blinked. "You think I have rough edges?"

Johnston met his look. "I think we have different ways of doing things," he said. "Not that I noticed anything wrong with your former lot, but you have to admit, there was little comradeship."

The statement took Harris by surprise, and he was still thinking of a suitable response as Johnston continued.

"Oh, you got results, there was no doubt about that, but where were your blokes when *194* was hit in the smoke?"

"If you're talking about the *Seydlitz* affair, we were last in line and, as you say, in a smoke screen. As soon as I signalled for assistance it came."

"That's what I mean, old boy; they weren't looking out for you. My lot are like Nelson's band of brothers." He considered this, drink in hand, before continuing. "Look after each other, we do. I dare say you'll find that a pleasant surprise – providing you remain with us, that is."

There was an emphasis in the last statement and Harris could not resist rising to it.

"You mean, I might not be accepted?"

"I mean I hope you are," Johnston corrected. "You're a good bloke, Harris, and a straight striper to boot; career officer – I respect that. But Coastal Forces is not the regular Navy; your lot are welcome, as long as you ditch some of that Dartmouth nonsense. Mixing with E-boats and VPs is hardly conventional warfare; more like a pub brawl and no room for Queensbury rules."

Few statements left Harris speechless, but this was one. Ostensibly he and Johnston were equal in rank – both lieutenant commanders. Only a few months and an appointment as Flotilla Senior Officer made the younger man his superior. But, to Harris' mind, such a difference was more than outweighed by the straight stripes on his own arm. Whatever Brooks might say, a reservist could never fully emulate one with a lifetime's training, yet Johnston was implying temporary officers were more suited to small boat combat and actually better at it. He collected his drink and downed it in one.

"That's the spirit, old boy," Johnston said, noticing this. "Get you another, shall I? Then how's about a spot of luncheon?"

* * *

Jelly made the Dover train with seconds to spare, only to find it comparatively empty. And neither did it seem in any hurry to be off, which was annoying as running through the London streets had left him quite out of breath. His compartment was close to the guard's van, and he sat panting while others clambered aboard a train which, by rights, should already have left. A whistle finally sounded, but doors were still being slammed as they began to pull away, and it was then that a figure on the platform caught his eye.

It was Geoff Pickering, a Geordie and one of his own boat's mechanics; there was no mistaking that gait, nor the burn marks on his face and chin visible even from such a distance. Without thinking further, Jelly leapt from his seat and flung the carriage door wide. The train was barely moving faster than a walking pace and may even have slowed slightly; certainly no one could have missed Pickering's shouts for it to stop, or Jelly's equally loud encouragement to join him. And it was done smoothly enough; first, the mechanic lobbed his duffel bag through the doorway, then jumped after it and, as Jelly grabbed at his shoulder, landed deep in the otherwise empty compartment.

"Nearly missed it," Pickering said, brushing himself down while Jelly slammed the door shut and they finally picked up speed. "Knew I shouldna had that final cup of tea at Lyons'."

"You're lucky, we're late pulling out."

"Train times are so up the chute they've stopped worrying," Pickering panted. "We're due in at Dover at five-and-twenty-past six, but will be lucky to make it afore lights out."

The pair had very different jobs; Pickering spent much of his time in the airless and noisy underworld that was the gunboat's engine room while Jelly's place of work was the W/T office just off the wheelhouse. And Pickering was part of a team of three, whereas Jelly held complete autonomy over his wireless sets. But there were no such things as strangers aboard a gunboat, and never could the term 'shipmates' be better applied.

"So, how was your leave?"

Pickering considered this. "What there was were canny enough," he said at last. "But I spent much of the time in a hospital getting larded up twice a day."

"Burns bad then?"

"They seen worse, an' I did an all while I were there. Some of them fighter pilots get proper roasted..."

"I heard they were bad."

Pickering briefly closed his eyes. "You wouldna believe," he said.

"What did you do after?"

"They gave me the last three days to myself an' I were next to a main line station so spent them in London, though the Lord knows why." The mechanic began to study his nails which, to Jelly's eyes, seemed oddly clean. "With Christmas over, the place were like a morgue, what pubs they had were filled with Yanks. Not a bit like where I'd just come from; no lasses were interested in a singed grease monkey."

"Never was one for the city myself."

"Me neither; ain't got the friendliness of places up north – or East Grinstead come to that."

"But you're okay, the burns I'm meaning?" Pickering was sitting opposite, and Jelly found it hard not to stare at the still-livid scars, while the first sprouts of fresh hair over his shorn head gave the man an almost comical appearance.

"Burns is right enough," Pickering sniffed. "All I wants is to get back to the boat." He looked directly at Jelly. "You don't get no one gawpin' at you in an engine room."

Jelly supposed that must be a consideration and quickly looked away.

"What about you?" Pickering asked. "London an' all, was it?"

"No, I went back to my folks."

"But you're from the smoke, surely?"

"Was. Parents moved away to Shropshire, so I reckon that's my home now, though it don't feel like it."

"Happy to see you, were they?"

"Happy enough, though I couldn't say the same for their new friends. Round their way the war's almost a side show. There's little industry so few raids and they don't even keep a reliable blackout. Most of the locals would rather pretend nothing were going on and a sailor turning up was a bad reminder."

Pickering seemed to understand. "The war means different things to different folk," he said. "You heard anything about the boat?"

Jelly shook his head. "No more than you; she's due to be ready but that don't mean much, not nowadays and what with

Christmas... Chances are we'll find ourselves detailed elsewhere."

"Be a pity." Pickering sighed.

"Telling me. I been with the skipper and his Jimmy for most of the war. Not saying they're perfect, but there're a lot worse."

"An' the rest of the lads ain't that shabby either."

"Them that are left."

"Aye," Pickering agreed more solemnly. "Them that are left."

"You know Price's gone?" Jelly said.

"The old coxswain? I knew he were wounded but didn't think it that bad."

"Bad enough to see him out of the Andrew. And Bishop, the gunner; we won't see him no more either."

"You're joking!"

Jelly shook his head. "Lost his nerve, or so they say. Last heard of he was heading for the funny farm."

"An' we didn't get that cruiser," Pickering mused. "Makes you wonder if it were all worth it..."

"Oh, it were worth it," Jelly said. "I heard a Jerry destroyer was sunk, but even without that, it was something we had to do."

"Suppose so." Pickering shrugged. "Can't have no German sailing down our Channel without doing somethin' about it."

The inner door slid open with a clatter and both men looked up as a further two seamen entered from the corridor.

"Make room for the Navy!"

"Navy's already here." Jelly regarded the pair. One was older and considerably heavier than the other; they might even have been father and son.

"Wey aye, it's Laurel and Hardy!" Pickering said as two more duffel bags were added to the overhead netting.

"You watch your tongue, sunshine," the older pointed threateningly. Then, on noticing Pickering's scars, his tone changed. "Been in the wars, 'ave we?"

"Been in one war," Pickering replied. "But then we're all in that."

"Aye, reckon," the newcomer agreed after removing his hat and taking a seat.

The train rumbled on for several seconds then Jelly spoke.

"From London, are you?"

14

"Stepney," the larger man said, then nodded at his companion seated opposite. "Though Len's a Bethnal Green boy."

"And you're both Coastal Forces?" Jelly had noticed the hat band.

"Aye and bound for *Wasp*. You?"

"Same."

"Active?"

"Oh yes: gunboats."

"Likewise," the older man nodded. "Name's Smith – Fred Smith. Lenny an' me is gun crew; Oerliks: he's me loading number."

"Good to keep a team together," Pickering said.

"Didn't 'ave no choice," Smith sniffed. "We're all that were left of our last boat."

"That right?" Jelly was morbidly impressed.

"E-boat jumped us an' took out our bridge and foredeck."

"Many wounded?"

The older man shrugged. "Pretty much everyone else bought it," he said.

"Even them in the engine room?" Pickering had a special interest.

"One got clear but pegged it later."

"Wounded, was he?"

Smith shook his head. "Ripe as ninepence, but we was nearly a day an' a half in the water, and nothing but a chunk of wood to hang on to."

"Sounds rough," Jelly said.

"It were," Smith agreed. "And cold."

"Were you there an' all, pal?" Pickering was addressing the lad who nodded silently.

"Lenny don't say much." Smith's tone sounded harsh, but might just have been defensive and he added, "Not since then," more softly.

* * *

"Lieutenant Commander Harris?"

After what turned out to be a frustrating day, Harris was eager to make his escape and had been heading for *Wasp*'s main doors when he heard the call. But at least it was a woman's voice,

15

so could not be Johnston. Sure enough, he turned to see a Wren approaching.

"This has just come down from Samuel Brothers, sir." She handed him a folded sheet of buff paper.

"Thank you." He unfolded the message and automatically braced himself. After the way things had been going he was prepared for the worst, but it turned out to be good news; by far the best of the day, in fact. *194* was ready or would be shortly. There were still a few final checks to be carried out, but a collection party could set off almost straight away. Harris' mind ran on. Anderson, his number one, was due back at any moment; he could raise a scratch crew and see her safely from Portsmouth.

Then a thought occurred: he might lead them himself. It was common enough for a commander to collect his own boat and, though he had only just returned, at that moment Harris wanted nothing more than to get a long way from *Wasp*. Or, more to the point, away from Johnston and his cronies.

After lunching with the man, and two more COs from his new flotilla, Harris' reservations had been confirmed and he was coming to the conclusion there were two distinct types of RNVR officer.

The first, like Anderson, his own number one, were dedicated men and aware of their own weaknesses yet determined to become effective officers. And then there was the second; the kind who viewed the war and their part in it as little more than an agreeable jaunt. This latter group were dedicated to a point, and some had done much that could be called commendable; feats far removed from a previous life filled with golf club parties and old-school junkets. But few showed real interest in the Navy or its traditions and, though they might play the part, Harris doubted any would become proper officers.

His mind went back to the interview with Brooks, the base captain, and realised it was only a few hours since his world began to fall apart. Harris sensed Brooks felt the same about Johnston; he'd certainly gone to great pains to emphasize the spell of serving under him would be short. Within a month, possibly less, Harris expected to be in charge of his own flotilla again. And for all he knew, wiser for the experience, although the possibility of a bunch of jumped-up lawyers and city brokers teaching an old salt like him anything of value was slight.

He stuffed the buff paper into his pocket and made for the glass front doors once more. Harris retained a room on the upper floors of the Grand Hotel. It was relatively close by, yet a world apart from the order and discipline of HMS *Wasp*. There he might find a form of sanctuary; a place to recover and regroup. He could meet with Anderson in the morning and decide what to do about collecting *194*, but at that moment he wanted to get as far away from the Navy as possible.

* * *

Gibson took a fresh ten bob note from his hat where it had been stuffed when the paymaster issued his fortnightly wages. Folding it once, he placed it in the envelope then, after licking the flap, pressed the thing closed, holding it for a moment while the glue – often unreliable these days – set. Then he scratched out the address in pencil. He had not enclosed any form of letter; his landlady would know who the money was from; there was no need to remind her of his name – not when the old girl might already have forgotten. Ten shillings more than covered his lodgings, but that had been thought out as well; once she received it her memories of him would be good. He walked across to the small counter next to the NAAFI entrance. A bored young rating looked up.

"Nutty, is it?" he asked.

"Stamp," Gibson replied, passing the letter across. "And post this will you?"

The boy pushed his paper to one side before reaching for a small tin.

"Tuppence halfpenny," he said, and Gibson tossed the coppers in his direction.

"I'll sell you a stamp, matie," the boy said, before licking the thing and pressing it down on the envelope, "but you can post it yourself; box is by the entrance."

Gibson, who had been in the act of walking away, stopped suddenly and turned back. The lad was holding his letter out and, with a move as fast as it was unexpected, he grabbed his wrist and dragged the young body half over the counter. The boy's protests faded as soon as he met those terrible eyes and, for a moment, there was silence. Then Gibson spoke again.

17

"No, you will post it for me," he said. "You will put it in the box just as soon as you finish your trick."

The lad nodded but did not speak as Gibson had more to say.

"And if you do not, I will find out. Find out and come for you. And then you'll be sorry."

The wrist was released as suddenly as it had been taken and Gibson was already heading for his room when he heard the sound of the boy falling back off the counter. He didn't look back, he didn't need to: the letter would be posted and nothing else mattered.

* * *

Anderson actually remained at the cottage for most of the day and, when he finally packed his books away and collected his luggage, the walk to HMS *Wasp* took less than thirty minutes. As soon as he drew near and returned the first salute from a group of liberty men, he felt he was back in the Navy. And when he saw the imposing frontage of the former hotel – his base and home for so long – it was as if his time with Eve had been weeks ago. The stone building looked solid and unyielding; even the occasional scars from bomb damage heightened its impregnability. And then, with a feeling of deja-vu, he saw a familiar figure emerging from the glass front doors.

Lieutenant Commander Harris had been Anderson's CO throughout his time in Coastal Forces and they first met in almost exactly the same place. Much had happened since, of course, and it took understanding from both, as well as a few disagreements, to finally forge a successful partnership. But though there were times when his captain's crusty manner could still irritate, Anderson was already certain there was no one better to serve under.

"Number One?" Harris only noticed his second in command when they were a few feet apart.

"Good afternoon, sir: I think we might have met here in the past."

"Almost certainly," Harris replied although his mind appeared to be elsewhere.

"I was thinking when I first joined *Wasp*," Anderson

18

explained. "That was at the end of a leave as well."

"Indeed it was," Harris agreed, although the distant look remained.

"Did you have a good break, sir?"

The senior man blinked as if momentarily floored by the question. "Good enough, though there've been one or two changes back here that I can't say I approve of. What about yourself?" Harris' set expression relaxed for a moment and came close to a smile. "Nose sorted, is it?"

"As well as can be expected," Anderson grinned, touching the still tender bruise. "And the boat, what news?"

"I've just heard, she can be collected after tomorrow." Now Harris seemed to be returning to the real world. "No telling exactly when of course; you know what private yards can be like."

"I could pick her up; I did that last time as well," Anderson reminded. He had yet to check in at *Wasp* but, after parting with Eve, would welcome a distraction.

"You did," Harris said, smiling at last. "Though that was a different boat and mainly a different crew."

"And a lot's happened since."

"Very well," Harris said, coming to a decision. "Round up some of the lads and leave tomorrow, you should be able to bring her back straight after, though may have to wait a day or so; the yard superintendent has something of a reputation."

"You mean she might not be ready?"

"It's likely; seems the fellow has it in for the Navy, even though we put enough business his way. Can't do much as repairs are closely costed, but he always tries to get one over. And avoid shaking his hand," Harris added, mellowing further. "He gets it dirty on purpose and you'll come away with goodness knows what on your mitt; seems to think it funny."

Anderson grimaced. "Thanks, I'll bear that in mind. And what of the flotilla? Have you met with the other COs?"

Now Harris' expression was replaced with something closer to anger. "That's one of the changes," he said. "The flotilla's no more. Shaw and Barton have already left for *St Christopher*'s and the others are being reallocated."

"Reallocated?" Anderson's mind had been on domestic matters for so long that the news hit with surprising force. "But what of *194*?"

"We will be joining Lieutenant Commander Johnston's lot," Harris snapped. "With immediate effect."

"But your position as Flotilla Senior Officer..?"

"...was only temporary."

"I don't understand, how can that be?" Anderson faltered. "And why Buster Johnston?"

"Is that what they call him?" Harris appeared both unsurprised and a little saddened.

"Some do, sir." He had forgotten how straight-laced his superior could be.

"Fact is we'll be putting up with him for a while at least," Harris continued. "And, from what I gather, it won't be easy." Then he brightened once more. "But I must say, it's damned good seeing you again."

Chapter Three

It was midday when Anderson scrawled his name on the acceptance sheet.

"Reckon she'll last you a fair while," the superintendent told him, watching with approval. "As long as you don't break her." Anderson passed the papers back without comment.

"You ought to see some what come in here," the man continued, tearing off a top copy and handing the carbon back to Anderson. "Right state they can be, bits fallin' off all over the place, unexploded ordnance rollin' about the deck, and you wouldn't believe some of the mess, yet they expect us to put everything back together and make it all nice."

"There's no telling with some people." Anderson noticed the civilian had removed his bowler hat and seemed to be wiping it against his right palm.

"Well, good luck with her anyway." Now the superintendent was holding out his hand. Anderson glanced at it; just as Harris predicted, it carried a generous coating of grime and there was a sly smile on the man's face.

"Thanks for all you've done," Anderson said, grasping the paw firmly. "Sorry if my hand's a little damp – fresh paint always makes me sneeze."

Yet it looked like the yard had done a sound enough job and, as the superintendent bustled away, Anderson made a closer inspection. Two of the Packards had been replaced and the third engine serviced. There were fresh fuel tanks and a new Oerlikon cannon, still packed in grease and with carriage blocks in place, sat on a rebuilt mount, while a slightly higher mast now rose from the radio room where the R/T and W/T sets would soon be glowing. However, part of the aft deck and upper hull were peppered with irregularly shaped tingles marking where shots had penetrated, while several larger areas of decking had been entirely replaced. The thick layers of paint covering these were mainly for protection, and a poor match to the original colour, giving the boat a vaguely patchwork appearance. But as they put out from Portsmouth and passed through Spithead, there was no mistaking *194* was behaving much as before.

Even while still in the harbour confines, the triple engines seemed keen to bring her up on the plane and the roar from the exhausts when they were finally given their head was as deafening as ever. Anderson only needed a scratch crew to manage the craft; no more than the coxswain, a telegraphist and two general hands, but in view of what had been done below, he'd made sure of a full complement in the engine room.

It was clear and amazingly bright for the time of year. With the current generally in their favour, they should make Dover in just over six hours, even at cruising speed – a distinct difference to the previous day's journey down when much of the time was spent in a variety of cramped railway carriages. Anderson was vaguely tempted to press on once they were clear of the harbour; coming up to close on forty knots would shave several hours off their journey time and see them arrive in daylight. But it had been impossible to take on a full load of fuel at the yard and with engines lacking the fine tuning he demanded, Carter, their chief motor mechanic, was unsure if they would get back on the little allowed. Should things get tight, Anderson might put in to one of the smaller depots to top up, but a deck log showing excessive speed might raise a few eyebrows.

Besides, he felt in no rush to raise Dover; with Eve many miles away the town held little for him, and it was good to simply be at sea again – with the added novelty of having overall command. He ordered the speed down, then glanced south as they passed an island fort; one of several built in the Solent nearly a hundred years before. That had been in preparation for an invasion that never materialised, though recently they were recommissioned against a new and far more potent threat. The structure looked particularly solid and almost welcoming as it caught the early afternoon sunshine, yet Anderson understood living conditions were basic and the posting unpopular to the extent that they were garrisoned entirely by non-swimmers.

Beyond the fort, a pair of destroyers competed for the harbour in a flurry of spray and swagger while a dilapidated sweeper was coming up on *194*'s larboard bow and would shortly be overtaken. A whistle from one of the voice pipes broke into his thoughts; he leant forward and flipped the cover open.

"What is it, Chief?"

"Engines are a bit rough but seem to be doing the job, sir, though the port wing dynamo's running a little hot." Carter's voice was hard to distinguish over the roar of machinery. "Might clear as the bearings run in though I'd prefer not to take any chances."

"Very well, will dropping a couple of hundred make a difference?"

"It would be welcomed, sir."

"Then we'll bring her down and keep me informed." He flipped the cover closed and looked across to the coxswain. "Back two hundred, 'Swain."

It was possible for those in the engine room to alter the speed but, with control being set from the bridge, the act would have been close to bad manners.

"Back two hundred, sir." Phillips' gloved hand eased the triple throttles towards him slightly. Phillips was a replacement for Price, their previous coxswain, wounded when they attacked the *Seydlitz*. Anderson found it hard to believe the hair-brained scheme that pitched frail hulls of high-speed launches against an eighteen-thousand-ton steel warship had taken place barely three weeks before. And hard also to think that a relative youngster – Phillips had just turned twenty-seven and was newly promoted to petty officer – could helm as well as veterans such as Price. He definitely lacked the mature assurance of his predecessor. His service record was exemplary, however, and Anderson was quick to remember this was turning into a war where prejudices and preconceptions were common casualties. For as long as Phillips carried out his duties competently, he would keep an open mind.

He steadied himself as the boat fell back slightly, although remained on the plane; they were still going at a fair lick so the reduction would not delay them significantly, though must be remembered when it came to plotting their course. The coast would be in sight for much of their journey; even the final, nighttime, leg should be relatively easy assuming, of course, the weather remained clear. Fog, or deep-sea mists, were common in January and could leave them almost literally feeling their way, at which point everything would depend on him and his ability to navigate.

The merchant captain who trained him had summed the practice up succinctly enough; a navigator's job was to bring a vessel to the point where he was no longer needed, and Anderson had immediately felt at home with the science. Despite the current abundance of land and seamarks, he would shortly go below and plot their first leg from Selsey Bill to Beachy Head then keep a running log throughout. For now, however, he was content to simply enjoy being in control of a lithe and powerful craft. *194* might not be fully manned, and the chances of running across an enemy in daylight this close to the shore were slight indeed but, even with only their half-inch Vickers, no depth charges, and an Oerlikon yet to be commissioned, he felt she could give a good account of herself, and almost hoped for the chance.

* * *

There was nothing exactly wrong with Johnston's plan, Harris decided as the group of gunboat commanders sat back from the table. The broad guidelines demonstrated were close to textbook instructions and worked well enough for other flotilla leaders in the past. Yet the man's manner had been as condescending as ever, and Harris longed to find fault.

Once more they were in the bar of *Wasp*'s officers' mess – a place Lieutenant Commander Johnston seemed to regard as his personal space. And with them were two of his more experienced gunboat commanders, as well as the other newcomer to the flotilla; Hopgood, a man everyone – except Harris – referred to as 'Happy'.

"Approve, do you, Bob?" Johnston enquired and Harris looked again at the crudely demonstrated plan before them. A collection of matchboxes represented a supposed German convoy, with matchsticks showing where the enemy escorts might be expected, while Johnston's own flotilla was marked by Woodbines that in turn protected an attacking force of British torpedo boats – or in this case, a cigarette packet.

"It looks straight forward enough to me," Harris said. "Though I think you are assuming a lot."

"Assuming?" As Johnston spoke there was a distinct chill, certainly from him and his tame COs, although Hopgood, the newcomer, appeared interested in what Harris had to say.

"Your flotilla covers our torpedo boats up to when they make their attack." Harris waved vaguely at the table. "Yet no

24

provision is being made for their escape."

"That's it," the newcomer said, "I knew there was something. We were shown a similar battle plan at *St Christopher*'s, yet there was a larger gunboat force, and several were stationed to see the torpedo boys get clear."

"Ah, but at *St Christopher*'s they had limitless boats," one of the other commanders – a lieutenant in the RNVR – said. "And crews that had not been at sea the night before, nor would be the following evening…"

"Would that we had such luxury!" the other officer agreed.

"But you have sufficient boats," Harris said. "Correctly handled, three MGBs are more than enough to cover an attack and still be there to see the MTBs out of danger."

Johnston gave a shake of his head. "I have no wish to leave our MTB friends in the lurch, old boy, but this is just a general outline; an example of my methods, if you like."

"One we have used on a number of occasions," the second RNVR officer added, "and each has proved successful."

Now even Hopgood appeared mollified, but Johnston had more to say.

"Besides, I think you'll find a more detailed plan can fall to pieces in the confusion of action."

Harris felt his jaw tighten: that was going too far. Hopgood was a raw recruit, but he had been in combat as often as anyone at the table. More to the point, he himself outranked all bar Johnston and was the only regular Royal Navy officer present.

"You don't need to tell me about being in action," he said.

"Of course not, old boy," Johnston appeared eager to make amends. "But you must agree, it can be difficult to allow for every eventuality."

"Of course, but there can be an overall ethos, and yours seems to be to let the torpedo boats look after themselves."

Now the geniality was fading fast; Harris sensed the experienced men eyeing him warily while Johnston's expression was extremely cold.

"Not at all. I have every intention of seeing the MTBs home." There was a faint tremor in his voice as he spoke. "But their own senior officer should be perfectly capable of organising their withdrawal."

"Their own SO cannot order gunboat support," he said.

"Maybe not, but they can request it," Johnston countered. "And if they did – *and if it were possible* – I would respond. What I cannot do is build in cast iron provisions for such an eventuality."

Harris knew Johnston was right, yet he could not resist arguing further. "But an escorting force is exactly that, there should be no limitations. A torpedo boat lacks the fire power of an MGB; it's our job to support them throughout an action. As it is, a British gunboat can barely stand up to much of what the Germans throw at us; an MTB has far less chance."

Johnstone sighed and this time there was more than a hint of condescension in his tone. "Let me put it this way, my initial concern is to get those MTBs into a position where they can damage the enemy far more effectively than we can. But once that's done, everything changes; from then on, the flotilla – *my flotilla* – takes priority. If the torpedo boys have done their job properly there ought to be at least one merchant and maybe an escort or two in difficulty. And I say again, if any vessel asks for help, I'll try to give it, but with that level of distraction, both forces should be able to retreat without anyone being mollycoddled."

Harris sat back. It was a point of view, although not one he approved of. The RNVR were known to be more casual in their approach but, until then, he had thought this to be limited to skipping some less important rules and a more relaxed manner of command. There might be something to be said for Johnston's methods. Certainly, in the cut and thrust of a night action it was hard – impossible sometimes – to keep track of every vessel, and attempting to escort a force of MTBs to safety could prove positively dangerous for all concerned. Yet still he felt the attitude went against the spirit of the Navy, and feared it could only lead to disaster.

* * *

It was later that afternoon when they were beyond the mouth of Chichester harbour and making to round Selsey Bill that Les Carter appeared on the bridge. Anderson was surprised to see their chief motor mechanic's stocky frame; those inhabiting *194*'s nether regions tended to shun the open air in favour of their hot and noisy hellhole, especially when anything amiss could be reported through a voice pipe.

He gave the man a friendly nod. "Dynamo giving trouble

26

again is it, Chief?"

"No, that's sorted now, sir, but we've problems with fuel. Number three tank's leaking like a sieve." Carter's reply contained the combination of informality and respect common in Coastal Forces vessels. "Right now our bilges are almost one hundred octane."

"I see." Anderson's eyes instinctively flashed forward; Daly and Gibson were on the foredeck and being battered by a headwind that made breathing difficult and smoking impossible. Neither Jelly nor Phillips touched cigarettes and no naked flames were permitted aft of the bridge so, for the moment at least, they were relatively safe.

"What do you propose?" There was no risk to discipline in asking advice from a junior man, besides, Carter was both a specialist and too good a petty officer to take advantage.

"Bill Newman's trying to save the rest of the load," he said. "Fault's a leaking union which the yard should have noticed, though they probably fuelled up at the last minute."

"And the bilges?"

"Pickering's clearing what he can with a hand pump. Once the bulk's shifted we'll open up a scuttling valve and take on some sea water, then flush that out as well. I reckon three sound rinses will see us safe."

Draining a seventy-foot hull by hand must be miserable work, especially when electric pumps were available. But the risk of a spark would be great, and Carter was right in seeing the procedure done manually.

"Do you think Newman can fix the problem?"

"Can't think of anyone better," Carter said. "Certainly isn't worth putting in to a yard."

"And what about fuel; do we still have enough to make Dover?"

Carter shrugged. "Hard to say until we know for sure what's left, though they didn't leave us much of a margin in the first place. We have an entire tank that's not been tapped which'll take us much of the way; it all depends on what remains in number three."

"I see." Anderson glanced back. Chichester was fast disappearing, yet it would take little effort to turn and make for the harbour. They might attend to the leak more easily in sheltered waters, then take on further fuel and be underway again within a couple of hours, although Anderson knew government dockyards of old. Completing the paperwork alone could stretch deep into the afternoon, leaving much of the remaining journey to be completed in the dark. In a poorly armed and undermanned boat, that would be too great a risk; far better to delay setting off until the following morning.

He had been in no rush to raise Dover but the thought of wasting an entire day did not appeal. Harris would understand, of course, and they were yet to be rostered for operations, yet any delay that could be avoided went against Anderson's instincts.

"You're sure Newman can handle it?" he checked. Being Eve's brother made him especially careful when dealing with the mechanic.

"If he can't, I will," Carter said.

"Very well, we'll keep her as she is." Chances were, they would have enough fuel and, if not, he now had just cause to radio ahead to one of the supply bases en route.

"Good on you, sir!"

Anderson sensed Carter was restraining himself from slapping him on the back.

"And if I might suggest, we can save a bit if we cut out the two wings."

That also made sense: a single engine running at higher revs would use less fuel than three almost ticking over, while the centre ran the boat's hydraulic system that powered the steering and both Vickers' mounts.

"Very good." Anderson was unused to being in command and could not help feeling encouraged by the engineer's reaction. "Does Pickering need a hand clearing the bilges?"

Carter grinned. "Nah, it'll do him good; that one can do with losing a bit of weight."

* * *

"Seems like a sound enough berth, eh, Lenny?"

The lad looked up. "Reckon," he said.

"An' the others are a tight bunch," Smith continued. "Least they look like it."

Godliman returned to stare at the newspaper although,

with eyes so set, he could not be reading. Seeking distraction, Smith glanced about the sparsely furnished though generally welcoming room. The row of iron-framed beds was broken only by lockers between each while a similar collection of utilitarian tables and chairs lined the opposite wall. All was clean and, with a lino floor, it would be easy to keep so. In truth, it was a fair billet, being large enough to contain all the ordinary hands for their gunboat with no interlopers from other vessels. Only the petty officers, the coxswain, and chief motor mechanic berthed elsewhere. And Smith had been in Coastal Forces long enough to know the value of familiarity. In a small vessel where one man could take the place of an entire department, it was important for shipmates to get on.

"Weren't like this at *Beehive*," he said. "Ours was the last boat in, and her crew were billeted all over the shop. Remember?"

There was no reaction from Godliman, although Smith was sure he'd heard. He stared hard at his friend. The pair first met while training at *King Alfred* and, despite appearances to the contrary, the lad was barely five years his junior. But growing up in his particular part of London's East End had given Smith far more street sense, and he quickly took Godliman under his wing. That was not to say the kid lacked spunk; Smith was never one to support hopeless cases.

After basic training, then gunnery school, a shared wish for action saw them volunteer for Coastal Forces and when both were appointed to HMS *Beehive*, the Coastal Forces base in Felixstowe, Godliman was as eager to get to grips with the enemy as Smith.

The change began after they were fished from the water when their gunboat was destroyed off the Dutch coast. At the time both were checked over quite comprehensively by the medical department, and there was even a short interview with an old fellow whose questions appeared unrelated to their being the only survivors from a crew of twelve. Before then, Godliman had been reasonably chatty with no sign of the long silences that later became common. Silences that would have got Smith down were he not so concerned for his mate.

Things deteriorated further when they were released and allowed two weeks survivors' leave. It was almost Christmas, and there was only one destination for a couple of East End lads wanting a good time. Godliman had been orphaned before the war, so Smith, who had no wish to meet up with his father and

29

stepmother, suggested heading further West. They'd checked into a cheap hotel near Waterloo Station, then set off to find what wartime London could offer. But, no sooner had they sunk their first pints and bought tickets for what sounded like the raunchiest leg show in town, than Godliman began to act strangely.

The stage was full of dancers; brilliantly lit and delightfully underdressed, and Smith had just begun to enjoy himself when he noticed Godliman weeping. He'd tried to ignore the lad's distress, but the sobs grew deeper and soon became noticeable to others. Eventually, he'd been forced to half drag the boy from the theatre, and they'd ended up back at their shared room.

There, and in the dark once more, Godliman calmed down and began to talk. With the City's blackout heavily enforced, the theatre had been unexpectedly bright, and it seemed the dazzling lights stirred up memories of the E-boat attack. Smith could understand this to some extent and agreed to take things easier, maybe break the lad in slowly: in time he would be fine.

It was to prove otherwise; even after avoiding the busier night spots, Godliman steadily drew deeper into himself; there would be long passages of silence that Smith could only end by physically shaking the kid or bawling into his face. Instinct still told him the lad would sort himself out and, as a mate, Smith would support him, but there was only so much he could do alone.

Godliman seemed to be holding his own for now and had yet to disgrace himself publicly, though he remained uncommonly quiet. Smith had noticed a few of their new shipmates eyeing him with interest and wondered how they would take it should he start to play up. And with the boat due back from the yard, it was only a matter of time before they were at sea once more and given another Oerlikon to handle. If a stage filled with prancing floozies could set Lenny off, Smith could only wonder what would happen then.

* * *

They were almost home; swift work from Newman saved much of what remained in number three tank and their bilges now smelled as sweet as nuts. Dover lay a bare fifty miles off and Carter felt there should be just enough fuel to see them there. And even if not, even if they were to fail and *194* ran dry with their base almost in sight, Anderson would be excused for calling up the rescue tug. However, the reduction in speed meant fighting with a contrary current for longer; darkness had fallen several hours before and a faint mist now threatened to wipe out all signs of the nearby shore.

On realising this, Anderson's first instinct was to gain more sea room, but it was one he decided to resist. They were nearing the narrowest part of the Channel – the French coast lay barely twenty miles off their starboard beam and any movement in that direction would increase the likelihood of running in with an enemy vessel. Of course, they were still in radio contact with *Wasp* and, though the wish to remain undetected limited their own transmissions, they should receive notice of any German shipping close by. Yet still he decided to hold his course; his navigation so far had been spot on and knowing they were almost home brought with it an odd feeling of security.

"Kye, sir?"

Their new seaman gunner had managed to clamber up the short ladder from the wheelhouse with two steaming mugs, one of which he now offered to Anderson.

"Thank you, Gibson." Anderson accepted the drink and felt the agreeable heat warm his chilled hands.

"Nearly there, sir?"

Anderson considered the new man. Despite the relaxed regime, it was unusual for an ordinary hand to strike up a conversation with an officer. But then he only met Gibson the day before and a slight over-familiarity might be covering shyness.

Although in this case he thought not; having to depend on others in extreme situations heightened Anderson's senses, making him almost an expert at judging the personality of others. And in Gibson, he found something mildly disquieting.

"Yes, shouldn't be long now," he said. "Better return to your post."

"Right oh, sir." Gibson passed the second mug to Phillips before disappearing as easily as he had come. A few seconds later Anderson heard the wheelhouse door slam shut, then a murmur of conversation from behind as the new man exchanged a word with Daly, stationed in the starboard turret. The pair seemed relaxed, although the only thing they had to worry about was keeping watch over a small patch of sea. Others could concern themselves with the state of the tide, what fuel remained, and

31

whether they would be bounced by a stray E-boat. That was what officers were for.

Anderson sipped at his drink. Running under a single engine meant *194* was making less than her usual din. It was even possible to hear faint sounds beyond the guttural mutter. He was reminded of the first time they had lain cut, with just the ticking of cooling engines as they waited for an unseen enemy to appear. He learned then that, even on the stillest of nights, the sea was never quiet.

But on that evening Anderson had no wish to linger; his only concern was logging the few miles necessary to bring them off the entrance to Dover harbour. And then another sound made itself known.

It was one he knew well and immediately brought with it a chill of foreboding; another low muttering, this time from diesel engines, and not the kind associated with slow-moving coastal craft or merchant traffic of any description.

He placed the mug down and listened more intently. Phillips appeared oblivious, but then he was new to Coastal Forces and had not spent the last few months playing hide and seek amid the Channel's many perils.

And it was the greatest of these that Anderson thought he could hear now; one that would be unwelcome at any time, but especially so in a vessel as poorly armed, shorthanded, and under fuelled as they were. Then, either borne by the breeze or some other quirk of nature, the sound increased and suddenly he was in no doubt.

There were E-boats nearby.

Chapter Four

"Bring her back, 'Swain," Anderson told Phillips before leaning forward to the voice pipe and ordering their engine cut. The deep rumble that had been a constant background for so long fluttered to nothing and, for a while, all they could hear was the wind in the wires and waves lapping against their hull. Then the sound of distant engines returned.

"I'd say there were three of them, sir – an' spaced a bit apart." Phillips spoke softly yet still his voice seemed unusually loud. Anderson nodded; he thought three as well, certainly more than one. But where exactly?

He replaced his black cap with a steel helmet though not for want of protection: the metal dome was thought to accentuate any sound. Sweeping his head from left to right, Anderson thought the noise came off their starboard bow but still could not be certain. He glanced back to where Gibson and Daly were listening equally intently in their respective turrets.

"Can you get a bearing?" he asked.

Gibson cautiously raised his hand and pointed forward and to starboard while Daly nodded in agreement.

That was enough, while Phillips also reached for a steel helmet, Anderson lowered himself down the short ladder to the wheelhouse.

The plotting table was as he left it an hour before, and it took no time to enter their progress since and get a rough fix. Once this was passed to Jelly to forward to Dover Command, along with a breakdown of the situation, he had done all that might be expected of him.

On the bridge once more, Anderson took stock. The sound had gone for now, though the Germans would still be close. They might even intercept Jelly's signal and decide to seek them out. With luck a British flotilla would be nearby, if not it could take anything up to an hour for help to arrive. Until then they could do nothing but lie cut and hope the darkness and mist would shield them.

* * *

Even stripped of machinery, *194*'s engine room would have been a cramped and deeply unpleasant place, but needing, as it did, to house the three massive Packards made it so much more so. The engines dominated the aft area; one, the central, was set conventionally and drove the gunboat's middle screw while the two wing units were reverse mounted and sent their power through V drives. Each of the colossal lumps was frequently too hot to touch, while their high-tension cables could kill a man outright if the exhaust gasses – never anything more than suppressed in their asbestos-covered manifolds – were unable to. And the place could be unpleasant in more conventional ways. Fresh air came through a combination of ventilators and electric fans and was at best adequate, while the absence of scuttles or any means of natural light meant the bulkhead lamps burned continually. Even being around when the Packards were at maximum revs could cause irreparable damage to a man's hearing.

But after running on a single engine for some time all that had changed. Now with even that silent, and their black hole oddly cool, aired, and relatively comfortable, those who inhabited *194*'s underworld were mildly disconcerted.

From his favoured spot in the central position – a place within touching distance of their main engine – Acting Chief Motor Mechanic Carter glanced uncertainly about. Robbed of power, the boat's hull rolled alarmingly and, never one blessed with a strong stomach, Carter wondered if yet another problem was to be added to what had already been a terrible day. He and his team had only boarded the boat that morning and bore no blame for the dynamo, although that later disaster with the fuel was perhaps a little different. Unions were inclined to leak, and the engine room stunk like a refinery when they arrived; it was a big mistake to put this down to a lack of attention when fuelling. They should have carried out a full check – more to the point, *he* should have ordered it. The fact that all was now sorted gave little consolation and this sudden order to lie cut when they must still be some distance from home worried him deeply.

It meant the enemy was about, which was always a concern when the boat's very safety often depended upon his machinery. It also seemed likely they would be ordered to crash start all three and, in anticipation of this, his two mechanics were carrying out the start-up procedures on their wing engines. Should that be the case, though, and the Packards needed to be run at full tilt, their meagre store of petrol would soon be gone. And then Carter knew it would no longer be a question of failing to make it back to harbour; they would be lucky not to wind up on the sea bed.

* * *

The Germans were on the move once more and sounded closer. Standing in silence, Anderson and Phillips were able to track them as they crossed *194*'s bows. And then, when the E-boats must be closing with the shore, the noise began to alter.

"Reckon they've sighted land, sir." The coxswain spoke in barely a whisper. "An' they've throttled back."

That was undoubtedly so; the pitch had dropped considerably and now could barely be heard. Whatever the Germans were planning they had no wish to betray their position by leaving a heavy wake.

"So which way will they turn?" Anderson was too used to having a captain by his side and had not meant the question for Phillips, but the coxswain took it in his stride.

"Sound's growing fainter, sir," he said. "Reckon they'll be aiming to follow the coast to Dover."

Yes, of course, the E-boats were heading for *Wasp*. Despite their low speed, they would soon be prowling around the harbour entrance ready to pounce on any departing British vessel before it had properly shaken down or even run a gun test. Quite why Dover's much vaunted RDF had missed them was not Anderson's concern; for as long as *194* remained in contact, he would have the best evidence of the enemy's presence. He flipped open the W/T office voice pipe cover.

"Make to base, Tel': 'Enemy heading east along the coast, we are following.'"

Then, to Carter in the engine room, "Start her up, Chief; centre engine for now but be ready with the wings, we may need them at short notice."

"Following, sir?" Phillips enquired.

"Yes, following," he snapped. "And bring her up to eighteen hundred."

The deck vibrated for several seconds before a slow steady rumble resumed. After so long in silence it sounded unusually loud and, when Phillips brought the revs up and *194* rose cautiously onto the plane, it was easy to imagine they could be heard as far away as Dover. But whether those at *Wasp* registered their existence hardly bothered Anderson; he was far more concerned about the enemy E-boats that lay in between.

* * *

Harris looked at his watch for what must have been the tenth time that evening. He was in the bar area of *Wasp*'s officers' mess which wasn't especially foolhardy as Johnston and most of his flotilla had left harbour several hours before. Of course, it was only a matter of time before he would be seeing more of them; once *194* was cleared for active service there would be training exercises and briefings, to say nothing of regular patrols and the occasional jaunt to the other side. But he was in no rush and, on that particular evening, it was Anderson and his own command that filled his thoughts.

He had spoken with Operations several times throughout the day and learned much of *194*'s progress, but his last call was less well received. There was no further news and a duty Wren had been quite abrupt in telling him so. Which was understandable, the night must be hotting up; being misty, but with a touch of moon, contact with the enemy seemed likely. Besides, Johnston's wasn't the only flotilla at sea and Ops would have more to think about than one errant gunboat. Yet Anderson had still not appeared and Harris was starting to grow concerned.

He finished his drink – ginger without Scotch – and considered his surroundings. For a government-provided bar, it was pleasant enough; the furnishings were comfortable and, though well worn, the place even had a carpet. And the clientele, mainly uniformed personnel with a scattering of guests, were what could be expected in countless other bases throughout the country. There were several other solitary drinkers, none of whom appeared to be abusing the plentiful, and inexpensive, supply. A group of reservist officers were gathered in the far corner for some form of celebration, and the base captain was at the next table. Along with two regular lieutenants, Brooks appeared to be entertaining an unknown admiral who was accompanied by an attractive young woman that Harris trusted was a relative. Other than that, all was completely normal.

The door from the reception area opened and a commissioned Wren entered. Harris watched with nothing more than idle curiosity as she inspected the room, then stiffened slightly as her eyes fell upon him, and made her way over.

"Lieutenant Commander Harris?" She had a pleasant face with neatly cropped brown hair while the tortoiseshell glasses gave her an academic air that was not unattractive.

"I'm Harris," he said, standing.

"Second Officer Morris, I understand you've been enquiring about *194*, sir?"

"She's my boat, I hope I haven't caused a fuss."

The fact that uniform disguised much, including age, upbringing, and even personality, rarely bothered Harris, yet this particular woman intrigued him. And, on deciding they must be roughly contemporaries, he felt strangely encouraged.

"Not exactly, sir, though they have run into difficulties."

"I heard there was some issue with fuel – or the lack of it," Harris began before realising how stupid the remark must sound.

"I'm afraid it's more than that, sir. Perhaps if you come with me, I can explain?"

She turned to go before Harris could reply, though he was quite happy to follow.

* * *

Once underway and with the revs increased, further clues about the enemy's whereabouts were masked by the noise of their central engine and, as the tension grew, Anderson found himself gripping the guard rail. The mist had grown significantly, now shielding what moon there was, bringing visibility down to well under half a mile, and he was starting to doubt the wisdom of his actions.

If Dover Command's RDF had missed the Germans' approach, there was every reason for *194* to follow. Stalking a superior force had been the task of small vessels since the Navy's inception, but when Blackwood tracked the Franco-Spanish fleet before Trafalgar it was from a sleek and speedy frigate, with every expectation of beating a swift retreat. Anderson's enemy was not only better armed and carrying more men, their triple diesels could carry them faster than his untuned Packards. *194* would be easy meat for one E-boat and he was facing three.

He flipped the lid on the W/T office speaking tube.

"Make to *Wasp*, Tel'," he said. "Enemy continuing to head east."

That was certainly the case as far as he knew it; if the E-boats had turned in either direction they would have been spotted, nor had they fallen back. For a moment he felt a measure of pride in knowing more than all Dover Command's fancy equipment. Then his eyes began to ache from staring into the mist and he turned away.

Phillips, at the helm, appeared as steady as any coxswain could be, but it wasn't enough. Anderson needed more; he needed a solid captain by his side, someone who had seen it all before, someone who knew, as if by instinct, how far matters could be pushed. Someone who would take the blame if it all went horribly wrong.

He considered reducing speed; throttling back would be a sign of caution rather than cowardice and might allow him to fix the enemy's course and position more accurately. But the idea was rejected as soon as it formed. If the Germans knew *194* was trailing them, he would soon know of it. More to the point, a gunboat flotilla should be on the way to intercept. The longer he remained on the enemy's tail, the greater the likelihood they would find them. And when that happened it would provide all the distraction necessary for *194* to beat a dignified retreat.

And then he saw the first sign of tracer – a streak of fluorescent green rising up immediately ahead – and knew the British had indeed arrived.

* * *

"Looks like the cavalry's here!"

Phillips' remark had been unnecessary, although Anderson was too engrossed in the turn of events to notice. But if the light show ahead was anything to go by, his colleagues had certainly found the Germans. With luck, it would be a dedicated task force of gunboats acting on his information, in which case there was little left for him to do, and it would indeed be wise to withdraw. Already the lines of tracer had increased and now an intense red added to the dazzling display.

"Bring her back, 'Swain, twelve hundred revs."

"Twelve hundred revs, sir." Phillips obediently eased the centre throttle until *194* slopped down from the plane and began to wallow in the swell. Anderson leaned forward to the engine room voice pipe.

"What fuel do we have left, Chief?"

"Last spell used a good deal, sir." Despite the tube, Anderson could hear the concern in Carter's voice. "Not sure how far we are from base, but I reckon we'll be lucky to keep one alight for more than an hour, and considerably less if you up the revs again."

Anderson allowed himself a brief smile. Carter's only concern was for his precious engines, he would know nothing of the tension the last few minutes had contained.

"Very well, shut her down for now. There's a bit of business ahead; once that's passed I'll need your most economical speed and we'll see how far we get."

He shut the voice pipe cover and was turning to Phillips when something in the coxswain's expression made him look forward instead. And the sight that met him was enough to turn the stomach of even the most seasoned commander.

Three E-boats had appeared out of the mist, with several British gunboats close on their heels. The Germans must be travelling at close to their maximum speed and were firing from their aft cannon – their forward-mounted guns remaining silent. But it was only a question of time before *194*, lying square in their path, was noticed and then everything must change.

* * *

Other than he was an utter fool when it came to speaking with women, Harris learned little from his time in *Wasp*'s Operations Room. The night was cold and there was a light fog, but he felt better being outside and by the sea, something he almost understood, than confined in a dark, smoke-filled, room. The place had been inhabited by shouting officers and submissive

39

Wrens, but Second Officer Morris was there and, somehow, he managed to insult her. He sighed and stared into the mist that he hoped would be thicker further out. For somewhere, probably barely forty miles away, his number one was fighting for his life.

Anderson had certainly got himself into a right old mess. Meeting with a bunch of E-boats is never a pleasant experience but having them block the way home, when *194* was barely armed, could turn out very badly indeed. But then Anderson was no fool; even if low on fuel, he should be able to avoid action and, providing conditions were as bad as the Met. Officer claimed, hide himself in the gloom. And if Dover truly proved unreachable, it should be possible to make for one of the smaller depots at Folkestone or Dymchurch; that or signal for the rescue tug to see them in. Those in Operations seemed to be taking things very seriously, however, and he stayed long enough to watch two flotillas of MGBs vectored towards Anderson's general vicinity.

Of course, he understood the attraction was not so much in rescuing *194* but seeing to the E-boats. Second Officer Morris was quite certain their RDF had not failed, yet that hardly made sense as a lone British gunboat – presumably also on their plot – had been allowed to stray dangerously close to a powerful German unit. Harris was not totally closed to new technology, and previous examples of RDF's capabilities impressed him greatly. Yet the miraculous tool was still very much in its infancy, and it was then that he made the fundamental mistake of pointing this out.

It seemed Harris' doubts about Dover Command's precious toy would have been better kept to himself. Until that point, he and Morris had been getting on rather well, or so he thought. And it was pleasant, for a while, to enjoy a spot of female company. Harris had been determinedly celibate since joining Coastal Forces and that would never alter, but the small talk they exchanged while she explained the situation was unexpectedly stimulating. It simply felt good speaking to someone different. Someone not directly connected with the business of taking noisy, high-powered launches to sea and the fact that he found her attractive was a definite bonus. As their conversation progressed an element of humour even crept in on her part which he quickly matched, and there were several times when they both laughed together. But once he made that crass remark everything changed and doors that were being cautiously opened were suddenly slammed shut.

She was clearly as protective of the equipment as any captain would be of their command, either that or Harris had been wrong in detecting interest in the first place. For whatever reason, Second Officer Morris' attention was soon required elsewhere, and he found himself being brushed off to a duty controller.

Which is why he came out to the pens where the gunboats usually berthed and was now trying to wipe the memory of the past few minutes from his mind. If Anderson was able to avoid the E-boats he may still run out of fuel, although the harbour tug remained secured against Green Wharf. This should mean *194* had escaped detection and was inching home on the last drops of petrol, that or the Germans had accounted for her, and he should start looking for a new boat and second in command.

He sighed; failing to make a favourable impression on Second Officer Morris had been disappointing, but it would be so much worse to lose Anderson. A lot depended on the young man being able to keep his head.

* * *

"Crash start all, Chief, and give me everything you have!"

Anderson didn't wait for a reply, and the starter motors were already clattering loudly as he slammed the speaking tube cover shut. The centre Packard was the first to light up and *194* was soon rising onto the plane. Then, with a surge of extra power, the two additional engines came on line and the gunboat began to accelerate properly for the first time in ages. But there was no time to enjoy the sensation, even as Anderson and Phillips steadied themselves their eyes were set on the oncoming Germans.

"Hard a port!" Anderson ordered and, equally ignoring protocol, Phillips did not reply as he wrenched the wheel over. The boat heeled savagely as the power continued to build, and Anderson briefly worried about losing stability. But *194* had been well designed and her triple screws simply dug deeper as the roar from her engines rose ever higher.

Gripping at the handrail, he looked across at the Germans who were moving equally fast and would soon be cutting across *194*'s stern. Their fire remained concentrated on the pursuing British, now equally visible less than a quarter of a mile off their quarry and clearly a major threat. Then the flash of tracer close by blinded him for a second and he realised with horror that Gibson, in the port turret, had opened up with his half-inch Vickers. A second later, Daly's gun joined in: Anderson drew breath.

"Cease fire!"

Neither man could hear over the sound of their weapons, or that of three supercharged engines mounted just below their feet. Desperately, Anderson turned and hit a plunger once with the side of his fist. Bells began to ring throughout the boat and, mercifully, the firing stopped.

Gibson's look was a mixture of anger and confusion but there was no time to rebuke or explain. Anderson turned to Phillips.

"Meet her, midships."

194 swung back and, for a few brief seconds was relatively stable, then Anderson's next order sent her turning, and rolling, in the opposite direction. He glanced cautiously towards the enemy once more. With British launches hard on their tails, the Germans might not have been aware of another vessel's presence, but as soon as his gunners opened fire there could be no doubt. Sure enough, the nearest E-boat's forward cannon burst into life sending a line of green tracer just off their beam.

"And back to port!"

He was playing a dangerous game that could not last forever, but Anderson was desperate, and they should be safely ensconced in the mist before long.

Now the enemy's tracer was in line, though passing overhead and it would only take a minimal correction for the German gunners to find their tender hull.

As Anderson turned the boat again, the trail followed, although they were definitely pulling out of range and the flecks of green had started to fade. Then the thought of further enemy fire became almost irrelevant as another, brighter, light took over.

It came from a British gunboat; one of those pursuing the Germans. Chasing E-boats was always a risky business, especially when the enemy craft carried weighty ordnance aft. One scored a direct hit on an MGB which immediately burst into bright and final flames. It was a sight Anderson had seen often enough in the past although that night the sudden eruption seemed unusually shocking.

As if stunned by their own actions, the E-boats ceased to fire and turned away, apparently setting course for their home coast yet, though unequal in firepower, the British continued to follow. With his boat no longer in danger, Anderson was within his rights to set an economical speed and make for safety. But though the initial explosion had been deadly, and despite the burning gunboat now being little more than smouldering ruins, he really only had one option.

The likelihood of saving anyone from such an inferno was small but he must try. He cleared his throat.

"Starboard fifteen, 'Swain, and bring her back to eighteen hundred."

"Starboard fifteen, sir. Eighteen hundred revolutions."

194 began a more gentle turn until she was heading directly towards what remained of the gunboat. Then Anderson ordered the speed reduced further and they began to search.

* * *

The ambulance passed Harris as he was making his way to where *194* finally came to rest. She had taken the temporary berth, which usually meant damage of some description, although Anderson seemed unconcerned as he walked to meet him.

"Trouble, Number One?"

The younger man smiled. "Good to see you, sir. No, not now. We plucked a chap from the water and were desperately short of fuel, so I grabbed the emergency bay."

"You did right, and I saw the ambulance – not one of ours then?"

"From another flotilla; a gunner, thrown clear when his boat went up." Anderson's tone became more serious and, as Harris drew closer, he noticed his second in command looked strained. "He was in a bit of a mess, but we did all we could."

"I'm sure of it, and you were short of fuel?"

"Carter reckons we made it back on vapours. Would you care to check out the repairs?"

He stood to one side to allow his captain to continue towards the craft, but Harris had other ideas.

"Later, maybe, first I'd like to talk, and you need some rest. It sounds like quite a journey."

"You could say that."

Though Anderson appeared happy to walk back with him, Harris sensed reserve in the younger man's manner. In the distance, they could hear a bell as the ambulance reached the main road.

"I doubt he'll make it," Anderson said.

"Maybe not." It was dark, and the mist was just as strong, though both men could see the other well enough. "But he'll have a better chance in Dover than stuck out somewhere in the Channel."

"I guess you're right."

"So, why the long face?"

Anderson shrugged and looked down at his feet. "It was just so frustrating," he said. "We were there, at sea, and with an E-boat in our sights yet, without a working Oerlikon could do nothing." He shook his head. "When Gibson and Daly opened up, I was almost glad."

"You fired on an E-boat with a couple of half-inch Vickers?"

Anderson gave an awkward smile. "It wasn't my intention; they rather took the initiative."

"That can never happen," Harris was insistent. "We'll have to speak to them. And it might go further. I can't have gunners unable to hold their fire."

"I think it was a mistake," Anderson said. "And probably my fault."

"Your fault?"

"I'm not used to being in command; I guess I lack a captain's presence."

"A captain's presence?"

Anderson shook his head. "Let's just say I doubt they'd have done it if you'd been on the bridge."

Harris gave a low chuckle. "You know, there's more to commanding a gunboat than being a bit on the gruff side."

"Oh, for sure," Anderson agreed. "Though you've got to admit, it must help."

Chapter Five

The following weeks were taxing for all but, as first officer, Anderson bore the brunt. Not only did the boat have to be prepared, there were new crew members to integrate while everyone needed to readjust to the disciplines of active service. And it was strange how, even after such a brief time ashore, familiar tasks and well-known procedures felt strange and awkward. But at least the boat was soon brought up to scratch. Once Carter and his team finished tuning her engines, *194*'s performance improved and in an equally short time the fresh faces had taken on a familiar look; before long it took positive effort to remember they had not always been part of the crew.

In fact, Anderson was especially pleased with the new recruits. Despite his disconcerting manner, Gibson turned out to be a natural with the half-inch Vickers and, though the garrulous Smith and more reticent Godliman might not appear an obvious team, they worked in perfect harmony on the Oerlikon. Phillips was perhaps the only one to give doubts. His thin frame was such a contrast to the stocky coxswain he replaced, there were times when Anderson looked twice at the figure manning their helm. And there was another, more subtle, difference that he noticed from the start and suspected Harris had also. Phillips was too inclined to let slip with the odd remark or quip, a habit that was out of place even within the relaxed order aboard a gunboat.

What was less easy to address was Lieutenant Commander Johnston's attitude. When Harris led his own flotilla there was the occasional friction between him and the RNVR officers under his command. However hard both sides tried, the gap dividing a career officer from the well-intentioned, but inexperienced, reservists remained. The fact they gave Harris every respect and did much to meet his exacting demands improved the situation and Anderson felt that, had the flotilla been allowed to continue, it would have become one of the finest in Coastal Forces. But now the situation was reversed; Harris was having to defer to Johnston's very different approach, and it was clear the pair would never get on.

To make matters worse, Johnston was not content to limit his authority to directing the vessels under his command, he wanted to control them and be involved in every aspect of their care and maintenance. There was a splendid blow up when Harris indented for replacement equipment without Johnston's knowledge, and even such routine procedures as refuelling or revictualling could become fraught.

Johnston's need for control was equally evident during exercises. Once fully worked up, nothing should have prevented *194* from returning to active service, but this had been delayed and the boat, her crew, and officers, were forced to face the indignity of further exercises until Johnston deemed them fit to meet the enemy.

It couldn't last, of course. *194* was a valuable boat and one that had proved herself in the past. Unless Johnston had genuine concerns, he could not delay her return indefinitely. Though hardly a matter Anderson could discuss with his captain, he was reasonably sure Harris had already spoken with Commander Brooks. Once they were given their head, and Johnston could see for himself how effective *194* could be in action, tempers might cool, although Anderson remained doubtful.

On the plus side, Harris' attitude throughout had been encouraging. Few regular officers would have taken such treatment from a reservist without objection, yet he seemed able to close his mind to it. There was no more than the occasional curt remark and, even when the pair clashed over small matters such as *194*'s order of fuelling, Harris took a surprisingly phlegmatic approach. Surprising because, though it seemed like an eternity, Anderson and Harris had only served together a relatively short time. And the man he knew now was very different to the crusty old-school commander who first took him under his wing.

There was no obvious reason for the transformation; as far as Anderson knew, Harris' leave had been undramatic, and their last operation together was hardly an outright success. Since then, he had lost his position as Senior Officer, watched his flotilla broken up, and been placed under the command of a man he could not respect, yet none of this daunted him. There were even times when Anderson suspected the old boy of developing a sense of humour. But he was certain of one thing; whatever had caused the change in his captain, it was for the good.

* * *

Commander R.E.D. Ryder – 'Red' to his friends – had something of a reputation. Since joining the Royal Navy sixteen years before he had served aboard, captained, and then lost, an inordinate number of her vessels.

One, the Q-ship HMS *Willamette Valley*, was torpedoed in the North Atlantic, after which Ryder spent four days clinging to wreckage, and HMS *Prince Philippe*, another former merchant, sank in the Firth of Clyde after colliding with a larger vessel. To balance this, Ryder also captained the topsail schooner *Penola*, transporting, then supplying, an expedition to Antarctica. And there was a brief private venture; together with other Royal Navy officers, he built and then sailed a thirty-ton ketch over sixteen thousand miles from China to England.

But it seemed the Admiralty had long memories, and that of the *Prince Philippe* sinking many miles from her nearest enemy had stuck. After "incurring their Lordship's displeasure", he was given the post of naval liaison officer, advising Southern Command in case of invasion; a position that hardly satisfied Ryder's need for immediate action.

It also involved a good many lengthy meetings and it was to attend one of these that he had journeyed to Combined Operations HQ in Richmond Terrace. To make what promised to be another frustrating afternoon worse, the train from his Wiltshire base had been delayed and, some time after the conference officially began, Ryder was still searching for the room.

"Excuse me, I'm supposed to be in a meeting."

The Wren paused and noticed the dark hair, strong chin, and single, white Polar Medal ribbon.

"I see, sir; can you tell me more?"

Ryder met her smile. "I don't think it's anything terribly grand," he said. "I'm from Southern Command, General Alexander's staff."

"Oh, then it will be the one at the end of this corridor," she said. "But the Admiral arrived some while ago; I think they may have started."

"The Admiral?"

47

"Sir Charles Forbes, C-in-C Plymouth..."

"...and Admiral of the Fleet." Ryder finished before pulling a face. "They don't get much bigger than that."

"Maybe not, sir." The Wren was fast approaching twenty-one and just coming to terms with being uncommonly attractive. "Though Lord Mountbatten is also attending."

"Mountbatten!"

"Yes, sir." She smiled again. "You'd better hurry."

"I think you may be right; end of the corridor, you say?"

The Wren nodded and was about to add more but Ryder was already bounding down the passageway.

There was only one door, although a sign made it clear there would be no admittance. But Ryder had never been one for obeying instructions and, after tapping sharply on the polished wooden panels, he entered.

"Ah, here's Commander Ryder now," an unknown voice announced. A paper was thrust into his hand and an empty chair indicated. He took it, then looked about the table.

Of the twenty or so present most were senior Army or Navy officers, with a fair amount of gold lace between them. Some he knew well; Mountbatten was seated at the far end along with Forbes and a Navy captain who looked familiar, but Ryder couldn't place. And on the military side, there were a number of brigadiers and generals, although it was the lieutenant colonel seated opposite that caught his eye. Despite a broken nose and two cauliflower ears, the man appeared surprisingly affable and was sending out a continuous stream of blue smoke from a pipe apparently welded to his mouth.

Some of the more junior men were even lower in rank than himself; Ryder quickly decided these would be aides who did much of the work. A Wren, taking minutes, was regarding him with interest, but by then Ryder had noticed a builders' model of what must be a dockyard sitting square in the middle of the table. He could only see one side and was angling for a better view when Mountbatten spoke.

"We now come to item five," he said. "Commander Ryder has been appointed to lead the Naval Forces under the C-in-C Plymouth." For a moment the great man caught his eye and Ryder thought he could detect a glimmer of humour. "Is that alright with you, Ryder?"

* * *

Harris had thought long and hard before visiting the Ops Room and even carried out a measure of research beforehand. Once familiarised with the section rota – a listing posted with surprising openness in the nearby common room – it was easy to discover the officers on duty at any time. More to the point, he could also tell when they would be leaving and it was at the end of the day shift, and in a place where he was bound to come into contact with anyone exiting the room, that he had laid his trap.

For that was how it felt. Making the most innocent of enquiries had been alien to Harris' character and carried a strong taint of espionage, but loitering in the corridor leading directly to the outside world was definitely an ambush.

And with his command still shaking down, a new position in a different flotilla, and the prospect of returning to active service shortly, there shouldn't be anything else on his mind; certainly not the adolescent fascination he had developed for Second Officer Morris.

Which, again, was how it appeared. As far as relationships went, Harris had never been lax; in the past, several developed to the point of seriousness and it was probably due to his own, fixated, attitude that he was still single. Which was how he expected to remain, certainly for as long as hostilities continued. He was a professional officer with an important job to do; one he had been preparing for since signing on all those years before. Others – the majority, it seemed – might consider war to be a time for affairs and only a fool could ignore the fact that standards – along with morals – were steadily slipping, but Harris wanted nothing that might distract him.

Yet, strangely he did not feel Second Officer Morris would become a distraction. Almost as soon as they first met – first argued, as he guiltily remembered – there was something about the woman that, rather than divert him from his duty, suggested she might become an enhancement.

Obviously, such an impression could not have been made over words exchanged in the course of a single, stressful, evening; that would definitely suggest a schoolboy crush. No, Harris had seen her on a number of occasions since; once in the officers' mess with other senior Wrens, and again in the company of a bunch of rather loud reservist officers. There was also a general briefing when she supported the speaker – a superannuated admiral – and only the previous day they had passed on opposite sides of the street and exchanged smiles.

Even such scant contact had not lessened his interest, however, and he finally decided the best way to cure himself of this fascination was to meet the woman properly. Chances were, his interest would be one sided; on a base like *Wasp*, she must have the pick of far more suitable officers, while any future conversations would probably end up in another argument. Still, he was there at the end of the day shift, standing like a fool and feeling just as awkward as any lad meeting his first date, when the door to the Ops Room opened and a familiar figure appeared.

Thankfully she was alone – Harris' thoughts had not extended to what he might do if she were in company – and equally, she instantly recognised him. And was there also, perhaps, a hint of pleasure in that expression?

"Second Officer Morris," he said and, though no actor, Harris was pleased with the element of surprise in his tone.

"Yes, yes it's Lieutenant Commander Harris; how good to see you, sir. Were you making for Ops?"

Again, Harris' preparation had not been foolproof and even such an inane question was enough to break his façade.

"No." A cold wave ran down his back as he made the terrible admission. "Actually I was hoping to meet up with you. I think you're owed an apology."

His eyes fell as an inner feeling told him there was nothing left to do now but leave. Attractive women must be propositioned a thousand times a week and she would forget this in time. On glancing up, however, Harris was surprised to see a look of genuine pleasure on her face.

"Why, that's kind," she said. "I must confess we didn't part on the best of terms."

"I believe I cast doubt on your RDF," Harris said, and she smiled.

"Which was probably deserved. It really is a marvellous gadget though not without faults, and we can be a bit protective. So, I suppose it should have been me who sought you out."

"It makes no difference," he lied, then extended a hand. "I spoke in haste and am truly sorry."

50

She gave a brief laugh. "Lieutenant Commander, you have nothing to apologise for, I was equally short – it was a tense night. Besides, you were concerned about your command."

"Not so much the boat, more those aboard." Once more Harris found speaking the truth the easier option and, once more, it had the right effect.

"Which equally does you credit. Look, I've just come off watch." She glanced at her wrist. "I'm on an early tomorrow but have nothing on until then. Shall we grab a tea – or maybe some supper?"

Harris blinked. "Supper would be good – but perhaps not on the base?"

"Absolutely, though I'm not sure there's much in Dover itself and we'll never get a taxi at this hour."

"I'm billeted at The Grand," Harris said. "The restaurant's nothing special but civilised enough. And we could walk it if you've a mind."

"A walk sounds equally good." She smiled and took his arm as if it were the most natural thing in the world. "Shall we start now? I must say I'm starving!"

* * *

After his late arrival, Ryder had done all he could to catch up. The model before them did indeed represent a dockyard; one with a large central basin and what looked like an equally oversized dry dock. There was also a small harbour along with all the expected buildings and even a short mole, topped by a charming lighthouse. From his angle, he could see little further detail, but it was obvious the model had been carefully made and presumably represented somewhere currently in enemy hands. The place seemed familiar, though Ryder was equally sure he had never actually visited, and was almost sorry such an impressive, and well thought out, facility was apparently being eyed up for destruction.

However, such a target would equally be well defended. No gun emplacements were included in the model but there would be anti-aircraft batteries in abundance, many of which could be brought to bear on shipping, in addition to the inevitable larger coastal guns covering any approach. And that was ignoring the fact that harbours were inclined to contain ships; even one minor battlewagon would be a definite obstacle while a detachment of destroyers lining the quays and wharves might make a land or sea-based raid impossible.

Which meant any attack must surely be the preserve of the Air Force, and then Ryder noticed the mass of buildings representing a town sitting plumb in the middle of the complex. There was a well-known moratorium on the bombing of civilian targets, which probably explained the presence of so many high-ranking officers from both Navy and Army. This was obviously to be a combined operation. More than that, he had been appointed to lead the naval aspect, which was definitely a step up from liaison officer and, impossible though the project might appear, Ryder's senses were primed.

As soon as the meeting broke up he set out to learn more on an unofficial basis and sought out the pipe-smoking military type noticed earlier. This turned out to be the lieutenant colonel currently attached to No2 Commando. Colonel Charles, as he had been introduced, had spoken extensively and was obviously a man used to action; Ryder was sure he would provide the one piece of information he lacked.

"Of course, such a raid will require quite a commitment from you chaps," the colonel mused after they had been talking for some while. "There'll be a fair number of motor launches involved. Have you any experience with small craft?"

"Only the rag and stick variety," Ryder replied, "though I've cadged a few lifts with the Glory Boys in the past."

"Well, never mind that for now, we're still very much at the planning stage, but I've a mind it will also need something bigger; a destroyer, perhaps."

"Whatever, I'm sure we can adapt." There was a natural pause. They were of equivalent ranks and, though the lieutenant colonel appeared a little older, he had none of the stuffed-shirt attitude common in military men. Yet what Ryder needed to know would rather open him up, and any form of malice in the man would soon be revealed. "I wonder if I might ask a question?"

"Of course." There was a frank yet understanding look in the Army officer's eyes and Ryder took the plunge.

"This dockyard we're supposed to attack," he began. "Where the hell is it?"

Chapter Six

"It's that man again!" Smith announced as Bill Newman, one of *194*'s motor mechanics, entered the rating's room. "Been out on the town, have we?"

"I been about," Newman admitted, approaching his bunk.

"I'll bet," Daly, the Irishman, agreed. "An' seein' all the sights I've no doubt."

"Not much to see in Dover." Jelly spoke over his book.

"Ah, but there is," Gibson assured them. "You just need to know where to look – ain't that the case, Billy Boy?"

Rather than comment, Newman slung his hat on the bed and sat down next to it before bending to unlace his boots. Experience had taught him not to rise to such bait and he was in too good a mood from being with Sophie for barrack room banter.

"Not dishing the dirt, then?" Gibson persisted.

"Ah, don't bother the lad." Pickering spent much of his working hours with Newman and liked the chap.

"I'm askin'." Gibson raised his hands in the air with a look of assumed innocence. "Not touchin'."

"Well, maybe he don't want to be asked," the Geordie added.

For several seconds the room was silent as the pair exchanged glares, and then Gibson, who knew better than to make enemies amongst his shipmates, turned away.

"So, when we going to meet some of your doll's mates?" This was Smith, from the other side of the room. "Hear she's a driver – some of them Wrens are fair corkers." He looked across to Godliman on the adjoining bunk. "Might find a friend for Lenny. You'd like that wouldn't you?"

The boy lowered his newspaper but made no response.

"Ah, but didn't we try that afore?" Daly said. "Fixed us up proper, so he did. Finest bunch of colleens you'd ever care to meet."

"And what happened?" Gibson was oddly insistent.

"Well, wasn't that the problem?" Daly paused in the act of

removing his vest. "Fine they were in every way, though no time for common sailor boys like us."

"But if Billy's good enough?"

"Maybe he's got sommat we ain't?" Pickering again, and once more Gibson backed down.

"So, where'd you go, Bill?" Jelly asked more softly from the next bunk. Newman shrugged.

"A walk mostly," he said. "Then, when it started to rain, we had a cup of tea in the Italian café. Soph's on lates for the next five nights so we probably won't see each other for a while."

"And we'll be back on the job soon," Jelly said.

"Aye, more'n like." Newman paused and appeared to be considering, before leaning closer to Jelly. "But she's got a friend," he said.

Jelly lowered his book. "Really?"

Newman nodded. "New girl, just joined and still findin' her feet – first time away from home, you know the sort of thing. She came with us."

"So there were three of you?"

"It weren't like that," he said more softly. "Soph felt sorry for her, and so did I – after a while. Bonnie lass; maybe a little direct, but that could have been nerves. Comes from your part of the world an all."

"London?"

"Aye."

"North or south of the river?"

"Not sure."

"But she's looking for a friend?" Jelly also now spoke in little more than a whisper although the rest of the room had lost interest and were arguing about toothpaste.

"Reckon," Newman said. "Soon as there's a chance, I'll introduce you."

"I'd like that." His book had been thrust to one side. "What's her name?"

"Ann."

"Ann?" He tried it out again for size and seemed happy.

"That's it."

Jelly nodded. "Ann," he said once more. "Nice name."

* * *

54

"So, you didn't feel disappointed about losing your flotilla?"

Harris discovered Second Officer Morris' name was Laura, that she came from Surrey and was a librarian by training, while also revealing quite a bit about himself in the process. Yet quite how the conversation came around to his current status was a mystery. That said, they seemed to have been talking nonstop for the past three hours, so he supposed it was inevitable.

"It took a bit of getting used to," he said.

Laura's smile returned which, Harris decided, was one of the reasons he was being so honest, although there was also something cathartic about speaking so. Maybe it was because she had no connection with the affair; Laura's role in Operations involved deploying craft, but she wouldn't know any of the personalities. Or perhaps she was just a good listener?

"But standing down has given me a bit of space," Harris continued. Despite what was turning into a magical evening, he had been careful not to pass any criticism on his fellow officer.

"Space?"

"A breather, I suppose. My old flotilla was exactly that; a rag-bag assortment of boats mostly past their prime. And many of the hands, and officers, had been active since before Coastal Forces was officially formed; they were tired and so was I."

"So, you intend to stay as you are for a while?"

"The base captain's made noises about me being in line for the next flotilla SO post and I'd welcome the chance, though not holding my breath."

From being reasonably full an hour or two before, the hotel's restaurant was now almost empty and Harris guessed they would be asked to move to the bar before long. Yet he was surprisingly keen for the evening not to end. And Laura, it seemed, was in no rush.

"If Commander Brooks has said so, I'm sure it'll happen."

"Oh, I don't doubt that, but he may not be here. Or Dover Command may change." He stirred his tea. "The war does strange things," he said. "Sometimes it feels like everything you considered normal is being turned on its head."

"I know what you mean, but now America's joined in we might see some real progress. A year from now they could be planning to retake France; then there'll be no need for any of this, or HMS *Wasp*."

"I can't see them sending us home quite yet," he said. "There'll still be action in the Med and elsewhere – maybe the Far East..."

She grimaced. "Not so pleasant. But you'll be sticking it out?" she asked, her eyes suddenly serious. "With Johnston's flotilla, I mean?"

He dropped the spoon on the saucer.

"Of course, why do you ask?"

"You're clearly not happy under his command."

"I haven't said so."

She smiled. "You didn't need to; you're not quite as poker faced as you might think."

He raised an eyebrow, this was unexpected.

"You're obviously a man who cares a great deal about others; that was clear the first night we met."

"It was?"

She nodded. "We'd never had so many enquiries about a late arrival; you were genuinely concerned about those on board."

"It turned out I was right, and they were in danger," he said.

"Oh indeed, though you'd been asking for some time before. And it's equally clear you don't get on with Johnston, or any of his captains, come to that."

"Is it really that obvious?"

Now there was a gentle laugh that Harris found quite delightful. "Not obvious, perhaps, though I could tell."

"I'd been trying to give a neutral account." He smiled despite himself.

"Which is how I knew."

The door to the kitchen opened and the waiter who had been serving them looked over to their table.

"I think they want us to go," Harris said.

"And I think we should. I'm on an early tomorrow so have to be up at five."

"Are you billeted nearby?"

"At *Lynx*, it's where they put most of the Wrens."

"That's not far," he said, suddenly awkward.

"No, it isn't," she agreed. "We can walk it in no time."

* * *

56

Matters had moved on apace for Commander Ryder. After discovering the primary target for their attack would be St Nazaire or, more importantly, the massive dry dock it contained, he set to work with a vengeance.

Everything previously feared about the port and its defences had proved correct. Not only was the approach restricted to a narrow channel, the nearby coast was positively lined with batteries of every size and description, while the dock gates themselves were massive affairs that would take an equally phenomenal charge to destroy. But though the difficulties appeared great, the need for action – and success – was greater, for this was no mere whim from on high. The dry dock simply had to be destroyed; more than that, it must be done in the next few weeks, otherwise the ramifications would be too terrible to contemplate.

As with so many matters affecting the war, naval supremacy lay at the root of it. *Tirpitz*, a battleship in the same class and more powerful than *Bismarck*, was currently sheltering in a Norwegian fjord. Were she to make for the North Atlantic, havoc would be wreaked amongst the convoys currently keeping Britain fed. More than that, with America now an ally, vast quantities of military machinery, as well as troopships carrying thousands of fighting men, would equally be at risk. Only a combined effort from both navies and the probable loss of several capital ships would neutralise such a threat.

But for Germany to expose her largest warship so, a safe harbour and repair facilities on the French coast were needed. The dry dock at St Nazaire was over a thousand feet long and had been built to service the liner *Normandie*, though it might equally attend to a fifty-thousand-ton battleship, and was the only one on the west coast that could. Were it to be destroyed, *Tirpitz* could not be risked on the North Atlantic although Ryder was aware of an equally important reason for the attack.

Public morale had risen greatly after *Bismarck*'s sinking and having America join them in the fight had strengthened it further, yet the BEF's evacuation was still very much on the nation's conscience. Much had been done to present matters in a good light and there was no doubting the heroism displayed, yet Dunkirk had still been a retreat and France, another important ally, was effectively abandoned.

Since then, Hitler's penchant for invading hostile countries had come close to including England; with America alongside, that might be postponed but the need for physical retaliation of some kind remained. An audacious strike at the heart of enemy occupied territory would provide this, while also mollifying a France still smarting from her apparent desertion.

There had been several minor raids of late; since Christmas, Combined Operations carried out two in Norway and a radar station on the northern coast of France was recently targeted. But Ryder's current project would be in a different league and involve more troops as well as a far greater naval commitment. If successful, it would signal a significant change in the capacity and fortunes of British forces, and it was better not to think of the ramifications were it to fail.

Quite how to address the problem was proving tricky, however, and Ryder was hardly helped by an unexpected lack of support. It was soon clear the Admiralty's need for protocol and order was in direct contrast to the buccaneer aspect of the operation; he had begun with no staff or office, no 'phone, no car or driver, only the vaguest outline of the vessels that might be available, and under a month to organise the entire operation.

This deadline was a practical one and totally immovable. The port itself was situated several miles inland; any force capable of carrying enough men and equipment must negotiate the shoal waters of the River Loire. Only when March's spring tides added significantly to the depth, would such a venture be feasible. And it had to be that March; they could not afford to wait.

Ryder had already made great inroads and the basic outline was more defined, but much still needed to be done and the final, definitive, plan was yet to be agreed.

The initial requirement included Fairmile B motor launches, craft commonly used by Coastal Forces for harbour protection and general duties. Their lack of draught and relatively large capacity seemed ideal. The pipe-smoking Colonel Charles, who was proving a staunch ally, estimated each would comfortably carry fifteen commandos plus their equipment. Their normal range of five to six hundred nautical miles could be increased to the estimated nine hundred needed by the addition of supplementary tanks, while the crafts' low profile should make a nighttime approach more feasible. Fairmile Bs were also quick and cheap to build so would not add greatly to operational costs, although this was one consideration both men kept to themselves.

However, they soon discovered carrying enough men and equipment to destroy the harbour installations required an impossibly large fleet, while transferring four-and-a-half tons of explosives to wreck the dry dock was unthinkable when under fire. Consequently, and at a relatively early stage, it had been decided a small ship – perhaps a sloop, frigate or maybe a destroyer – was also needed, which created yet more problems.

The Admiralty maintained their spirit of non-cooperation and refused to spare even their most dilapidated warship, whilst the draught of any such vessel would mean an approach could only be made at the very height of the spring tides.

There was the possibility of using a Free French destroyer. The *Ouragan*, currently serving as a depot ship at Portsmouth, might be available although Ryder was reluctant to investigate too deeply as secrecy was vital. It was generally known the enemy expected some form of attack on the French coast, although the possibilities were wide and included the ports of Brest, Lorient, and La Rochelle in addition to St Nazaire. Were any hint of their target revealed it must mean an early cancellation. Furthermore, it would be impossible to involve a warship from another country without allowing their nationals to crew the vessel and neither Ryder nor Colonel Charles relished the prospect of mounting such an operation using two languages. Eventually, the Admiralty's hand was forced and a former American warship, supplied under the 1940 destroyers-for-bases agreement, was made available.

HMS *Campbeltown* had been launched after the end of the First World War and originally served in the US Navy as the USS *Buchanan*. Her flush deck and four funnels revealed her age and it was often mentioned that the only damage she caused while under the white ensign was accidental and to British shipping. When Ryder and Colonel Charles first viewed her, she had been anchored at Portsmouth; neither went aboard as the colonel was in uniform and security may have been compromised by an Army officer inspecting a commissioned warship. But she appeared ideal and was swiftly moved to Devonport for the necessary work to begin.

This involved removing her torpedo tubes and four-inch guns, replacing the latter with eight separate Oerlikons, which

Ryder felt would be more effective, both against light shore defences and air attack. The bridge required armour plating and her twelve-pounder was to be moved to the forecastle. It was hoped these changes, together with the removal of two funnels and adapting those remaining, would give a superficial resemblance to a *Mowe* class German warship.

Explosives had caused another headache. They had been fortunate in recruiting experts from both forces: Lieutenant Nigel Tibbetts RN and Captain Pritchard, Royal Engineers. It was agreed the content of twenty-four depth charges would create a sufficient blast to destroy the dock gates providing *Campbeltown* was brought into direct contact. This would mean effectively beaching a twelve-hundred-ton ship against the caissons themselves; no mean feat and one that must also be done without detonating the charges.

The dockyard had estimated two weeks to fully adapt *Campbeltown*, which Ryder felt was optimistic, although that only left them a further fourteen days to actually launch the raid and there was still so much to plan.

A signal had just come in from the Admiralty. After much debate, they were grudgingly allowing four more boats from the 20th Motor Launch flotilla. Together with the eight already promised, that gave him twelve Fairmile Bs, which at least made the current plan feasible, although he would have liked more. And he needed a sizeable gunboat – something along the lines of a Fairmile C as the Bs were simply too slow to act as a command vessel. His indent had been sent several days before and, doubtless, one would be supplied eventually. And – eventually – he should probably have everything but, unless the Admiralty dramatically changed their ways, it would be at the very last minute. Which only added frustration to what was already a hard enough task as, at that point, Ryder felt minutes were practically all they had.

Chapter Seven

The time had finally come for *194* to join Johnston's flotilla on a regular patrol. Leaning over the starboard side of the bridge, Harris gave the orders in a clear, loud voice.

"Let go for'ard – let go stern rope – hold on to your aft spring..."

The other two craft detailed for that night's sortie were already fired up and easing from their moorings; all *194* need do was follow. Her central engine had been running for some while and both wings would soon be properly warm but there was still time for an embarrassing breakdown.

"Slow astern starboard, stop starboard, slow ahead starboard – slow ahead port."

A flicker of light from the master's office gave them permission to leave and then, with *194* last in line, the three gunboats rumbled slowly away from the pens.

As they passed out of the harbour, Anderson gave a wave to the group standing on the wall before setting his mind to that night's activities. Their patrol would take in several areas where E- and R-boats had been spotted and one that Dover Command suspected of being a target for mine laying; not quite as exhilarating as a coastal raid or intercepting an enemy convoy, but sufficient to get the blood pumping. The weather was fine and dry, with a fair number of stars and a rising moon, although they had been warned of mist forming later, with the likelihood it would lead to dense fog. A click from the R/T repeater broke the expectant silence and then Johnston's voice came through.

"Very well, I'm assuming all is functioning correctly but if there are problems, message me immediately. We'll be making for Echo Two first to check for mine layers. Position yourself on my port quarter, Happy; Bobbo can take the starboard station. We'll have a gun check when properly clear; watch for my signal."

Harris and Anderson exchanged glances, but Johnston had more to say.

"And please remember, however experienced some might

consider themselves, neither of you has been out with me on a proper job. This will be very much a school run, and I shall be watching extremely carefully."

The repeater went dead and for a moment there was silence. Then Harris spoke.

"Bobbo?"

"I think it was meant in jest, sir."

Harris pulled a face. "Damned cheek, and I shall tell him so."

"It's his manner." Anderson could tell Phillips, at the wheel, was amused. "And an unfortunate one, but I really don't think the SO means anything by it."

"Maybe you're right," Harris said although he was clearly not convinced. "Frankly, Number One, I'd prefer it if he took a step back occasionally," he continued more softly. "We're all perfectly capable of organising our own fuelling and setting schedules for maintenance. That sort of interference can't all be down to an unfortunate manner."

"I think he's just concerned for the state of the flotilla," Anderson said, "and our welfare. You may remember making similar provisions when you were an SO."

Harris seemed to accept this, and Anderson was hoping the subject would be dropped when his captain spoke again.

"Well, I hope I didn't sound quite so much like a schoolmaster."

There was nothing Anderson could say to that. Privately he didn't care much for Johnston's attitude, but also knew Harris took exception easily. If only one of them would unbend enough to see the other had the right idea all might be fine; as it was, he doubted they would ever get on, and only wished Harris' own flotilla would hurry up and materialise.

The early moon picked out a tumble of water as Johnston increased speed. Hopgood's boat, being next in line, followed suit, and then Harris ordered their own engines up. The pitch rose steadily and soon *194* was on the plane, with only the aft part of her hull actually touching the water.

Travelling behind the other launches made the ride uncomfortable, but Hopgood soon took up station allowing Harris to adopt the opposite position off Johnston's starboard quarter. A flicker of blue from the flotilla leader signalled the gun check and, after Smith released several rounds from the Oerlikon and both Daly and Gibson liberally sprayed the air with tracer, a ten-degree turn to port was signalled and they could finally settle down to the night's activities.

As the boat stabilised, Harris turned to Anderson. "How far to Echo Two?"

He would shortly go down to the wheelhouse and begin to plot their course but, like any good schoolboy, Anderson had done his homework. "At this speed, little more than an hour."

"Very well," Harris said. "Let's see what the night will bring. And I must say it's good to be back in business."

* * *

In the cupboard that was optimistically referred to as *194*'s W/T office, Jelly closed down the bridge repeater. Though a relatively new recruit – he joined when hostilities began – Jelly knew all about security protocol and disapproved of their new SO's overuse of radio telegraphy. But at least they had increased the revs and were properly on their way. Experience of many such patrols had taught him all should be quiet as *194* travelled to the first waypoint.

When riding on the plane, with the boat half sailing, half flying, speeds of close to forty knots could be reached, which meant a distance conventional vessels took days to navigate would be covered in a single night. From the feel of the boat, Jelly knew they had several hundred revs in hand, yet *194* was still moving at quite a pace. And he was glad; when travelling fast, she was far more stable, meaning the bucket by his feet might not be necessary.

There were no windows or scuttles in Jelly's tiny cell; the only time he was likely to see the outside world was if called on to assist in a depth charge attack; that or abandon ship. Yet he was probably the best informed of all the ratings as much of his work entailed relaying updates to Dover Command and passing on information from their base in return.

Apart from the lack of human contact, being cooped up so was no hardship and actually had an advantage; the glow from numerous valves in each set was enough to keep his space pleasantly warm and, once seated behind the minuscule desk,

Jelly didn't notice the lack of room.

There should be no more from their loquacious senior officer for some while, so he flipped a switch on the W/T. A flurry of Morse filled his headphones, altering in pitch as he turned the dial, but the pencil that was almost a permanent fixture in his right hand remained motionless. For this was routine stuff: messages to and from those currently in the Channel; requests for weather updates, reports of floating wreckage or suspect sightings out of sector, and often simply idle chatter. He carefully selected the frequency for Dover Command and, at a suitable point, logged in and received a brief confirmation that *194* was on the plot. Then, after setting the incoming message alert, he switched to R/T and repeated the process.

There the wavelengths were clearer as communication was by speech although the traffic broadly mirrored that in Morse. He eased the volume up as a foreign voice came through. There may be Free French vessels active nearby and the Dutch were starting to be posted further south, although experience told him he was listening to the enemy.

Jelly had no ear for languages, his few stock German phrases having been learned from the music hall or cinema. And none were in use that night, though it was equally clear the speaker posed no threat. He may even have been reciting a comic monologue as there was the occasional interjection from another, more distant, voice and often one or the other would succumb to laughter. Jelly had heard a thousand similar conversations from bored radio operators, be they German or English, and soon, he supposed, the Americans would be joining in.

Quickly he returned to W/T and switched to the frequency agreed with their SO. He knew his opposite number in Johnston's boat reasonably well. White came from Manchester and had been in the same training batch as Jelly; if it wasn't for his lamentably lax approach to the craft, they would have been friends. But Chalky would never be a natural telegraphist; even at the end of the ten-week course, he was still rusty on Morse and never understood the simple pleasure in taking a set to pieces. That he had survived for so long in the SO's boat was a mystery, though Lieutenant Commander Johnston had already approached Jelly to suggest an exchange.

A knock came at the door, which immediately opened

outwards, and the scarred face of Pickering, the mechanic, was thrust into his tiny world.

"Hey up, Wobbler, how's it with you, man?"

All knew of Jelly's weak stomach and most understood if they had suffered in the past.

"Well enough, Picks; Carter let you escape, has he?"

"Engines are running smooth so he said I could do a char round. You want some?"

"That would go down well," Jelly said.

"Long as it stays that way." The mechanic gave a brief smile before closing the door, leaving Jelly alone with his radios.

* * *

Reg Gibson, womaniser, thief, all-time wastrel and – more recently – murderer, was bored. After settling in *194*'s port turret, and then the obligatory testing of his twin Vickers, he had been singularly unoccupied and a mind like Gibson's should never be allowed to grow idle. For much of the time he had been watching the other British vessels with little consideration for what lay ahead; his calculations being of a more practical nature.

He had started with his own craft. Being American built and part of what had become Lend-Lease, *194* was difficult to value but both the flotilla leader's vessels and the one almost parallel to his own were British Powerboat products. And, like so much war machinery regularly purchased by public subscription, their cost was openly publicised. Gibson had no idea if these prices were adjusted, but reckoned the cost of an Elco, like *194*, must be close to seventy-five-thousand pounds. Which was roughly the same as three-and-a-half Wellington bombers and nearly two of the new four-engine Lancasters everyone seemed to be talking about. On that basis, he guessed their little trio of gunboats was worth close on a quarter of a million pounds.

He licked his lips; this was important money, enough to change a man for life, along with the lives of many others. And though he could think of no direct route to such an amount, it was obviously disposable. By morning several thousand gallons of high-octane fuel would have been expended while, if it proved a busy night, so would much of their ammunition. Furthermore, it was possible – likely even – at least one of the miniature warships

65

would shortly end up on the seabed – that or in a thousand pieces. And in time each would be replaced; superseded by more advanced vessels at a considerably higher cost.

Gibson fiddled with the breach of one of his guns. Petty crime had been a major feature of his life; burglaries, extortion, and outright intimidation having provided a comfortable living only interrupted by one short spell in prison. But accounting for that postmaster had definitely placed him in a different league. After several weeks of hearing nothing, Gibson now considered himself safe and, if he could carry off a major crime with so little planning, there was no end to future possibilities.

The idea of something significant definitely appealed; a crime to set him up for life while leaving others in awe of his brilliance. He was in no rush, of course; with a steady wage along with all living expenses paid, Gibson was doing alright and, as nighttime patrols had finally returned, his appetite for violence should be sated. Before him lay two lethal weapons especially provided so he could kill and kill again. In the past, he had accounted for two enemy aircraft and heaven only knew how many German sailors.

That very night they might be needed once more and, if so, he would return to praise and a hero's welcome, rather than a bunch of sour-faced rozzers. And while he was living off the King, suppressing his animal instincts and planning the big job, there was always the chance of a bit of petty larceny on the side.

His present crowd were a dull lot, but there would be others in the Navy equally enlightened; he need only meet up with a few and there would be devilment indeed. At that moment Gibson had no idea what this major crime would entail and was keeping an open mind. Yet of one thing he was certain; when the right chance came, he would know and be ready.

* * *

"Cold enough for you, Lenny?" Fred Smith grinned cheerfully at his loader, but the young seaman made no response other than to pull his rubber goon suit closer.

From their position at *194*'s main armament, a 20mm Oerlikon mounted aft, they could see little other than the English coast being steadily swallowed by the growing mist. And though it was undeniably cold, both were seasoned enough not to notice – until the fact was pointed out. But the chill of open water was no great hardship; rather than ice, there was little more than heavy condensation on the metalwork, and both had known far worse.

"Simple patrol, or so they reckons," the older man continued. Smith needed to shout above the roar of engines mounted below, but they were used to communicating over such a din. Besides, he considered it a duty to engage his friend in conversation, even if Godliman insisted on limiting his speech to essentials and what was required when on duty.

The latter came as some consolation. In exercise, Godliman was as good as ever; just as efficient when changing magazines while also appearing to know exactly what Smith was targeting. Indeed, despite his partner's change, they still worked perfectly as a team and, if Smith was any judge, may even have improved.

Quite what that night would bring was another matter, though. The difference between action and exercise was vast and if a line of spot-lit trollops could turn Godliman into a sobbing mess, how would he react when the guns began to fire in anger?

And there was a subtle drawback to patrol work. Were this a proper raid on an enemy convoy, or even a hit-and-run against shore emplacements, they would know what was in store and could prepare for it. Chances were strong tonight's little escapade would end up peaceful, with the rounds used in test the only ones fired. Yet, a meeting with the enemy was likely to be both unplanned and unexpected, and Smith didn't think Godliman would cope with that sort of surprise.

Such an encounter probably meant E-boats; superior craft in every respect although most enemy vessels could outgun *194*. Even the slower VPs – *Vorpostenboote*; little more than converted fishing boats bearing an almost benign appearance – carried 88mm cannon and were protected by heavy gauge steel and slabs of concrete. Smith's own gun was by no means feeble and, carefully handled, brought dramatic results yet it could not be fired far forward of the beam and, as most of their armour closely resembled straw mattresses, it would always be an unequal fight.

But then the concept of fairness was one of the reasons the pair had chosen Coastal Forces in the first place. For Smith the decision was simple; though no politician, he did know right from wrong and was a vehement defender of the former. That any man, party, or country could behave as Germany had offended him deeply and he was determined to stop further outrages, especially if the recent horror stories had any basis in truth.

And for Godliman the cause was even plainer. Though it was years since being inside a synagogue, he'd also heard the rumours, along with more verifiable accounts from distant family members forced to abandon their homeland before the war. Their stories might lack the awfulness of those in current circulation, but still told of a prejudice verging on evil, which was enough for him.

The sinking of his previous vessel only strengthened Godliman's convictions as well as his hatred of all things German. He knew how others viewed this and appreciated Smith's efforts to reawaken the happy-go-lucky Lenny of old. But after seeing so many of his friends die at close hand and realising more – including himself – were likely to follow, he had no further need for humour. Instead, Godliman's life was now dedicated to destroying any aspect of the country he now despised.

It was indeed cold, but he barely noticed the condensation from his breath. And though many considered their rubber suits uncomfortable, Godliman appreciated the clinging embrace of his, and that it contained a warmth springing from the anger that burned inside.

* * *

"We're nearing Echo Two now." Anderson had come up from the wheelhouse that doubled as the boat's chart room and, though the plotting table was lit by a red lamp, it would be several minutes before he had full night vision.

"Very good," Harris said. "No sign of minelayers and the SO's been agreeably quiet."

As his eyesight steadily improved, Anderson decided much was as before. Hopgood's craft lay off their port beam and Johnston's the port bow; all three gunboats were travelling at a reasonable speed and *194*'s engines had been running for so long the noise could almost be ignored. The moon had yet to rise fully and there was more mist, yet anything within a mile would still be in plain sight. And on the French coast – to his certain knowledge

68

no more than three miles off – an occasional stray light could be seen.

"Seems empty enough," Anderson agreed. "I wonder what the SO has in mind."

A whistle from the W/T voice pipe drew their attention and Anderson flipped the lid open. "What is it, Tel'?"

"SO's reporting the area clear to Dover Command." Jelly's voice could just be made out over the drumming of their engines. "He's planning on heading for the next waypoint."

"Nice of him to let us know." This was Phillips, at the helm, and Harris frowned.

"That will do, 'Swain."

Anderson bent forward to the voice pipe once more. "Thank you, Tel', keep us advised."

"How far to the next waypoint?" Harris asked.

"About ten miles to the northeast," Anderson said. "I gather three E's were spotted by aircraft earlier this afternoon."

Harris shrugged. "Should be long gone by now, but we may as well be sure."

Anderson had opened his mouth to reply when the R/T repeater burst into life and Johnston's voice cut in.

"We have a contact on our RDF. Two jigs bearing red oh-nine-oh. I shall be turning shortly; you fellows stay on my tail but fan out: we'll see if we can't surprise 'em."

Once more Harris and Anderson exchanged glances; as instructions went, they were hardly comprehensive, and it was risky using the R/T so close to the enemy shore.

"There he goes," Phillips said as Johnston's boat turned to port and her speed increased further.

"Port fifteen, 'Swain, and bring her up to twenty-one hundred."

Phillips dutifully repeated the command and the boat lurched forward as the engines' pitch rose still higher. Soon they were scudding over the dark waves, the very fabric of *194* vibrating in sympathy with her Packards.

Johnston's contact came into view less than ten minutes later. The wind was picking up, making the mist roll and in one of the eddies, a low hull could just be made out. Daly and Gibson noticed it simultaneously and announced the fact.

"Appears to be stationary." Harris lowered his glasses and

glanced towards Johnston's boat. "Though the SO's going in at full tilt."

That was certainly the case. Johnston altered course only slightly before making straight for the contact at what must have been over thirty-five knots. For all anyone aboard *194* knew, he might have flashed a challenge, but there was no reply from the mystery hull, and they had little choice other than to follow.

"I'd give a lot to see that RDF screen," Anderson shouted.

"Wouldn't do much good." Harris was peering through his binoculars once more. "Whatever their gizmo's picked up will only become an enemy when we get a proper visual fix."

"But Johnston said they'd spotted more than one," Anderson pointed out, and the glasses came down again.

"That he did," Harris agreed. "And it would be nice to know where."

* * *

They soon found out; just as the mystery hull was becoming more defined, a series of flashes from her bridge caught their attention.

"Answering a challenge?" Anderson suggested.

"Hardly." Harris raised his glasses once more. "Lamp's pointing east, we're only getting the edge."

Both officers looked across as the unmistakable outline of an enemy R-boat emerged from the mist off their starboard bow.

It was a common sighting in the Channel. Though slower than an E-boat, the R would be larger and carried more crew, as well as a formidable armament that easily out-gunned the British craft. This particular example lay closer than the original sighting and Harris immediately hit the firing gongs.

But no shots followed: the fresh target was beyond the effective range of *194*'s machine guns while they would have to turn considerably to allow her aft Oerlikon to speak. The enemy was better placed, however, and a stream of green tracer began to play about Johnston's boat.

Why doesn't Johnston take us to port?" Harris demanded. Anderson glanced over; they could disobey orders and make the move themselves but that would take them across the SO's wake; a perilous move at such speed, while they might also collide with Hopgood.

70

Johnston's boat remained at the head of the pack and was returning fire from her light machine guns, though tracer showed the shots falling short. Anderson watched in silent horror; for as long as their leader's craft remained the centre of attention they need not worry, but soon it must be hit, at which point the Germans would look for further targets. He glanced back; Smith and Godliman had the Oerlikon trained as far forward as possible, although it would be a while before the enemy came within their arc.

"We have to steer to port," Harris shouted. "There's cover in that bank!"

Sure enough, a thicker area of mist lay close to that would conceal them all. Quite why Johnston had not made for it was a mystery but with German shells raining about his ears, he may have been distracted.

"Bring her back, 'Swain!"

Phillips, at the wheel, looked over to check, but Harris was adamant. "Drop to fifteen hundred and take us ten degrees to port!"

The boat slowed just as further fire erupted from the first sighting, now revealed as yet another R-boat. This time *194* was the target but her sudden reduction in pace was enough to throw the German gunners off, and a flurry of tracer landed forward of her bows.

And then they were turning; as *194* passed over Johnston's wake a series of shudders shook her fragile hull and for a few desperate seconds Hopgood lay almost dead ahead. Then the other gunboat's speed cleared the way allowing Harris to aim more purposefully for the bank of heavy fog. As he did a deep clatter aft told them their Oerlikon finally had sight and a stream of red tracer was being sent towards the nearest R-boat's foredeck.

"Johnston's seen sense, he's turning!" Harris was having to bellow now as Daly's Vickers had also come into range and was adding to the bombardment.

Anderson looked forward; their SO's boat was indeed making for shelter and, as he watched, Hopgood turned to follow. For several seconds the nearest German was treated to the concentrated fire of all three gunboats then, finally, they reached the safety of the fog bank.

At first, it seemed the mist would be too light to fully shield them, but in no time they had lost sight of all other craft and *194* might have been alone in a dark and very private world.

"Bring her back to twelve hundred." Harris' order seemed to break some kind of spell, and when Phillips replied, and the engine note dropped yet further, Anderson felt himself relax.

"Proper peasouper," the captain added. "Though welcome nonetheless."

Anderson leant forward to the W/T office voice pipe. "Anything from the SO, Tel'?"

"His telegraphist's just reporting the contact, sir," Jelly replied, then, "Hold on, he's coming through on R/T."

The monitor cracked twice, and then Johnston's voice echoed around the bridge.

"Right, well that wasn't entirely to plan..."

It was the first time Anderson had heard their flotilla leader sound at all shaken, but then he supposed he had a right to be.

"Bobbo, you were out of line breaking formation like that, though I accept the fog looked inviting."

Harris turned to his second in command who matched his look of shock, but Johnston had more to say.

"RDF shows the Germans turning back, they clearly didn't like what we dished out."

"They wouldn't like it any more if we continued," Harris muttered.

"Frankly a pair of Rs is too much for us to take on," Johnston continued. "I've reported them to Dover Command. They'll detail a larger force to intercept."

"But shouldn't we stay in contact?" Anderson asked, and Harris shrugged.

"Next waypoint is southwest of Echo Seven." Johnston was sounding more positive now. "Once we're clear of this mist we can reform and make for that."

"Echo Seven is considerably to the north," Anderson added.

"Keep the revs down and stay alert," the SO continued. "We should be in clearer air soon. And when we do group up once more, can we all try to remain in formation?"

* * *

"I'm not saying we should have taken on both those R-boats," Harris said later that night. The rest of the patrol had proved uneventful, and they were heading back for *Wasp*. Anderson had taken the helm to allow Phillips to use the heads and the officers were able to talk in relative privacy. "But when suspect craft are detected, a little more decorum is called for."

"Rather than charging in at maximum revs," Anderson agreed.

Both men knew speed was probably a gunboat's greatest asset, and may have saved their senior officer's craft from certain destruction. But the resource should be used with care.

"A staggered line ahead formation might also have been wise," Harris added.

"As it is, we're being blamed for breaking formation."

"I know, and it galls," Harris sighed. "Brooks said to keep my head down and I really thought I could, though now it doesn't seem quite so easy."

Anderson considered this. *194* was back to being a slick and effective gunboat. For that, and the prospect of leading their own flotilla, to be jeopardised because her captain did not get on with the senior officer seemed foolish in the extreme.

"You could try speaking with the man?" he suggested.

"Oh, I shall, don't you worry," Harris replied. "He may be the SO, but we're still the same rank. And if he doesn't listen, I shall take it up with Brooks."

Anderson nodded. That did not sound good, but he could hear Phillips talking with Jelly in the wheelhouse and knew their brief time of privacy would soon be at an end.

Then Harris cleared his throat before lowering his voice and adding, "But first I'm going to stop him calling me Bobbo."

Chapter Eight

"You handled them magazines perfect," Smith told Godliman. "Just like in the past – I were proud of you."

Both had taken full plates from the NAAFI servers but, while Smith had almost finished his breakfast, Godliman still picked at his food.

"So, what d'you reckon?" the older man persisted. "We're not rostered for a couple of days, an' there's only the usual service to do on Bertha so we'll probably be given liberty straight after. Fancy a run into town?"

Godliman shrugged and continued to annoy the beans with his fork.

"We could go for a walk – you'd like that. Maybe see if we can get up on them cliffs?"

There was no response.

"Come on, China!" Smith was starting to lose patience. "There's nothing of you, get some food inside or you'll waste away."

More to the point, if Godliman carried on as he was, the PMO would start taking an interest. Their shipmates were reasonably tolerant, but all must have noticed the boy's behaviour; it only needed an unwelcome word, and his pal would be whisked away by the white coats.

"Room for a little one?"

Smith looked up; Gibson, their port gunner, wanted to sit at their table.

"Help yourself," Smith told him. The three joined *194* at the same time; all were gunners, and all came from London; facts that should have made for instant friendship, yet Smith, for one, had no wish to be close. There wasn't anything wrong with Gibson, though he did have an air about him that Smith definitely did not like. More than that, it frightened him.

"Not feelin' hungry, then?" The newcomer addressed Godliman through a mouth already full. The youngster shook his head but said nothing.

"It's being so cheerful that keeps him going," Gibson told Smith.

"He's tired after last night, that's all," Smith said.

"Is that right?" A piece of bacon leapt from Gibson's mouth as he spoke. "Now me, there's nothing I likes more than a busy evenin'. And if I get to fire me guns, so much the better."

Godliman had put down his fork and was looking pale.

"Yeah, well we won't be going out again for a while," Smith said. "We was just talking about heading off base, ain't that right, Lenny?"

"Hit Dover?" Gibson brightened. "I'd be up for that if you've a mind. Maybe check out a few of the dames." He spoke the last sentence in a bad American accent. "Though if we don't find local talent there's a number of likelies on base I've me eyes on. Know what they say: 'up with the lark and to bed with a Wren'!"

Gibson gave them the benefit of a toothy grin.

"That weren't what we had in mind," Smith said.

"What then?"

"Lenny and me was thinking about a walk."

"A walk?"

"It's what we likes." Smith was mildly defensive. "Get away from this place and stretch our legs: a bit of fresh air."

"I gets all the fresh air I want at sea." Gibson was now well into his breakfast and had started casting occasional glances at Godliman's still-full plate.

"Well, that's alright then." Smith gave a quick wink in his friend's direction. "We weren't planning on making you come."

"No, I'm up for it." Gibson wiped his plate with a piece of bread, then began to lick each of his fingers. "Never know who you might meet on them cliffs. And, if you get lucky, there're always bushes. Hey Goldie, you done with that breakfast?"

"No!" For Godliman to speak at all was a rare occurrence and his voice sounded unexpectedly loud, at least to Smith's ears. Gibson instantly withdrew his outstretched hand.

"Alright, alright, I were only askin'."

"And no to the walk!" the lad added, before taking a deliberate forkful of beans and thrusting them into his mouth.

"Well, someone's got out of bed the wrong side," Gibson said, though Smith noticed a slight blush on his face.

"You're not coming." Godliman was now positively digging

into his breakfast.

"Fine, though that's hardly the way to talk to a shipmate."

"He don't mean nothing by it," Smith explained. "It's just me and Lenny likes our walks."

"You're welcome to 'em." Gibson was standing now. "And you're welcome to each other. And, while you're about it, stay away from me, 'cause I sure ain't interested."

"Seems to have touched a nerve," Smith said after Gibson left.

"Good riddance." Godliman had now finished more than half his meal.

"Hey, that's better," Smith said, noticing this. "Bit of grub'll do you good." He glanced at Gibson's empty plate, beside which stood an enamel mug still filled with tea. "And our friend seems to have left a mug of char behind; fancy that an' all, do you?"

* * *

"I know Buster Johnston well, and it sounds just like him!"

Harris blinked. He genuinely thought Laura's position in Ops would have isolated her from seagoing personnel. But then she was stationed at *Wasp* and, if a recluse like him had met up with her, others would have also. Still, he didn't like the sound of Johnston being a friend.

"You didn't say that," he said, "not when I mentioned him before."

She smiled. "Maybe you wouldn't have been quite so forthcoming if I had."

"And perhaps I'm being unfair," Harris said. Being in her company certainly made him less dogmatic. "It's probably just a clash of personalities."

"It does rather sound like it."

The heavily framed glasses distracted from her eyes which, now that he could look at them properly, Harris found especially lovely. They were lunching in the dining room at The Grand which, after a brief dalliance with other Dover restaurants, was the best of a bad lot. And, as they both often worked late into the night, daytime meals had also become the norm.

"You called him Buster," he said.

"His nickname apparently, though chosen by himself, I

76

think."

"Aren't all nicknames?"

She laughed. "Probably, though it isn't what the Wrens call him."

Laura didn't smoke, Harris liked that, and they both enjoyed a pot of tea after a meal, one of the few things The Grand did well.

"So, he's generally known to all at *Lynx*?"

She gave him an odd look. "Now that I wouldn't know, but he is a regular visitor."

"Is that sort of thing allowed?"

"*Lynx* isn't *exactly* a convent," she said, replacing her cup. "Gentlemen callers are permitted. Of course, it has to be by written invitation, and only during daylight hours. And naturally, there must be a middle-aged chaperone present at all times."

That did surprise him. "Really?"

She laughed. "Oh Bob, you're such a fool! No, of course not. He can come to the Wrennery; anyone is allowed if they're invited. We're officers after all. If they can't trust us to keep our legs together, what are we doing handling official secrets?"

Harris had spent all his adult life in the Navy and considered himself immune to any form of vulgarity, but Laura's words shocked him deeply.

"One of his captains is seeing my roommate," she continued, oblivious to this, "though I think our friend Johnston has his eyes on her as well."

That did not surprise Harris. "So, what do you call him?" he asked.

"I'm not sure I should say."

After what he had already learned, her reticence seemed ridiculous. "You may as well," he said.

"Alright then, we call him Bubbles."

"Bubbles?"

"Yes, rather good, don't you think?" Laura collected the teapot and filled both their cups. "Next time he gets you down, just think of that."

* * *

77

Gibson took a second look along the street; there was still no sign of movement. The lock was a standard one and only three levers – it might as well have been there for decoration. He inserted his specially adapted screwdriver and felt for the tumblers. They moved as he expected, and the bolt eased back. Another look around. Nothing had changed. The door opened easily. Gibson slipped inside.

There was the faintest hint of staleness in the air, but no more; the house was lived in, though currently empty. He moved down the hallway and into a tiny kitchen. A pile of dirty crockery lay on the draining board and the table was covered in crumbs; the feeling of relaxed domesticity struck a chord somewhere deep in Gibson's subconscious.

"Messy buggers," he told himself firmly.

A greatcoat hung on the back of the kitchen door and there was an ordinary Wren's hat on the sideboard; these must be married quarters. Gibson pulled a face then moved across to the three-ringed cooker and touched the kettle with the back of his hand. Cold, whoever lived there must be working the dayshift; he had all the time in the world.

Still Gibson would be brief: it was the safest way. Moving back, he considered the stairs but chose instead the living room. This was tidier, although still carried the same horrible homeliness that was the last thing he wanted in his life. The remains of last night's fire had not been cleared and two ashtrays needed emptying. He noticed a glass-fronted cabinet, which held no sign of silver, just a few ill-matched glasses. There would be nothing of value for him here; even the pictures were cheap prints, and the cloying cosiness was quite repugnant, yet Gibson continued to explore further.

The needlework basket might be more promising, such things had contained all manner of treasures in the past although this one held nothing more than needles and thread. He removed the top tray and dropped it on the floor. Beneath, there was only a darning mushroom, thimbles, and a collection of buttons. The box was also discarded, and Gibson moved on.

There was a wireless – a large one and too big to carry down the street, while such things were easily traced. The sideboard might be worth a shot though; two drawers and a double cupboard beneath. He bent down and opened one of the doors;

there was an assortment of plates and what looked like a tea service; no use to him. He checked the next and found nothing of further interest then, leaving both doors open, Gibson moved up to the drawers.

The first came out fully, spilling its contents on the floor. He glanced down; mainly stationery: envelopes, notepaper, and pens. An ink bottle had smashed and was spreading its contents across the floorboards. He reached down and collected a line of stamps then slipped them into his pocket.

The second was locked; usually a good sign. Again, the bent screwdriver came into its own and he jemmied the drawer free amid a mass of splinters. Once more Gibson opened it fully, this time looking more carefully at the papers that fell out. He kicked them over with his boot; what might have been a will, and some certificates – educational mainly and several were marked Royal Navy. One might have been for a birth, but they were no use to him. There were also some photographs; the ink was already spreading onto them.

A vase on the sideboard shelf caught his eye. He tipped it over but all that fell out was a small key – presumably for the locked drawer. The vase fell to the floor where it smashed.

There was nothing else of interest – at least nothing to excite the senses of one such as him. It was just the usual clutter ordinary folk accumulated and worthless; the senseless paraphernalia of their comfortable lives. Gibson gritted his teeth and moved on.

A narrow staircase reached up to an equally mean landing. From this, two rooms led off. He checked the first; a pair of single beds, lots of boxes and a couple of suitcases; maybe this wasn't married quarters after all, although the Navy definitely owned the place. He moved across to the window and peered down at a tiny garden – another miserable affair with an outside jakes by the back door and an Anderson air raid shelter. Some effort was being made to grow vegetables and a woman's bicycle leant against the fence.

Back across the landing to the front room. The door was closed; he had to push hard to make it open and when he did the darkness took him by surprise. The curtains were drawn – something he had missed on checking out the place. A Bakelite switch was by the door, and he flicked it down. The low-wattage bulb was just bright enough to show him the room.

Again, two single beds; one was made but the other looked slept in; the sheets being pulled back. There was also a warmth, probably explained by the drawn curtains and closed door. Gibson glanced about; a shabby wardrobe and a small chest of drawers, all as cheap and nasty as they came. He was definitely wasting his time, though this must be better than prancing around the cliffs with Laurel and Hardy.

He moved across to the chest and opened the lowest drawer. A quick rummage assured him it held nothing other than crisp white shirts. Tossing them to one side and leaving the drawer open he moved up to the next which was slightly more interesting.

It held women's underwear; stockings, suspenders, and the like. Lingerie held only a basic attraction for Gibson although he had found any amount of valuables stuffed inside a pair of knickers. But his rapid search only left a heap of lace on the uncarpeted floor. Gibson took a final look before deciding to call it a day, and it was then that he heard the back door close.

He froze. It was a terraced house so presumably whoever it was had come from the garden, yet there was no one there when he looked. Then he remembered the jakes.

Realisation ran through him like an electric shock. Someone must have been asleep in the nearby bed and, just before he entered, slipped outside to relieve themselves.

There were footsteps in the kitchen; not loud, probably a woman's. Then he heard the stairs creak.

Gibson had been in similar situations before and was used to controlling his emotions. He might try for the window, but that would mean turning his back on whoever it was, and his instinct was to confront them.

The bedroom door was only half closed. He thought he heard a slight intake of breath and then, slowly, it creaked open.

He was right, it was a woman, a young one. She was dressed in a plain pink bathrobe and wore fluffy slippers while the short, brown hair was ruffled. Yet it was a pleasant face and one Gibson felt immediately drawn to.

On seeing him she jumped visibly, then pulled the robe closer as her mouth opened. But there was no scream and, as Gibson moved nearer, he sensed there never would be.

"So, you're Ann," Jelly said after Bill Newman and his girlfriend had left them.

"And you're David."

He was dressed in his number two serge suit while she wore a Wren driver's uniform. Neither outfit exactly flattered and standing outside a boarded-up greengrocers was hardly the most romantic of places. Her eyes were dark brown and kind and, though not exactly slim, she exuded a warmth that Jelly found disturbingly attractive.

"Are you really called Jelly?" she asked.

"That's my surname," he admitted. "Friends call me Dave – that or Wobbler."

"I think I prefer Dave."

Yes, they were definitely nice eyes, and she had freckles; it was just a shame her hair was mainly hidden under that cap.

"I think I do as well," he said. "Look, do you want to go for a walk, or something?"

"A walk sounds good, but we'd better not be long; it'll be getting dark soon."

Being a Wednesday afternoon, those shops still in business were closed. Only the nearby Italian Café remained lit and, as Newman and his girl had been heading there, it was denied to them.

"What say we make for the cliffs?" he said.

"You mean Dover Castle – isn't that off limits?"

He shook his head. "Round by the Western Heights, it's much closer."

"I thought that were an' all."

He shrugged. "Some parts are; they got land mines, guard dogs and everything. And there's a coastal battery covered in barbed wire." She was still assessing him, so he gave a reassuring smile. "But I know a way through," he said, "and it's a clear day, so we'll probably get a good view of the sea."

They began to walk and quickly fell into step.

"I'd have thought you'd be sick of the sea in your job," she said.

"Fat chance," he laughed. "Most of the time I'm stuck in the W/T office."

"Posh."

He shook his head. "It's about the size of a broom cupboard."

"Can you see the sea?"

"No windows," he said, "though I still get sick."

She glanced at him sideways. "What, you mean seasick?"

"Yup, our boat dips about like nobody's business."

"But you're a sailor!"

"That might be how I'm dressed." He added a laugh, though inside was cursing. Only a fool would have admitted to failings so early on, but then Jelly had never found socialising easy.

"So, what d'you do?" she persisted. They were almost at the end of the town now and had reached the path that would lead them to the woods beyond. "I mean when you feel ill?"

He shrugged. "Well, sometimes I'm sick." No, this definitely was not the topic for a first date. Ann, though, appeared intrigued.

"But how d'you do your job; send all them messages and things? And talk to the other boats?"

"You just have to close your mind to it," he said. "Most times it gets better after a while and, if we're at sea for long, goes completely."

"That's amazing."

He stopped, certain she was joking, and she paused also.

"No, I mean it," she said. "I were car sick as a kid, messed up my uncle's Riley something rotten. Ended up I had to stay at home when he took us out, though I weren't sorry." She thought for a while, then began to walk on more slowly. "'Cause it's the most horrible feeling in the world," she said. "An', if I had it now, there's no way I could be a driver, yet you carry on going to sea..."

"I don't think it's the same when you drive." Jelly realised they were now speaking quite intensely and was unsure how to continue. "I mean, if they let me steer, I probably wouldn't get so ill." He'd meant that as a joke, but she was taking it seriously.

"Have you tried, steering I mean?"

"Only the once, and it were alright, though we were in action at the time. I prefer to be with my radios."

She shook her head. "So you go to sea, but are stuck in a cupboard, get seasick, though still have to work *and* fight the Germans?"

"That's about it." There remained the feeling she might be laughing at him, although her face was serious; concerned even. And that initial attraction – which, to Jelly's mind came close to electrical – was still very evident. Some strands of dark brown hair had worked loose from her cap and now trailed around her face making her look both respectable and oddly reckless. And though she might lack conventional good looks, to him she was breathtakingly attractive. It was just a shame they'd started off on such a foolish subject.

"Well, I think it's wonderful." Ann turned to look at him again and suddenly the words would not come. Worse than that, Jelly knew he was staring.

"Hardly," he said at last.

"No, really. Putting up with all that when you might end up injured – or worse – that's marvellous, Dave." There was a sudden look of concern. "You don't mind me calling you Dave?"

"No," he said. "I don't mind at all."

* * *

They had just finished the weekly intelligence briefing, a time when confidential information relevant to the flotilla was shared with the boats' commanding officers, and the last thing Harris wanted was to be collared by Johnston. But the man had made a beeline for him as soon as the meeting dispersed and now placed a comradely arm around his shoulder.

"It's about your boat, old boy or, more to the point, her crew."

Harris had managed to stop Johnston from calling him Bobbo, but suspected 'old boy' would prove harder.

"What about my crew?"

Ever since *194* joined his flotilla, Johnston had been making oblique remarks about reassignments and this, Harris suspected, was what he wished to discuss.

"Come, let's take the weight off our feet in the bar; not too early for a snifter?"

"It is for me," Harris said, but he allowed himself to be steered in the direction of the officers' mess.

"From what I gather, yours is an eclectic lot," Johnston began when they were both seated.

"Eclectic?"

Johnston nodded. "They come from all parts of the country."

"Mostly London actually," Harris said, "though we do have a few northerners as well, and an Irishman." He'd ordered a club soda but even that seemed inappropriate before noon.

"Commendable, of course, and I gather they work well as a team, though it rather goes against naval tradition."

"It does?"

"Oh, certainly. Even in Nelson's day, it was customary for ships to have a geographical bias; he favoured men from his native Norfolk while Collingwood – a Northumbrian – preferred Geordies."

"You seem to know your history." Harris sipped at his drink. For Johnston to lecture him about naval tradition went against the grain although constant exposure, along with Laura's insights, was slowly making him immune to the man.

"I take such things extremely seriously." Johnston collected his own drink and sniffed appreciatively. "I may not be a dyed-in-the-wool bod like yourself, but the Navy means a lot to me, and I intend to abide by its customs."

Harris said nothing; there would be more, he could sense it.

"As a matter of fact, I was only reviewing my own men the other day and, though generally pleased, there's an anomaly I'd like to address. You see, one's from Manchester."

Harris raised an eyebrow. "That's hardly a crime."

"Oh, don't get me wrong, excellent fellow and all that, though I'm equally conscious the rest of my lads are southerners."

It would soon be noon and the morning spent, while Harris feared this would end in one of Johnstons' invitations to lunch. And despite neither of them being rostered for that night, he was suddenly determined not to waste the entire day.

"You'll forgive me, but I have urgent matters to discuss with my number one," he said, glancing at the mess clock and then reaching for his drink. "You're wishing to poach one of my men; if you'd care to tell me who, I'll do all I can to keep him."

Johnston shook his head. "Now come on, old boy, there's no need to be like that. I'm only doing what any good SO would – I'm sure you'd have done the same had you remained in post."

"You mean disrupt content and well-balanced crews?"

"*Creating* content and well-balanced crews is my aim," Johnston insisted. "Your fellow, Jelly – from London, or so I hear?"

"My telegraphist? Yes, I believe so."

"And you don't think he'd be happier amongst his own? While my lad, White, comes from further north and you've several from his area."

Harris shook his head. "My chaps are fine as they are," he said. "Primarily because I, and my first lieutenant, see to their needs."

"Ah yes," Johnston agreed, and Harris wondered briefly if anything he said could really shake the man. "Your number one; Anderson, isn't it? Another southerner..."

Harris leant forward. "Let me make it plain; if you have further thoughts about pinching any of my men, *especially the officers*, I will bring it to the highest level possible."

Johnston blinked but did not seem surprised.

"Which you would be entitled to do, old boy," he agreed. "Within the bounds of military procedure, of course. But I think you'll find I'm within my rights as the senior officer," Johnston continued. "Indeed, many would regard my motives as admirable and back me to the full."

"Maybe so but, step out of line, and you'll regret it."

Johnston shook his head and tried a smile. "Look here, Bobbo, I only want to run a successful flotilla," he said. "Yet all you do is mess things up. Why is that?"

Harris shrugged. "I'm afraid you're going to have to work that one out for yourself, Bubbles."

* * *

"Oh Bill, it was terrible!"

Newman pressed the receiver to his ear, knowing instantly it had been a mistake to use one of the NAAFI 'phones. He'd wanted to talk with Sophie before going on duty yet could barely hear her over the clatter and chatter of breakfast. And this sounded important.

"What happened, Soph? Tell me."

"We was burgled," she said. "And the man what done it

85

were still there!"

"What, you surprised him?"

"Not me, Carol – one of the girls."

Newman had met Carol; a northerner. This was her first time away from home and he had been wondering about pairing her up with Pickering. "Is she alright?" he asked.

"I think so, she's been with the PMO since yesterday evening."

"Is that when it happened?"

"No, the bastard broke in during the afternoon; Carol was on nights and surprised him. I met you straight after coming off an early; same as Ann and Shirl'. We only found her when we got back, and she were in a dreadful state."

"I'm sorry."

"It's okay; they've taken us all off duty and we'll be moving back to *Lynx* ASAP."

"It's a shame." The words were inadequate, but he really did not know what else to say. "Such a nice little cottage."

"A shame for Carol. And I'd like to get my hands on whoever did it."

Newman nodded slowly. "So would I," he said.

Chapter Nine

194 was once more at sea and travelling fast. Anderson had returned to the bridge after checking their position and could see the other two gunboats close by. They were also on the plane, their chine hulls barely touching the water as they powered through the dark sea. As his vision improved, he could make out more; further off and also to port, another trio of high-speed launches, torpedo boats this time, were moving equally fast. Though armed with fewer guns, they were far more menacing as each carried a pair of weapons that could sink a vessel many times their size.

"Stirring sight!" He was barely inches away, yet Harris needed to shout above the roar of the triple Packards.

"Definitely," Anderson replied.

Actual conversation might be tiring but the determination evident in the light craft certainly inspired. That they could travel at such a rate on a less than placid sea was rousing in itself and, considering each would soon meet with a more powerful enemy, called for extra respect. There was also something classically beautiful in the sight. The moon was just beyond the full and had barely risen but still it picked out the torrents of water following each craft. It was a display equal in beauty to many more natural scenes while the backdrop of scudding clouds and translucent waves completed an image worthy of any latter-day Turner.

For a moment Anderson considered mentioning this to his captain before rejecting the idea. The continual engine noise was bad enough, but Harris was never at his most approachable when heading for action and a bellowed allusion to fine art would not go down well. He glanced about the gunboat's tiny bridge. Despite the insane speed, *194* was keeping perfect station off the SO's starboard quarter. Though a good deal younger than his predecessor, and lacking Price's maturity and tact, Phillips was proving a competent helmsman.

Which was all they required of him, Anderson decided. All they required of any aboard *194* really. Most involved in Coastal Forces were amateurs, certainly as far as seamanship and combat were concerned. All they need do was carry out a series of odd, esoteric, and occasionally grisly duties without being killed and eventually the whole dreadful thing would come to an end. At which point they might go back to living normal lives again, and it was then that Anderson pulled himself up short.

For thinking so was wrong when they were heading to meet with the enemy. And this might not be like previous engagements; it was far too easy to forget Harris was no longer their senior officer. Once more they would be subject to Johnston's whims and, though previous patrols had returned with all boats more or less intact, it was not a pleasant prospect. He would be wise to take a page out of Harris' book and set his mind solely on that night's target.

Which was a convoy heading north out of Boulogne. By now it should be somewhere off their starboard bow. The mist, light at present, was expected to increase; even if they carried out a successful attack, simply finding Dover again would be no picnic. Anderson focused on the white expanse of cloud that lay ahead. If his calculations were correct, the French coast was less than ten miles off although that was irrelevant; the convoy ought to be lying far closer and must soon be detected.

Being northbound it would probably be carrying coal to Sweden, although that was not his immediate concern; *194* and her fellow MGBs were under instructions simple enough to survive even Johnston's habit of breathing down his captains' necks.

The convoy was thought to be made up of two merchant ships escorted by five smaller craft. Yet radar – as RDF was starting to be called – was not infallible and had yet to reach the degree of sophistication where vessels could be identified beyond a rough estimation of position and speed. For all they knew, this might be a flotilla of far more powerful warships travelling at convoy pace to conceal their identity. Such mistakes had happened in the past, although the possibility did not worry Anderson unduly; the five escorts they were expecting would provide a formidable enough opposition. There were few, if any, German warships smaller than *194* and, though some might not be as fast, the vast majority were better armed.

Whether as a result of Harris' criticism or not, Johnston was starting to plan his operations with a little more care, and this would be a variation on a classic convoy interception. Rather than their torpedo boats leaving early and taking up position on the eastern – enemy – side they would be attacking from the west. As soon as German shipping was spotted, the MTB's senior officer should take his craft northwards before lying cut close to the enemy's path. Meanwhile, Johnston intended a more direct attack from the south; with luck, the Germans would think this the only attention they faced and, when the torpedoes began to strike, they should be unexpected. As soon as their deadly fish were launched, the MTBs would make straight for home and, if *194* and her fellow gunboats did their job correctly, the German escorts should be too involved to follow.

Which was likely, Anderson reminded himself. Although Kriegsmarine craft were superior in both numbers and size, their captains trod a cautious path and rarely followed a retreating enemy. Providing the MTBs exposed themselves no more than was necessary, they should make it back to Dover; he just wished the same could be said for the gunboats.

"How long before we're in position, Number One?"

"I'd say another fifteen minutes, sir. Which would place us about a mile off the convoy's estimated course."

The older man nodded but made no other response. Anderson was reasonably sure of his figures although nothing could be certain at night and when travelling at such speed. But there was someone close by who must know for certain, and both instinctively glanced across to the launch lying off their port bow that was leading them into action.

Johnston's boat carried radar; not the most sophisticated of sets, perhaps, but enough to give a more direct fix on the Germans. For all they knew, the enemy might already have been spotted; a small series of 'jigs' that Johnston was preferring to keep to himself. Such reticence was certainly in keeping with the man's general attitude.

In the past few weeks, *194* had accompanied Johnston on a number of patrols when he made it clear initiative was not expected, or allowed, from those serving under him. Only when they were actually in the thick of things was any amount of autonomy permitted, and even then, it was closely monitored. And this especially applied to Harris' boat, or so it seemed. Should they deviate in any way from the prescribed plan, Johnston was quick to comment. And neither did he confine his remarks to subtle

89

flashes from an Aldis lamp, preferring to use an open R/T channel so the entire flotilla might benefit from his wisdom.

Of course, such apparent prejudice could be an illusion; Johnston's manner of command was different to what they were used to, so it was likely *194* would deviate more than other boats, while Harris definitely had a bee in his bonnet as far as their senior officer was concerned. And probably with good reason, Anderson decided, whereas he did not; his own position had changed very little since the captain's demotion, yet he also found serving under their new SO frustrating in the extreme.

More than that, Anderson realised with a twinge of guilt, Johnston's style of leadership had a further and more subtle defect. It could send his officers' thoughts elsewhere, when really they should be concentrating on nothing other than the forthcoming action.

* * *

Though colder than he would have liked, Gibson was reasonably content at his station. The twin half-inch Vickers machine guns were housed in a turret, although the only protection this offered ended well below his shoulders and could only be depended upon for keeping out the odd ambitious wave. But the weapon itself met with Gibson's full approval.

Despite being designed to fight in a previous war, each gun could empty its belt of six hundred and fifty rounds in under a minute; time enough to down an aeroplane, knock out a searchlight, and, though it might not actually sink another vessel, make a proper mess of her crew. All these Gibson had done, in some cases several times, so it was hardly surprising ending the life of one elderly postmaster barely affected him. The incident was now very much at the back of his mind and would soon be totally lost amongst many equally violent, most of which he had performed in the King's name.

And he was just as confident about the affair with that girl. There was no end of a fuss at first, with those from the Regulating Branch, as well as conventional coppers, asking all manner of questions, but so far he had avoided attention. And he would continue to do so. On leaving the house, Gibson legged it as far as The Red Lion, where he made sure most present saw him. And Alf, the landlord, would certainly remember his visit; Gibson spent the best part of a week's pay buying drinks for the old soak, along with others at the bar. By the time he left all were three sheets to the wind and none of them would remember exactly what time he first appeared. His mind ran back to that afternoon's activities and, for a moment, a faint smile appeared on his face. Then Gibson began to consider his weapons again.

The Vickers also had the advantage of a powered mount; remarkably little pressure was needed to sight the twin barrels on any sector and at a speed that made the gun feel almost part of him. Admittedly Laurel and Hardy's heavier Oerlikon could fire further and with greater effect, but he was quite content with his weapon. It gave him total autonomy and Gibson was always at his happiest when he worked alone.

* * *

"I think I sees somethin' to starboard, gentlemen."

Phillips' announcement came a second before the more official reports from both *194*'s lookouts, and Harris turned his binoculars in that direction. All launches had throttled back some time before; since then, everyone on the gunboat's bridge had been staring into the mist.

"Damn right," Harris said.

"Is it the convoy?" Anderson asked.

"I'd say. Think we should notify our glorious leader?"

Both men looked across to the leading MGB.

"No sign of a signal," Anderson began, and then a crackle of static came from the R/T repeater.

"Okay chaps, we've found Jerry." Johnston's voice was loud enough to cut through the sound of their rumbling engines. "Charlie, take your torpedo boys off to port and lay up while I lead my lot to starboard and make a bit of noise."

Harris lowered his glasses and glanced at Anderson. Yet again Johnston was using R/T transmissions to order an attack; surely an unnecessary risk when a workable plan was already in place. The Germans were perfectly able to monitor British wireless communications; a flickering Aldis would have been far more confidential.

"Bob and Kipper, follow me and step on it!"

91

Even as he spoke the words, Johnston's boat began a graceful turn that set *194* rocking in her wake.

Harris sighed. "You heard the man, 'Swain." Then he and Anderson took hold as the boat accelerated into a tight turn. Soon the trio of gunboats had become a staggered line ahead with Johnston's craft leading. Harris looked to Anderson once more. "Hardly subtle," he shouted.

That was indeed so. If the mist concealed the stream of phosphorescence they were kicking up, the enemy were bound to hear nine supercharged engines at close to maximum revs. But then the intention was to cause a distraction, and Harris supposed Johnston had not done anything exactly wrong. Even to have used the R/T might be considered worthwhile if it drew attention away from the three MTBs now taking up position in the convoy's path.

He looked across and already there was no sign of the torpedo boats. If all went to plan, Charlie Hunter's craft should switch to their auxiliary engines, near silent Ford V8s, which would bring them to a place where the precious torpedoes would create the most damage.

"Merchants for sure," Anderson said, and Harris nodded. A stately collier was in plain sight with another, slightly ahead, only vaguely concealed by the patchy mist. Then Harris noticed a flicker of light shining from out of the gloom.

"There's an enemy signalling!" he shouted.

The lamp was roughly equidistant from the leading merchant. An otherwise invisible escort must be there, probably an R- or E-boat, and was sounding them out. In the past, several German convoys had been attacked by their own high-speed craft and whoever had command must be keen to avoid a repetition.

"Looks like Johnston's replying," Anderson said as a flickering of blue came from the leading British boat. "Probably repeating their signal."

It was a common ploy though one that usually worked. An enemy cautious enough to send a challenge would be disconcerted by any response, and one approximating the original message could buy considerable time.

"Well at least he isn't using the R/T," Harris yelled in reply.

Now the outline of that escort was becoming clearer along with others lying closer to the merchant ships. They appeared smaller than any E-boat and sat far higher in the water.

92

"Minesweepers," Anderson shouted, and Harris nodded.

They had not messed with R-boats since their first patrol under Johnston, and the memory of that lucky escape still haunted Harris. About the only advantage the British gunboats had was speed; flat out the enemy's twin diesels could barely take them to twenty knots, yet Harris had almost twice that under his control. Such power could be potent though and, properly handled, *194* would create merry hell with their lethal, if sluggish, opposition. Yet until Johnston gave them their head there would be no room for daring or independent manoeuvres.

Thoughts of his flotilla leader naturally led Harris to look towards the speeding boat ahead. They were well within range and, were he in command, Harris would have started to weave, or even broken up the tight line of British gunboats. But it was only when the nearest escort began sending green tracer over Johnston's craft that the repeater crackled into life once more.

"Okay, break it up, chaps. Make as much of a nuisance as you can though don't get in the MTB's way or stop any of their fish."

It was the signal he had been waiting for and Harris immediately ordered them to starboard and then nodded at Anderson who sounded the firing gongs. If Johnston had been more prompt in breaking formation, there would have been no danger of interfering with the MTBs. But, as they banked steeply, Harris was finally free to find his own prey and safety.

The turn had brought the nearest R-Boat within reach of their main armament and, even as the German minesweeper sent lines of green tracer in their direction, Smith and Godliman's Oerlikon opened up with a far more accurate trace of its own. Harris watched as the red flashes punched deep into the vague outline of the German craft. The relatively light cannon would have little chance of sinking an enemy, yet such an onslaught must be disconcerting to the German gunners and, as *194* continued to power through the steady swell, no enemy shell found her.

"Green fifteen; vessel in sight."

That was Daly in the starboard turret. Until then he had been more or less redundant yet was keeping a good watch. The sighting appeared to be a VP this time, an escort even slower than an R-Boat yet more heavily armed and protected. As Harris watched, Daly sent out lines of red tracer from his Vickers, although it would take more than a couple of half-inch machine guns to silence such an enemy.

Both merchants were still plodding steadily towards the place where the MTBs should be lying in wait; the last in line was almost level with them now. Harris glanced back; Johnston was engaging another escort but of the third British gunboat – or any of the MTBs – Harris could see nothing. He caught Anderson's eye.

"I'm taking us round the stern of that collier," he shouted, pointing at the merchant's dark hull.

Anderson nodded and Phillips began to turn even before his captain finished issuing the order.

Now there was chaos indeed. The mist was steadily increasing and *194* would be heading into a particularly dense spot. For several deafening seconds the clatter of every gun competed with that of their engines, turning her into a high-speed cacophony, but there was no time to consider, or even notice this. Shells from the R-boat were creeping alarmingly close and it would only be a matter of time before the VP's gunners found their mark.

"We'll take her deeper still," Harris bellowed. Closing with the enemy merchant should certainly silence the VP's cannon and it was unlikely the R-Boat would continue when their charge was placed in danger. Then another thought occurred, and he looked to Anderson.

"Depth charges, Number One!"

It was not planned, indeed, interference with any of the merchants had almost been prohibited by Johnston yet, as the bulk of the sternmost collier came steadily closer, it was a chance too good to miss.

Anderson immediately picked up on the idea and left the bridge. Harris watched him go; below he would find Jelly and make for the two depth charges *194* carried. Each contained enough amatol to blow the stern off a sizeable vessel if correctly placed. Harris had no expectation of anything quite so dramatic, although an explosion nearby would create even more confusion and further distract the enemy from an MTB's attack.

Now the darkened hull of the collier lay close to, and both escorts had ceased to fire. Harris swallowed; once they passed the trader he could expect more enemy warships on the other side. He

94

might also be effectively trapped, though such a risk was worthwhile if it meant a close release of the charges.

"Very well, 'Swain, take her in and wait on my word!"

Phillips eased back the throttles and the gunboat slumped forward slightly as the power came off. Usually, Harris would have allowed his coxswain complete control over the operation, but Phillips was perhaps a little too inexperienced. Anderson had taken up position aft and was signalling the charges primed. Harris raised an arm. The minimum depth setting was six yards which would be nearly instantaneous and could seriously damage *194*'s hull should she not beat a hasty retreat. Some commanders attached empty oil cans to their depth charges to slow the descent and make for a more effective anti-shipping weapon; he doubted Johnston would agree to such an innovation.

The hull was nearing quickly now. Phillips obviously knew his business and was taking them almost alongside the vessel's rudder while Harris fancied he could hear the sound of rifle fire from the merchant's deck. He looked back; Anderson and Jelly were ready; it was the perfect time.

Lowering his hand, Harris gave a shout and both charges were released.

"Maximum revs, 'Swain!"

194 surged up amid a cloud of spray and, though stumbling slightly, Harris turned quickly enough to see the first charge detonate. A tower of water briefly obliterated the collier's stern and was soon joined by its twin, although both explosions were too far away to do great damage.

"Vessel green ten." Again, this was Daly, and again Harris was amazed the man had the sense of duty to keep watch forward with such a distraction aft.

"Port fifteen. And bring her back to fourteen hundred!"

194 turned, slowed, and began to run alongside the merchant's hull. There was a wicked pleasure in using the enemy trader as a shield, certainly no shots were released from the new sighting, and neither was there fire from the further escort that appeared to starboard shortly afterwards. Such security could not last, however; Harris knew he must prepare for the moment when his unwilling guardian protected them no longer.

The leading collier was coming into sight now, she lay less than half a mile off – a distance that could be covered in a matter of seconds even at their current speed. He supposed there would be little wrong in continuing the ploy with that vessel, so long as they returned to the other side of the convoy when their task of distracting the escorts finally came to an end.

And then Harris realised it had. Just as *194* cleared the first collier, a fountain of water reared up beside the leading merchant. There was no explosion that he could hear, and neither did he see signs of flame or fire, yet the vessel was clearly hit and her heavily loaded hull staggered visibly.

Harris instinctively looked for his second in command, but Anderson was still aft; he would have to see to the next stage of the operation on his own. Once in open water he ordered the helm across and watched as Phillips dutifully obeyed. With luck, none of the escorts on the convoy's western side would expect their sudden appearance and it should be possible to head straight for home, something Harris would be pleased to do. Yet still he missed the presence of Anderson alongside.

* * *

In fact, *194*'s first officer was already heading forward when the depth charges exploded. After he and Jelly had set the fuses to almost instant detonation, neither wished to stay aft longer than was necessary. Jelly had taken the port route, meaning Anderson needed to duck under the fire from their Oerlikon, then again dodge what was apparently an even more ferocious onslaught from Daly's twin Vickers. He reached the starboard wheelhouse door just after the telegraphist entered from port. The two grinned briefly at each other before Jelly made for his W/T office. And it was just as Anderson was checking through the shuttered forward screen that he saw the leading merchant hit.

For a moment he was transfixed; with Phillips helming from the bridge, the wheelhouse was empty and there was no one to share either satisfaction or pleasure. And then Anderson wondered if either were truly appropriate.

The merchant was already starting to list and, low in the water as she was, would probably sink before morning. Such a gentle departure should not cause additional casualties – even a fully laden collier would retain some stability when hit by a single torpedo. Yet a perfectly good ship had been destroyed, not to mention a cargo, probably mined by prison labour at great expense to life. Anderson had learned much since joining the Navy but would always remain a civilian at heart. Yet there was something about the loss of a ship – any ship – that tugged at his conscience.

And then he saw sense; there were still the western escorts to face and Harris would need him on the bridge. Yet even as Anderson turned to go, he could not help thinking the whole exercise had been oddly futile.

* * *

In the port turret, Gibson was also looking back at the stricken collier and thinking along similar lines. They had scraped past the first merchant too close for his guns to reach its deck; he had punched a number of dents in the solid plating, but the pleasure that produced soon paled. The sinking coaster was far more interesting. In wartime, the value of that rusted hull, along with its cargo, would be truly eye-watering. Such riches were beyond his reach, yet would soon be on the bottom of the sea, lost to all, and the fact of their destruction had also affected him.

At that moment countless other incidents must be taking place, with vessels similar to the collier lost and, though each were bound to be regretted and recorded by their appropriate governments, the war would continue. All Gibson needed was some way to tap into that loss and he would be a made man.

* * *

Harris acknowledged his return with little more than a nod although Anderson sensed his presence on the bridge was welcome. *194* was now heading west, and for the coast of England, yet several obstacles still stood between her and safety. The mist had deepened further although it was being cut through by tracer flying from several otherwise invisible vessels and much of it was green. A major source lay ahead and off their port bow which, from the amount of fire, Anderson presumed to be VPs, while another craft travelling at speed to starboard was probably an R-Boat. To counter them, long trails of red were being directed at both: these could be Johnston and Keane's gunboats or possibly two of Charlie

Hunter's MTBs though all appeared to be heading hell for leather for their home shore.

"I'm taking her to starboard and upping the speed," Harris shouted, and Anderson nodded in reply. That made sense, if other British boats were fighting it out ahead, *194*'s sudden appearance might attract friendly fire. There was an R-Boat close by, but they would be faster, and turning now should avoid attention from the VPs altogether.

194 heeled dramatically as her helm was put across and soon they were passing the damaged coaster. Even in the poor light it was possible to see the hole blown in her hull, just aft of the bows; no vessel wounded so could sail far without a considerable feat of seamanship; even as they cleared her lee, the way was being taken off her.

A stream of green flashed by close to port; something was firing at them from astern. Anderson looked back to see the R-boat following, but she was making less than half their speed and would soon be out of range, while Smith and Godliman were returning fire from the Oerlikon.

Harris turned the boat to starboard for a few seconds, then corrected until the barrage grew more vague; they need only continue for a minute or so before being able to turn fully west then make for home. And it was then they saw the MTB.

The R-boat remained uncomfortably close as Harris brought the speed down. The British vessel was clearly in trouble and, like any wounded creature, on the defensive; a series of red lines erupted from her aft guns and began to play about *194*'s bows.

Harris acted instantly. Slamming down on a button, *194*'s short mast was suddenly illuminated by the three white and three red lamps that formed that night's emergency recognition signal. He paused for barely a second before extinguishing the glow, although there had been time to attract the R-boat's cannon and they were forced to make a savage turn to avoid the attention. With danger temporarily averted, they could close with the now silent MTB and Harris switched on his boat's PA.

"What's the trouble?"

There was a pause before another voice crossed the short distance. "Ruptured fuel line; we're running on auxiliary."

"We'll take you in tow, but be sharp, there's an R on our

98

tail."

"No need; should be back in no time."

"I'm not leaving you, prepare to take a line."

The crew of the MTB needed no further encouragement. Even as Phillips brought the gunboat alongside, three ratings were ready to pounce on the hawser Smith passed and, within twenty seconds of announcing the manoeuvre, *194* was firmly attached and taking the strain.

"Bring her up, 'Swain."

But the R-boat had found them and was closing; soon bolts of green were flying about once more. Phillips steadily increased the power until *194*'s engines came close to maximum revs, and both craft were set firmly on the plane.

"We'll keep her like this for a mile or so." Harris' eyes were alight with excitement. "Then take her round and make for home. Can you give me a course, Number One?"

After the confusion of the last half hour Anderson's dead reckoning would be wildly out, but the English coast could not be more than fifteen miles away: all that was needed would be a rough indication. He turned to go but Harris was grinning and had more to say.

"It'll be good to take a passenger with us." Both men looked back at the MTB, now bouncing perilously in their wake.

"I wouldn't be aboard her for the world!" Anderson shouted. "Though it beats being jumped by an R-boat."

"Never mind that," Harris said. "What do you think the SO will make of our rescuing a torpedo boat?"

Chapter Ten

"It was outright stupidity!" Johnston roared.

They were in the base captain's office with Commander Brooks present although no one was seated. Instead, Harris and Johnston stood toe to toe, their noses inches apart while Brooks watched from behind his desk; a headmaster regarding a pair of bickering pupils.

"I did what any competent captain would do." Harris' tone was considerably lower than Johnston's.

"No competent captain would order an ad hoc depth charge attack on a merchant," the latter spluttered, "and as for messing with Jimmy Joseph's boat while under fire..."

"I would have thought both to be particularly brave acts," Brooks interrupted. "The depth charges may not have caused any appreciable damage, but the diversion they created must have been impressive. And that was your brief, as I recall?"

Johnston blinked as the base captain continued.

"And as for rescuing Joseph's MTB, I'd say that showed quite a degree of courage."

"But Jimmy's boat picked up almost immediately," Johnston said. "Once their mechanics sorted the fuel feed the main engines were back on line!"

"Maybe so, but there was an R-boat close by."

"Who wouldn't have known of their existence if Harris hadn't brought it down on them!"

There was an impasse as Johnston looked from Harris to Brooks before closing his eyes and releasing a deep sigh. "I can see I'm getting nowhere," he said. "You straight stripers always stick together." Then turning, he stormed out, slamming the door in his wake.

As the echo died Brooks cleared his throat. "We seem to have upset the fellow," he said, "though I must say he does have a point."

"A point?" After the taxing night Harris was in no mood for compromise.

"Well, he's right, damn it." The base captain sat down heavily. "I've spoken to Lieutenant Joseph; he was pleased to see you, for sure, but less so when you brought that Jerry to the party. And his CMM was able to sort the engines out – another instance of Packards not being totally compatible with Vospers, it seems."

"I couldn't tell that," Harris said. "When a vessel's in distress, I go to its assistance."

"Of course," Brooks allowed. "Anyone would. But Johnston's right about the Service as well. Nine times out of ten reservists and regulars get on fine, yet in a situation like this I suppose there was always going to be trouble."

Harris lowered himself more gently onto one of the guest chairs. His problem had more to do with the kind of man Johnston was, not the insignia he wore on his sleeve.

"It's clear you cannot remain under his command," the older man continued, "and neither can I conjure up another flotilla simply to give you a position. There might be something else, though it's not in my gift: more a favour to an old shipmate, I'll have to make enquiries."

"If it means freeing me from that buffoon, I'll take anything," Harris said, and Brooks looked him full in the face before smiling slightly.

"You may not think so when you hear it," he said. "Now get some sleep; we'll talk again in due course. And, strictly off the record, you did well."

"Thank you, sir, but it was a group effort."

Brooks' smile broadened. "These things usually are, but your performance tonight might just tip the balance for what I have in mind."

* * *

Leading Motor Mechanic Bill Newman was eating his breakfast in a rush. He had much to do on the boat and Mr Carter had also asked him to check the timing on the larboard wing engine. But calling Sophie was another priority, and there was already a queue for the two NAAFI telephones. He scraped his plate clean then dumped it and the eating irons next to the gaff bin before heading

101

for the queue of waiting ratings.

Often there would be a warrant officer on hand, ostensibly to see no one hogged a line, although any leaking of confidential information would also be stamped upon. However, on that morning they were free of supervision; the pair currently using the 'phones had been there for some while and were set to remain.

Newman cursed silently as he fingered the coppers in his pocket. He had enough for a two-minute conversation with Sophie then a bar of nutty from the shop afterwards. But it was gone seven and she may already be on duty, while he would be needed for fuelling at eight. He glanced around the busy room. To one side breakfast was still in full swing. Powdered eggs, beans and heavily salted bacon were being shovelled out with the usual generosity while others queued at one of three tea urns for their first dose of char and – it was rumoured – bromide. There were three in front of him and a handful behind; were a petty officer on hand all could have made their calls by now but those on the 'phones remained entrenched.

"Waiting for the blower, are you?"

Newman turned to see Gibson had joined the tail of the queue.

"Aye, an' have been for a while."

"Been ten minutes or more," another member of the line informed them.

"Have they now..?" Gibson was looking speculatively at the backs of those using the 'phones.

"Aye," another confirmed. "Hoggin' it they is."

"Sounds long enough to me." So saying, Gibson pushed his way next to Newman.

"'Ere, don't you know there's a queue..?"

"You want trouble, matie?" Gibson asked, and the protestor turned away.

"They look like office bods," Newman muttered.

"Then they shouldn't be holding up sea-going personnel." Gibson's tone was low and threatening although he flashed a grin at Newman before approaching the two men.

It wasn't violent; all he did was place a hand on each of the ratings' shoulders before turning both round to face him. One dropped his receiver, the other flushed red with anger, but they stopped dead on seeing Gibson's expression.

"Hop it," he told the nearest while collecting his receiver with one hand and shutting down the call with the other.

"You got a bleedin' cheek!"

Gibson eyed the man for a second. "That's right," he said. "I have."

* * *

Anderson was also making a telephone call but, in an attempt at privacy, had spurned those in the despatch room unofficially allowed to officers. Instead, he stood in the draughty remains of a telephone box outside the entrance to HMS *Wasp*. What glass remained was held in place with brown tape and the rumble of a nearby tug firing up sounded as loud as the dialling tone as he fumbled for the number. He and Eve had an arrangement; they would call each other on alternate days, usually late in the afternoon – when her shift was over and his often just starting. But she hadn't been in touch for some while and, when he'd tried the day before, the girl that answered was singularly unhelpful.

He finished dialling and waited; it was a communal 'phone in the refectory – or so Eve told him – and often took several rings before being answered. Finally a female voice came through and he inserted the first of his pennies.

"Eve Newman please," he said. "She's in B section."

"I'll call," the woman told him, and he winced as she did.

He waited.

"No one's answering."

"Can you try again?"

"If you like, but there's not many here."

His mind raced. "Okay, don't worry, can you try Jean Farebrother instead?"

There was a pause. "Playing the field, aren't you?"

"She's Eve's friend," Anderson said, and the voice rang out again.

This time he was in luck and Jean answered.

"I'm sorry to bother you, it's Ian Anderson," he said. He'd met Jean on his one trip to London, but Eve seemed to trust her. "Look I'm trying to get hold of Eve."

"But she's no longer here."

"What do you mean?"

103

"Don't you know? She's been transferred."

"Transferred?" Anderson's mouth dropped for a moment before sense took hold. "Where to?"

It wasn't a great line, but he was sure there was hesitancy in the woman's voice.

"Look, you know how it is, I really can't say."

"You can tell me," he insisted. "I need to know."

"Sorry, Ian, really; Eve'll probably be in touch."

"Probably?"

Again, that pause. "I can't say more; I'm sorry."

He held the receiver to his ear long after the line went dead. Then, as the tug's whistle blew three long blasts, Anderson returned the instrument to its cradle and left the telephone box.

* * *

Ryder and his hastily assembled team had been installed in a requisitioned seafront hotel that looked over Falmouth's Gyllyngvase Beach. The place was crowded, though mainly due to his own efforts. From the conservatory which had become his centre of operations, he could see the frantic comings and goings of personnel from both forces. Some were military, and Colonel Charles' concern, but the Wrens were on official detachment, while most of the staff officers had been blatantly poached from Plymouth Command. Also present, and appearing far less anxious, were several RNVR officers; the archetypical Glory Boys whose launches were anchored nearby.

Ryder had seconded twelve Fairmile Bs from the 20th and 28th ML Flotillas, supposedly for use on extended anti-submarine patrols. It was a task they were eminently suited for; he only hoped their true mission, which was now quite advanced, would prove as fitting.

Much had already been done to equip the vessels. Each now boasted a five-hundred-gallon fuel tank to either side of their superstructure while work was currently underway to uprate their armament. The obsolete Hotchkiss three-pounders were to be replaced by a single 20mm Oerlikon – a weapon far more suited to the work they would be undertaking – with additional Lewis guns mounted aft. The end result might not be impressive but should give adequate cover when the boats were travelling in company.

Little could be done about the engines, however; Fairmile Bs were powered by twin Hall-Scott petrol units that gave a top speed barely in excess of eighteen knots. This was slow compared with the majority of Coastal Forces' craft, but where they truly scored was in their carrying capacity. In addition to a twelve-man crew, each launch could carry fifteen commandos and their equipment in relative safety – if such a word could be used when describing such frail vessels.

Of their destroyer, Ryder was more confident. The Devonport yard had really come up trumps; nine days being all that was needed to convert *Campbeltown* into a ship that might have been made for the job. And the work was good; the newly enclosed bridge might not withstand heavy fire but should at least give confidence to the command group sheltering within, while the old girl positively sprouted further Oerlikons. Of more concern was her draught; after extensive lightening, the destroyer now drew slightly under eleven feet, as opposed to her original fourteen, but that was only when travelling at speeds lower than fifteen knots. Any faster and she would ground on the five miles of shoal waters that led to St Nazaire.

A lieutenant commander had been found to captain her. Stephen Beattie was roughly his own age and almost as experienced; Ryder liked him on sight and, more importantly, sensed they would work well together. Yet, as with every decision made of late, Ryder had the feeling he might be consigning men to their deaths.

After their initial reluctance, the Admiralty finally became more supportive. Two *Hunt* class destroyers were to escort his force to the Loire estuary and the RAF equally promised a diversionary air raid at a time he could pretty much choose.

And Colonel Charles was also pulling out all the stops. Ryder had worked with commando units in the past and never failed to be impressed by the strong and mainly silent men. At that moment they were being trained in specific tasks, those detailed for offensive work were undergoing intensive instruction in street fighting, while others endlessly practised the laying of separate charges to destroy other installations. The latter were currently further up the coast at Southampton where the lock gates and many of the dockyard buildings closely resembled those at St

Nazaire. Such an important aspect could not be overlooked, yet Ryder had been reluctant to allow too many into the secret. It was Colonel Charles who finally came up with the answer and, once more, subterfuge was necessary.

His troops were working under the cover story of practising demolition in case of invasion. This was generally accepted by Southampton's top brass, and Ryder understood the commandos' regular 'raids' to plant plasticine explosives often drew quite an audience.

There remained several matters he had yet to address. Ryder was still concerned about actually getting his force to the mouth of the River Loire. Coastal Forces had been stepping up their efforts of late, but E-boats still prowled the area. Fairmile Bs, with their ponderous engines, weak hulls, and limited defence, would prove easy meat and even destroyers lacked the agility to combat such nimble enemies. The obvious solution would be to commandeer further gunboats to act as escorts though, there again, he was hit by the problem of range.

Now modified, the Fairmiles could make the return trip without refuelling but not so high-speed launches. Rather than a couple of low-compression engines, they boasted three supercharged monsters that drank petrol as if it was going out of fashion. Even with auxiliary tanks, they would be lucky to make it all the way south and a short time in combat might see them stranded.

He also had to accommodate himself, Colonel Charles, and Lieutenant Green, the navigating officer, along with other members of their staff. *Campbeltown* was the obvious choice; once she was in position against the dock gates, they could take their chances with the rest of her crew and escape aboard a Fairmile. But the old destroyer was not the most manoeuvrable of vessels, and there was still a good chance of her grounding or being hit on the approach.

Mountbatten was hardly being helpful either. Even this close to the raid he seemed to be having second thoughts: that or the man simply enjoyed causing problems. Recently he directed Ryder to organise some practice sea time. A passage out into the North Atlantic had been chosen, and the entire force of commandos would soon be embarked on a three-day round trip. No destroyer escort was available; the launches must rely on their numbers for safety and, were the enemy to get wind of such an operation, it could be a massacre.

An order was an order, however, and Mountbatten didn't like to be ignored, while Ryder had another problem which looked like making things more complicated still. He was being lumbered with a crackpot.

Apparently, some obscure RNVR sub-lieutenant had the bright idea of modifying an MTB to make an attack on the battleships *Scharnhorst* and *Gneisenau* while they sheltered in Brest harbour. Both ships had long since sailed, and Southern Command was desperate to justify the expense of fitting the boat out. Consequently, Ryder was supposed to find a use for a solitary high-speed launch capable of firing special motorless demolition torpedoes at close range.

Quite how this could be incorporated into his plans remained a mystery. He presumed the boat started life as a standard MTB, so would have all the problems associated with range, while a brief investigation revealed the genius who cooked up the idea and now commanded her had, until recently, been an Army officer.

And finally, there was the nagging doubt that, well supplied with launches though he had been, he might still not have enough. Twelve was sufficient to carry the necessary troops, though with no allowance for casualties. It only needed two or three of the Fairmiles to be taken out on the approach for them to be short of commandos and, if it proved impossible to form a proper bridgehead, the entire operation would dissolve into chaos.

So, what to do? Put in for more craft now, then fill the available space with further commandos? Colonel Charles would provide, he was sure of that, but they had already decided on the optimum number. Or maybe push for the extra boats and spread the existing force more evenly?

Ryder didn't know, but that did not mean he didn't care. Only a couple of weeks before, the mission had seemed little short of fantastic yet, as every apparently insurmountable obstacle was overcome, he was starting to think otherwise. Much – *too much* – could still go wrong, although the chances it might actually succeed were growing. And at that moment, and for reasons too numerous to list, success was all he wished for.

Chapter Eleven

Smith's suggestion that he and Godliman go for a quiet drink had been half in jest, as much of their free time was spent in silence. But the lad accepted with a nod and when Pickering and Jelly, also in their room at the time, made noises about wanting to come along, he could see no harm in it. However, once they found a table in The Red Lion and saw Gibson sitting alone at the other end of the bar, he was not so sure. A shipmate should never be allowed to drink on his own, yet there was something about the gunner he did not like and, though never discussed, Smith sensed the others felt the same.

They had hardly started on the first round when Gibson noticed their presence and made his way over.

"Well fancy that; maties out on the oil and I'm not invited."

"You are now," Pickering said, though his tone lacked warmth. "Bring your beer across."

"So, what about a game of arrows?" Gibson asked when he'd settled.

"Not me," Jelly replied.

"Me neither," Pickering agreed.

"Scared about playing against a gunner?" Gibson's eyes roamed about the table, finally finding Smith's. "What about you then, Smudger?" he asked. "Your eye good enough, is it?"

Smith met the gaze. "Alright," he said. "I'll give you a game."

The board was close by, but Smith had no darts and needed to collect the house set from Alf behind the bar. By the time he returned, Gibson had wiped the scoreboard clean and was taking practice shots with three elegant brass affairs that might have been hand turned.

"What is it, five-oh-five, easy in?" Gibson rolled a dart in his hand and had the air of an expert. "Diddle for the middle: you can throw first."

Smith took his stance at the oche and eyed the board. It would be one dart from each and whoever landed nearest to the bull would play first – an important advantage.

He threw and was pleased to see the dart land less than an inch from the centre spot. Gibson took his place and spent some time apparently weighing his dart while examining the board in minute detail.

"It's the bit in the middle you want." Pickering's suggestion brought a round of laughter although neither player appeared to notice. Then Gibson released his dart.

And despite the preparation, and quality of his tools, it was clear he was not a good player. The dart landed by the double nine, several inches from Smith's.

"Me to open then," Smith said, taking up position once more.

His first three darts took him below four hundred, which Gibson followed with a poor thirty-seven and in no time Smith was doubling out on a nine, leaving his opponent still struggling in the three hundreds.

"Best of five?" Gibson asked.

"Why not?" Smith agreed. Winning so easily had come as a relief, and it was a pleasant surprise to find Gibson a good loser. But though he might not be the most accurate player, Gibson definitely had a talent when it came to adding up the score.

"Mugs away then," he announced and, before Smith could agree, he had already thrown the first of his darts.

The second game was more of a contest as Gibson went below forty before Smith. But rather than doubling out, he continually overshot, allowing Smith to finish the leg with a double eighteen.

"Well, it's clear you've played before." Gibson wiped the board clean while Smith grinned back at his mates. "What say we have a little wager?"

"Wager?"

Gibson nodded. "Five bob for a win; ten if it's by more'n a hundred."

Smith shook his head. "I thought we was playing for sport."

"It is sport; an' a bit of spice'll make it more so. Come on, mugs away!"

Gibson's first darts might have been drawn to the board, with two scoring a triple twenty and one only missing by a fraction of an inch.

"One-forty," he announced, stepping forward to collect them. "Looks like I've got my eye in; let's see if you can do better."

Smith couldn't. He made eighty-four and that was soon trumped by another post one-forty from Gibson who, in no time was playing for a double.

Which came with the next throw – a double nineteen that was followed by two outer bulls for good measure.

"Nice darts," Smith said. "An' it looks like I owe you ten bob. Hat's on the table."

"And it can stay there," Gibson beamed. "Best out of five, or don't you remember? We got two more games left!"

* * *

Harris gave three stout taps then opened the base captain's door.

"You wished to see me, sir?"

Brooks looked up from his desk. "Indeed, Bob, take a seat."

It was five days since their last operation and, though Johnston's flotilla had been in action since, *194* was not rostered. The fact hardly played heavily on Harris' mind; the less he saw of the jumped-up prig the better, but there was another side to it. If his command had been relegated in any way, it would eventually affect his crew which was a definite consideration.

"*194* alright, is she?" Brooks asked.

"Top line, sir." Harris was determined to keep his tone neutral. He did have a perfectly good boat; if Johnston chose not to include her that was his problem.

"And she's an Elco..." Brooks was almost pondering. "Remind me of her range."

"Not so very different to a comparable British craft," Harris shrugged, "at least those fitted with Packards. I think our cruising limit is somewhere in the region of six hundred nautical miles. Though, were we travelling at speed it would be considerably less." He regarded Brooks quizzically. "It's not something we usually have to consider, sir."

That was certainly the case, and for Brooks to ask such a question had piqued his curiosity. With Dover so close to enemy territory, range was almost immaterial. Maybe they were to be transferred, in which case *Beehive*, in Suffolk, seemed likely as much of their work was carried out on the Dutch coast. Then a terrible thought occurred; supposing it wasn't an operational base at all – maybe a training depot? Was Brooks proposing to put him out to grass?

"That's very much as I'd thought, though obviously there's no reason why she couldn't take on extra capacity?"

"None that I can think of."

One of the qualities of Coastal Forces' craft was their adaptability; gunboats had been created from anti-submarine launches and nearly all could be converted to carry mines should the need arise. After alterations, one launch had effectively become a high-speed merchant, making regular runs to Sweden for consignments of ball bearings.

Harris' mind ran on. "If it were carefully done, *194*'s range could be increased considerably, or even doubled though the added weight may mean removing some of her ordnance."

"Fine, though that might not be necessary. From what I gather the project is already quite advanced and provisions have been made for the supporting craft."

"Project, sir?" Harris was starting to get interested.

Brooks leant back in his chair. "It concerns a friend of mine; most folk know him as Red Ryder. We trained together and were both on the China station. When our time was drawing to a close, we decided to make our own way home. Together with a bunch of other chaps we designed and built a thirty-ton ketch."

Harris raised an eyebrow; this was a different side to the base captain.

"Made it to Blighty, then saw a modest profit on the boat but since then we've rather drifted apart," Brooks continued. "Red spent three years in Antarctica commanding the supply schooner under Rymill – won the Polar Star as I remember. When war broke out, he was posted to a Q-ship and after that, an assault vessel, though lost them both. Now he's been given something else – something special." Brooks pulled a face. "Probably as punishment..."

That might be the case, but Harris was not one to judge: he had also lost a command. This Ryder fellow sounded interesting.

"He won't say much about it, secrecy and all that, though I gather this is a little more confidential than most. Operation Chariot – have you heard of it?"

Harris shook his head.

"It's hardly been in development long but already things are advanced so I'm afraid you'll be one of the last to join. And I don't believe it's a major role."

Major or not, Harris was keen.

Seems Ryder wants a gunboat and yours will be ideal, only the Admiralty are saying no. Consequently, this will be very unofficial," Brooks continued. "As far as anyone is concerned, *194* is being detached for special service – we can make something up. I expect you to be away for up to a month. By the time you return, there may be other boats available and you can revert to your former position as Flotilla Senior Officer, otherwise it's back to running around under Johnston, but at least you'll both have had a break. How does that sound?"

A few weeks away from Johnston's interfering? It sounded perfect.

"This wasn't exactly what I had in mind," Brooks added, "and there are no promises. That said, if you put on a good show at Falmouth, I'd say you're a shoo-in as the next flotilla leader."

"Falmouth?" That would be HMS *Forte* – not a base Harris was familiar with.

"That's right, it'll be your new home for a while at least and a pleasant place by all accounts, though I don't expect there'll be much time for exploring. Give Red my regards, I'm sure the two of you'll get along famously. And I understand this'll be a combined operation, you'll be working extensively with the Army and Bomber Command."

"I see," Harris lied. "And will we be the only Coastal Forces craft?"

Brooks smiled. "No, Bob, you certainly won't be alone."

* * *

"Anyone else fancy a game?" Gibson enquired.

"You're barmy if you do." Smith was reaching into his hat. He had a little short of a pound in there with nothing more due for over a week. If he was to pay Gibson, he'd have to get a loan from his mates, which would naturally mean Godliman. And asking him for a rubber felt like taking advantage.

"I'm fine," Jelly said. "Just came out for a pint."

"What about you, Smiler?"

Smith realised with a shock he was talking to Godliman, who seemed unusually alert.

"Chuck a few darts about, will you?" Gibson persisted. "Whiles away the time."

"Now hold on…" Smith began, but Gibson was in control. "Who are you, his mother?"

"Go easy, he's just a bairn," Pickering added.

"No, I'll play him." They were the first words Godliman had spoken all evening and the shock stunned the others into silence.

"That's my boy!" Gibson said. Then, turning to Smith, "Come on, mum, hand over your arrows."

* * *

"Operation Chariot?" Anderson shook his head, "Means nothing to me."

"Nor me," Harris agreed. "And frankly I don't think Brooks had much of a clue either."

"But he said there'd be other Coastal Forces craft?"

"I got the impression quite a few."

Anderson scratched at his chin. "Can't see what good launches'll be as far west as Falmouth – unless we're going for the Channel Isles."

"Any campaign there would be based at Dartmouth, more'n likely, and Brooks did say range might be a factor."

"HMS *Forte* is used for clandestine operations," Anderson said. "SOE and the like. And we'll be cooperating with the military…"

"Though also Bomber Command – which doesn't sound terribly clandestine. It's really a mystery."

They were in the officers' mess at *Wasp*. The flotilla was not detailed for duty that night so Johnston had taken several other gunboat officers on a jolly to Canterbury. Anderson was invited but declined on hearing his captain had not been included.

"When do we go?" he asked.

"Pretty much straight away." Harris took a sip at his Scotch. "I gather there's a bit of red tape to sort out, but we can fuel up after the service boats and set off the following morning."

"So, a daylight run?"

Harris shrugged. "No reason why not. Be a change to see a

bit of sun."

"What do we tell the lads? They'll be thinking we're joining another flotilla."

"That certainly isn't the case; *194* is being seconded, no more. She'll remain attached to Johnston's lot, in theory at least."

"And when will we be returning to Dover?"

This was obviously a far deeper question and Harris rested back in his chair. "Frankly, Ian, I haven't a clue. Special Operations are exactly that; one-off jobs, so no telling how likely they are to succeed, or the attrition rate if it comes to it. We could be back in a couple of weeks, or possibly never. But one thing's certain, we've seen our last of Dover and HMS *Wasp* for the time being. And, more importantly, seen the last of Bubbles Johnston..."

* * *

Gibson fingered his darts with increasing anxiety. It wasn't supposed to be this way; the boy, Godliman, wasn't even a proper gunner – his job was to see a crummy Oerlikon didn't run out of shells. That said, being a gunner was no guarantee of competence, yet it was strange how many considered themselves gifted. Most turned out anything but and, when up against a persuasive tongue, coupled with his own special skills, usually turned out to be a walkover.

But not this time, not with this eighteen-year-old kid who rarely said a complete sentence yet handled his arrows like they were an extension to his body. Gibson watched while Godliman stepped up to the oche to take his turn. There was no pause to size up the board. Damn it, the child was still walking when he released his first arrow, yet it found the triple twenty. The second followed, then the third and, for a moment, Gibson took heart. Godliman's last throw missed the sweet spot completely and ended up just to the right on a solitary one.

It hadn't taken long for others in the pub to realise they had a genius in their midst and this final arrow brought as much of a reaction as if Godliman had nailed a one-eighty. Gibson looked again. He was not mistaken, the kid definitely hit the one, and then realisation dawned. That last dart brought his score to an even forty; Godliman had laid the perfect path to hit a double twenty with his next throw.

Gibson's jaw tightened as he took his place at the oche. He was way behind on two hundred and ninety-seven, the best score from three darts would still leave him woefully short. And to make matters worse, he'd agreed terms and gone straight for the kill, with no warm-up matches to soften the young mark. Consequently, Gibson would shortly be down ten whole shillings and, unless he did some quick talking, it would only get worse.

He finished his round, which reduced the score by a mere hundred, then surrendered the oche to Godliman who took his stance with that same impassive expression. Gibson looked away as the thump of a single dart echoed for a moment before the roar of approval told him he had indeed been taken to the cleaners.

There was nothing else for it, and a bit of smooth talk might salvage something.

"Nice darts, Sunshine. Looks like I owe you some cash; what say I buy you a drink into the bargain?"

The lad was considering him with the same vacant expression. "We play again," he said.

"You want another?"

"We agreed," Godliman insisted. Gibson glanced at his watch.

"Maybe so, but I can't spend the whole evening here."

"You heard him right enough."

Gibson turned to see Pickering, the grease monkey, standing behind and he was not alone. Others from his table were gathered alongside and it felt as if the entire pub might also be watching.

"Lad don't talk much but, when he does, he means what he says." This was Smith, the goon Gibson had already beaten that evening.

"A quick one then," Gibson temporised, "though I can't stay longer."

"You agreed to the best of five." Pickering again. "That's at least two more games."

"He's right, we all heard you," Smith added.

If there was one thing Gibson prided himself on it was knowing when he was beaten. "Right-oh then, mugs away, is it?" he said, collecting his darts. He leant forward and threw one that landed just north of the treble twenty. It was an omen, he knew that, just as he knew he was in for another pasting.

Chapter Twelve

194 left Dover in the early hours of the morning and spent the day running at her best economical speed. It was an uneventful passage; an enthusiastic armed trawler – crewed presumably by volunteers of some variety – challenged them off Portland Bill and they reported several large pieces of wreckage that might cause problems if encountered by small craft at night. But even though it was almost a pleasure cruise, by the time they sighted the entrance to Falmouth harbour and made their number, all aboard were in need of a rest.

Which was hardly surprising; the seventy-foot Elco had not been designed with comfort in mind, and neither were regular long passages envisaged. *194*'s catering arrangements were meagre and confined to a single stove; adequate enough when it came to boiling up char or kye, but the vegetable soup attempted by Daly and Newman was undercooked and challenging. To make matters worse, their living spaces were littered with luggage ranging from duffel bags and suitcases, through several larger cardboard boxes and culminating in a chest of tools and spares belonging to Jelly.

Anderson had attempted to break the monotony by switching posts amongst the crew; Phillips was forced to give up his precious helm to the ministrations of gunners and motor mechanics who, in turn, gave brief instruction in their own dark arts. Some way off St Catherine's Point, Newman and Pickering were given charge of the Oerlikon and set to work sinking a collection of drifting planks – a task they found satisfying despite it being all but impossible – while numerous sea birds were either frightened – or not – by Phillips and Jelly trying their hands at the half-inch Vickers.

As *194* rounded Pendennis Point and began to run deeper into Falmouth harbour, it became clear their brief holiday was over and all aboard grew more serious. The engine pitch lowered and Daly went forward to handle the berthing wires while Smith stood by aft. On the bridge, both officers were taking note of the assorted shipping as it was revealed, and one particular vessel caught their attention.

"*Princess Josephine Charlotte,*" Harris said as he surveyed her stern through his glasses. "Must be close on three thousand tons."

"Obviously meant for the passenger trade; I doubt her builders intended that particular shade of grey."

Certainly, as *194* rumbled past, the only clue to the ship's previous life was her generous proportions, while several nests of anti-aircraft guns gave her a more warlike appearance.

"Think she's an LSI?" Anderson asked.

"Landing Ship, Infantry?" Harris considered. "It's a possibility. They did say this would be a combined operation."

"And there's more," Anderson said, pointing over their starboard bow to where a collection of motor launches lay in the Carrick Roads anchorage.

"Fairmile Bs," Harris said, his mind running back to when his previous command had been suspected of sinking just such a vessel. "Wonder what they're doing here."

"And why such a colour?" Anderson added. The light was steadily fading but the launches' fresh paint was obvious. And rather than the standard Admiralty grey, or even one of the more esoteric camouflages, the Fairmiles were decked out in a deep pinkish mauve that made their ordnance appear mildly ridiculous.

"Never seen anything like it." Anderson shook his head.

"I have," Harris said. "Some of the merchant lines adopted it early on. Reckoned it made their ships near invisible at dawn or dusk. As I remember they call it Plymouth Pink."

"Sounds more like a drink to me."

"Maybe so, but why use it on Fairmile Bs?"

From what Harris could see, the launches carried a single Oerlikon at the fore and were not fitted with torpedo tubes. Which meant they might have been converted for mine sweeping – or laying. Or there could be another use in mind – anti-submarine work perhaps. Most had figures swarming about their deck, so they appeared fully crewed which was also strange with land so close.

"And there's another gunboat." Anderson was pointing deeper into the harbour. "Fairmile again, but this time a C, so quite a bit larger than us."

"Almost twice as long again," Harris agreed, "and a darn sight heavier – though not as fast..."

"Do you think any of this is significant, sir?"

Harris pursed his lips. "I haven't a clue, Number One. Though something tells me we're about to find out."

* * *

But Harris was wrong. Even after they were directed to a pontoon berth some way from the gunboat, and *194*'s cooling engines could finally tick quietly in the early evening calm, no one appeared eager to greet them.

"What do you think?" Harris asked. "Go ashore and make our number?"

"Could do worse, though they don't strike me as an especially friendly lot."

"Wait a while, there's a bunch heading our way."

They watched as a group of twelve approached.

"Dockyard workers," Anderson said as they drew nearer.

"Look like Wrens to me," Phillips commented from the helm.

"Thank you, 'Swain," Harris grunted. "We had noticed."

The women moved on with no more than curious glances and *194* continued to be ignored. In fact, it was close on half an hour before a greatcoated sub-lieutenant, accompanied by a chief petty officer and two ratings, made directly for them and asked permission to board.

"Name's Peters from Combined Operations HQ," the officer announced when salutes had been exchanged. Harris and Anderson came down from the bridge to meet the new arrival and naturally expected to accompany him ashore, but Sub-Lieutenant Peters had other ideas. "I wonder if we might speak in your wardroom?"

"No reason why not," Harris said, "though if what you have to say is at all confidential it's hardly the place."

"Indeed, sir," the young man agreed. "Though I've brought CPO Oats with me; he'll address your men while we talk. Perhaps they could be assembled on your mess deck?"

Harris glanced briefly at Anderson; this was hardly the welcome they expected, if indeed it could be called such. But there

118

was no point in arguing.

"Very well, Sub, though we've just been transferred; the ship's full of luggage so you might not find it convenient."

"I totally understand, sir, and am sure we'll manage."

* * *

Manage they did, but only just. *194*'s wardroom was remarkably similar to a good-sized larder, with an outer wall that inclined steeply to a low deckhead. The narrow settee doubled as a single bunk and was positioned below another that could be folded out. Apart from that, and a collapsible table, there was no furniture although two large grips, a steamer trunk, and three suitcases took up the rest of the space.

When Anderson had stacked these into a more economical pile, he just had room to help Peters off with his coat and direct him to a seat next to Harris before perching against the table's edge. While these preparations were being made, the sound of a resonant voice could be heard as CPO Oats addressed *194*'s remaining crew on the other side of a plywood bulkhead.

"You'll have to forgive me, gentlemen," Peters began. Now freed of his greatcoat Anderson noticed the man was painfully thin and could not be older than twenty. "But security in this particular operation is a major concern. We're immensely careful with anyone hoping to join us."

"But we *are* joining," Harris said. "At least that was the impression."

"And you may well be, sir," Peters agreed. "Though that has to be confirmed. And even then, there may be areas where you are not fully briefed."

"This is clearly a large undertaking." Harris again.

"Oh indeed, sir – I can at least tell you that. And a combined operation; Army, for sure, and some assistance from the RAF."

"We noticed some Fairmile B's," Anderson said.

"They also form a major part." Peters was more wary.

"And a troopship?" Harris added; the young officer smiled.

"I should let my superiors brief you further," he said. "My brief is to see you and your men comfortably quartered. Arrangements will be made ashore for billets though I'm afraid you'll have to spend tonight aboard your ship."

Anderson glanced about at the crowded wardroom. "Is that really necessary?" he asked. "There's hardly room for us both here and the men'll be just as cramped. Surely you have an officers' mess or some form of barracks we can use?"

"You've already noticed our accommodation ship," Peters said, "though I'm afraid she's full to the gunnels with commandos and five of their officers are already sleeping in the wardroom bar. I'll try to find you rooms together, but it might not be easy."

"Did you say commandos?" Harris asked.

"I did," Peters admitted, "and that may have been a slip on my part. But some things cannot be hidden, and I think you'll soon discover this really is a major enterprise."

* * *

The following morning dawned clear and bright. They had been given no orders about fuelling and, with the upper bunks stripped and folded away, *194*'s mess deck was more or less reinstated. Yet luggage still filled most of the usable space making moving about awkward and the stale smell from nine men sharing the same small area forced most on deck.

"Any news of breakfast?" Gibson's question was rhetorical; no one had visited the boat since the previous evening; the only food available was crusts from last night's sandwiches and rather too much of the vegetable soup.

"You've had your tea," Daly said, "that should keep you goin' a while."

"It takes more than a mug of char to fill me up."

"Well maybe that's where the skip' and Jimmy have gone," Jelly suggested. "Rather than food, his need was for the heads but, being as they were in harbour and *194* had no holding tank, there were bound to be complaints from those on deck.

"Aye," Daly agreed with a grin. "Them'll be off to find us a proper feast, then show us back to the plush hotel they has a waitin' for us."

"With a bunch of canny lasses to see we has all we needs," Pickering agreed.

"Well, I ain't waiting for somethin' to happen," Gibson said.

Jelly regarded him with concern. They had been told to remain aboard ship, yet this was a British harbour, with all the usual facilities within reach. And there was no one with any real authority on board; the captain and first officer having left earlier, while Carter and Phillips, their two warrant officers, were yet to emerge from their shared berth amidships.

"Think I can smell bacon..." Smith had a twinkle in his eye and, once the thought had been put in their heads, all quickly agreed.

"I could handle a bacon stottie right now," Pickering said. "All runny with fat, an' a dose of sauce."

"What in heaven's name's a stottie?" Gibson asked.

"Soft roll," Pickering said. "But not the kind you get down south. A decent stottie's real scran – heaven on a plate."

"If it's from Newcastle they probably makes it from coal," Daly said.

"Don't know about breakfast, I could do with something else." This was Smith again and, from the expression on his face, Jelly sensed he was not alone in needing the heads.

"So, what say we take our chances ashore?" Gibson was standing up and eyeing them expectantly. "Hit the town an' see what we can see."

"Breaking ship are you, Gibbo?" Smith asked, although it was clear he cared little either way.

"Think the natives'll be friendly?" Daly added.

Jelly cleared his throat. "Friendly or not, we were told to stay aboard."

"Don't give me that." Gibson glared at his shipmates in turn although each stared back in modest defiance.

"Go if you want," Daly told him. "I'm for stayin' and seeing what comes about."

"Wey aye, that's the best move," Pickering agreed.

"I'll show you the best move." Gibson had already started for the pontoon, and they watched as he clumped down from the boat, then made for the nearby quay.

"He's off then." Smith had a hint of envy in his voice.

"That he is," Jelly agreed.

* * *

121

Peters proved as good as his word. At first light Harris and Anderson had been collected from the boat and escorted to the Tregwynt Hotel to meet with Commander Ryder. Their staff car drew up outside a three-storey building on the other side of the peninsula and Peters led them to an upstairs room. There, a small dormer window gave an impressive view of the wide sweep of sandy beach, now sadly marred by defence measures. Pendennis Castle was also prominent on the eastern headland and the sight of such a magnificent monument to past wars added gravity to the occasion.

"Commander Ryder will be with us shortly," Peters said when they were seated at a plain deal table.

Harris glanced about the room which had been stripped of most of its previous furnishings. Apart from the table, there was a line of filing cabinets while, in place of pictures, several large maps filled two of the walls, with a blackboard that had been clumsily wiped taking up another. One of the maps covered the Western Approaches, another the west coast of France, and the third was of a far larger scale and centred on a sizeable estuary that slimmed down to a wide river.

"Is this your centre of operations?"

Peters smiled. "No, we use this room for interviews and small meetings. Commander Ryder's office is actually a conservatory in the grounds."

That sounded anything but private though the entire hotel had been made over for government use. And security was remarkably tight with armed sentries generously scattered throughout. Harris was still considering this when the door flew open and a regular Royal Navy officer strode in.

He was immediately struck by the man's presence; an air of authority was emphasised by a forceful chin and, as they shook hands over Peter's introduction, he also noticed a determined look in Commander Ryder's eyes. Yet there was the suggestion of humour there as well, and he lacked any trace of arrogance.

"You will forgive me, gentlemen, but I must be brief," he said, taking a seat and indicating they should do likewise. "This entire operation is being put together double quick; I'm due to meet with Colonel Charles in ten minutes. I understand you've brought the gunboat Brookie promised and wish to know more about our little excursion. Which is understandable, though in view of the time constraints I suggest we skip the pleasantries and crack on."

"Of course, sir." Harris settled himself in his chair; he was definitely warming to Commander Ryder.

"Obviously much of what I am about to tell you is confidential. You will speak of it to no one on the outside and even be circumspect with those actually involved in the raid. Colonel Charles has briefed his men and most officers are also in the know, but not the ratings; is that understood?"

Harris exchanged a glance with Anderson then cleared his throat. "Let me get this straight, sir, you are expecting our seamen to put out to an unknown destination?"

Ryder nodded. "I realise how it sounds, but there's good reason. Naturally, the general hands are aware some form of land assault is being planned and most have a good idea of the type of target we have in mind, just not exactly where. We hope to inform them closer to the event, but it might have to remain a secret until we're actually on our way."

"Yet this Colonel Charles has informed his soldiers?"

"He heads 2 Commando," Peters, the sub-lieutenant, explained. "They are an elite force and being accommodated aboard the *Princess Josephine Charlotte*, the LSI in the harbour, but not even they know our exact destination."

"Though they have been told more than our boys?"

Ryder's smile owed much to politeness. "Most of the general ratings are from Coastal Forces," he said. "These Glory Boys – as I think they like to be known – are mainly 'Hostilities Only' so have not been sufficiently cleared for security. Those from the Fairmile Bs are remaining aboard their craft for now, although I can see a time when they'll have to be brought ashore. *Campbeltown* has a handpicked crew to see her on her final voyage. We're calling them the steaming party, and most are already billeted in the town and regularly mix with civilians, so you can see we must be especially careful where they are concerned."

It was a reasonable explanation, yet Harris still felt mildly offended that the Army was being trusted more than their own men.

"We are to attack a major port on the coast of France," Ryder continued. "It's an important target that, due to a high civilian population, cannot be reached from the air. We've explored the idea of using the Special Operations Executive, but a veritable army would have been needed to manoeuvre the explosives necessary for what we have in mind. And so it's down to us..."

Ryder paused as if only just realising the enormity of what lay ahead, although Harris and Anderson were already in no doubt.

"HMS *Campbeltown* is a former American destroyer which has been altered to resemble a *Mowe* class torpedo boat." Ryder broke off to give a quick smile. "I understand the term is misleading; in reality they are quite substantial vessels."

Harris nodded; the *Mowes* were all of eight hundred tons and should really be classed as destroyers.

"She's due here tomorrow and I think you'll be interested to see the changes made in her appearance. However, altering the silhouette has only been part of the work. Much of her armament has been replaced or moved; her bridge is now fully enclosed, and her draught greatly reduced but, more to the point, she now carries several tons of high explosive in her bows."

"Her bows?" Despite the commander's obvious wish for brevity, Harris could not contain the comment.

"Indeed," Ryder agreed and once more fixed Harris with those eyes. "You see we propose to ram her into an enemy dry dock and blow the lock gates off."

Chapter Thirteen

Ryder's revelation left Harris slightly stunned. As plans went it was verging on the fantastic, yet there was a piratical element that he found oddly appealing.

"But if your target's a major port it's bound to be heavily protected," he said. "Do you expect the Germans to allow a destroyer so close?"

"Not merely expect, we're depending on it," Ryder grinned. "Our approach will be unorthodox and should catch the enemy napping. And it will be a considerable flotilla; *Campbeltown*, accompanied by the motor launches you have no doubt already noticed."

"Fairmile Bs!" Harris protested. "They're patrol vessels, little more than pleasure craft. You can't use them to attack an enemy harbour!"

"I'm afraid they're essential; the route we envisage will be by river and contains a fair amount of shoal water."

"A destroyer cannot negotiate shallows." Harris could not help being adamant although Ryder only looked mildly disconcerted.

"Not normally maybe, which is why we have reduced her draught," Peters interrupted. "And the raid is scheduled for the height of the spring tides, which explains our need for haste."

"Each of the launches will be carrying members of 2 Commando led by Colonel Charles," Ryder continued. "After being landed at predetermined points, their job will be to overpower what defences there may be and then destroy specific facilities in the harbour itself. These include pumping stations and ammunition stores." Once more he paused to smile. "Though I understand the colonel has a hankering to sink a few U-boats into the bargain."

"You mean there are U-boat pens there as well?"

"Oh, yes."

Harris sighed; in which case there was even more reason for the Germans to maintain a strong defence. Despite Ryders' obvious sincerity, this was starting to sound frighteningly fanciful. But the commander was talking again.

"Meanwhile *Campbeltown* will be steered for the gates of the harbour's graving dock."

"Steered for the gates, sir?" It was Anderson this time. "You really are intending to use a destroyer as a ram ship?"

Ryder switched his gaze. "Indeed, Lieutenant."

"Actually, it's quite ironic," Peters added. "The gates we have in mind were originally supplied by the Germans as part of their repatriation payments."

Harris sensed further comments would continue to be ignored and had almost ceased to listen.

"And as I have mentioned, *Campbeltown* will be carrying a large quantity of explosives," Ryder continued. "These will not detonate immediately, enabling her crew and additional commandos to disembark. The troops will cause more devilment ashore before everyone makes for the launches waiting to take them home. If all goes to plan the charges aboard *Campbeltown* will detonate the following day, making the dock unusable."

Ryder had finished but Harris and Anderson were still too startled to talk. In Harris' case, he had rarely heard a proposal that relied so much on luck. Wherever this port may be, it would take a dark night indeed for so many vessels to approach undetected, let alone a twelve-hundred-ton destroyer and, should the force be spotted, Fairmile Bs were not the most robust of vessels.

Their hulls might be longer than *194*'s, but the construction was remarkably similar, with a mahogany skin that could be penetrated by anything larger than a rifle bullet. Even the lightest German shore battery would shatter them to pieces and, with an additional cargo of commandos, it would be carnage.

Then there was the problem of using a ram ship; though amazingly responsive on the open sea, destroyers were pigs to manoeuvre in harbour. Without the aid of tugs, whoever had command must simply aim the darn thing at the dock gates with no chance of going back for a second try.

And as for the suggestion of evacuating the landing party, even supposing every launch arrived safely – which must be in doubt – they were then expected to take on their original passengers as well as those previously carried by the destroyer, while the Germans would be far more vigilant on the way out.

Really it was unbelievable.

Yes, unbelievable was the word, Harris decided, although those higher up must think otherwise and a Royal Navy commander had been put in charge, so who was he to criticize?

"And what would our part be in this?" he asked at last.

"We'd like you to ride shotgun," Ryder replied. "Two *Hunt* class destroyers'll see us to the mouth of the river and take care of any larger surface vessels, though they might not cope with anything fast. Should an E-boat decide to follow us downriver it would be like a wolf let loose in a sheep pen."

There was no disputing that; in restricted waters, a cluster of Fairmile Bs would be easy prey.

"We need a gunboat to act as back marker to see such a danger off."

Harris scratched at his chin. "*194* might match an E for speed, but little else; what the Germans call their S craft are larger, stronger and better armed."

Ryder considered Harris more carefully. "Forgive me, Lieutenant Commander, I was given to understand you had already sunk at least one E-boat and damaged several more."

"That's so, sir, but a lot of luck was involved."

Ryder nodded and the smile briefly reappeared. "Your modesty does you credit, but we won't pursue the matter now. I simply need at least one small, fast, and well-armed boat on hand in case the situation arises."

Harris realised their involvement was to be treated as casually as any other part of the operation. "Unless your target is within a hundred miles of Falmouth, we shall need auxiliary tanks," he began. "Which will naturally slow us considerably while also..."

"On the subject of fuel, I can reassure you," Ryder interrupted. "We propose to tow your boat behind one of the destroyers. Once we reach the enemy coast it will be released but until then your men can sit back and enjoy the ride."

"And will we be involved in the actual attack?"

"No. I'll be heading the assault in a Fairmile C gunboat while you protect the rear; were my vessel to be disabled you may be asked to lead the withdrawal but there should be no need for you to even touch the shore. Oh, and there'll also be an MTB equipped with special torpedoes designed to destroy stationary targets at close range. Her commander is keen to be in on the action, though if you'd rather take a back seat that'll be equally fine."

Harris went to reply just as Ryder glanced at his watch then rose. "Forgive me, gentlemen, but I really have to leave you now. We'll doubtless meet again before the operation. Any further questions can be answered by Sub-Lieutenant Peters."

Harris and Anderson stood and the three men shook hands before Ryder swept from the room. Peters eyed the pair warily.

"I'm sure there's more you wish to know," he said. "We may as well get everything sorted now."

* * *

Gibson hadn't gone far, and neither was he in search of breakfast, not when a new port might produce all manner of fresh opportunities for one such as him. From leaving the boat he'd made for the nearest building, which was some sort of storage shed. He found it deserted with the door firmly locked and every window barred but from there he spotted a line of Nissen huts that looked more promising. They were equally well secured although Gibson was considering a panel that might be less so when the voice stopped him.

"Alright, Popeye, what's your game?"

He turned slowly and was surprised to see a soldier, rather than the expected naval guard. And this one wasn't dressed like your normal bullet stopper; he appeared far more casual with loose-fitting tunic and baggy trousers that had two prominent pockets on the thighs. He also wore a tightly knitted hat in place of a cap. But what caught Gibson's attention most was the machine gun pointing at his own boots.

"Fall out of a movie, did you?" Gibson enquired.

By way of response, the soldier cranked the gun's slide with a menacing click, then raised the barrel until it aimed at Gibson's belly.

"Hey steady there, matie, I ain't doin' no harm."

The sentry's teeth showed white against his tanned face. "You're right there, Popeye, now keep your hands where I can see them."

"Hands ain't going nowhere." Gibson raised both palms

128

up. "Now where I can get a spot of breakfast?"

"Where you from?"

"My boat's moored nearby."

"One of them launches?"

Gibson shook his head. "Gunboat," he said.

"Make you as sick, do they?"

"Sick?"

"Never mind, you'd better get back to it and sharpish."

"Don't I get breakfast?"

"I can arrange it," the soldier said. "Though it won't be up to much. Then there'll be a bed for the night; several nights actually. And after that, you'll get a spell in jankers, or whatever you salty types calls punishment."

"Hey, I were only takin' a look about."

"Well, you don't do that in a restricted zone, 'specially not when there's a job about to go down. Now get back to your boat and sharpish. And think yourself lucky I didn't turn you in."

"Grateful, I'm sure."

The soldier gave him a sideways look. "You didn't ought to be," he said. "Glasshouses are a darn sight safer than where you'll be headin'."

* * *

"The first thing I'd like to know is when we go."

Peters appeared mildly uncomfortable. "As Commander Ryder stated, we're very much dependant on the tides." Harris waited and the young man swallowed. "But it should be towards the end of the month," he said.

So much had already shocked Harris that morning that this final nugget barely left an impression; they were already well into March. "And you really intend to embark your entire commando force in a handful of Fairmile Bs?" he asked.

"We're hoping for more," Peters replied. "But the Admiralty do rather blow hot and cold. And, of course, some will be travelling aboard *Campbeltown*."

"Which is to be sacrificed," Harris reminded. "Meaning the launches will need to carry more back than they take."

Peters wriggled in his seat. "A mission such as this will inevitably involve casualties..."

129

"No disagreement there," Harris grunted. "And you're happy to anticipate taking back only a fraction of the original force?"

"I'd hardly say happy." Peters gave a weak smile. "We're hoping for quite a large fraction."

"Still a trifle dispassionate, don't you think?"

"Perhaps, sir, but it does rather emphasise the mission's importance. I cannot explain more at this stage, but a successful outcome will save more lives than might be lost in a single commando raid."

There was a pause, and Harris sighed. "Very well," he said. "You're obviously committed to the operation; I only hope whoever planned it truly understands the risks."

"I believe that's the case, sir." Peters appeared to have taken on fresh life. "But while we're being frank, could you explain more about your dealings with E-boats?"

Harris looked up. "It's something we try to avoid," he said.

"But you do encounter them on a regular basis," the young man persisted. "Or so we understand."

"Oh yes." Harris' mind was still on the anticipated loss of those commandos. "And usually give them a run for their money," he added. "But run is what they tend to do. You see E-boats are mainly used against our merchant shipping. If they can get beyond the escorts and sink a coaster, they'll have done their job and head for home. There's little gained and too much to be lost in delaying to engage the likes of us."

"A merchant ship being more valuable than a high-speed launch," Peters supposed.

"Even without considering her cargo," Harris agreed. "It takes several years, the use of a shipyard, and a good deal of resources to build an ocean-going trader."

"So quicker to build a gunboat."

"Quicker and cheaper," Anderson confirmed. "And the work can be carried out in any yard with access to the sea."

"I understand." Peters seemed to be taking everything in very carefully.

"We do run into them when attacking their convoys," Harris added, "and occasionally in open water though, again, they tend to play it cautiously."

"Which is definitely to our advantage," Anderson said. "An

E is larger, faster and better armed than most Coastal Forces vessels; when it comes to a showdown, we're very much on the back foot."

Harris was considering the young officer carefully. "You're not seriously intending to use *194* as the sole defence against E-boats?"

"That was what we had in mind, sir. Records show them being sunk or disabled on a regular basis."

"Yes," Harris agreed, "when they are on the defensive. To protect your flotilla against a concerted attack would need almost as many gunboats as there are Fairmile Bs. And they'd have to be substantial vessels, maybe steam-powered affairs, or a squadron of the new British Powerboat MkV's: something with a forward-facing gun at least."

Harris stopped. The young sub-lieutenant was regarding him with the same look of absurd confidence so obvious in his superior.

"We do have one other MGB," the young man said. "The Fairmile C that'll be carrying Commander Ryder and Colonel Charles into action. I believe she has a forward-facing gun."

"But no power." Anderson this time. "She'll be lucky to make more than twenty-five knots; an E can almost double that!"

Peters pulled at his chin. "I'll pass on what you've said to Commander Ryder, though doubt much can be done in the short time available."

"How long do we have exactly?" Harris asked.

"I can't give a precise date." Peters was now looking decidedly shifty, "but it'll be soon, sir. Very soon."

Chapter Fourteen

"A pub!" Smith exclaimed. "We got ourselves a bleedin' pub!"

Shortly after Gibson's return to the boat, *194*'s ratings were met by a pair of military policemen who ordered them to collect their belongings. Then, after a walk that lasted no more than ten minutes, they rolled up outside the brown-tiled exterior of The Rose public house that stood on the corner of Dewbury and Denmark Streets.

"Don't get too keen," one of the MPs said as he and his partner prepared to go.

"Aye, there won't be much chance of a razzle," the other agreed.

They were the first words from either man since leaving *194*, yet the ratings' enthusiasm remained as strong and, as the front door opened, they filed eagerly inside.

Though all was not as they expected. There was a bar, for sure, and several small tables; even the aroma was similar to countless other public houses throughout the country. But rather than a row of beer pulls at the counter, or optics on the wall behind, glass cases contained various cakes and buns while an industrial-sized kettle was sending out a continuous stream of steam.

"Ah, the naval gentlemen – my first guests!"

The woman was in her late forties and overweight, yet there was no mistaking the delight in her eyes as she stepped forward to meet them. "We've rooms for you all upstairs, though some'll have to share – I'm sure that won't bother you. I'm Jenny Lott, though everyone calls me Mona and I really don't mind. Now do you want to see the accommodation, or shall I cook you breakfast first?"

"Breakfast would be welcome," Jelly told her. "And I'd appreciate the chance to wash my hands."

"Of course, the gents is on the right, it's really like a normal pub!"

"So why isn't it, Missis?" Daly asked as Jelly and Smith

made for a heavily panelled door. "A pub, I'm meaning. To be sure, it looks just like one."

"Oh, but it is," Mona gushed. "At least it was – and will be again I've no doubt. For now, though, the WVS have taken it over. Me and my ladies hope to make you boys very comfortable."

"But no beer?" Gibson checked.

"Not even southern muck?" Pickering added.

"No, no beer, no alcohol at all. Just plenty of tea whenever you want it and lots of home cooking."

"Could be worse, I suppose," Gibson glanced around.

"Aye," Newman agreed. "At least they still got the dart board."

* * *

Once they had deposited their luggage and argued about who was sleeping where, the ratings returned to the bar and made themselves comfortable at a corner table. And it was there that Mona and another lady served them a first-rate breakfast.

"That looks like heaven on a plate, Mona my love," Smith told her when his food arrived.

"Tea whenever you want it." Her face was a picture of ecstasy.

"Hardly the canny lasses I were expectin'," Pickering muttered when the women left, "but if they feed us like this, you won't hear me complaining."

"Well, that'll be a first." Smith glanced over to his mate. "Dig in, China!"

"So what are we to do, boys?" Daly asked once the initial pangs of hunger were sated. "Stay here until they sends for us?"

"The boat'll need toppin' up," Pickering said.

"And the starboard wing might be slightly advanced." Newman was hardly looking at his food, although the mechanics of eating continued.

"Well, they knows where to find us," Gibson said.

"Aye, what say we sink this lot then stick about for more char and maybe a wad?" Smith had already demolished most of a substantial breakfast and was looking speculatively at Godliman's. "If you don't want that sausage, Len old chap, I could find it a home."

133

"Not tasted bangers like them in ages," Jelly said. "Reckon they must come from a local farm."

"That's what you get for living in the country," Smith again. "Ration's a joke round these parts; eggs a plenty, butter an' all, and they just got to pick up a gun to have rabbit for supper every night."

"Never thought of that." Gibson stopped eating for a moment.

"Makin' plans are you Gibbo?" Pickering asked.

"Aye," Daly agreed. "Gonna fill the boat up with dead bunny to take back to Dover?"

"They got rabbits a plenty round there an' all," Jelly said. "Just that we never get to see them."

"Maybe that's what someone should try when we gets back?" Gibson said.

"Wey aye, a rabbit hunt!" Pickering exclaimed.

"To be sure, and couldn't I bring me Vickers?" Daly added. "Wouldn't that be a fine thing?"

Fuelled by the food and company, the table was soon vibrating with good humour. Only Gibson remained silent.

"Well, this don't taste like rabbit." Smith pointed at the sausage Godliman had donated. "An' the bacon's kosha an all."

"When do you think we'll get back to Dover?" Jelly's second meeting with Ann had gone as well as the first, though he was unable to tell her his boat would be seconded.

"Will you listen to the fellow?" Daly grinned. "There's us not been in Cornwall more than five minutes and already he's wantin' to get back."

"Got a lass there, have you Wobbler?" Pickering enquired.

"Never mind that," Smith said. "Do we stay here or head back for the boat?"

"We stay." Gibson was adamant. "There're no POs about to tell us otherwise."

"That's true," said Jelly. "What did happen to Carter and Phillips?"

"Probably laid up in some fancy hotel, like." Pickering again.

"So, we stay, but what do we do?" Smith asked.

Newman nodded towards where Mrs Lott was moving tables. "Looks like Mona's got her work cut out."

"Aye, we won't have the place to ourselves forever," Jelly

said, "Most times it's a WVS tea shop, probably get packed later."

"What, *our* pub?" Smith exclaimed.

"Face it, lads," Newman said. "We might have to share."

* * *

The mystery of *194*'s officers' accommodation was easily solved. Harris and Anderson were given a room each in a nearby hotel while Carter and Phillips bunked together in the same building. Anderson had spent much of the day attending to *194*'s need for fuel and other supplies while Harris remained at the hotel in the hope of discovering more about Operation Chariot. Both dined aboard the *Princess Josephine Charlotte* at different times and, though they had not arranged to meet up, each was pleased to see the other on the hard that evening.

"*Hunt* class," Anderson said as they considered the two trim destroyers freshly anchored in the roadstead. "I saw them come in this morning."

"Then I expect they'll be part of this little lot. Must say it feels strange coming in so late."

"I know what you mean," Anderson agreed. "Everyone's so busy yet we've got damn all to do. I spent most of the afternoon trying to get 20mm shells for the Oerlikon."

"And did you?"

Anderson shook his head. "Nothing doing. There's some sort of shortage though it only came to light after half an hour's arguing. Took me that long to convince them MGB*194* existed, and that she was part of the operation. It's almost as if we were someone's last-minute whim."

"If I knew who it was, I'd give them a piece of my mind."

"I think you'd get it thrown straight back," Anderson said. "This entire plan's wildly optimistic, but there's no doubting all involved are devoted to it. And they're the toughest bunch I've ever come across."

Harris considered this. The day had been uncommonly hot for March, and it was still warm standing on the hard, even though the sun was close to setting. "I dined with the chap heading the commandos," he said. "Genial bod; everyone calls him Colonel Charles and as nice a bloke as you could meet. Even played piano at the end of the meal; not my sort of music, but he was good. Yet all the while I felt that under that affable exterior lay a heart of cold steel."

"Did you learn any more about the raid?" Anderson asked.

"Not from him, and everyone else seems tight-lipped, but some of the Fairmile skippers were more inclined to chat."

"Aren't they all stuck out on their boats?"

"Officers are allowed ashore," Harris said, "though they're as much in the dark about the destination as us."

"Can't be many enemy ports that big within striking distance," Anderson said.

"Maybe not, but until we know which one for sure, we're floundering."

"Did you discover anything else?"

Harris shook his head. "Not much, except four more Fairmile Bs are joining shortly. That'll bring their force up to sixteen."

It was a fair number, though Anderson could not rid himself of the notion that allowances were being made for wastage – of the human variety.

"What about the colour, did you ask about that?"

"The pink?" Harris grinned. "Oh yes, and it's a moot point. Everyone's blaming Mountbatten."

"*Lord* Mountbatten?"

"That's right, he's a bee in his bonnet about that particular shade."

"Really?"

"Apparently when his lordship was on convoy duty, one of the merchants was always the first to disappear at night, and the last spotted in the morning. She was painted Plymouth Pink and, as he has a say in the matter, all motor launches are being decked out in it."

"What about the destroyers?"

Harris shrugged. "I doubt there'll be time. It's a miracle they got the Fairmiles done, but then miracles and this raid are undoubtedly linked."

"And what about *194*?" Anderson asked as the possibility occurred. "Will she get the pink treatment?"

"Who can tell? Though for all the attention shown so far, I reckon there's a good chance we might get forgotten."

Anderson shook his head. "It all sounds so haphazard – so

last minute."

A faint smile played about Harris' face. "You're not wrong. It seems they had an exercise a couple of days before we showed up. The entire force of Fairmiles set off to invade Devonport."

"Devonport?"

"That's right; brass hats played it up as a test of the harbour's defence measures but really it was to find out how the motor launches would behave when attacking in formation and at night."

"And what was the outcome?" Anderson wondered if he really wanted to know.

"Terrible. Several got lost and overshot, others were blinded by searchlights, while those ashore saw them coming a mile off – literally."

"So, a complete failure?"

"Some did find their target, though more by luck than judgement. Admiral Forbes wants them to have another shot though I gather they learned enough. And from the one before."

"There've been *two* exercises?"

"Seems so. The first was a week ago. Ryder took the commandos on a jaunt into the Atlantic proper, under the auspices of an anti-submarine patrol."

"They took soldiers on a sub hunt?"

Harris nodded. "I doubt anyone was fooled. The intention had been to give the troops experience of heavy weather sailing. Turned out it was just a bit too heavy; they didn't get further than Scilly."

"I bet most were seasick."

"Of course. You know how *194* bucks about in a swell; apparently, Fairmile Bs are far worse."

"Doesn't bode well for what they're about to face."

"I just hope bad weather has been taken into consideration," Harris said. "All the planning in the world'll be no good if they land a bunch of queasy commandos."

As Harris spoke, something in the distance caught Anderson's eye. A large vessel was rounding Pendennis Point and at speed. "What do you make of that?" he asked.

"Destroyer," Harris replied as the vessel drew nearer. The Fairmiles were anchored close by, but the warship came on regardless. "Though not like any I've seen before."

"Nor me," Anderson agreed.

"Hull's like something from the Great War, and she's flush-decked, yet only two funnels."

Anderson clicked his fingers. "She must be the *Campbeltown*," he said, "the four-stacker Commander Ryder mentioned. They were making her look like a *Mowe*."

"Can't say it's a great resemblance," Harris said, "though the light's reasonable of course."

"And she's riding high, though that'll be to see her over the mud flats."

The destroyer was approaching her two younger sisters now. There were several loud blasts from her klaxon before she reversed her screws in a flurry of foam and dropped a forward anchor."

"Fellow seems mighty sure of himself," Harris grunted.

"Let's hope he remains so in a few days' time."

"It's hard to realise that's all we've got. To be frank, Number One, this feels like everything's going off at half cock."

"There's certainly a good deal of haste. But one thing worries me more than any."

Harris turned to look at his second in command.

"It's what Ryder said this morning; about the commandos being briefed but not our chaps."

"Yes, that didn't sound entirely fair," Harris agreed.

"Especially when you remember most of the green jobs are professional soldiers, whereas our lot are mainly conscripted."

"I'm afraid it's worse than that." *Campbeltown* was now at a standstill and even from such a distance the two men could hear derisory shouts coming from the crews of all three destroyers. "It's something else I learned today," Harris continued. "Seems the commandos have been given the chance to opt out, with no mention of it on their service records. But our lads won't even know where they're going, not till they're halfway there."

* * *

After taking on fuel, *194* returned to her pontoon berth though nothing more was required of her. It was as if she and her men were an addition no one knew what to do with. Their introductory lecture from the CPO had been annoyingly vague, though it was clear they were needed for something more ambitious than minelayer protection or a raid on enemy shipping. Exactly what remained a mystery although the presence of so many motor launches may have been a clue. And then there was Falmouth itself.

Ordinarily, it would have been a pleasant seaside resort but the presence of so many military types made it more akin to a garrison town. Most were built like houses and definitely a step up from the common conscript. More to the point, each carried themselves like trained fighters and none of *194*'s ratings were keen for a close encounter.

So, when the boat had been thoroughly cleared and cleaned, they were given liberty. And, despite the prospect of a fresh town on their doorstep, they had no intention of exploring. Having their own pub, albeit a dry one, was still a novelty and their breakfast that morning had been spectacular in both quantity and quality. So, they quickly agreed to forgo the delights of Falmouth and test out The Rose's evening fare.

Which definitely went down well with Mona and her helpers. The men soon discovered this was a new enterprise and, though carried out under the auspices of the WVS, something of a personal venture.

Living in the West Country provided few opportunities to support the war effort and, when the lack of holiday trade forced the pub to close, Mona joined with several other women to take on the lease. The intention was to provide homemade food to service personnel and with the sudden influx of those concerned with Operation Chariot, they had been expecting far more in the way of business. But whether it was the back street location or simply too much choice, they were all but shunned by the new arrivals. However, after downing generous portions of steak and kidney pudding, *194*'s ratings were certain of one thing; there was nothing wrong with Mona's cooking.

"That were real beef!" Smith sat back as they surveyed their empty plates with wonder and regret.

"Aye, not a whiff of Dobbin," Pickering agreed.

"An' none of it from a can," Jelly added.

"Oh, you wouldn't find us opening no tins, my lover." Vera, one of the assistants, was collecting the plates. "There's one thing you can be sure of in the country: proper food." Then, closing one eye and tapping the side of her nose, she added; "If you know who to ask, that is."

"Said as much," Gibson muttered when she had gone. "There's money to be made round here, see if I'm not wrong."

"Whether you are, or whether you're not, I ain't interested," Smith said. "Those old girls are going out of their way to see us fed: you won't find me takin' advantage."

"Nor me," Pickering agreed.

"Nor any of us," Jelly added with a purposeful look at Gibson. "Though I'm surprised they're quiet. Town like this and with a positive army in residence, they should be doing a roaring trade."

"Yeah, well I ain't so keen to share with no military types," Smith said. "Not if they were like them we saw earlier."

"Nothing wrong with pongos," Newman said. "An' at least this lot are well presented, not your common 'hostiles'."

"Looked more like parachutists to me." The meal had made Gibson unusually content, though he would rather his shipmates took him a little more seriously. "Think they got anything to do with our mission?"

"They calls them paratroopers now," Newman said.

"And they drop them from planes, not Fairmiles," Daly added.

"'Less they got low-flying launches!" Smith spluttered.

"Now wouldn't that be a fine thing?" Daly agreed amid the laughter.

"I didn't mean that." Gibson glared at his shipmates and the merriment stopped as quickly as it started, although no one appeared particularly intimidated.

"We don't care what you meant," Daly told him slowly. "You say something funny, and folk'll take the mick."

"He's right, Gibbo," Pickering said. "Better get used to it."

There were several seconds of silence, and then Gibson appeared to back down. "Never met such a bunch of coconuts," he said.

"Well, ain't that a shame?" Smith grinned. "But then I always knew we was special."

* * *

140

The good weather stayed with them for the following morning and showed every sign of remaining. *194*'s crew were ordered to assemble at the boat at 08.00 hours when it seemed it wasn't just the motor launches that would be getting an extra coat of paint.

"I wouldn't say the old girl's lookin' that bad," Smith said as he and Godliman finished unloading a selection of pots and brushes from the dockyard truck.

"Not now maybe, but wait till she gets a dose of this." Jelly had opened one of the cans and was staring at the contents.

"Lummy!" Smith exclaimed, looking over his shoulder. "Looks more like primer!"

"Give it a stir, Wobbler," Daly suggested. "Maybe it'll mix in."

"If it does it'll be the first," the driver told them.

"So, we ain't gonna cop another coat of grey on top?" Smith checked.

"Not likely." The superintendent pointed across to the launches anchored nearby. "End of today you got to look just like them!"

"That'll take a fair few layers." Daly said. "We're half the size of a Fairmile."

"Spare us the humour." Both men were already making for their truck. "Just get one good coat on and you can call it a day," the superintendent added.

"He serious?" Gibson asked of no one in particular as the truck drove off.

"Don't see why not." Daly had collected a can and was reading the label with a sceptical look. "There ain't nothing else to do, and no officers about to tell us otherwise."

"So, what happened to the skip' and Jimmy?" Jelly had found a length of wood and was beginning to stir the paint.

"Carter and Phillips is missin' an all," Gibson added.

"Reckon they'll be at some sort of briefing." Smith was regarding the boat speculatively. "What say we start at the stern and move forward together, then we won't get in each other's way."

"An' we're just doing topsides?" Gibson checked.

"Nah, they've given us a stage." Smith pointed towards a plank of wood and several lengths of line.

"Though no one'll be expecting a pucker job," Jelly said. "Reckon if we put our backs into it, we can be done by lunchtime."

"Come on Lenny." Smith collected a brush and headed for the painting stage. "You an' me can handle the hull."

Daly clambered on board and began dosing the deck next to the CSA canisters. "What happened to Pickers and Newman?" he asked.

"Went below to see to their precious engines," Jelly said. "Looks like we got the job to ourselves."

"Still like to know where the officers have got to," Smith said. He and Godliman had rigged the painting stage and, such was the lack of *194*'s freeboard, their heads remained level with the deck.

"It's what happens before a raid," Jelly said. "Officers are told what's going on and we just get to obey orders."

Smith charged his brush. "Aye, mushrooms, that's what we is!" he said.

"Mushrooms?" The sound of Godliman's voice made those on deck stop for a moment.

"That's right, lad," Smith gave an encouraging smile. "Mushrooms it is, 'cause we're kept in the dark, see, an' fed on muck!"

Godliman smiled and started to paint, and soon the others were following his example.

Chapter Fifteen

Anderson left Harris after breakfast to check on *194*'s repainting and, after noting all was well with much of the aft deck already transformed, found himself at a loose end. As would be Harris, he reminded himself. Since their arrival, there were few of the briefings both expected; the very reverse, in fact. But rather than return to the hotel, only to become embroiled in yet another card game with Phillips and Carter, he decided to take a look around and maybe clear his thoughts.

Of course, Eve was at the centre of them. After trying unsuccessfully to raise her by telephone from Dover, then again when they arrived at Falmouth, he considered speaking to her brother. Apart from being a first rate mechanic, Bill Newman was a reliable hand who never mentioned the fact that Anderson was courting his sister. Yet though he might know more, approaching him could be stretching the officer–rating relationship too far. Instead, Anderson had resorted to the Royal Mail.

The only address he had was her training establishment although, in a world where transfers and redeployments were common, using that should find her eventually. Despite being inordinately long, he was aware the letter lacked any real content. After all, there was little he could tell her about his work and any mention of Falmouth and their current deployment was definitely out. Yet still he hoped she would read beyond the inane lines and realise things had moved on since they last met.

Since they last met; it was a shock to realise that was almost three months ago, and nearly two weeks since speaking on the 'phone. Should anything dreadful have happened both were listed as the other's first contact; it had been one of the early signs of their relationship's importance, although didn't rule out other, less drastic, events. And he was equally conscious they now lived very different lives in very different environments. Anything could have happened during their separation; for all he knew there may now be a fresh first contact on her records.

But it was too fine a day for such thoughts. The weather,

spectacular since *194*'s arrival, was holding out; as he stared at the roadstead, he could feel the sun's warmth on his face.

There was movement aboard all three anchored destroyers and some additional work must be in progress aboard *Campbeltown* as two bright pinpoints of light were noticeable even in the dazzling sunshine. Closer to, the Fairmiles were equally active with what looked like improvised keep-fit classes being held on several. Though they were considerably larger than *194*, Anderson knew how claustrophobic small craft could be when riding at anchor. Their first officers must be running out of ideas for keeping the crews amused.

The sound of far-off engines caught his attention and he looked up to see a small craft rounding Pendennis Point. It was yet another Coastal Forces vessel but closer in size to his own boat. From her prominent whaleback, she appeared to be a Vosper, although something on the foredeck looked amiss, and it wasn't until she had been signalled to berth on the adjoining pontoon to *194* that he realised it was a pair of torpedo tubes.

Intrigued, Anderson made his way over. It was customary for Vosper MTBs to mount their torpedoes amidships, either side of the superstructure. Having two tubes so high on the forecastle made them look like some form of oversized shotgun and must do little for the vessel's stability.

And that was not the only abnormality; Anderson arrived as the craft was being secured and was struck by her extraordinary colour scheme. The boat boasted almost every shade of Admiralty paint, though not in any of the prescribed patterns. It was as if a child had been let loose with a painting set; erratic lines and shapes ran over the hull and topsides making her appear about as lethal as a patchwork quilt.

What must be her CO was on the bridge, although he looked nothing like a conventional Royal Navy officer. A battered black cap was worn on the back of his head and there was a pipe sticking from his mouth at an equally jaunty angle. Seeing Anderson, the man gave a friendly wave before disappearing below and finally emerging from the wheelhouse.

"Ahoy!"

That one word said much. Its speaker wore a tattered regulation tunic top with a single RNVR stripe although the trousers were definitely of a civilian cut and could have started life as part of a dress suit. And as he skipped down to join Anderson on the quay, he was obviously an individual.

"Names Wynn," he said. "Micky Wynn, just in from Pompey. You must be the welcoming committee."

Anderson took the hand. "Not me I'm afraid – just an idle spectator."

Wynn drew closer and Anderson could see the intensity in his eyes. "But you're a part of this Chariot set-up, surely?"

"Oh yes, number one of that gunboat." He pointed briefly at *194*, now almost half covered in fresh paint.

"Odd choice of shade."

Anderson grinned. "We're all getting it: Mountbatten's orders."

Wynn glanced back at his own boat. "Really, it would be a shame to change the old girl, I rather like her colour scheme."

"That'll probably be the first in quite a list of disappointments."

Wynn looked concerned. "Disappointments?"

Anderson shrugged. "I suppose surprises would be better. Not to put too fine a point on it, all involved in Chariot are unusually protective about their little plan. Apart from an initial briefing, we've spent much of the time kicking our heels."

Wynn nodded. "I sensed this wouldn't be easy. It took quite a bit of pushing to get aboard in the first place." Now he had spoken further, Anderson could place his accent as Welsh and cultured, though that hardly matched the man's appearance. "But now I am, I can't wait to get going."

"Quite a vessel you have there."

Wynn turned again to appreciate his command. "*74*? Yes, my little project," he said. "She were doing remarkably little when I took her over, so we chopped her about a bit."

"Was there a reason?"

Wynn looked back and was suddenly deadly serious. "I should say so. If everything had gone to plan, she would have taken out the *Scharnhorst*."

Anderson was suitably impressed. "Quite a feat," he said.

"It was when she were in Brest," Wynn explained. "But wouldn't you know, the buggers got wind and ran off before we got the chance..."

"Germans all over," Anderson sighed. "Easily intimidated."

The remark amused Wynn who removed his pipe before slapping Anderson heartily on the shoulder, sending fragments of glowing tobacco down his own tunic. "I say, I'm in need of a brew. Take me to where we can get some breakfast."

"What about your number one?"

Wynn glanced over to where three ratings were securing the boat unsupervised. "He'll be fine, spent most of the journey asleep in the wheelhouse. Come on, I want to see the sights of Falmouth!"

* * *

It was actually nearer to one o'clock when *194*'s painting team finished. By then a thick layer of drab pink paint lay wet and stinking on most of her surfaces with only small areas around hinges and clips still showing a defiant grey.

"It's quite a sight," Smith said as they regarded their handy work, and it seemed an appropriate comment.

But it was done reasonably well, and in good time. Apart from an initial annoyance when Pickering and Newman insisted on starting one of the engines, sending waves of exhaust fumes over the workers and shreds of carbon onto their wet paint, it had even been moderately enjoyable. Then, once the mechanics finished below and joined them for the final push, they began working as a team.

"So, is it back to The Rose?" Daly asked.

"I can't see much happening around here," Jelly replied. "Anyone going on board'll get covered in Plymouth Pink."

"I could handle one of Mona's pasties," Pickering said.

Smith was looking towards the pens where four newly arrived launches were already getting a coat of paint. "Them seeing to the Fairmiles 'ave got themselves a catering truck," he said. "They might have sent one to us!"

There was a rumble of discontent.

"What say we goes and joins them?" Jelly suggested.

"Share their grub?" Daly asked. "You think they'd let us?"

Smith shrugged. "Bound to if we give them an 'and after."

"Give them a hand?" Gibson sounded mildly insulted.

"What else you gonna do this af'ernoon?" Pickering asked. "Let's slap on a bit more paint and 'ave a natter; maybe suss out why we're 'ere."

"I'm up for it," Jelly said, although Gibson still looked sceptical.

"And me," Godliman added, and all automatically turned to him.

"Well done, lad," Smith told his mate. "You're becoming quite a talker."

* * *

Anderson usually took secrecy extremely seriously and had not forgotten Ryder's warning of the previous morning. However, since then they had been all but ignored and, after walking with Wynn for no more than a couple of minutes, his tongue became increasingly loose. But then Wynn had an air about him that encouraged familiarity and, after discovering they had both been at Dunkirk, it was as if they were old friends.

"I'd just been demobbed from the Army," Wynn revealed. "It was on medical grounds, and there was nothing I or my family could do to change matters, though all seems to have cleared up since."

"Fortunate." Anderson did not comment further.

"Whatever. After a bit of pressing, I was taken on at an Air Sea Rescue base and given a launch to play with. But once we began to retreat, they started seizing anything bigger than a tin bath for the evacuation."

"I remember."

"Not that I wouldn't have gone anyway though knowing my old mob were still out there was one hell of an incentive."

"And did you find them?"

Wynn shook his head. "Did I, hell? But we made five trips and brought back a bunch of other chaps until the launch got badly shot up. We only just made it into Ramsgate; after that, they wouldn't let me try anymore."

"Still, you did your bit."

"Oh, I wasn't finished," Wynn said. "I heard of a Norfolk fisher going spare so persuaded a couple of my boys to come along and we tried the beaches south of Calais."

"And?"

Wynn sighed. "Still no sign of my lot, but we found a load

147

of others and it gave me a taste for the Navy."

"So, when all this happened you were still a civilian?"

"Officially; they let me join up proper later. Mind, I borrowed a Navy jacket to wear on the beaches," he winked. "No sense in being shot as a spy!"

They were at the outskirts of town, yet neither seemed in any hurry and Anderson was enjoying talking with Wynn.

"So, what's the story behind your boat?" he asked when his companion paused to clear out his pipe.

"Ah, that's a long one," Wynn said, filling the thing once more. "I was based at Gosport, see, and training up with you Glory Boys. *74* was an early boat and mainly being used for milk runs. The Army taught me a little about explosives so, when they were working on ways to take on *Scharnhorst*, I came up with my plan."

"Which was?"

"Engineless torpedoes." Wynn produced a match which he lit on the back of his trousers and was soon half hidden in a cloud of smoke. Anderson wondered if he had heard correctly but the statement was repeated, and Wynn explained further.

"You see the German battlewagons were protected by torpedo netting, but I reckoned if a boat could get close enough it should be possible to shoot a couple of fish over the top."

"I see."

"And mounting the tubes on the foredeck should have given us the height, though we couldn't be certain."

Wynn had the air of someone who cared little either way and, once his pipe was properly alight, the pair began to walk once more.

"Hang on, if the torpedoes have no engines..." Anderson said.

"I'd worked out there'd be enough power in the launching charges to send them a good distance, and with an extra dose of explosive, they'd only need to be under the ship." Wynn took two deep puffs before continuing. "Having no motors or gas tanks left more space; by the time we'd finished, each fish could hold eighteen hundred pounds of amatol, that's enough bang to blow a sizeable hole in pretty much anything."

"And how were you going to get out?" It was an obvious question, yet Anderson still felt awkward asking it.

Wynn shrugged. "To be honest, I didn't give that much

thought," he said. "But you know what it is with our craft; takes a lot to catch 'em."

"And now you're going to try your little toys on Operation Chariot?"

"That's about the size of it. I've spoken with Commander Ryder, and he seems a decent sort."

As proposals went, Wynn's was remarkably casual, although that hardly differentiated it from much involved in the coming attack.

"Of course, my father had a hand in it as well," he admitted.

"Your father?"

"Yes, the old boy must be running out of ways to finish me off. It was him who arranged my command of *74* in the first place and financed the weapons."

"He sounds an influential fellow."

Wynn puffed at his pipe some more before turning to Anderson.

"Always has been, always will be," he said. "But then it helps that he's a Lord."

* * *

It was as if The Rose had reverted to her previous entity. Without a sniff of beer in the air, and in direct contrast to the previous two evenings, the place was as crowded as a pub on payday with Mona working harder than any barmaid. But she, and her fellow WVS helpers were not alone; most of *194*'s ratings had picked up the baton and were clearing tables or delivering food with all the grace and delicacy of blacksmiths.

"Corner table, egg 'n' chips, four times," Smith announced as he collected a handful of china mugs full of tea from Vera at the urn, and slopped them onto a tray.

"Be ten minutes," Mona said.

"Tell 'em, Lenny." Smith shoved the tray to Godliman for delivery. "Oh, an' they wants bread 'n' butter, if there's any left."

Mona made a note on her pad, then glanced at the china crock behind the counter. "I can do this and maybe a couple more, but the butter won't hold out forever. An' neither will I," she added under her breath.

"Go on, Mona my love," Smith said. "You're as strong as an 'orse."

"One heading for the knackers, maybe. Why can't they get their meals at the base? Don't they feed them?"

Smith looked back on the crowded room with an element of pride. "Your fault for serving such luverly grub," he said.

That was the case, although Smith equally knew many were there because of him – and his mates, of course. The previous day they'd brought a crowd from the newly arrived Fairmiles while limited leave was finally being granted for those at anchor. And though many would later be heading for Falmouth's more conventional pubs, they'd been starved of proper food as much as drink. As a consequence, the place was positively heaving which, in their innocence, *194*'s crew thought would please their hosts. When it proved otherwise all they could do was help.

And not all the guests were men. Word about The Rose's fare must have circulated, and a good few Wrens came in search of a real meal. Like the men, they would only be in Falmouth a short time which was enough to break down many barriers and all were in a holiday mood. Yet though the talk was loud and, occasionally, risqué, the atmosphere remained good-humoured.

"Lady gave me a penny."

After returning with his tray, Lenny was holding a copper coin up in puzzlement.

"What she do that for?" Smith asked.

Godliman shook his head. "Said I were a dark one and wanted to pay for me thoughts."

Smith focused on the corner table and smiled. There were three ratings and one Wren; an older woman with blonde hair, red lipstick and a look of pure iniquity. His mate must have caught her eye over those of her companions and, as he watched, she looked towards them and gave a generous wink that was definitely meant for Lenny and Lenny alone.

"Reckon you're in there, China," he told Godliman. "Why not take 'em their bread and butter?"

* * *

150

Dining aboard the *Princess Josephine Charlotte* was more sedate, although the wardroom appeared no less crowded. Harris and Anderson were invited to join Commander Ryder, Sub-Lieutenant Peters, and Colonel Charles for what promised to be a tense and possibly sterile meal. But when Anderson noticed Micky Wynn already at the table, his spirits lifted. And the atmosphere was surprisingly relaxed, almost as if *194*'s officers had finally been admitted into a very private group; one that was planning the most audacious raid of the current war.

"You made good progress painting ship," Ryder told them during a break in conversation and Anderson smiled uncomfortably. There had been little input from him. Even without supervision, *194*'s ratings had done a workman-like job painting while Carter claimed their starboard wing engine now ran smoother than ever.

"And I believe your chaps were decent enough to help with the Fairmiles just in," Peters added.

"They're a good bunch," Anderson admitted.

"And how is it with *74*?"

The focus switched to Wynn, seated near the end of the table. He still wore the same tattered tunic and took the attention in his stride.

"Well enough in most respects, Commander," he said. "Though we've problems in the engine department."

"And they are?" Ryder was suddenly deadly serious.

"We can make a good nine knots on the twin V8s," Wynn replied. "Just when engaging the Packards we run into trouble."

"You won't get far at nine knots." Colonel Charles gave a genial smile, but it was clear he was just as concerned.

"Don't worry about that, sir; *74*'s a cracking boat. She'll get to wherever you want her to go."

"But not on main engines, perhaps?" Again, that smile.

"My motor mechanic thinks he can sort two of them, though one definitely needs replacing," Wynn admitted. "Fortunately we have another on board; I brought it with me as deck cargo; only needs to be fitted."

"Which will be impossible, considering the time." Ryder turned away. It was as if Wynn had excluded himself from the mission and warranted no further attention.

"Lovegrove's a wonder as are his team," Wynn insisted.

151

"All they needs is a winch and perhaps a couple more willing bodies."

"The loan of a winch we can organise, but the dockyard's fully stretched at present." Ryder's tone still held the air of finality. "74's presence was unexpected and, though your remarkable weapons would have been a welcome addition, we'll have to count you out."

Anderson flashed a meaningful glance at Harris, who looked back uncomprehending. Then he took the plunge.

"Perhaps our lads can help?" Anderson now had everyone's attention and there was a grunt of surprise from his captain. "Our CMM's well versed with Packards, as are his mechanics," he said. "I'm sure they'd respond well to a request."

"Then that's settled," Wynn exclaimed. "If you gentlemen arrange access to a hoist, I'll prime my lads to have 74 in position first thing. With luck, we'll have everything in place and fully tuned by this time tomorrow."

It seemed a bold assumption but, as Wynn was involved, no one appeared very surprised.

* * *

The Post Office proved to be a life saver. Jelly had only met Ann a few times and, though each occasion was special, with their mutual attraction deepening, he would always be a pessimist. So, when 194 transferred to Falmouth it was as if all hope had been taken from him; she would hear of the boat's relocation and was bound to give him up for lost. Yet a remnant of faith encouraged him to write a note and send it almost as soon as they arrived.

Of course, it would have been foolish to give any indication of where they were, or when they might expect to return; all mail was censored and he would end up on a charge, with the letter potentially destroyed. There were no government restrictions on feelings, however, and, in this last-ditch effort, Jelly allowed his to run free.

Consequently, when a warrant officer handed him the small white envelope, he opened it with mixed feelings. Though unable to recognise her writing, he was in no doubt of the sender; none of his family ever wrote and the bare address of name, boat number, and flotilla was a perfect example of Annie's practical common sense.

Yet his letter to her had contained anything but; rather than give a broad outline of the situation and send hopes for an eventual reunion, it was an exercise in prose of the purple variety, and expressed his love in a manner as novel to him as the emotion itself. Quite how level-headed Annie would respond was all too easy to anticipate and his hands were shaking as he opened the envelope.

At least there was no need for blue pencil. Annie's thoughts were expressed in a more disciplined manner and without the need for poetical allusions. Instead, the single sheet was covered on both sides with neat writing that told him with commendable clarity that the affection he expressed was not only appreciated, but fully reflected, and Jelly was more than satisfied.

* * *

Carter and his team proved as keen as Anderson expected. And, with nothing else to do, were better off working on another boat than lounging around in Falmouth, so Harris was pacified. By midday, the blown Packard had been neatly plucked from MTB74's engine bay and a fresh unit, still sticky with grease, now sat in its place.

"Take a while to plumb her in," Lovegrove, Wynn's chief motor mechanic, said. He was well built, with what must be permanently untidy hair and a goatee beard, but very obviously a natural mechanic and Carter took to him instantly.

"And they usually take a bit of settling," he said.

Lovegrove flashed a penetrating look. "How long?"

Carter rubbed a smudge of oil into his chin. "A week or so, in my experience."

"We don't have a week," Lovegrove said. "Nothing like it."

Newman was wiping a paraffin-soaked cloth over the new engine and well out of earshot while Pickering had gone forward for a brew with the other two mechanics.

"Do you know exactly?" Carter asked.

When Lovegrove nodded he looked more like a pirate than ever, but there was no humour in his eyes.

"Buzz is, day after tomorrow," he said.

Carter considered this. Forty-eight hours had been enough

for them to get *194* ready, but it would be a miracle to see this one fully operational in that time.

"We've managed in the past," Lovegrove continued. "In fact, with a skipper like ours, we get used to doing the impossible."

"Right oh then," Carter sighed. "We'd better get down to it."

* * *

Once more the officers were dining in the assault ship's wardroom and the table was roughly as before, except Colonel Charles and his adjutant were attending their troops and two young Naval officers had taken their places. The senior newcomer was an RNVR lieutenant by the name of Dunstan Curtis, a polite yet oddly serious young man who sat quietly at his end of the table. Anderson failed to catch the name of his junior, a sub-lieutenant and equally reticent. And they were not the only ones to keep their own counsel; in direct contrast to the previous night, an element of tension had returned.

The meal, though nothing approaching the excellence of those served by Mona Lott, was good enough yet, sensing the mood, most ate sparsely. And when the table was cleared and a substantial bread and butter pudding appeared, only Wynn showed interest. Then, after coffee was served, Ryder leant forward and caught the attention of every man present.

"You'll have noticed we're an exclusively Naval party tonight," he said. "More than that, you all command vessels with important roles in the forthcoming raid."

He waved a hand in the direction of Curtis and the young officer who must be his second in command. "Dunstan here has MGB*314* which will not only be leading the attack but also have the unenviable task of taking me, Colonel Charles, and our staff into action."

There was a murmur of polite laughter as Curtis nodded in acknowledgement.

"Micky here we know about," Ryder continued. "He has a specialist craft and I understand has worked wonders to get her back on the top line."

Wynn also recognised this, although in his case there was a hint of appreciation as his eyes flashed towards Anderson.

154

"His initial target will be the graving dock gates, should *Campbeltown* not beach herself correctly. That said, Sam Beattie's a good man and I've every confidence he'll get through. In which case Micky will have a choice of targets for his little toys."

All eyes turned to Wynn who was obviously relishing the prospect.

"And then there's Bob," Ryder continued, and the attention switched to Harris. "His is the widest brief; the protection of our Fairmiles. In this he'll need to be ready should small craft appear during our approach, then stand guard outside the harbour and see they make good their escape. Much of the time he'll have to use his initiative and – this is the point, gentlemen – he will not be alone."

Anderson was conscious Ryder had the undivided attention of all at the table. And though his voice was low, and the noise from others in the wardroom constant, no one missed a word.

"Obviously in a raid such as this, all must think on their feet to some extent, although those commanding the Fairmiles will be in company, and under the direction of their flotilla leaders. Tweedie and Jenks, who captain the destroyers, will work together and enjoy the security of a decent-sized vessel under their feet, and Sam Beattie, in *Campbeltown*, can rely on Major Bill Copeland and roughly eighty commandos to give him all the advice he needs."

Again, another round of polite laughter, although Anderson sensed something extremely serious was about to be announced.

"But you'll all be relying on your wits. Things may not go according to plan – there's bound to be more than an element of confusion – but if everyone does what they feel is right, there'll be no repercussions."

That was comforting to a point, though it did rather highlight the raid's haphazard arrangements. And there was more to come; Ryder still carried an air of expectancy, and all remained captured by his spell.

"And finally, I have the main news of the evening," he said. "We'd pencilled in the twenty-seventh as the ideal date for departure. Bearing in mind our expected transit time, this would have seen us arrive at the very height of the spring tide. However,

I think you'll agree the weather has been exceptionally mild and, as the Met boys consider it'll remain so, this has been changed."

Now the tension increased further, and most were sitting forward as Ryder continued.

"Consequently, we'll be setting off a day earlier. All boats must be ready for departure tomorrow afternoon, is that clear?"

Wynn, who was looking uncharacteristically serious, raised a hand.

"And are we able to brief our crews before they go?"

Ryder shook his head. "No. Until every vessel has left Falmouth, they are to be told nothing, other than we expect to be gone for several days."

"And what about us?" Harris asked. "Are we to be kept in the dark as well, or do we get to know where we're bound?"

Ryder eyed him thoughtfully for a moment, then sighed. "I don't see why not," he said at last. "The colonel will be telling his men first thing."

Noise from the other diners seemed to grow, although those around Ryder's table were deathly silent. And then he spoke again.

"Gentlemen, in two days' time we shall be mounting an attack on the dry dock at St Nazaire."

* * *

Three hours later Ryder sat in the cabin that had been allocated to him aboard HMS *Atherstone*. He was about to turn in when the photographs arrived and, after the briefest of glances, passed a message to Colonel Charles to join him at the earliest opportunity. And as he studied them more carefully the doubts grew further.

They'd only just brought forward the departure date; that could be cancelled. Or perhaps the bombing run the RAF was planning for the evening of the assault could be increased, with a larger number of planes and a more specific target? Both should ease the situation to some extent but, in a raid that already left much to chance, they might be pushing their luck too far.

Footsteps sounded in the corridor and were followed by two sharp raps on the door. Then Colonel Charles entered, and Ryder noticed his normally benign face was showing signs of strain.

"Is there trouble, Red?"

Ryder handed over the photographs without a word.

"When were these taken?"

"This morning," Ryder replied.

"And you know these ships?"

"They're from the German's 5th Torpedo Boat Flotilla, which seems to have taken up residence at St Nazaire."

"Torpedo boats?" the Colonel questioned.

"Don't let the name fool you; each is armed and built like a destroyer. With them about, our lot won't stand a chance."

"So, what do you intend?"

"I was trying to decide when you arrived," Ryder said, "And think I might have come to a decision."

The Colonel waited.

"Nothing. We go ahead as planned."

"You think we can land my troops and take out the dock gates despite the presence of these warships?"

"No, but I think they might go – at least I hope so. St Nazaire isn't their home port; the likelihood is they've put in for fuel or possibly revictualling."

"And, if they do leave, we can still go ahead?"

"Yes, though with the knowledge there's a force in the vicinity that can totally wipe out ours, destroyers and all. I've messaged the Admiralty asking for back up and am hoping for a reply first thing."

"They've hardly been supportive so far, what if they say no?"

"Then we take our chances."

The Colonel looked doubtful. "There've been enough chances already, Red."

Ryder smiled suddenly. "Then a few more shouldn't make any difference," he said.

Chapter Sixteen

Falmouth's fine weather was holding out; the following day dawned clear and bright and the sun was soon warm on the backs of those preparing *194* for sea. Yet despite this, there were areas where the fresh paint remained tacky and, by the time they had taken on additional victuals, water, and other essential supplies, most of her crew had managed to mark their clothing in some way.

They worked in genial silence, as it was hard to take the task seriously. All now knew *194* intimately, with some having been with her during the tightest of scrapes, yet had only needed to sleep aboard when she was in harbour. Consequently, it was with an air of unreality that they stowed provisions for several nights at sea.

Anderson supervised the preparations while Harris attended a final briefing and, when he returned with the all-important orders of sailing tucked protectively under one arm, it was finally accepted they would be putting out that afternoon. More than that, the much vaunted raid – whatever it might be, and wherever it took place – was not a figment of someone's imagination but would shortly begin.

Gibson and Daly checked over their weapons, greasing slides and making sure the ready-use ammunition was exactly that, while their further supply in the main magazine would be sufficient. And Jelly, in the W/T office, went through that day's codes and frequencies until they might have been engraved upon his brain. In the engine room, Carter and his team fired up, then brought each engine to working temperature before checking timing and fuel flow, then cleaned every filter while Phillips checked and lubricated each of the steering unions and all throttle lines. But Smith and Godliman had less to do than most. After treating their weapon to a full strip-down the day before, neither felt the need to do more than carry out a cursory check. And in their case, there was no additional ammunition to worry about.

This was the first major obstacle any of them had encountered so far. When provisioning for extended deployment at Dover, additional supplies for the half-inch Vickers had been provided, but not so the Oerlikon. Ammunition for *194*'s main gun was usually so widespread no one had been concerned; it was only after Anderson investigated the problem that they discovered a general shortage of 20mm shells. It seemed the motor launches had less than half the eighteen hundred rounds of ammunition usually provided for each gun, and much of that was donated by Lieutenant Commander Jenks of HMS *Atherstone*.

194 was actually carrying more than this and the thousand rounds currently in her main magazine had always been enough to see them through the toughest operation. The forthcoming raid would be so much more than an evening run, yet Smith and Godliman lacked the foresight to worry further.

But Harris and Anderson remained uneasy; without their main armament, *194*'s only weapons were the machine guns, which might prove useless against the kind of target they could expect.

And other matters were causing them concern. For much of their journey to St Nazaire *194* was to be towed behind a destroyer, meaning the only petrol used would be the meagre amount needed by her generator. Which was fine in theory; were an enemy to appear that called for speed and manoeuvrability there would be plenty of fuel to deal with it and still allow for cruising time outside the harbour. But what if there were problems on the return trip? Either destroyer could be diverted, disabled, or even sunk, leaving them on an enemy coast with no support and empty tanks.

Much would depend on the success of the raid, of course, and the Admiralty must be aware of their vulnerability, yet only that morning Ryder had made a passing reference to the possibility of enemy warships in the area. Were these to meet with the British destroyers it would be a disaster, as Harris told Anderson later. Even if *194* avoided being sunk, she might need to be paddled home...

But all such worries were very much for the future. Ryder's covering story was the 10th Anti-Submarine Strike Force – a fictitious unit created to mislead enemy agents – would be going on a sweep in cruising order number one: the broad, flat, arrowhead beloved of such patrols. Only when they knew themselves clear of prying eyes, both ashore and in the air, would they turn to the south west, and the journey to St Nazaire could begin.

* * *

The flotilla set off without incident and a routine was soon established. They remained in the same sailing order, with *Atherstone* leading the heavier ships and their Fairmiles spread to either side. Each of the destroyers took one of the high-speed launches under tow so *194* was bobbing astern of HMS *Tynedale*. And Ryder was correct in his initial statement, those aboard the gunboat did have little to do, although that hardly applied to every vessel under tow.

"She's starting up again," Carter told Pickering. With little to do in the engine room, both men spent much of the afternoon on deck, yet it was as if they were naturally drawn towards the stern, and neither ventured further forward than the Oerlikon.

"That's the second time in an hour," the mechanic agreed.

"Lovegrove, their CMM, said something about tuning the new mill while under tow," Carter muttered, "but I thought he was having a laugh."

A cloud of black smoke erupted from *74*'s exhausts, and then the engine apparently died.

"Judging from that, they've still got a way to go."

Further forward, Smith and Godliman were relaxing on their weapon's bandstand, their bare backs resting against the splinter matting as they absorbed all they could of the spring sunshine.

Daly and Gibson were in their turrets, even though nothing had been called for from them since testing the weapons and there should be little need to fire again for some while. An empty horizon stood out boldly in the crystal air and with the only aircraft in sight a Hurricane watching over them – this could almost have been a pleasure cruise. The boat itself was even strangely quiet with only the generator's faint burble to challenge a gush of water from their bows as *Tynedale* pulled them ever onwards.

In the wheelhouse, Phillips was equally idle. The helm only needed cursory attention, so he retreated below and was keeping watch at the secondary steering position.

Jelly, in the W/T office, was more occupied. Most signals

between vessels were being sent by Aldis lamp, but there were still regular updates from Southern Command, while he was also keeping a watching brief over enemy channels. All seemed mercifully quiet yet, even in his tiny space, the sense of anticipation was almost palpable.

And especially so on the bridge. Freed from the restraints of the coxswain's presence, and with both turret gunners far enough away to give a modicum of privacy, Harris and Anderson were able to talk openly. Which is what they had been doing for some while although to no great conclusion.

"I had the feeling it might be St Nazaire," Harris said. "All things pointed to it; the massive dry dock and U-boat pens while having a town so close ruled out an effective bombing raid."

Anderson nodded. "Yet it must be one of the most heavily defended ports outside of Germany."

"A bit like Jerry making an attack on Portsmouth," Harris agreed.

"Didn't our lot have a bash at Devonport?"

"And made a hash of it by all accounts," Harris grinned briefly. "Though frankly, that isn't my main concern."

Anderson waited.

"Well, what exactly are we expected to do?" Harris continued.

"Remain at the rear of the column and see no one follows them in?"

"So, we stooge about in case an E-boat gets past the destroyers?"

Anderson considered this. "I guess so," he said at last. "While drawing fire from the shore batteries."

"I suppose we might do that to some extent; at least this old girl has a decent turn of speed as well as a measure of manoeuvrability. But what if we do encounter an E? We're hardly better armed than the Fairmiles; in the confines of an estuary, they'll take us to pieces!"

Anderson could only agree. "Commander Ryder believes we can do more and, going on our track record, I can see why."

"Then we only have ourselves to blame." Harris sighed. "Well, whatever happens, it's going to be a busy few days and, now we're at sea, I suppose there's no harm in telling the hands exactly what they're in for."

"It's something that should have been done a while ago. Shall I call them to assemble?"

Harris was about to reply when a whistle from the W/T office speaking tube interrupted. Anderson flipped the cover open. "What is it Tel'?"

"Message from Commander Ryder to all vessels, sir. MGB*314*'s telegraphist has reported a problem with their R/T transmitter and is asking for assistance."

"What kind of assistance?" Harris had overheard.

"Sounds to me like the main board's gone down and they aren't carrying a spare."

"How does that affect us, Tel'?" Anderson asked.

"I've one, sir – always carry anything like that."

"And can you fit it?"

"Oh yes; it usually takes about three hours."

"Three hours in which we'll be without a radio op." Harris pointed out.

"That needn't be, sir. If their telegraphist swaps with me while I do the work, you'll be covered. I can return when the set's back online."

Anderson blocked the speaking tube with his hand. "What do you think, sir?"

"I see no reason why not. There won't be much going on here; Jelly might as well be doing something useful."

"Okay, Tel'." Anderson had returned to the speaking tube. "Make the offer, but we want you back here sharpish. And before you go, the captain's about to address all hands."

* * *

No one discovered if Harris' news altered Jelly's mind in any way, but he left the ship less than half an hour later and a freckle-faced youth was taken aboard in his place.

"Jenkins, sir," the new man said in reply to Anderson's question. "Ordinary telegraphist."

"You'd better take a look in the W/T office and acquaint yourself. From what I gather our chap's made quite a few alterations."

"Very good, sir."

The boy saluted smartly enough and must have been of a

reasonable standard to be aboard *314* in the first place. It was just a shame he lacked the skill to change a board.

Moving aft, Anderson noticed the hands had returned to their previous places and there was an air of stillness that had nothing to do with the lack of engine noise.

"This won't do," he told them. "You heard what the captain said, we'll be at sea for several days; you can't remain at actions stations, or even on deck, all the time."

Smith, seated next to his beloved gun, eyed him warily but no one spoke; it was as if Harris' words evoked some unearthly spirit leaving them stunned and torpid. But then discovering they were part of a mission that would bring them close to death was likely to have such an effect. Anderson wondered how the news was being received aboard the motor launches; it must become apparent the commandos and Special Service troops they carried had known of their destination for some time. And *194*'s crew were used to being in action; a good proportion of those aboard the Fairmiles would be far less experienced with some only recently plucked from safe shore jobs. For those whose sea time consisted of the occasional jaunt out of harbour, this would be a shock indeed.

"Gibson and Daly; I want one of you in a turret at all times with the other below and resting. Mr Carter, kindly detail one of your men to take the second turret to act as lookout while the other is also on the mess deck and make time for sleep yourself. Smith and Godliman, you can alternate in the same way, and I shall be relieving Mr Phillips at the helm." With luck, Jelly would be back before nightfall although, even then, he knew the feeling aboard *194* would be some way short of normal.

"Very good, you can make individual arrangements but if I find everyone on deck again, will impose set watches."

In the relaxed regime they were accustomed to, that felt like the right course and, as he turned to make for the wheelhouse once more, Anderson thought he heard mutterings of agreement. This was certainly not the time to impose rigid discipline, or treat the men in any way harshly, not if he expected them to give of their best for the rest of the mission.

* * *

163

At sundown, the Hurricane that had been carrying out high-level reconnaissance for so long finally lost height and passed low over the flotilla. Then, with a wagging of wings, the fighter turned north and made for the English coast, now many miles over the horizon. Aboard the destroyers, white ensigns were lowered, to be replaced with the blood red flag of Germany – a ruse decided upon in case they came across fishing vessels closer to the French coast. Scuttles were closed, all external lights extinguished and those on watch assumed the cold-weather clothing appropriate to a March night at sea. And as the light steadily faded and darkness finally shrouded the eclectic group of shipping, a sense of acceptance, and possibly understanding, slowly enveloped every vessel. But not peace.

Chapter Seventeen

The following morning dawned as bright and clear as those preceding it and, though all aboard *194* had, at best, slept only fitfully, the men seemed to have come to terms with what lay ahead and it was as if a new energy now filled the gunboat. Jelly had failed to return; the problems with *314*'s wireless appeared to extend beyond the relatively simple replacement of a single board. A message flashed from him at first light was optimistic, however, and the fact that Jenkins, his replacement, was proving adept at preparing breakfast on the boat's primitive stove meant his absence was barely noticed.

"Luverly grub," Smith told the youngster as he helped himself to a second bacon roll and settled back against the Oerlikon's splinter matting.

"Wey aye." Pickering sat on one of the smoke floats and was still working through his first roll. "Though this bacon is nee a patch on Mona's."

"It's salty, to be sure," Daly agreed. "But you can't go blaming that on the young fellow." He nodded towards Jenkins. "He can only cook with what he's got and we're a long ways from T'Rose."

"Too far, if you ask me." Smith spoke through his breakfast, though there was nothing unusual in that. "An' did you see the look on the old girl's face when we left?" he added. "Like we were her own sons goin' off."

"Probably wondering how she were going to manage the evening rush," Pickering said.

"Anyone know exactly where we are?" Jenkins, Jelly's replacement, asked.

"Far enough to make no difference." Bill Newman wasn't thinking about their digs in Falmouth; it was several days since he last spoke to Sophie and there would be no chance to do so again for some while, yet that hardly lessened his desire.

"France is over that way," Smith indicated with the remains of his roll.

"And when do we land?" Jenkins again.

"We don't land, son." The last bite was safely deposited, and Smith should have been finished, but there was one more roll on the plate. "Didn't you catch what the skipper said?"

"I weren't around when he spoke," the youngster confessed. "No one's said nothing aboard my boat, least they hadn't before I left."

"Then you don't want to go worrying," Daly told him.

"Aye," Pickering agreed. "We're bound for St Nazaire; canny spot by all accounts."

"And when we get there?" Jenkins asked.

"Well, we sails in, and we sails out." Pickering reached for the last roll and, if he heard the hiss from Smith, it made no difference. "Trust me, it'll be a piece of cake," he said.

"Signal from *Tynedale!*" Gibson was on lookout duty and his voice cut through their conversation like a knife.

Smith turned to Jenkins. "Better get yourself back to the wireless," he said, and the boy ran off.

"Casting off the tow!" Anderson's voice came over the ship's PA but already everyone knew something was up, and unfinished breakfasts were tossed aside in their hurry to take up action stations.

"Good on yer, Len!" Smith said as Godliman appeared. "Make with the ready-use, I think we're gonna be in business."

Those aboard the destroyer were as good as their word, the tow parted, and for a moment *194* was allowed to drift aimlessly. Then, as *Tynedale*'s accelerating screws began to bite, there was a rumble from below. The gunboat's central engine erupted into life and a cloud of black smoke was expelled through the exhaust. Soon this was joined by the wing units and *194* was under her own power once more.

On the bridge, Anderson and Harris took up their appropriate positions as Phillips guided them closer to *Campbeltown* and *Atherstone*, both still with their launches under tow. A whistle came from the W/T voice pipe but when Anderson replied he was greeted by a different voice.

"Message to all ships from Commander Ryder," Jenkins reported. "*Tynedale* has a suspicious contact on the starboard beam and is investigating."

Harris looked back at Gibson.

166

"Nothing sighted, sir," the gunner said.

"Very good." Being a taller vessel, *Tynedale* could sweep a wider horizon.

Anderson leant forward to the speaking tube. "Any further R/T signals can be patched through to us on the bridge repeater, Jenkins."

"Bridge repeater, yes sir."

Anderson sensed hesitation. "Is there a problem?"

"No sir, not really. Only it's something I've heard of but never used."

"But you were detailed to the lead boat."

"Yes, sir, but as a replacement. The regular telegraphist were taken ill."

Anderson supposed he should not be surprised. The entire raid had been cobbled together far too quickly. "Very well, do what you can," he said.

"What do you think, Number One?" Harris asked as Anderson flipped the speaking tube lid closed.

"Difficult to say, sir. Starboard beam would suggest something substantial, but it might only be a deep-water trawler."

"In which case we should shortly be making eastwards." Harris glanced across at the eclectic collection of shipping. "If anyone spots this little lot, they'll be asking questions. And the last thing we need is a couple of Jerry destroyers coming to take a look."

"Signal from *Tynedale*!" This was Daly, once more in position in the starboard turret, but Gibson was already reading the message.

"Object is enemy submarine. Engaging."

"A U-boat," Harris said. "That's all we need!"

Anderson looked west; the destroyer was already halfway towards the horizon and kicking up a sizeable bow wave.

"With luck, she won't have seen this little lot," he said. "And even if *Tynedale* doesn't sink her, she should keep her under long enough for us to get clear."

Harris nodded. "Well, we'll just have to hope she does."

* * *

Aboard HMS *Atherstone* there was also hope in the air. Ryder had been using the warship as his headquarters for some while, so much was already in place. And he was conscious of a strong feeling of relief as what had often appeared to be an impossible task was finally underway. Consequently, when the submarine was spotted, it didn't trouble him greatly. With two highly capable destroyers on hand, the enemy posed little immediate danger; it was only after considering the matter more fully that the doubts began.

A submarine on its own might, at worst, sink one destroyer and, as long as the vessel concerned was not *Campbeltown*, that could almost be tolerated. But were the enemy allowed to report their presence, even in the vaguest of terms, it would not only spell the end of the raid but potentially every vessel in the flotilla.

Ryder had received no specific reply to his request for additional escorts, and neither was there an update on the position of those German warships in St Nazaire itself, yet he remained set, hoping against hope that something would turn up.

On the plus side, he had a first rate team behind him and so much was already going well. Mainly there had been little, if any, friction between seamen and soldiers – two groups that were notoriously incompatible. Even the expected frustration of leading an operation aboard a ship captained by someone else had not materialised; Lieutenant Commander Jenks had shown himself to be a seasoned officer and sympathetic to his position.

A whistle came from one of the voice pipes which the first lieutenant answered.

"W/T says *Tynedale* is reporting the contact to Southern Command," he announced, and it was significant that he spoke to the bridge in general, rather than his captain.

"Very good," Jenks replied.

It was the right procedure for a lone destroyer chancing upon an enemy; Tweedie, in *Tynedale*, was keeping his head. He would also know the flotilla would be monitoring his signals so had not contacted them directly.

"*Tynedale* has answered the sub's recognition signal..." the first lieutenant continued.

That was encouraging and suggested the U-boat remained surfaced. Ryder glanced across but their recent change of course, and *Tynedale*'s speed, had put the confrontation well beyond the horizon; they only had the telegraphist's relayed commentary to rely upon.

"... and now she's opened fire!"

The tension rose further, yet Ryder could still hope Tweedie had found the time to exchange his German ensign with a white duster first. Several minutes went by when anything could be happening, and he began to fidget noticeably although it was Jenks, the destroyer's captain, who broke first.

"Is she hit?" he demanded.

"I'm afraid not sir," his first officer replied after a pause. "She's gone under; they're starting a box pattern search."

Tynedale must have lost contact; a bad mark for Tweedie.

"Do you think this means trouble, Red?"

Ryder turned and was surprised to see Colonel Charles had come up onto the bridge.

"Not if Lieutenant Commander Tweedie can keep her under," he said. "And we have changed course significantly. A U-boat's conning tower is pretty low so, even if the destroyers were spotted, she could hardly have seen the smaller craft."

"Then there's nothing to worry about?" the Colonel checked.

"I wouldn't go that far, Charles," Ryder said. "But it could be a darn sight worse."

* * *

In MGB*314*'s W/T office, Jelly knew nothing about any submarine; indeed, he was only vaguely aware of the time. A rating delivered a sandwich the previous evening, and he had dozed intermittently in his chair during the night, but even the scent of breakfast failed to penetrate the tiny space while, so cluttered was it with various parts from the errant wirelesses, last night's meal had been pushed, untouched, to the back of his desk.

Replacing a board would have been simple enough though was not the answer, and neither had the problem been confined to one set. Jelly's initial examination showed failure in the power supply effectively blew out both units and he began by rebuilding the transformer.

169

Fortunately, that proved relatively straight forward and, by early evening, he was able to start on the wirelesses themselves, replacing each part in order. Some had come from the small number of spares carried in the boat, but most relied on his own more comprehensive stock and, even then, he had needed to cut corners and fit the occasional modified part. Now the transmitter was almost completely rebuilt but he was yet to start on the second unit.

A tap came at the door, and Jelly looked up in annoyance; if this turned out to be someone else bothering him with food, they'd get short shrift. But the door was pulled open by Lieutenant Commander Curtis, the boat's captain.

"I hear you're still having problems," he said. "Is there anything we can do?"

Jelly shrugged. "I don't think so, sir; the transmitter should be operational shortly – the receiver'll take longer."

"We need both," Curtis said. "You know we're down to head the attack?"

"Yes, sir."

"Commander Ryder's due to come aboard at any time, but without wireless support we'll have to think again."

"We could transfer a receiver from another craft," Jelly said.

"That's an option, though a submarine's been spotted and the entire flotilla's travelling at speed. It might be something to consider for the future, otherwise another vessel will have to act as leader."

Despite his present concerns, Jelly realised this would probably mean *194*, yet that didn't worry him unduly. From what he had learned before leaving, the forthcoming raid would place every light craft in danger, while they were actually going to sacrifice an elderly destroyer; *194* might as well be at the head of the line as the tail.

"Never mind, do what you can, and if you need any help, shout."

"Yes, sir."

The small door was pushed closed and Jelly returned to his work. He didn't want help, what he really needed was time.

* * *

Harris and Anderson were in the otherwise empty wheelhouse with a heavily creased chart stretched out on the plotting table.

"This is the general plan." Harris spoke softly, though not for fear of being overheard by Jenkins in the W/T office or Phillips directly above them at the helm. Some of the crew would be asleep further forward and the last thing he wanted was to wake them.

"You will note the Loire Estuary is reasonably wide, though there are coastal batteries on both shores." He indicated with his finger. "Searchlight stations here, here, here, and here. Then the Ack-Ack positions, which are even more liberally distributed..."

Anderson nodded. He had looked up St Nazaire the previous evening, but the standard Admiralty pilot gave no indication of the defences they were to face.

"At the time of our approach, it has been arranged for a force of Whitleys and Wellingtons to make a diversionary bombing run."

"Diversionary?"

"The town of St Nazaire is right inside the dockyard complex and has a population of over fifty thousand."

"So, the fly boys cannot actually bomb?"

"Not unless the target's particularly clear, and even then it's unlikely. But their presence should at least act as a distraction, as well as sending most of the Ack-Ack guns pointing skywards."

"Enabling us to approach undetected?"

Harris had a quizzical look. "I hope so," he said. "There's a dredged channel to the north known as the Chapenters but you'll see why it cannot be used."

Anderson could indeed. Taking that course would bring them right under the guns of several coastal batteries as well as the more numerous anti-aircraft positions on the northern shore.

"After passing the Le Vert buoy we'll close more with the southern coast. There'll still be one major battery and two searchlight stations, but it's the best route."

"Are we sure there'll be the depth to take something as large as *Campbeltown*?"

"Ask me again tomorrow night, but for now we have to assume there will."

Anderson smiled, though Harris remained deadly serious.

171

"We approach the harbour itself with Commander Ryder leading in *314*," he said. "*Campbeltown* will be following, then two columns of motor launches. Behind them'll be us, and Micky Wynn's torpedo boat."

"Why's he in the rear?"

"His engines are untested," Harris explained. "For all we know *74* won't be able to maintain the set speed needed as the main force goes in. If everything behaves as it should he can cut through the pack later."

"I see, but we remain as tail-end Charlie?"

"That's about it; light batteries on both shores cover the harbour entrance, it'll be up to us to keep them entertained while the Fairmiles go in and deliver their troops."

"And *Campbeltown*; what happens to her?"

"Her target is the gates to the dry dock," Harris continued, "which does explain a lot. With that out of action, Germany won't be able to maintain a capital ship on the French coast."

"*Bismarck* had been heading for St Nazaire when she was sunk," Anderson remembered.

"Exactly, it was the only place that could take her. And it could take her sister just as easily."

"*Tirpitz*?"

"That's right. With her on the loose our convoys would be severely threatened, to say nothing of the battle waggons needed to neutralise such a threat. Once the dry dock's gates are destroyed there'll be nowhere for *Tirpitz* to repair and any plans to use her in the North Atlantic will fall to pieces."

"I see," Anderson said although, with everything else to consider, it was a lot to take in.

"As the flotilla approaches the dock, *314* will turn to starboard leaving Beattie, in *Campbeltown*, a clear run. They reckon he'll have to go in at twenty knots to set her right against the gates, which will be no mean feat."

Anderson nodded. He had no experience of conning anything larger than a minesweeper and, after *Campbeltown*'s bridge had been heavily reinforced, visibility would be limited.

"Should he fail, other measures will be taken," Harris continued. "Micky Wynn's torpedoes for one, but there'll be troops landing in two main areas of the harbour, by the Old Mole here," he said, pointing to the chart once more. "And by the secondary entrance to the main basin here."

The two points were just over five hundred yards apart; with the force they were carrying it should be possible to hold such a space, although that was assuming the men could be landed in the first place.

"Plans have been made to establish a headquarters next to the basin, and specialist teams will then proceed to destroy various other installations."

"So, the dock gates are not the only targets?"

"The dock gates are the most important," Harris said. "If it seems unlikely *Campbeltown* or Wynn's torpedoes are going to work, the demolition parties will centre all their energies on them, otherwise there're a dozen or so facilities that need their attention, including U-boat pens to the opposite side of the basin.

Anderson shook his head. "It's a far more... ambitious plan than I'd expected."

"I think it took us all by surprise," Harris agreed. "And can't help thinking they've bitten off more than they can chew, but let's not dwell on that. The longest Colonel Charles and his men can stay ashore is two hours, and at any time they can expect additional opposition in the form of six thousand crack troops stationed nearby. With *Campbeltown* due to hit the dock gates at 01.30, they must be gone by 03.30 at the latest."

In which case *194* must spend two hours under fire from coastal batteries. It was not a pleasing prospect, although one Anderson preferred to actually going in with the Fairmiles.

"When the time comes to leave, we'll be in the lead," Harris said. "And have specific instructions not to delay for any reason. Should a boat be disabled it must be left. Likewise, we're not to stop for men in the water."

There was nothing Anderson could say to that, and Harris quickly moved on.

"Then it will be a case of finding the safest way out. However easy our approach might have been, the enemy gunners will be waiting for us and, with no bombers to distract them, it could get dicey."

"And then we rendezvous with *Atherstone* and *Tynedale*?"

"That's the idea." Harris paused. "As long as the Germans haven't accounted for them."

Anderson blinked.

"You see, Commander Ryder also mentioned the possibility of enemy warships in the area," Harris said. "Should that be the case, the force will be more than capable of dealing with a couple of *Hunt* class destroyers."

"I understand," Anderson said, and finally he did. All too clearly.

Chapter Eighteen

The day continued with an air of restraint masking the fact that all aboard *194* knew they were heading for the toughest battle of their lives. Without further intervention from Anderson, her crew settled into their own, truncated, watch system of two hours on and two hours off. Whether those below were actually asleep, no one cared to check, but the mess deck became a peaceful area where conversation was discouraged, and men could simply be.

By eleven o'clock a faint mist descended over the entire flotilla although the sea remained as calm, something that was welcomed by the commandos packed aboard the motor launches. *Tynedale* proved unsuccessful in sinking her U-boat and came hurrying back with all the bluster of an errant puppy. *194* was taken under tow once more and there were no further signs of the submarine or any enemy forces she might have summoned. Being slightly ahead of schedule, Ryder was able to order a general decrease to eight knots, and so minimise the bow waves and wakes that might betray them to passing aircraft and all settled down to a long day's steaming.

Then, just after noon and a further scratch meal, fishing boats were spotted. The eventuality had been planned for; in the case of Spanish vessels, German ensigns would be flown from the destroyers, while all smaller shipping made for the opposite horizon in the hope of remaining undetected. However, reacting to French fishermen was more tricky.

Being allies, and civilians at that, they should have enjoyed immunity although some were known to carry German observers equipped with radio. So, when three trawlers flying prominent tricolours appeared almost directly in the flotilla's path, a different course of action was called for.

Which directly involved *194*. Once more she was released from her leash and, while *Tynedale* made to intercept two on the port bow, Harris was ordered to seize that to starboard. And whatever the state of mind of those on board the gunboat, they enjoyed the brief time away. As Phillips pressed the throttles fully forward and *194* rose onto the plane, it was as if she was returning to her natural element and a fresh wave of optimism swept over all on her newly vibrating decks. The Frenchman heaved to long before they came alongside, and Anderson's less than formidable boarding party was surprisingly well received.

He explained their presence in halting French, only to be mildly humiliated when the captain replied in far more eloquent English. A brief explanation sufficed; they were on a mission that would significantly weaken the German invaders and, it was hoped, hasten an end to the war. The news was taken in good heart and the Frenchman handed over his vessel's papers, orders of sailing, and any other necessary documentation. The fishing boat's crew proved as cooperative and, in addition to their personal belongings, brought with them most of the previous night's catch, something that was greeted with horror by Jenkins and almost immediately made *194* smell like a fishmongers.

Before they rejoined the flotilla, Harris entertained the trawler's captain in his tiny wardroom. After an offer of gin was refused, he suggested his guest might wish to travel to England aboard one of the *Hunt* class destroyers. That offer was also declined as the Frenchman had a wife and three children depending on him. Then, when Harris repeated his regret, he replied with a shrugged, "*C'est la guerre.*"

After he and his fellow fishermen were taken aboard *Tynedale* to await eventual repatriation, their vessel was sunk by gunfire.

Meanwhile, aboard *Campbeltown,* there was almost a holiday atmosphere. To avoid rousing suspicion, the doomed ship had been victualled for a normal deployment and, with the likelihood the precious supplies would soon be destroyed, all felt obliged to raid her stores. Copious quantities of eggs, butter, bottled beer, and even a case of sherry was discovered and randomly distributed, while packets of cigarettes were wrapped in condoms – equally available in profusion – to make them watertight.

194 did not resume her tow. Instead, she was despatched to circle the small fleet instructing every boat to minimise their use of Aldis lamps. Until then messages flashed between the launches proved a pleasing distraction and there were instances of Fairmiles bombarding each other with potatoes fired from their

Holman projectors. But the time for games had passed, their long approach was nearing completion, and a more mature attitude would soon be necessary.

Then, late in the afternoon, *Atherstone* and *Campbeltown* also cast off their respective tows, giving all the high-speed launches the freedom of their own power. Ryder and his staff, along with Colonel Charles, his adjutant, and Gordon Holman, a war correspondent, transferred to MGB*314*. There was some comfort in the fact that the gunboat now had working radios; both W/T and R/T sets had effectively been rebuilt by *194*'s telegraphist; a tired young man that Ryder went out of his way to thank. It was a shame that, with *314* now leading, and *194* the back marker, it would not be possible to return the lad to his former ship. Instead, Ryder supposed he would prove a reliable deputy to Leading Signalman Pike, a man brought along for his ability to speak, and send W/T messages, in German.

One of the Fairmiles then suffered an engine failure. The subsequent request from her captain to pause while repairs were carried out had to be refused, and she was left to make slow progress home.

And then came confirmation that two more *Hunt* class destroyers had left England and were heading their way. This was followed by a further signal from the Admiralty suggesting the enemy warships previously reported in St Nazaire harbour *could* have moved further upstream to Nantes. With no evidence to support this, the message was more frustrating than useful; those taking part in the raid could guess as easily as any safe in England. And there was some consolation in the fact that, were Ryder to know for certain the enemy force still lay in St Nazaire, it was unlikely to alter his plans in any way. He would soon discover if they were there, and then it would be too late for reinforcements.

Next, Ryder ordered the Fairmiles to cover their wheelhouse glass with grease or paint to prevent glare. Then the order of battle was altered yet again with MGB*314* remaining at the head, and *Campbeltown* roughly a quarter of a mile behind. To either side, two columns of motor launches followed and *Tynedale* and *Atherstone* took up position with Harris, in *194*, and Wynn's MTB*74*, at the stern. With barely fifty nautical miles to cover, the mouth of the Loire would soon be in sight. And then Ryder increased their speed to fifteen knots.

* * *

The haze increased further; already it was softening the harsh silhouettes of individual members of the flotilla, and a major waypoint would soon be due. But Ryder was not concerned; HMS *Sturgeon*, an *S* class submarine, had been detailed to position herself opposite the mouth of the Loire and should be hard to miss. And even if they did, or if something delayed the sub, Bill Green, their navigating lieutenant, had taken a sighting earlier and was reasonably confident of their position. But a focussed, flickering, light was soon reaching out to them and what appeared to be random flashes were quickly identified as the letter 'M' in Morse code.

It was the last of any outside help the flotilla could expect for some time. As they passed the barely surfaced submarine, some exchanged greetings, or ribald comments with those on her conning tower. Then, on turning eastwards, and as *Tynedale* and *Atherstone* prepared to leave them, the mood changed yet again. They were now heading for the river itself; soon this apparently haphazard collection of shipping would be several miles inside enemy territory and deep within one of the largest, and best protected, docks in occupied France. Things had begun to get serious.

* * *

"You haven't missed much, sir," Anderson told Harris when he returned to the bridge after a brief trip below. "The launches have been draining their deck-mounted bunkers."

"Makes sense." Harris raised his glasses to inspect. Each Fairmile B was fitted with auxiliary tanks to either side of the superstructure. In battle, these would have proved a positive liability, so they were tapped first and provided fuel for the journey so far.

"Looks like they're refilling them with seawater," Harris said.

"To cut down the chance of fumes, I expect."

"Not that it'll do much good," the captain added more softly. "Their regular tanks below are hardly any more protected,

178

and there must be several hundred gallons in them."

"Not something I would wish to carry into battle."

Harris lowered his glasses and gave an ironic smile. "Yet we are, Number One, we are!"

The mist continued to thicken; that, and the remarkably placid sea, showed at least the elements were with them.

"It'll be strange being without the destroyers," Anderson said as *Atherstone*'s faint form was gradually swallowed by the darkness.

Harris now focused on Wynn's boat, roughly a hundred yards off their port beam. "Ask me, this entire venture's been odd from the start."

"It's less than a week since we were in Dover," Anderson agreed, then gave a short laugh. "Do you know, I almost said 'safe'?"

"Whatever happens tonight, a run across the Channel will never seem the same." Harris returned his binoculars to the nearest Fairmile, before lowering them once more. "I doubt there'll be much for us to do for a while," he said. "Just follow this lot."

"It'll be different for Jelly," Anderson said.

"Jelly?"

"He's still aboard *314*, the leading boat."

"Of course, right in the thick of it." Harris considered this for a moment before adding, "I hope he'll be alright."

Anderson nodded. "I hope we all will," he said.

* * *

Actually, Jelly felt remarkably safe. Though he knew, in theory at least, the danger his adopted boat must be in, *314*'s radio room was remarkably similar to his own. And he had already met up with, and detected a fellow spirit in, Bill Pike, the specialist telegraphist with whom he would be sharing wireless duties. After seeing both sets back to working order – something Pike considered a minor miracle – he caught a couple of hours' sleep and now felt reasonably bright.

R/T had been silent for some while, but then he expected that, and those in England were now leaving them to their own devices as the W/T was equally quiet, yet Jelly was not bored. He

179

had the letter from Ann in his trouser pocket and, though he knew every sentence by heart, it never hurt to read again.

Which is what he was doing when Pike returned with a couple of steaming mugs.

"Pusser's kye," Pike said, passing one to Jelly, then collecting the small stool that had been outside the W/T office and slotting it alongside.

"You don't want the chair?" Jelly checked.

"Na, you have it. We're both extras aboard this tub, but you've been here longer. Did you get the chance to read through those notes?"

"I took a glance," Jelly said, slipping the letter back.

"Well, it probably won't come to it, and I'll be answering Jerry directly in any case. But if I'm not around you might find this of use." He passed across a small sheet of brown paper. "That there's the German emergency code for vessels being fired upon by a friendly force."

"Handy, but do you think they'll take notice?"

Pike took a deep sip from his mug. "They might," he said. "Long as we don't do anything daft like fire back. If you ask me this whole caboodle's been drawn up on the fly, with much depending on outright chutzpah. So, anything that might baffle the Hun's worth a shot."

* * *

Aboard *Campbeltown*, Major Bill Copland, Colonel Charles' second in command, had called a meeting in the destroyer's wardroom. Present were those in charge of the eighty or so commandos the ship carried, and the atmosphere was cheerful and confident. After a recap of their duties, there was a brief discussion on what might be expected. With still no definite news of the German warships, Copland decided to make no mention of them. If they were there, they were there, and planting further doubts in the minds of men already sufficiently burdened was not his style. Instead, he closed the meeting with a formal 'Action stations, gentlemen', and each officer went to join their troops.

Meanwhile, Lieutenant Nigel Tibbetts, *Chariot's* explosives expert, was approaching the concrete encased charges mounted below *Campbeltown's* forward gun position. After much

180

debate, this was selected as the optimum place for the revised charge of three-and-a-half tons of amatol. Were they successful, and the ship made contact with the dock gates, some degree of buckling and compression could be expected. If placed too near the bows, the explosives might detonate prematurely, killing most on board, while too far aft may leave the gates undamaged. There had been no time for simulations or experiments, like much associated with the mission, the calculations relied on experience, combined with a fair amount of guesswork. So now, as he carefully inserted each fuse deep into the heart of the deadly mass, Tibbetts added a prayer for good measure.

* * *

At just gone midnight the atmosphere on *314*'s crowded bridge was tense and expectant. They had already heard the drone of aircraft and the skies ahead were filled with searchlights hunting for the RAF raiders.

"Bomber Command promised something larger," Ryder said.

"Though I expect they sent enough to draw attention," Curtis, *314*'s captain replied.

"As long as Jerry doesn't think they're carrying paratroopers."

"Which might mean the enemy's elite troops are brought in early," Curtis said. "I hadn't thought of that."

Ryder gave a wry smile. "Neither had I," he said.

Any hint of that day's warmth had long since vanished and all were wrapped in greatcoats and oilskins as the flotilla ploughed on through the darkness. Sandwiches had been sent up some time before and Ryder was taking a bite from one when the lookout reported a buoy.

It was the first of very few they could expect, but a vital one, as it marked the beginning of the shoal waters. Ryder finished his mouthful, then asked Curtis to bring them to starboard.

Looking back, *Campbeltown*'s outline was obvious enough even in the poor conditions, while none of the launches following could miss her bulk. He turned his gaze forward again and was momentarily shocked as another hull loomed out of the gloom.

"*Lancastria*," Curtis announced, following his gaze, and

Ryder nodded. Less than two years ago the British troopship had been a major part of Operation Aerial, the evacuation of British nationals and military personnel from France. When a cruise liner, *Lancastria* was licenced to carry thirteen hundred passengers, yet over four thousand lives were lost when German aircraft bombed her. Rumour had it she went down in less than twenty minutes, which probably accounted for the tremendous loss of life.

"Tragedy," the gunboat's captain added, but Ryder made no reply.

Four thousand was actually a conservative estimate, many unofficial sources claimed more, and the Admiralty remained suspiciously mute about the entire affair. But there was no such doubt about those who survived. The press reported less than twenty-five hundred were rescued which meant an attrition rate of almost two out of three. He hoped his current expedition returned with better figures.

"Twelve miles to run, sir." This was Green, the navigating officer. Twelve miles meant less than an hour at their current rate. Ryder looked to port where the northern shore could just be picked out. They had already passed one of the main batteries with no sign of activity but were in shoal waters and, even allowing for the height of the tide, there could be little depth. Were *Campbeltown* to ground and remain stranded it would be foolish indeed and a simple matter for the enemy to pick her off with the dawn.

"Very well, kindly reduce to eleven knots."

The coxswain repeated the order as he brought *314*'s revs down, and then Curtis awkwardly cleared his throat.

"Should we make that to the flotilla, sir?"

"No, I trust Sam to notice," Ryder replied. "And if any of the launches miss *Campbeltown* slowing it'll serve them right."

He took another bite of his sandwich. Even such a small reduction in speed would lessen the destroyer's draught aft by several inches. All they could do was hope it would be enough.

Chapter Nineteen

Although at his action station, nothing had been called for from Smith for several hours and, if his luck held out, nothing would. However, that did not mean he was bored, even supposing such a thing possible aboard a wooden boat penetrating deep inside enemy territory. Godliman was with him and seemingly alert as he sat on a box of ready-use ammunition, but the recent progress Smith felt personally responsible for seemed to have disappeared and the boy hadn't said a word in ages.

"It comes from being a back marker." Smith leant against the bandstand rail that surrounded their gun and resumed his monologue. "None of our lot are supposed to be following, so anything we spots astern is liable to be an enemy.

"Ah, you say..." he looked hopefully at Godliman, who had remained silent, "...Ah, then we opens fire!" He paused, though there was still no response from his mate. "But you'd be wrong, see, that's the worst thing we could do. We has to remember what the skip' said: 'there'll be no firing of any sort less we're specifically ordered'. Until then we keeps quiet, even if Jerry starts shooting."

He'd expected that to provoke more from the boy, but Smith was far from beaten. There'd definitely been improvements of late, and he still hoped they would continue.

"You see, we're trying to pass off as German shipping," he said. "Which is why the old *Campbeltown* were cut about so. The moment we starts returning fire our cover's blown. So, we just have to shut up an' take it."

Still nothing, and Smith began to worry. Despite being deep into occupied France, they'd been in tighter spots. And simply being quiet was alright, but should action be called for, and Godliman decided not to make with the shells, it would be a sorry state of affairs. He tried another tack.

"I've never been abroad," he said. "Not properly, like, though I seen the coast of France often enough. And the funny thing is, the one chance I get to hit a foreign port, I find out that's what I has to do!"

183

Pleased with his joke, he grinned at Lenny; there was still no reaction though he seemed to be listening. Encouraged, Smith tried again.

"Did I ever tell you about the hop picking?" he asked.

The lad looked blank.

"We were living in Stepney at the time, but every autumn moved down to Kent to help with the harvest. You know about hops, don't you? Nasty spiky things that taste foul; they use them to put the flavour into beer."

There was no reaction from Godliman, and Smith continued.

"It were like a holiday, though all of us had to work and work hard. In the evenings we went down to the local pub, and some of the older ones got to sample what we'd been picking. I weren't included, mind, but that didn't mean us saucepan lids couldn't sit out in the garden. And that's when the old guys told us about the ducks what landed arse backwards..."

Now there was a stirring from Smith's left. Godliman was starting to pick up on his story.

"Course, we thought they was stringing us city folk a line. Whoever heard of ducks landing arse backwards? So, me an' the other kids decided to challenge 'em."

There was still no verbal reaction from Godliman, though the boy was definitely listening.

"One of 'em said we could see for ourselves next morning, and to be at the local pond bright and early. We agreed and met up, though nothing happened for a while. Then a flock of ducks came up from the marshes and before long one of them landed on our pond."

Smith waited; then, out of the darkness, Godliman finally spoke. "And?"

"And it was like the old guys said," Smith continued. "Darn bird got lower and lower, till it landed – arse backwards. The others flopped about a bit, then did the same thing."

"Arse backwards?" Godliman enquired.

"Of course arse backwards," Smith said. "You'd hardly expect a duck to land arse forwards now, would you?"

* * *

184

Campbeltown ran aground for the first time by the Banc du Chatelier. It was not a heavy impact, no grinding crunch or sudden jolt, just a gentle rubbing of her hull against the mud and sand beneath. All aboard were instantly aware, however, and Christopher Gough, the destroyer's first lieutenant, strode forward to peer through one of the armoured slits that surrounded much of the modified bridge.

"Still underway, sir," he said, "though we've slowed considerably.

The hull rocked; this was uneven ground.

"Very good," Beattie replied, "Keep her as she is."

The temptation to increase revolutions was strong but might only see them more firmly held; while they had motion it was better to wait.

Another tremble from below, but this time there was a sudden increase in speed that made some stagger. And then the warship was fully released and surged forward as if sprung from a trap.

Beattie caught Gough's eye. "A close one, Chris," he said.

"Close indeed," the lieutenant agreed. "Let's hope it's the last; we'll soon be back on station."

And then she grounded again.

* * *

MGB*314* passed the Le Vert beacon shortly afterwards; it was now a little more than five miles to the port itself although the shallowest, and most dangerous part of the journey was still to come. At this point, the estuary narrowed and the northern batteries on the Pointe de L'Eve would have them in range. Yet if they could only keep up their current speed, they would be at the harbour entrance in under forty minutes.

Campbeltown's brushes with the riverbed had gone unnoticed by those aboard Ryder's boat. Even the second, which detained the old ship for longer, was only apparent to those directly concerned. But they were now far deeper into enemy territory, and passing through what should have been shallower waters, so all were intently listening to the solid ping of the gunboat's ASDIC as it recorded the path ahead.

185

Soon the disused tower of Les Morées appeared off their port bow. Passing it would mark the two-mile point and it seemed impossible that such a flotilla should have come so far without being noticed. Yet no one was prepared to question their good fortune, while a succession of six heavy-flak batteries lay ahead which they must pass closer to than any before. An 88mm anti-aircraft shell could sink any of the launches with ease and do serious damage to a destroyer.

And then their luck ran out; from the northern coast, a single point of light began to cut through the misty darkness, illuminating *Campbeltown* like a bit performer caught early on stage. In no time searchlights on either bank burst into life and soon every vessel was floodlit, making their bold venture appear brash and futile in the combined glare.

"Two miles to target." Lieutenant Green's tone was almost expressionless despite the cruel light that had robbed all of their night vision.

Ryder swallowed. Two miles, or twelve minutes at their current speed; it was vital they used every second to delay the inevitable.

"Signal from the northern shore!" This was one of the lookouts and Ryder turned to Pike. The telegraphist had been on the bridge for some while and now would come into his own.

"What are they saying?"

"It's a simple challenge, sir."

Another lookout announced a second signal from starboard and all spun round to see flickering from the south. Ryder opened his mouth to speak, although Pike had already begun to work his lamp, aiming it to port before turning to the opposite shore and sending a shorter message.

"I just sent what we agreed, sir," Pike said when he had finished. "'Two damaged vessels in company; request permission to proceed without delay.'"

"Very good, and what did you say to the other lot?"

The young man grinned. "I told them to wait."

Several of the searchlights went dark, but enough remained to make everyone feel sufficiently exposed. Then a series of flashes made them all turn back towards the northern shore.

An enemy flak cannon had opened fire and there was a dreadful pause as all waited to see if a British gunner would reply.

A single shot from the smallest weapon would make it difficult – probably impossible – to complete the mission. But the trail of green tracer soon stopped and then the only sound was a gentle chug from their engines.

"Did anyone sight splashes?" Curtis enquired, but there was no response.

Pike began to work his machine again.

"What are you sending?" Ryder demanded, but the signalman remained mute until he finished his task.

"It's the standard German response when a vessel's under friendly fire," he said, adding, "Sorry, sir, it needed to be sent quick and I had to complete the phrase."

"Of course."

For several precious minutes the flotilla inched closer to the port itself; soon individual buildings could be made out as well as the start of the harbour wall. Then batteries on both shores erupted with a fusillade of dazzling tracer.

"Time for our trump card." Ryder produced a Verey pistol and leant over the starboard rail. The first enemy shots were landing close to *314* as he held the device up and squeezed the trigger, but rather than sending a host of coloured light into the heavens, the flare rose barely ten feet before falling impudently into the dark waters.

"It was something I ordered especially," Ryder's face bore a rueful grin. "And was supposed to give a German distress signal."

"Reckon they issued the wrong cartridges, sir," Pike said. "Them's the kind what should be fired from a plane."

Ryder nodded. "I think you may be right." Another burst of tracer flayed the water to port and more searchlights began to reach out to them. "Well, there's nothing else for it, gentlemen," he said. "We may as well change ensigns and return the compliment."

* * *

Below, in the W/T office, Jelly cooly relayed Ryder's instruction to the rest of the flotilla, although every vessel was already following *314*'s example. Soon waves of shot and tracer were washing over the nearest battery as well as more minor anti-aircraft positions. There was even the rattle of light machine gun fire from some of the commandos, both aboard *Campbeltown*, and the motor launches.

With only a mile to go, and their cover effectively blown, there was no longer any point in remaining in the shallows. With *314* in the lead, the flotilla – now under British colours – turned to port and, on gaining deeper water, accelerated to twenty knots. As they drew nearer, the northern signal post was revealed to be a guard ship moored off the east jetty. Her light camouflage paint and tall superstructure proved a tempting target, and she was soon engulfed in the combined fire of several vessels. But *Campbeltown* was equally compelling to the Germans; even as the old warship's speed increased and she summoned her final bow wave, the shore-based guns drew a bead on her and both hull and superstructure were pelted by shells digging deep into her steel casing, causing carnage and confusion within.

On her heavily protected bridge, Sam Beattie peered through the slits at the blinding tangle of tracer and searchlights. The dockyard itself was in sight, but individual areas were hard to discern. They appeared to be passing the Avent Port where a separate lock led into the main basin. His target lay deeper in the harbour complex itself; there was still some way to go.

At least they were beyond the range of the major northern batteries. Only one, to the south, could still reach them, as well as a dozen or so lighter weapons. Beattie consciously closed his mind to the damage these were causing to his command; *Campbeltown* need only hold together for another half a mile, and her task would be complete.

The searchlights' glare was distorted by mist and, with the closed-in bridge giving limited visibility, it was hard to keep track of their progress. A series of industrial buildings could now be seen to port, and beyond them must be the more domestic dwellings of the town itself. Which meant the Old Mole, a substantial granite structure rising up from the river bed and stretching deep into the channel, must be close by. Should *Campbeltown* run into that, the entire operation would come to a premature, and farcical, ending. Yet, with no clear sight forward, it was a distinct possibility.

Then, as if on cue, a stray searchlight lit up a lighthouse on the port bow. Beattie knew one was sited at the mole's very tip and it was far enough off to be no danger. His target lay five hundred yards upstream; it was time for the final approach.

"Five degrees to port."

He had no way of knowing their exact speed, but dockyard buildings were passing in an apparent blur. Their coxswain, CPO Wellsted, had been killed at his post some while before, his place being taken by a signalman who fell shortly afterwards. With the bridge then lacking suitable replacements, Lieutenant Tibbits, the explosives expert, had taken the helm. Beattie caught his eye.

"Prepare to ram, Nigel!"

It was the only instruction needed; all knew what they had to do. The next few seconds would be the culmination of so much work, so much worry.

The old ship shuddered slightly as she tore through a line of torpedo netting, and then the giant gates finally came into sight. They were closed, just as all were hoping, making a veritable wall of iron that towered high above and stretched for many feet to either side. It was an entrance wide enough to take a battleship, and each caisson had been built to withstand the pressures of the massive dock that lay beyond; was it really possible for an outdated destroyer to do more than dent such a thing?

"Ten degrees port."

Tibbits calmly turned the ship until all that lay between arrow and target was a diminishing stretch of dark water. The dock gates drew closer, and closer still. Soon all that could be seen was their immense bulk that blocked out everything, even the glare of searchlights.

Then, with a grinding crunch that travelled throughout the ship, HMS *Campbeltown* rose up and wedged herself firmly against the heavy metal entrance.

There was silence for a moment, even the German gunfire ceased as if shocked by such an outrage. Beattie held his breath, *Campbeltown*'s forecastle had buckled for at least thirty feet and in the reflected glow he could see a shimmer of heat rising from the splintered decking.

Sparks and assorted wreckage continued to fly for several seconds, and smoke was billowing from a lower wound. A small fire broke out under the destroyer's foredeck, it was soon quenched and a cloud of steam followed, but the charges had not detonated.

Beattie exhaled. Whether the fuses chose to fire later was another matter, but it should be relatively safe for them to leave;

their particular part of the operation was over.

"Okay," he said, "we seem to have arrived."

He glanced at his watch; it was 01.34: they were exactly four minutes behind schedule.

Chapter Twenty

As soon as *Campbeltown* steered away from the shallows, Harris ordered his command to take up a defensive position at the rear of the flotilla. Then, when the motor launches had also been shepherded into deeper water, *194* turned once more and for a moment lay stationary across the channel while Gibson and Daly wafted tracer over the northern gun emplacements and Smith, at the Oerlikon, fired more deliberately at those to the south. In this he was well served by Godliman, who kept up a ready stream of ammunition that gave almost continuous fire, making the light but accurate cannon even more deadly.

On reaching the deeper water, Micky Wynn in MTB*74* took off in a flurry of wash and spume, then proceeded to dodge recklessly through the twin columns of Fairmile Bs. Seeing this, Harris decided it was time for them to move also.

"Bring her round, then up to fifteen hundred, 'Swain," he ordered, "but keep us at the rear!"

For several seconds the searchlights lost them, although the brief reprieve was of little use as every eye was dulled by their penetrating beams. Harris glanced back; he was sure nothing had followed but that did not mean they could desert their post. *194* was starting to catch the rearmost launch; it was time for them to truly earn their place.

"Bring her up to twenty hundred, and start weaving," he said. Then, when they had the outer harbour almost to themselves, "Very well, you have control..."

Now they would discover if Phillips truly knew his craft. *194* was smaller, faster, and more agile than the stately Fairmiles; a good coxswain would use such advantages to the full, and make the gunboat an inviting, yet impossible, target for the shore gunners. But such a task called for a sensitive hand on the wheel, along with the heart of a lion.

Almost instantly the gunboat reduced speed before turning sharply to port and then accelerating once more. In no time all aboard were being thrown about like beans in a barrel forcing both

Harris and Anderson to grab for support. Her erratic progress was equally confusing those on shore, however; no searchlight held them for more than a second, and the lines of enemy tracer began to weave strange and intricate patterns as the German gunners sought to pin such a tempting target down.

Harris gritted his teeth as he clung to the guard rail; Phillip's actions were also silencing their own guns; those in the midships turrets had almost given up while even Smith, at the Oerlikon, was finding it hard to bear on any target. But it was equally noticeable that fewer enemy weapons now trained on the Fairmiles, who must soon be nearing the point where they could decant their passengers.

He briefly caught Anderson's eye; Phillips was doing well, but they were by no means out of the woods. And if protecting the rear of the flotilla was proving difficult, seeing all safely home, past gunners eager to make up for missing them on the way in, may well be impossible. No one aboard *194* knew about *Campbeltown*'s successful beaching, or that the first wave of commandos was even now landing on enemy ground. And even if they did, it would mean little; they had their own job to do, and it was by no means an easy one.

* * *

Ryder had been equally unaware of Beattie's success. As the destroyer prepared for her final approach, *314* turned to starboard to give the larger vessel room and immediately ran into further fire from the shore. This was from three anti-aircraft positions to the south of the dry dock, and it was only when they had been silenced by their forward gun, that he could look back and catch the moment of impact.

"No sign of my lads." Colonel Charles was also on the bridge and staring at the beached warship.

"Give them time." Ryder spoke slowly, his eyes fixed on the crumpled bows of the battered destroyer. For the past few weeks he had headed a project that appeared hopeless from the start, so had accustomed himself to not expect much. But it was possible, probable actually, that *Campbeltown* was in the perfect position.

192

Should the charges detonate as planned, the lock gates must surely be damaged; in which case the raid could already be deemed something of a success.

"Here they come!" The colonel's shout alerted them all, although the sight on *Campbeltown*'s forecastle made the distraction worthwhile. A grey mass that must be commandos was moving forward along the deck. Bright pinpoints of lights showed where several returned fire, and then ladders and ropes started to be thrown down.

"Some are climbing on the gates themselves!" Curtis said, and that was certainly the case. Already a stream of men had leapt onto the caissons and were now descending like ants down a stalk. On landing, one group made for the nearest gun emplacement, while others headed for other targets.

"They'll be established in no time!" Colonel Charles was fidgeting with excitement.

That might be so but there was no room for further speculation, *Campbeltown*'s hull was still being targeted by shells of every size, while Ryder knew he must secure *314* as close as possible and then release the commando officers to do their duty.

He glanced at Curtis. "Very well, Dunstan, take us in."

The gunboat described a tight circle in the central channel before turning back towards the northern shore. As they approached, *Campbeltown*'s hull shuddered slightly, and faint explosions could be heard from within. These would be the scuttling charges and meant those still aboard were keeping their heads. He went to comment on the fact to Curtis, but the young officer's eyes were all for his ship; bringing her to a mooring under the very noses of the enemy would not be easy. There should be three further anti-aircraft guns positioned beyond the destroyer and no telling if Beattie had silenced them on his way in. If not, Copland's lot would soon be engaging them, but the likelihood was strong that one or all remained active. Yet as they passed the beached ship's stern there was no welcoming barrage of fire, and Ryder breathed again.

Curtis gingerly nosed *314* alongside the eastern wharf at the mouth of the Old Entrance. Ryder could see walls bedecked with posters and advertisements appropriate to holiday traffic carried before the war. Then he noticed Colonel Charles and his staff on the gunboat's foredeck. All had jumped ashore before she was even secured and were soon lost in the darkness.

Ryder turned to Curtis. "That was well done," he said. "Now we must hope the rest goes as smoothly."

* * *

194's Oerlikon had not been silent for long. Despite the gunboat's erratic performance, Smith soon began to get a feel for the situation. It was as if the shore-based targets that were equally trying to find him had become etched on his mind. Whenever Phillips, at the helm, turned the boat, Smith was ready with a stream of 20mm shells that found them with unerring regularity.

And in this he was helped by Godliman. From the start, the lad was right there with every change of magazine and even had time to empty the canvas bag that caught their discharged cartridges. But latterly his mate was doing more; he began a running commentary on the boat's course or where the next target could be expected, and Smith found he heard without consciously listening.

"He's taking us right again: watch the bugger in the middle."

As the boat completed her turn, Smith was ready and sent a succession of shots in the correct direction, adjusting his aim only slightly when return fire pin-pointed the enemy's gun more accurately. Then the stream of green tracer died, and they knew that particular threat would not bother them for a while.

"Next it's the one to the left," Godliman yelled as the boat turned once more. Smith glanced at his mate; the lad was definitely back to his old self, with no sign of hesitation or caution.

"Good job, Lenny," he told him and there was a flash of teeth from the youngster.

"Good job yourself, Smudger," he said.

* * *

"Take her in deeper," Ryder ordered.

314 was too exposed where she was but, with the nearest anti-aircraft positions now out of action, limited safety might be gained from the small inlet next to the Old Entrance. Curtis ordered the boat released and brought her forward before finally turning about and coming to rest under the lee of a substantial dockyard building. Meanwhile, Ryder made his way down to the deck. A group of Naval ratings were waiting on the jetty.

"From *Campbeltown*?" he asked, guessing them to be part of the steaming party that brought her in.

"Aye, sir. We was told to make for this boat."

"Any officers amongst you?"

"No, sir, but some of us is wounded."

"What of your captain?"

There was no answer.

Ryder nodded. "Very well, come on board, we'll do what we can for the injured."

Then it was his turn to jump ashore, and as he did, Leading Signalman Pike, who had armed himself with a broken bayonet, followed.

Ryder regarded his unlikely accomplice. "Shouldn't you be in the W/T?" he asked.

"Jelly's a good bloke; he can cope," the lad grinned. "And I doubt the Germans'll be sending us many more messages."

There was no time for discussion. Men were clambering off *Campbeltown* by a variety of routes, all commandos or Special Service troops and used to improvising. The rest of the steaming party must be evacuated, along with probably more wounded.

Ryder began to run towards the beached warship. His first job was to make sure she was perfectly seated against the lock gates, and it took no more than the briefest inspection to confirm this. *Campbeltown*'s bows were ideally placed for an effective explosion, all they need do was trust Tibbitt's fuses to fire at the right time.

"She's down at the stern, sir," Pike pointed out, and that was equally good. Scuttling the destroyer had been an important part of the process; the last thing they wanted was for the Germans to tow her back into the channel. Satisfied, the pair hurried along the hard, only stopping when a dark figure stepped out of the shadows brandishing a machine gun.

"War Weapons Week!" The man was sporting a short, scruffy beard and there was no humour in his voice. For a second, Ryder was nonplussed, then he remembered Colonel Charles' password and response – both specially chosen as a German speaker might have difficulty in the pronunciation.

"Weymouth," he replied, and the gun was lowered. "Are you from *Campbeltown*?"

The soldier looked confused.

"That ship," Ryder pointed at the massive hull close by.

"No sir, we was landed from a launch."

"Very good, carry on."

That at least meant some of the Fairmiles had got through, but Ryder should still look to those aboard the destroyer. Colonel Charles would be close by; he must find him and see how advanced they were with the evacuation.

At that point, a concrete winding house to the other side of the gate erupted in a mass of flame and rubble. Though out of immediate danger, both men were momentarily stunned. Ryder was the first to recover.

"That's our boys," he said, "and they're doing their business; expect more."

Pike nodded in silence, although Ryder was already moving on. Knowing some commandos had been landed and were carrying out their orders was reassuring, but he still had to find Colonel Charles. The most likely place was the other side of the ship, although to get there meant leaving the relative shelter of the quay.

Another explosion, and a small building further away disappeared into dust and rubble. It was followed by two more as they neared the beached destroyer. Soon Ryder was staring up at the dark hull knowing at any moment it might be torn apart by an eruption to put all these minor blasts to shame. And then he saw Colonel Charles.

In company with Copland, he was seeing to the disembarkation of those on board, which would include the rest of the steaming party. Light shells were continuing to bite into the ship's superstructure and upper hull, but those on the ground must be out of reach. And then Ryder noticed several seamen had already made the perilous journey and were standing nearby. The Colonel was gesticulating to those preparing to go, and the damn fool still had that pipe stuck in his mouth. Then, as if feeling Ryder's eyes upon him, he turned in his direction.

"Alright, Charles?"

In the circumstances, it was an idiotic question, but the Colonel took it in good heart.

"First rate, Red. Just getting the rest of your chaps off, then we'll be out of here."

"*314*'s by the Old Entrance," Ryder shouted. "But if she has to go, I'll do my best to send others."

The Colonel gave a grim smile and an offhand salute, which was all the indication Ryder needed. With *Campbeltown* in position and being effectively evacuated there was nothing left for him to do but head back. Micky Wynn should have made it through and would need a target for his toys.

He turned away and almost ran into Pike, who had been fingering his bayonet reflectively.

"Come on, we'll be needed at the boat."

"Very good, sir." The young man slipped the weapon into his belt and, after a final glance at the massive, beached hull, followed the departing figure of his leader.

* * *

The time for *194* to draw fire from the launches had passed. Most of the Fairmiles were deep into the port by now and some had already been hit. Harris could make out at least one hull burning brightly in the haze and, as he watched, another exploded, sending a sheet of flame high into the sky. Whether either had landed their troops was uncertain, although he held his own thoughts on the matter, as he did the wisdom of *194* remaining where she was.

He turned to his second in command. "I'm taking us in, Number One." Then, before Anderson could protest, Harris ordered Phillips to steer for the harbour.

The guns which plagued them earlier were quieter now, but it would not be the same for those in the port. And it was as if the whole of St Nazaire was alight with *194* heading for hell itself. But in his current mood, nothing would have persuaded Harris on any other course and when Anderson attracted his attention with a gentle touch on the shoulder, he did not appear to be objecting.

"What do you intend?" The younger man's face was lit by flickering light from the conflagration.

Harris gave a brief smile. "I haven't a clue, Ian," he said. "But I'm not standing about while our boats are being shot up."

"Very good, sir."

Harris glanced cautiously at his second in command, but it was clear he was sincere.

"You might want to slow down as we approach," Anderson added. "There may be men in the water."

* * *

Bad news awaited Ryder on his return. Six Fairmiles of the starboard column had been detailed to land their troops next to the dry dock, but most were now destroyed or had been forced back with their men still on board. To balance that, Micky Wynn was there and the sight of his grin was a tonic in itself.

"Get over to the basin entrance," Ryder told him, pointing at the nearby gates. "See what sort of mess your toys can make of that lock. We've still to secure that area; there may be enemies ashore, so keep your head down."

"Right you are, sir." Wynn appeared totally at ease with the mission and Ryder knew if it could be done, it would.

"When you're finished come back and take on what wounded you can, then head for home."

Wynn gave a casual salute and was gone. Then there was Rodier, the captain of another Fairmile, presumably awaiting instructions.

"Did you land your men, Mark?" Ryder asked.

"As ordered, sir." The lieutenant spoke as if it had been the easiest thing in the world.

"Very good, then get your boat closer to *Campbeltown*," Ryder said. "You'll find Colonel Charles there and probably Major Copland. Take any wounded they may have along with the steaming party – officers as well," he added. "And if anyone argues, tell them those are my orders."

"Yes, sir."

"Then you can beat it also."

* * *

198

In MGB*314*'s W/T office Jelly was troubled. The gunboat's radio mast had been hit and, rather than the comforting glow of valves, both sets were steadily cooling. Before him, his signal pad still bore several unsent messages as well as the start of the first reply from England, which he had been unable to acknowledge. As soon as the trouble became apparent he powered down, then went to check on the mast itself and the conditions topside were sobering indeed.

Moored as she was, the gunboat appeared relatively safe, with only the occasional stray round finding her. But the damage on deck showed exactly how deep she had been in the thick of things. Not only was the mast a complete write-off but there were several jagged holes where shells had struck and, in one case, passed through both hull and superstructure, while nearly every gun was wrecked. And all the while an odd smell – similar to burning and just as menacing – hung over her.

From the battered bridge, someone noticed his presence and demanded to know why he was there. Jelly thought this was Curtis, the boat's captain, but the blackened face staring out from under a helmet could have belonged to anyone. After explaining, Jelly had been ordered below and now was back in the closest thing to a sanctuary he knew.

Yet with both sets cold, even that small space felt lifeless and unwelcoming. The unsent messages stared back accusingly. He shivered, partly from the temperature and partly due to what he had seen on deck. One of the Fairmiles from the port column was ablaze from stem to stern, although men remained on board. And just as he was clambering into the wheelhouse, another launch went up like a Roman candle. His present boat was bigger than *194*, but Coastal Forces craft were not built with protection in mind and the open sea, with the relative safety it offered, still lay several miles off.

And what miles they would be. On their approach, they had found the enemy's wavelengths and Pike gave a running commentary on the German's casual chatter. From what they heard there were several major artillery batteries and many smaller emplacements within range. Both lads found the exercise amusing; a large British flotilla was passing under their noses, yet all the Germans could do was exchange rude jokes. Now, though, the situation was far from funny.

No one on the estuary banks could be unaware that St Nazaire had become the focus of a violent and prolonged attack; even without a direct command, those in charge of the enemy's defences would want to make up for missing them on the way in. There would be carnage, of that he was certain.

Without the wireless sets, there was little for him to do, however, and the W/T office offered about as much protection as the average garden shed. He might take refuge below, but that only added the prospect of being trapped, and they must still be carrying more than half their load of high-octane petrol.

He jumped as the door was pulled open and Pike's face appeared.

"Sets down, are they?" he asked.

"No aerial."

Pike nodded; he looked flushed but alert.

"Where you been?" Jelly asked.

"Ashore!" The young man grinned. "It were great; destroyer's in position, all it's got to do is blow and the lock gates'll be history."

"Are we in control?"

Now the smile became doubtful. "In places, but I can't see us making plans to settle. Ask me, we wanna be ready for the fastest evacuation in history." He paused. "Shame about the aerial."

"I could try and rig another. There's no mast but I might improvise." Despite the obvious danger, Jelly liked the idea of being active.

"Without a mast there'd be no range," Pike said. "Besides, once we're underway topsides'll be a dangerous place."

"So, what do we do?"

Pike shrugged. "I'm sticking in the wheelhouse; you can see quite a bit – care to join me?"

Jelly shook his head. It might be better to have a distraction but even the company of cold sets was preferable to watching the slaughter outside.

"I'll stick in here," he said, and Pike grinned before shutting the door once more.

Jelly sank back into his chair. The image of that exploding Fairmile came back to him and was followed by others, each more terrible. There had been men in the water, he'd seen them swimming amid patches of burning fuel while the raw sounds of battle could still be heard through the thin walls surrounding him.

He closed his eyes and was considering prayer when something more constructive occurred. Reaching into his pocket he brought out a tightly folded piece of paper and, after smoothing out the creases, Jelly started to read. And as he did, the tension in his face began to ease, to be replaced by the faintest of smiles.

* * *

Rodier was able to manoeuvre his launch alongside *Campbeltown*'s stern and roughly thirty men were taken aboard. These included wounded from both forces as well as Beattie, her captain, and Tibbits, the explosives expert. Throughout, enemy shells continued to rain down on the larger vessel but eventually it was done and, easing past the remains of the torpedo netting, ML*170* could finally turn and set her bows for home.

* * *

The Fairmiles from the port column had been detailed to land their troops by the lighthouse at the Old Mole, a quarter of a mile downstream from the Old Entrance. As a drop-off point, it was hardly ideal, even with an abnormally full tide, the solid granite jetty was considerably higher than any of the launches' decks and its narrow slipway lacked protection. Then, to top it all, there was the small matter of a pillbox set just below the lighthouse that was proving impossible to silence.

ML*447* was the first in and carried an assault party trained to deal with such a menace, but she was hit and set alight while still some way off. A few that survived were rescued by another boat which proved equally unable to land her troops. Only ML*457* was able to battle through the blistering fire to despatch her commandos. The achievement was short-lived, however; after delivering the men to what looked like certain death, she withdrew, only to be struck by several shells that turned her into a blazing wreck.

ML*307* was next and almost fulfilled her mission but was driven back when still several yards from solid ground. Together with three other Fairmiles, she pulled out and turned for the open sea; in the circumstances, it was the only option.

Meanwhile, Ryder was getting restless. *314* remained moored in the lee of the dockyard buildings yet they had been in the port for more than an hour. In that time much was achieved though at a cost far higher than even the most pessimistic estimates. They had also taken on a considerable number of wounded from *Campbeltown* who needed professional attention; he must rejoin the destroyers as soon as possible.

First he had to take a more comprehensive view of things, however, and at a muttered request, Curtis brought the gunboat back into the main channel. And once there, the picture became clearer although no more optimistic.

As they approached the Old Mole, the wrecks of several Fairmiles became obvious, as was the fact that the enemy remained very much in control. Tracer fizzed towards them while smoke and fumes from the petrol-topped water stung eyes already smarting. Of all *314*'s guns, only the forward two-pounder remained undamaged, and this was being put to good use. Despite being horribly exposed, a single gunner had taken control and was sending a stream of shells into the pillbox mounted beside the lighthouse.

"Bill Savage," Curtis announced, noticing Ryder's interest. "Able seaman and as tough as they come; never was a name more fitting."

But Ryder's thoughts were elsewhere. "This is no good," he said. They had failed to establish a bridgehead and, with so many launches already accounted for, would no longer be able to. "We'll have to go back for Charles and his lot."

Curtis ordered the boat about and soon they were heading away from the gunfire, although their destination appeared no less hostile, with tracer, and the beam of searchlights, coming from every direction. Then, as they neared *Campbeltown*'s stricken hull, Ryder noticed someone remained on board.

Silhouetted against the glare, a single rating was manning one of the destroyers Oerlikons, systematically raking German strong points with steady fire, and pausing only to act as his own loader when a magazine became exhausted. Ryder was about to draw him to Curtis' attention when an enemy shot silenced the gun forever.

Several buildings were now ablaze which only added to the

light; indeed, apart from the occasional patch of black sky, it might have been midday.

"What do you think?" Ryder demanded, yet he was not seeking to delegate responsibility.

"We're already carrying over forty wounded," Curtis shouted in reply, "and have few fully fit men ourselves. I say we pull out."

Ryder glanced at Green, the navigator.

"I agree, sir. There's no room for Colonel Charles or his men, and we still have the guns downriver to negotiate."

That was certainly the case; gambling the lives of those already rescued on the vague chance they might save more was not a risk Ryder felt entitled to take, and the fact they lacked the room for extra must be the final clincher. But Beattie, *Campbeltown*'s captain, was still missing, along with so many who had been vital to the raid and, as he glanced back at the destroyer's hull, now gleaming with the reflection of a thousand deadly lights, the thought of leaving them behind saddened him deeply.

"Very well, take her downstream," he said at last. Then after a final glance at the stricken ship added, "We'll just have to hope the old girl finishes the job."

Chapter Twenty-One

194 was the only British boat still travelling upstream, and she did so in relative safety. Standing with Harris on the bridge, Anderson looked out to the northern shore, but there was little sign of local gunfire and even the searchlights mounted behind the town itself were directed elsewhere. The glare of flames, tracer and an occasional explosion reflected in the sky ahead while the rattle and crack of weaponry was almost constant. He wondered for a moment if there was a lack of emplacements this close to the harbour – it seemed unlikely and went against their intelligence. Perhaps the full-scale battle being waged to the east was simply too much distraction but, whatever the reason, Anderson was glad they were being ignored.

Earlier their foredeck had been raked by light machine gun fire and several heavier shells struck her stern but, apart from knocking away one of the smoke canisters, little actual damage was apparent. Yet even this casual brush with the enemy demonstrated the fragility of *194*'s hull; if anyone had been unaware of the gunboat's vulnerability, they could no longer be in doubt.

"It's mainly flak batteries now."

The engines were running at under fifteen hundred revs, yet Harris still needed to shout, and Anderson strained to hear. There had been no communication from Ryder's vessel for a good half hour though the Fairmiles were using the R/T to excess. And their messages did not inspire confidence; most speakers were close to panic, and it was equally plain not all was going to plan. If *194* was to be of any help they would have to rely on their wits and instinct.

"The main fighting seems to be at the Old Mole," Anderson bellowed in return and received a nod from his captain. But as they drew closer it was hard to see what, if anything, could be done.

Light from several wrecked and burning Fairmiles lit the water, picking out the floating debris that seemed to be everywhere. *194* remained unnoticed, although it could only be a matter of time before her freshly painted hull was targeted.

"We'll have to get in closer!" Harris said, and Anderson was about to agree when there was a cry from Gibson, in the port turret.

"Blue light! On the quay and almost level with us."

Anderson scanned the nearby land, but it was several seconds before he saw the faint flicker. Considering the brilliant display nearby it was remarkable Gibson made it out at all.

"What do you reckon, Number One?"

"The commandos' torches have a blue lens," Anderson replied. "It's to aid identification – like their white webbing straps."

"Well, somebody's got hold of one and is flashing Morse." Harris paused. "It's pretty basic stuff; a simple SOS..."

"I suppose it could be a trick..."

"And it could be our lads," Harris said. "Take her in, 'Swain."

Phillips started turning the wheel to port, then stopped and looked back. "Beggin' your pardon, sir, but I think we've a problem with the steering."

* * *

Aboard MTB74, Micky Wynn was still very much involved in the action. After months of waiting, and one abandoned operation, it was finally time to release his personal weapons on an unwitting enemy and he could think of little else. The lock gates Commander Ryder had singled out were close by and gave direct access to a massive basin also serving the U-boat pens beyond. It was a target worthy of what some were pleased to call his toys. Wynn gritted his teeth; he cared little that others regarded him as something of an eccentric; one who took matters lightly and bore little respect for authority. But where MTB74 was concerned and, more specifically, the pair of engineless torpedoes she carried, he was always deadly serious.

The boat pulled away from the quay and accelerated into a high-speed turn in the very centre of the river. Then, slowing slightly, Wynn lined up his tiny craft on the short, narrow channel and ordered her in.

It was still too fast; the launching charges should easily see both missiles in place, and little good would be served if *74* was sent piling into the gates after them.

"Throttle back further," he ordered. Then, when it was clear their way remained too great, "Engage reverse."

This was the time to see how the new engine performed, and whether Lovegrove was really as good as Wynn thought. The deck beneath him gave a sudden jolt as the drive was changed but they were in the channel now and the black wall that must be the lock gates was growing ever closer.

"Now!" he bellowed and was pleased to see both torpedoes blast forward from their specially designed mounts. For less than a second, they remained in sight before hitting the water at a commendable speed, then disappearing into the black beneath. Whether their momentum would sink them close enough to the lock gates was anyone's guess, there had been no time for trials; all would be revealed when the charges detonated. His part in delivering was over however, and, with the briefest feeling of anti-climax, Wynn turned his attention to seeing the boat clear.

Reverse was now fully engaged, and he edged *74* back towards the port side of the channel. With tracer, flames and the bright white glare of searchlights reflecting off the concrete, it was easy enough to see and adrenaline, rather than experience, told him there was room enough to turn.

Which he did, but only just. Moving forwards once more and under hard starboard rudder, the boat's port beam came dangerously close to the opposite side of the channel but *74* was accelerating before she had fully straightened out. There would be wounded to collect from *Campbeltown*, and possibly those commandos whose tasks were done. Wynn could afford a few minutes to collect them, then nothing would stop him from hightailing it home. He glanced at his watch; within an hour they should be in the wardroom of one or other destroyer drinking gin and swapping lies; the time could not come quickly enough for him.

* * *

"It's not that I can't steer her," Phillips said, "but she's hellishly stiff. I reckon them shells aft must have done more damage than we thought."

That was probably the case, although Harris had more to think about. Whether or not he tried for the men ashore, they must still turn and at that point the river was wide enough to use the engines if necessary. Then he might rig an emergency tiller at the stern, although that would be his last option. Steering so worked in some situations, but where immediate response was necessary, it could equally lead to chaos.

"Very well, bring her about if you can, but stand by with the throttles in case they're needed."

By now the blue light was well off their port quarter and fast disappearing while the Old Mole lay directly ahead. The stone structure stretched out into the main river and, in addition to the lighthouse, carried two fixed gun emplacements. One had been silenced and now sent a stream of smoke into the already polluted air, but a second, lying closer to land, was active. And movement ashore suggested enemy troops were taking cover behind the mole's low wall.

Sure enough, as *194* finally dipped into a stiff turn to port, a barrage of small arms fire pelted her hull and superstructure while something heavier – probably an Oerlikon almost identical to their own – sent a flurry of green tracer in their direction. Daly returned fire from the starboard turret, but it was long range for a half-inch Vickers, and he soon switched to sweeping the mole itself. Only when they were halfway through the turn, and *194* could fully present her starboard beam, did Smith's Oerlikon come into play, and the shore-based gun was finally silenced. Then, as *194* began to retreat from the menace, both turrets could speak once more, and there was no further attention from that quarter.

"Smell something, Number One?"

Anderson sniffed. "Electrics," he said. Then, leaning forward to the voice pipe, he called up the W/T office.

"Better take a look," Harris said when there was no answer.

"If you're sure..."

"I'm sure but get back as soon as you can." Harris turned to Phillips as his second in command left. "How's the steering, 'Swain?"

The coxswain jiggled the wheel experimentally.

"Still stiff and doesn't like turning to port, sir," Phillips replied. "But I don't reckon it's the hydraulics."

"There's no time for a full investigation: as long as the helm works to some extent we have to carry on."

194 was approaching the quay now and Harris would have liked Anderson alongside. The flickering blue light was now less than a hundred yards off. Two gun emplacements were mounted further downstream but posed no threat. Being on the same stretch of quayside, neither could depress their barrels sufficiently while any shots fired over *194* would endanger the enemy's own troops on the Old Mole.

He leant forward and sounded the gunboat's klaxon. Its deep guttural wail seemed insignificant against the din of battle but was heard by both forces ashore. Those commandos that could, broke off and began heading for apparent safety while some of the enemy started targeting *194* with small-arms fire.

Soon shots were being taken over much of the boat, forcing those on deck to find what shelter they could. Yet Harris was resolute; they had come to do a job and if that meant staying still while enemy soldiers took pot shots, then so be it.

The remaining commandos came with a roar that would have chilled any standing against them and, as they leapt for the doubtful sanctuary of the gunboat's deck, some began offering thanks.

"Secure yourselves," Harris bellowed. "We're about to pass several Ack-Ack positions, and they'll be waiting for us."

A quick look ashore; the only figures he could see now were enemy soldiers gathered at the water's edge; soon his command would be facing a positive barrage of light calibre fire. He nodded to Phillips; the engines roared and *194* was already rising onto the plane when the first shots found her.

* * *

As Anderson entered the wheelhouse the acrid smell grew stronger. He looked about; apart from two holes next to the shuttered windows and the starboard outer door that hung drunkenly from a single hinge, there was nothing obviously wrong, although the stench was definitely electrical and decidedly unhealthy. He turned for the W/T office and reached for the door, which opened unexpectedly easily as the body of Ordinary Telegraphist Jenkins had been leaning against it.

He glanced down, but only briefly; the lad had taken a direct hit from a shell and there was nothing that could be done for him. Then light from the wireless sets caught his attention and he was spurred into action.

Both units were smouldering, he could see actual flames within the transmitter while the receiver sent out a deep pall of smoke that stung his eyes and made him want to retch. He grabbed at the nearest extinguisher, aimed it at the transmitter and squeezed the trigger.

Methyl-bromide enveloped the hot metal to little immediate effect other than a further repugnant smell, and for a moment Anderson came close to panic. Yet he kept the jet directed until enough chemical penetrated and the flames eventually died.

By then his extinguisher was empty yet the receiver continued to smoulder. The desk lamp still shone brightly through the haze and by its light Anderson noticed a bulkhead-mounted fuse board with isolating switches. Desperately he flicked each up; the light went out, and a buzzing noise not previously noticed stopped. He reached for his torch and shone the beam about; smoke continued to filter from the receiver's grill, but he sensed there was no immediate danger. Then a jolt told him the boat was underway while a rattling noise suggested they were under fire once more.

In which case Anderson's place was on the bridge and, stepping carefully over Jenkins' body, he made for the wheelhouse ladder. The fire should be under control but, if not, at least he must have lessened it somewhat. The important thing now was for them to get the hell out of St Nazaire.

* * *

For the second time, Ryder approached the carnage by the Old Mole. It seemed their earlier action against the pillbox had been effective as there was no longer any sign of activity there, and the second gun position, slightly inland, was equally quiet. However, they were close enough to the shore to make light machine guns effective and twice his boat was struck by short bursts from unseen enemies. Able Seaman Savage had returned to the fore two-pounder and was raising dust along the mole and quayside while some rescued from *Campbeltown* were equipped with Thompson sub-machine guns. As the boat edged towards the wrecked Fairmiles, the commandos sent short zips of fire towards their unseen enemies. But other than being appalled at the devastation caused aboard their sister craft, and avoiding the patches of burning petrol, there was little Ryder could do.

For whatever reason, the port column had failed to land sufficient men to hold the Mole even temporarily and, with no sign of life, he could only hope those who had made it ashore were now prisoners.

"Very well, we'll pull out," he said, after yet another suspected survivor was revealed to be a piece of floating wreckage. Curtis gave the order and Ryder sensed relief in his voice. And why not? A captain's first duty is to his ship and MGB*314* had already taken a pounding; sailing amid the debris of similar vessels so recently destroyed could hardly have been pleasant.

The boat picked up speed though still felt mildly sluggish. Whether this was down to the extra bodies crammed into her living spaces or something more serious Ryder could not tell, and Curtis had enough to think about guiding the craft out of harbour.

They were passing the Old Town and would soon encounter three further flak emplacements on the harbour wall. Judging by their failure to gain ground at the Old Mole, the commandos would not have dealt with these, and a few well-placed enemy shells could end their journey there and then. But once more Curtis was on the ball and steered the gunboat to port. The tide had turned some while before but would still be sufficient to see them to safety over the shallows.

"Vessel in sight to starboard."

The lookout pointed off their bow where another launch was also heading for the open sea.

"That looks like *194*," Curtis said, "call her up on the Aldis."

Harris' gunboat should have been considerably downstream; presumably, he had found the temptation of following them in too much.

"Reply from *194*." There was a pause while the lookout focused on the flickering blue light. "Do you require assistance?"

"Make, 'state position'."

The nearest enemy gun burst into life, but no searchlight

found them, and the shots fell wide.

"Steering damaged, carrying wounded."

Ryder was right, *194* must have strayed too close to the action and now the escort they were relying on to see them safely back to sea was damaged herself. But there could be no blame, presumably her wounded were either soldiers or crew from the Fairmiles, so the risk had been worth taking. And, with so much of his force destroyed, there was little left to face the heavier shore batteries they would shortly encounter.

"Make, 'continue to rendezvous point' and 'good luck'," he said, just as another gun emplacement opened fire.

* * *

The damage to *194*'s steering did not appear crucial, and her hydraulics were indeed unaffected. Which, as Carter dolefully reported, meant the problem must be aft in the tiller flat. With all three engines now running in the twenty-hundreds, it would be impossible to inspect; they could only hope matters would not grow worse. Besides, Harris had other concerns.

Their speed had been enough to see them clear of the harbour guns, yet there were still six flak emplacements on the northern shore, with a heavier battery mounted to the south. And then he would be in the estuary proper with a choice of taking the deep water route, passing by further flak and coastal artillery, or making for the shallows once more, where another sizeable battery awaited them.

But Harris had already made up his mind. "Take her to port, 'Swain," he said. Then, on noticing the man's momentary hesitation, added, "if you can."

All watched as Phillips took a firm grip on the helm before wrenching it anti-clockwise. The wheel turned, though only slowly, and Harris thought he could sense the bent linkages twisting under pressure. Should any one of the unions snap, *194* would be left rudderless and under enemy fire. They might still use the engines to manoeuvre, but only at the cost of a good deal of speed and the chances of being picked off would rise considerably.

Yet they were gradually turning and the headland of Le Pointeau was coming into view. Harris' notes indicated the heavy guns of a coastal battery would be found there, he must bank on

211

194 being too small, and too fast, to be caught by the ponderous weapons.

"Beggin' your pardon, sir, the helm's getting stiffer."

He turned to the coxswain who was holding the wheel gingerly in one hand.

"Can you bring her to midships?" he asked.

Phillips took a firmer grip and bore down in the opposite direction, but it was some time before the boat responded. Harris glanced uncertainly at Anderson; that last turn to port must have caused further damage; they couldn't trust the steering again, although it had been important to centre the rudders if they wanted to use their engines to the full. Without the instant response of a wheel, it would be far harder to dodge between shells when the shore batteries had them in their sights.

At least they could keep the speed up for now, though quite what those below were feeling could only be guessed at. With all engines running close to a scream, *194* must be approaching forty knots.

Sadly, it was not fast enough to avoid the searchlights. One caught them almost immediately and soon the gunboat's hull was enveloped in an eery white glow that made strange shadows on her topsides and only emphasised her lack of bulk. At the aft Oerlikon, Smith tried a few ranging shots, but the searchlight station was considerably beyond the battery, and his tracer fell foolishly short.

The first of the shore guns spoke soon afterwards, raising a fountain wide to starboard. Harris swallowed; he had no idea of the size of shell, but this was dedicated coastal artillery intended to sink ocean-going warships; quite what such weapons would make of a wooden launch didn't bear thinking about. Another shot followed, and two more after that, all equally ill-aimed. This was to be expected; both gunners and their weapons would need to settle. He could expect better shooting shortly.

The next shell arrived with a strange whirring noise that grew louder as it passed close overhead. Three more followed at the same range although two veered to port and one starboard. Yet *194* was still travelling fast and making definite progress; Le Vert could be made out, and shortly they would be passing the Pointe de St Gildas. Harris' notes suggested they could expect more fire from that quarter; he must risk another turn but this time using the engines.

"Full ahead port, half starboard!"

"Full ahead port, half starboard!" Phillips bellowed the acknowledgement while his gloved hand brought the starboard throttle back and *194* began a more graceful turn to the north.

Further shots came from the battery astern, but the searchlights lost them for a second and all fell short. Then a fresh cluster of flashes was spotted off their port bow; the emplacement there must be expecting them and was firing at the very edge of their arc.

The shells landed in line, though considerably ahead, but the fact that several guns spoke simultaneously caused Harris to wonder. They might have encountered a different standard of gunner; it was a reasonable assumption as the battery reached deep into the Atlantic and must be the enemy's first line of defence.

"Full ahead all engines!"

The boat straightened and was now heading across the estuary. It was simple enough to turn her so but there could be no violent manoeuvres.

Another salvo; again, closely grouped and this time off their port beam, then more shots from astern showing the battery to the east had not given up. Le Vert flashed by in a blur, they were now in the very teeth of the southern battery and a line of flashes signalled another barrage was on its way.

Once more that deadly whirring sound, and once more the shells barely cleared the gunboat's superstructure. Harris glanced at the coxswain; Phillips was hardly holding the wheel; the steering must have all but locked up.

"Throttle back all – hard!"

For a fraction of a second, the coxswain looked around before discipline took charge and he snatched back on the controls. *194* dipped violently, throwing all on the bridge off balance while there was a smack from the bows as she slipped down from the plane. A further salvo landed directly ahead; the line of fountains being close enough for a faint tinge of yellow to be seen in the searchlight beam.

"Now all engines full – maximum revs!"

Harris had no idea what damage he was doing to Carter's precious Packards, but if they held out for the next two miles or so he would be satisfied. *194* reared up as if fighting for breath, and then suddenly it was as if she had landed in the midst of a maelstrom.

Wind and water beat against all on deck, causing Phillips to cough while Anderson fell sideways against the rail, his helmet clattering onto the duckboards. Harris, who had been thrown back against the aft bulkhead, pulled himself up and looked about.

"Straddled!" he said.

Phillips had only just steadied himself while Anderson still lay on the deck. Both must look after themselves, Harris knew *194* could not be lucky twice: he would have to risk the rudders again.

"Full ahead starboard, half port and port your helm!"

It was asking a lot from the coxswain, and possibly a great deal more of their steering gear but Phillips at least was up to it. Raising himself slightly, he bore down on the wheel while his right hand adjusted the throttles and the boat all but spun into the tightest of turns.

"Straighten up now – meet her; midships!"

Phillips shifted his weight and, mercifully, the boat recovered. Another salvo, again a near-perfect grouping, this time off their starboard quarter.

"Full ahead all." There was nothing from the easterly battery and the searchlights seemed to be losing power, but *194* remained in immediate danger.

"*Lancastria*'s on the port bow!"

Anderson had recovered himself and was pointing to the left. Harris nodded; the wreck might grant them sanctuary.

"Full starboard, half port!"

Harris did not wish to risk the wheel again but, with two engines at maximum revs, there would be speed enough and the turn should be deceptively subtle.

Which is how it proved; the next salvo landed off their starboard quarter as did the one that followed.

"Full ahead all engines!"

Steadily the port wing gained revs until it was screaming with its brothers, but the upturned hull of HMT *Lancastria* was closer now and they should be passing it to starboard.

"As soon as we're clear I want the starboard engine all but cut," Harris bellowed, "then give me all the starboard wheel you can manage."

Phillips was focusing solely on the approaching wreck and

gave a distracted nod; if they cleared the hull, it would only be with feet to spare.

Another salvo, this time two of the shells hit the derelict troopship causing a minor explosion just as *194* swept into her lee. Then, their starboard engine note dropped, and the coxswain hauled down on the wheel once more. But this time there was no corresponding surge to starboard, instead, Phillips cursed as the wheel slipped from his fingers and began to spin freely.

"Steering's gone!" he shouted.

"How are the rudders set?"

"Near enough centred," Phillips replied, "We'd not started the turn."

Anderson was saying something, though Harris could not catch a word. They were due for another salvo, but the battery was oddly quiet. Then it fired again.

"They've switched targets."

This time Anderson's words got through and Harris nodded. Obviously, a more favourable prey had come into view, possibly another small craft escaping from St Nazaire, and whoever controlled that particular battery had given *194* up as a bad job.

"You might be right," he said.

And, though it meant someone else now faced the punishment they had just endured, none of them were sorry.

Chapter Twenty-Two

Micky Wynn had also been heading for home when they sighted the Carley float. With an agile craft once again able to show a fair turn of speed, he chose the northerly channel. The route had the advantage of being slightly shorter and, though there were more shore batteries, most were of the heavy coastal variety intended to sweep the estuary or even reach out to sea. Not being tied to the sluggard pace of a Fairmile B, MTB74 could raise over forty knots, especially on sheltered waters. Wynn was banking on this, and the fact that they would be passing almost under the enemy's guns, but the lookout's shout stopped all that.

"What do you make of it?" he demanded, as the dismal sight rushed into view. If they were to stop it must be soon.

"Definitely a float, and definitely one of ours," O'Connor, Wynn's second in command, reported. "And I'd say it was occupied."

Wynn looked across at the nearby shore. He was right in his assessment, 74 had been able to shoot under the larger guns without any getting a bead on her, although the lighter anti-aircraft pieces were more of a nuisance. They would shortly be entering the next battery's arc and the Carley was annoyingly placed firmly within its reach.

It appeared to hold two British seamen that must be part of Chariot. Standing orders prohibited the collecting of survivors, but Wynn had never been one to take notice of rules. However, he did understand and respect himself and, were he to leave men behind, knew it would remain on his conscience forever.

"Throttle back," he ordered, then, "I want two stout hands on deck with boat hooks – we can't afford to hang about..."

The boat swerved then came to a near stop just short of the float, and its passengers began paddling furiously in their direction. 74 was close to the shore and though a searchlight soon found her she was on the very edge of its beam. There was a chance, a slim one maybe, they remained invisible to the gunners.

Wynn's first lieutenant beat his fist against the bulkhead as

216

they waited, and the coxswain's hand hovered over the boat's triple throttles, although their captain seemed almost composed. *74* had already dodged fire from several batteries with some quite outlandish manoeuvres, this current halt might be considered as just one more.

The first survivor had been hauled half on deck and the second was reaching up; it could not be long. A line of green tracer streamed towards them from the shore but fell considerably short. All held their breath.

The second man must be wounded and was being dragged against the boat's side. Wynn winced in sympathy but the lives of many more depended on their getting under way immediately. Then, just as he was about to give the order, the first shells found them.

Once more it was anti-aircraft fire – explosive rounds intended to halt aircraft many miles up – and *74*'s eggshell hull crumbled easily. The initial hits were enough to signal her end; even if able to move again, water would be flooding in, and the boat must be abandoned long before reaching the waiting destroyers. But further shells penetrated the engine room while others dug deep into her fuel bunkers and the subsequent explosion put an end to all doubt.

* * *

Meanwhile, closer to the harbour, MBG*314* was in a bad way. Not only were all bar one of her guns out of action, she was without any form of wireless communication and carried over a foot of water in her bilges. Below, every available space was filled by wounded and, with no medically trained personnel on board, their third officer, Sub-Lieutenant Worsley was giving what comfort he could. Ryder had been reasonably sure theirs was the only boat in that particular stretch of water, but as the Les Morees light came into view, there was a call from the starboard lookout.

"Looks to be a launch, sir," the rating added, and soon all on the bridge could make out the dim shape.

"ML*156*, that'll be Les Fenton," Curtis announced as they began to pass. The Fairmile was from the starboard column and should have landed her troops at the Old Mole before joining Colonel Charles as a reserve. No one could tell how successful their

CO – a noted actor before the war – had been, but his boat looked to be in a bad way and was making poor progress.

"Call them up," Ryder instructed. "See what the trouble is." Even a masked Aldis could attract attention that close to the shore, but he considered it worth the risk and a few minutes later they had the answer.

"Extensive damage to hull and superstructure," Pike reported. "One engine's disabled, she's steering by tiller and has seven wounded."

Now it was mentioned, Ryder could see a huddled figure at the boat's stern; not an enviable job. Normally he would have taken the launch under tow but, at the last count, *314* had over forty shot holes and was leaking badly while she also carried far more wounded.

"Very well, tell them to make what progress they can, we'll see the escort doesn't leave without them."

* * *

Of those blown from *74*'s bridge, her captain was probably the most fortunate as he, at least, remained on board. But as Wynn lay in the wreckage of the wheelhouse, he didn't feel exactly lucky. His left hand was shattered, he needed to fight for every breath and there was no sight in his left eye. Yet through the right he could see the figure of Lovegrove standing over him quite clearly.

"Alright, sir? Taken a bit of a tumble, have we?"

"You could say that..." Wynn began, but the mechanic was already easing both arms under his body and lifting him as if he were no more than a child.

"There we go," he said, rising slowly. "We'll get you outside, then see about leaving the boat."

"How'd you know I was here?"

"I didn't." The wheelhouse door had been destroyed by the blast, although Lovegrove was able to manoeuvre his load through the massive hole left in its place. "Knew we'd have to leave sharpish but thought I'd better take a look round first."

"Glad you did," Wynn muttered and, despite the weight, Lovegrove smiled.

"So am I," he said.

218

* * *

On reaching the estuary proper, Ryder decided to give the northern batteries a wider berth, and soon MGB*314* was a good four miles from the heavier coastal guns. In the darkness, he had hoped they might even scrape by without being noticed, but fire from the shore soon told him otherwise. And the Germans were making good practice; for several seconds it looked like the gunboat would be sunk in mid-channel, so making smoke was the obvious solution.

314 carried internal CSA apparatus capable of producing a fog that could mask far larger vessels. But after several attempts to start the mechanism, Worsley, the third officer, was forced to resort to one of the smoke floats. Rather than following the boat, these left a stationary cloud that could be just as effective, although the unit was started by a chemical reaction and the flame this produced must initially reveal their position.

And so it proved; almost as soon as the process fired, the boat was raked with gunfire causing Worsley to fling the heavy unit bodily over the side. Though soon left in their wake, the float continued to burn and, believing they had scored an important hit, attracted attention from every available enemy gun. For several seconds the water around the smoking unit boiled with the impact from a dozen assorted weapons and, in the darkness and confusion, *314* escaped.

As if by telepathy, many of those aboard decided this must be their final brush with danger and a sense of apathy began to settle over the small craft. After living on their nerves for so long, the dawn most had not expected to see would soon break and should reveal two far larger, far more friendly warships. Some began examining minor wounds while others sought what comfort they could amid the crowded, bloodstained, mess deck and there was even the occasional snore as the battered craft ground steadily through the dark waters.

"Kye, sir?"

The rating was carrying a tray full of steaming mugs and, as he handed them out, Ryder saw blood on his sleeve. Then he noticed Curtis leaning against the starboard side and approached.

"Won't be long now, Dunstan," he said. "*Tynedale* and *Atherstone* should be in sight at any moment."

"If they're still there," Curtis replied before taking a sip of his drink. "Remember the talk about the German's Fifth Flotilla?"

Ryder felt a wave of guilt wash over him. Though barely believable, this was the first time he had considered the threat since leaving the destroyers several hours before. Throughout their approach, and while inside St Nazaire, there were other matters to consider. But he remembered them now, and that five eight-hundred-ton enemy warships would easily outgun and overpower two British destroyers.

"Last we heard, there were a couple more *Hunt* class heading this way," he said. "With any luck they'll be here before noon, and I think we can hold out until then."

"Oh, I'm sure of it, but then we're the lucky ones." Curtis was now looking into the distance. "So many have been left behind."

At this, Ryder simply nodded. When last seen, Colonel Charles had been fit and in charge of a fair number of troops; he might have made it to one of the other launches. But not just him, Sam Beattie was also missing, and Copeland. Indeed, so many.

Then there were the seamen – his men; those given little choice in the matter. How many of them were casualties? And even those who remained alive long enough to be captured, how long would they be prisoners? Probably the rest of the war – the Germans were not exactly keen on repatriation. Even if they survived, their lives would be changed forever.

And for what – what exactly had been achieved? Beattie did well in placing the old *Campbeltown* correctly, but until Tibbetts' explosives did their stuff, the Germans' use of the berthing dock would only be delayed, not made impossible, while winding houses and pumping stations could always be rebuilt.

This was not his first time in action and Ryder recognised the depression that frequently accompanied the end of combat, yet this was something more. Unless genuine results were revealed, Operation Chariot could go down as one of the most ill-conceived and expensive raids in history. And he had led it.

"Green ten, vessel in sight!"

Ryder stirred himself at the lookout's call. "What do you see there?" he demanded, throwing his drink to one side.

"Small – could be another launch." Curtis had also disposed of his mug and was studying the image through binoculars.

"Better make for her."

The chance of any minor sighting being anything other than one of their own boats was slight and they were surely close enough to rescue for nothing further to go wrong.

But Ryder was mistaken. Even as they flashed the usual challenge, the mystery vessel sprung into life and was accelerating towards them as her guns opened fire.

"Hard a port," Curtis ordered. "Full ahead both!"

314 heeled dramatically as she was wrenched off course, while Able Seaman Savage, at the forward gun position, sent a lively stream of fire in return.

"Looks like a Jerry harbour launch," Ryder shouted.

"Indeed," Curtis agreed. "Ironic really..."

But the German was better armed than any Fairmile B; green tracer swept down the British gunboat's hull and then began to play about her midships. Curtis' sudden turn had been effective, however, and the two vessels were soon drawing apart and at speed.

"Hard starboard rudder – now meet her, midships!"

Ryder was staring back, but the enemy launch apparently matched them in their reluctance to fight and was already disappearing into the night. After several minutes there was still no sign and he turned back to see Curtis finish speaking with a petty officer.

"A close one," he said.

"Indeed," Curtis pulled a face. "Our fuel tanks were hit; quite how they failed to explode is a mystery."

"We certainly got off light."

"Sadly, not all. I understand Bill Savage, our forward gunner, was killed."

"I'm sorry." The words were inadequate, but Ryder could not help that. "He'd come so far and done so much," he added.

"You could say the same about quite a few tonight," Curtis replied. "Let's hope it was worth the effort."

* * *

"You done well, kid," Smith told Godliman. "Handled them magazines perfec'. An' keeping me up to scratch with targets: that were magic."

"Came natural," Godliman shrugged.

"Maybe, but it were grand," Smith insisted. "And you seem more your old self now," he added.

"Think so? I don't feel no different."

"Well, you are, just like the old Lenny."

There was a pause, then Godliman said, "It was good, Smudger. Real good – better than I expected."

Smith was surprised but let the lad continue.

"I mean, we didn't sink nothing, and got bashed about a bit ourselves, but we were givin' it back."

"Aye, we were that."

"It kinda made up," Godliman persisted.

"Made up for what?"

"For when they killed our mates, sank our boat, and almost wiped you an' me out."

Smith considered this for a moment. "I suppose you could think that," he said at last.

"I do." Godliman was positive. "They've not got the hold on us no more. We're back on top."

* * *

The other survivors from MTB74 were already crowded aboard the Carley float, unconsciously provided by those they'd been trying to rescue.

"I have the skipper," Lovegrove said when the raft came alongside. "He's badly wounded, you'll have to make space."

One man slipped silently into the water and took hold of its surrounding rope as the captain was heaved on board.

"What about you, Chief?" a voice asked.

"I'll hang on to the side as well."

The shell that knocked out their centre engine also peppered Lovegrove's legs with shrapnel. Having to save his captain proved a perfect distraction from the nagging pain, but the salt water soon reminded him. He took hold of the rope and looked about. 74's fate must have been registered by those on shore; if rescue were swift, they might not lose too many. Yet it was not long

222

before the injured did begin to die.

Some were not wounded, however, and a couple of healthy seamen decided making for the nearby land would be worth the risk. The space they left, along with that from the body of a gunner who had given his all, allowed Lovegrove to join Wynn, and he could finally care for the man properly.

With limited medical supplies, this amounted to breaking open a pack of syrettes and squeezing morphine into the chilled veins, then stopping major bleeding with a combination of field dressings and clothing. Even before the drug, Wynn was barely conscious and Lovegrove's constant monologue mostly went unheard. Yet, though the situation appeared hopeless, the mechanic was not despondent. In four hours it would be dawn and after that, a watery sun could be expected. He just had to keep the captain alive to see it.

* * *

194 was first to find the destroyers. Initially, Harris had been cautious about approaching the larger ships as their outlines remained indistinct. Only after a wary challenge received the correct reply did he bring his boat within their grasp and, even then, was unable to accept the night's activities were truly over.

Once they had come alongside *Atherstone*, and their wounded were transferred, Harris joined the destroyer's captain in his sea cabin, just off the bridge.

"I wasn't aware you were to follow the main force in," Lieutenant Commander Jenks told him after he was given a mug of tea laced with a generous dose of whisky.

"I wasn't," Harris agreed, "and it's something I'll probably have to answer for, though we were able to collect a fair number of wounded."

"Which makes it worthwhile, I'm sure," Jenks added quickly, "though it's fortunate no stray Hun appeared at the wrong moment; an E-boat at the tail of the flotilla could have been disastrous."

"It was disastrous anyway." Despite the difference in their commands, he and Jenks were of equal rank, although at that point Harris would have addressed an admiral no differently. "To be frank, I'm not sure what Ryder and his lot expected, but what they got must have been a darn sight worse."

"I see."

Harris was sitting on the bunk with Jenks leaning against a small basin that was practically the only other piece of furniture in the tiny room. "From what we gathered *Campbeltown* made her approach as expected, and ended up against the gates, but after that, nothing came through from the lead boat."

"Nothing?"

"We continued trying to raise her, of course," the destroyer's captain continued, "but she appears to have lost her radio."

Harris felt mildly guilty about not insisting on Jelly's return, and now the feeling increased.

"Have you heard from anyone else?"

"'Fraid not. My wireless boys picked up quite a bit on R/T but it was mainly between the Fairmiles."

"Did you learn much?"

"It was chatter mainly, and not encouraging. Until we saw you, we weren't sure anyone would make it out."

That was not good news; Harris guessed his boat would have been the least involved, and they had only escaped by the skin of their teeth.

"But whatever you chaps started in the town made an impression. You could see the glow for miles."

"Glad to hear it."

"That said, we had our own problems," Jenks added. "Ran in with a bunch of Jerries a couple of hours back; Fifth Flotilla."

Harris looked up; "Did they do any damage?"

"Hardly engaged, as soon as we opened fire, they made a run for it."

"In what direction?"

Jenks sighed. "St Nazaire, I'm afraid."

Which meant any other escaping small craft were likely to run in with a force of German Type 24s. And eight-hundred-ton steel warships would not be so reluctant when it came to fighting wooden boats less than a tenth their size.

The terrors of that night came back to him, the scattering of wrecked launches and a sky full of searchlights and tracer; the very water had been on fire. Quite how many had died was still a mystery, although there was some consolation in learning

224

Campbeltown made it to the lock gates.

"Well, I'll have to leave you," Jenks said. "Put your head down here if you wish, or you may want to return to your boat; I expect *Tynedale* will take her under tow again, so you won't have anything more to worry about," he gave a brief smile. "From now on you can just sit back and enjoy the ride."

* * *

Harris had indeed intended to return to *194*. His number one was perfectly capable of preparing her for a tow, although Anderson would be as tired and shaken as any of them. Yet still he sat for a moment simply enjoying the security of a solid warship while the images and sounds slowly began to subside. When he did finally leave Jenks' sea cabin, dawn had broken clear and bright and there was a commotion on the bridge.

"Definitely two, sir," the destroyer's first lieutenant was reporting, and Harris paused in case the German Fifth Flotilla had returned. Noticing his presence, Jenks turned to him.

"It would seem you're not the only one to have got out," he said. "Commander Ryder's boat's in sight and less than a mile off. She's in company with one of the Fairmile Bs, which looks to be Charlie Irwin's *270*."

Irwin was the seventh flotilla's SO; Harris had met him a couple of times and liked the chap, though whether he himself had made it through was another matter.

"And there are a couple more on the horizon," Jenks added.

That meant of the veritable flotilla that entered St Nazaire, only five were returning; an attrition rate of more than two out of three. But at least Ryder's was amongst them so they might learn exactly what had been going on. And, of course, it meant Jelly was probably safe.

Chapter Twenty-Three

The Germans came for what was left of Micky Wynn's crew later in the afternoon. By then only three were still alive, and they were in a bad way.

Lovegrove was marginally the fittest; he had spent the time attending to his wounded captain, keeping up a steady stream of one-sided conversation while doing what he could to stop the bleeding and regularly topping up with morphine. Providing such constant attention weakened him considerably and, after what had already been a harrowing night, his hands were starting to shake and the increasingly nonsensical monologue was harder to produce.

The third survivor was a young stoker who boarded the float without serious injury. His overalls were thoroughly soaked, however, and he quickly lapsed into an intensive shivering that closely resembled a fit. As dawn broke exposure to the weak sun warmed him to some extent but, without the distraction of keeping another man alive, he soon grew listless and, when the patrol boat drew near, barely acknowledged the fact.

Consequently, Lovegrove was the only one to truly appreciate their rescue and caught the line thrown from the launch.

"English?" the German seaman enquired as they were hauled closer.

"Yes, English," Lovegrove confirmed.

"From the boats?" His accent was strong, but the open face appeared friendly and it was not the welcome Lovegrove feared.

"Yes, from the boats, the ones that came last night."

"I thought as much and said so to my friend." The seaman tipped his head towards a heavily built fellow staring at the trio in open-mouthed wonder. "Klaus and I will take care of you. It is not so far to the harbour; you will be there soon."

Lovegrove nodded, and there was a faint groan from Wynn's recumbent body; returning to St Nazaire was the last thing any of them wanted, though neither did they wish to remain floating aimlessly in the estuary.

"You will find it a different place," the German continued as the float was made fast.

Lovegrove eyed him cautiously. "In what way?"

"Your big ship, it blew part of the dock to pieces."

There had been the sound of an explosion around midday but, so intent was he in his care for Wynn, Lovegrove barely noticed it.

"The dry dock?"

"Yes, the dock gates." The man had a twinkle in his eye. "Though I could never see what use such a monstrosity could be. And they were French gates, so we did not mind so very much."

"I see."

"Come, we must take you back and you can see for yourself."

The larger seaman – Klaus – was the first to board and made the float tip alarmingly. But his friend soon joined and together they collected the stoker's body tenderly enough before returning for Lovegrove's patient. The Carley had kept them alive for so long, yet Lovegrove followed without a backward glance and, on feeling the reassuring solidity of the launch, breathed out for what might have been the first time in hours. There was a brief pause before the engine rumbled into life and then they were underway and once more heading for St Nazaire.

* * *

Lieutenant Commander Jenks was mistaken; those aboard *194* had plenty to do.

After rendezvousing with the waiting destroyers, then transferring their dead and injured, Anderson was able to address what repairs he could to the boat. Surprisingly the damage to hull and topsides was relatively minor; tarpaulins stretched across part of her fore and stern made the deck sufficiently watertight, and the wheelhouse door was secured. More attention was needed below; even with the wounded removed, evidence of their presence remained, and the W/T office, redundant now and a place best avoided, was simply sealed and left for another day. However, nothing was done with any enthusiasm; it was as if the recent action had sapped every ounce of energy, and several were found sleeping in unlikely places.

Meanwhile, the rest of their small force was assessed. Fenton's ML156 was considered too badly damaged and promptly scuttled, while *Atherstone* resumed her old role as Ryder's headquarters ship and took the remains of MGB314 under tow. 194 was similarly picked up by *Tynedale* and, with the two remaining Fairmiles chugging manfully in their wake, the dramatically reduced flotilla started for home.

An hour later they were joined by *Cleveland* and *Brocklesby*, the promised reinforcements and Ryder was finally able to pass on overall command to *Cleveland*'s captain, who was senior to him. Then, after further discussion, it was decided the battered Fairmile Bs would slow their eventual arrival. They, too, were despatched by gunfire, along with MGB314, whose leaking hull was becoming a liability. Of the force that entered St Nazaire, only 194 remained, and it was questionable if even she would see British soil again. For speed was a necessity; with so many wounded to care for, they must raise England in the shortest possible time. And so the nightmare journey began.

Though nothing like 194's potential, running at more than fifteen knots under tow was verging on the foolhardy. The hawser parted twice and, both times, Anderson expected their gunboat to be disposed of in a similar manner to 314. But whether it was Harris' dogged determination to save his command or the thought that at least one from the raid should return to tell the tale, her presence was tolerated, and the misery continued.

On several occasions they were attacked by fighter bombers, but the destroyers' excellent anti-aircraft armament came into its own and the enemy were driven off. They finally made Plymouth three days after setting out from Falmouth although to many it might have been a month.

But once secured, and after the truck sent to collect their ratings and petty officers had left, Harris and Anderson were reluctant to leave. Standing on the now empty bridge, it was hard to believe they had even been part of such a venture. And the sensation was not entirely down to exhaustion; 194 was directed to a quay some distance from the destroyers and, for all the attention given to the larger ships, she might not have existed.

"Rather like our arrival at Falmouth," Harris said, as they watched another group of enthusiastic visitors boarding *Tynedale*.

"I suppose it comes with being a latecomer to the party."

Anderson was not so sure; Micky Wynn's boat had turned up after them, along with *Atherstone* and *Tynedale*. Technically even *Campbeltown* put in at Falmouth following their appearance, yet all were accepted into the fold. And it couldn't be that *194* proved supplementary to requirements; fourteen trained commandos now back on British soil would be prisoners had she not collected them, and he liked to think their covering fire had been of some use to the Fairmiles. Of course, there was no way of gauging the mood aboard the destroyers; despite the apparent party atmosphere, some might feel the same sense of anti-climax; so much would depend on the mission's overall success.

Which was especially difficult for either of them to assess. Without a working radio, or even a telegraphist, there had been no chance of a comprehensive de-brief. They only knew *Campbeltown* was correctly positioned for an explosion, while several of the dry dock's secondary installations were no more. But whether that was worth the loss of so many lives remained in question and having been forced to leave such a significant proportion behind must surely tarnish any eventual success.

Indeed, losing the Fairmiles was an aspect that hurt Anderson deeply. The plucky little craft had been designed for harbour defence duties, and the fact that these were later stretched to incorporate the laying, or sweeping, of mines, and even coastal convoy escort work, was a credit to them. But their hulls were never intended for long-distance, deep-sea travel, and neither were they meant to face the full force of coastal batteries. Anderson had no idea how many seamen had perished in the recent nightmare, but it would take a significant result to justify such a loss.

And the commandos; he felt less immediate affection for men of another force yet remembered still the sight of so much fighting, both on the Old Mole and deeper in the harbour. For those who made it ashore, seeing the remains of their flotilla effectively abandoning them must have been hard to accept. And with them were Colonel Charles, Major Copland, and others; men he knew well and had dined with so very recently.

"We might learn more later." Harris must have been mirroring Anderson's thoughts. "But you know how these things are. Those in authority tend to keep a good deal close to their chest."

"And that's even supposing they know," Anderson said. "There should have been at least one reconnaissance flight by now, and it would be obvious if *Campbeltown*'s charges had exploded or not."

"But will that tell us if the gates were wrecked?"

Neither spoke for some while and then Harris let out a deep sigh. "Must say, I could use a rest."

"And I need a bath," Anderson added.

Harris grinned. "That as well." He paused, and his face fell as he said the words that Anderson had been expecting, yet also dreading.

"Well, what do you think, Number One; was it worth it?"

Anderson shrugged. "I guess we'll find out in time."

* * *

Surgeon Commander Simmons had spent many years in general practice and was adept at treating most common ailments. And despite the isolation of a small country surgery, he kept up to date with the latest drugs and techniques, although not to the extent that the personal needs of his patients were ignored. Early in his career, he discovered an extra five minutes at the end of a consultation could reveal far more than any list of symptoms and often uncovered important clues that might otherwise be missed. This habit of paying attention to the person, rather than their ailment, was acknowledged by his colleagues, although many suspected it to be a way of upping his bill. But to Simmons it went further than good bedside manners and was more an indication of the need to heal he had felt all his life.

When the war came, along with a commission in the RNVR, there was little call for this aspect of his skills. Being too old to serve aboard ship, much of Simmons' time was spent treating mundane ailments, especially venereal diseases, at which he was relatively inexperienced. Occasionally he would be asked to advise on diet for seagoing personnel and was also charged with organising fitness regimes for new recruits or those needing to convalesce. None gave the same satisfaction as working in general practice though. There, every name on his books was known to him, with many having been guided into the world by his own hands, yet he remained content to help the war effort in any way he could. So when the call came for additional doctors to attend the Royal Naval Hospital, Stonehouse, where a number of healthy young men had returned from combat, he immediately volunteered.

And, in the main, they were healthy. It was clear the action had been particularly brutal, with many fatalities, while the number of seriously injured currently being treated in the medical wards was also higher than expected. It was this sudden influx that led to his summons; with every hospital bed taken, and many cases proving complex, the regular staff were fully occupied. Yet even those apparently fit needed a medical examination so, for the past day and a half, Simmons had met with a succession of extremely lucky young men.

One was before him now, a pleasant lad, and obviously bright. David Andrew Jelly was a leading telegraphist and, though listed as a Hostilities Only rating, appeared dedicated to both his craft and the Service. He was also generally fit, as was to be expected of a twenty-one-year-old on a good, if basic, diet, with none of the deficiencies Simmons occasionally noticed in those on extended sea time. Apart from a mildly raised temperature, and a pallor that might be a symptom of sleeplessness – something Jelly readily admitted to – Simmons could find nothing wrong with the fellow and was inclined to send him on his way. Insomnia was a common ailment and one modern drugs could address to some extent, although a decent spell of leave – something Simmons felt all his patients were due – would provide a more permanent cure. There were three more in the waiting room and the afternoon was already half spent, yet he was in no rush. This was as near as he had come to general practice in months, and Simmons preferred to write up his notes with Jelly still present.

"I gather you intend to remain in the Navy, when this lot is over, I mean."

"I'd like to, sir. I've learned a lot, especially about electronics."

"You had no knowledge of such things before?"

"None whatsoever. I'd been helping out on a building site when I got my papers."

Simmons smiled. "I think I'd rather work with a soldering iron, or whatever you do," he said.

"I just seem to understand it. I mean, I read a lot at school, but not much went in, yet anything to do with electricity comes easy."

Simmons nodded; Jelly had discovered his vocation: a lucky man.

"Well, I'm pleased to say you're physically fit," he said. "If the sleep problems persist see your MO; some take it seriously and some do not, though it rarely hurts to report."

Both were smiling now and stood together, and it was only when Simmons offered his hand that he noticed the first sign that something might be wrong.

Jelly appeared awkward; perhaps he was not used to being on friendly terms with officers, although a salute, when one wore a white coat and the other his underwear, was hardly appropriate. For a moment the young man stared awkwardly at the outstretched hand, then his eyes rose and there was torment in them.

"Show me your hands," Simmons said, and Jelly held out two clenched fists, fingers down.

"Now the other way up."

This time it took a second or two for Jelly to respond. Then slowly the wrists turned, and Simmons examined the hands.

Which appeared remarkably normal. Perhaps the grip was a little tight, but the boy had been through much and needed a good night's sleep. And then he noticed a scrap of white peeping out of the left.

"And now open them."

This time Simmons thought Jelly would refuse. For several seconds the fists remained clenched and only after both began to shake did the fingers uncurl. And when they did a scrap of paper was revealed.

"What's that?" he asked.

"A letter."

If that was the case, it could be little more than a note. And, from what Simmons could see, much of it was already reduced to pulp.

"Who's it from?"

A pause, then: "My girl."

"And she is special?"

Jelly nodded.

"There's nothing unusual in that." Simmons relaxed slightly as he spoke. "In fact, I would say retaining a keepsake is completely normal and to be encouraged. But why are you holding it so tightly?"

Again, Jelly seemed lost for words; this was a very different chap to the one Simmons had been examining a few minutes before.

"Because its important," the young man said at last. "It's all that kept me alive."

* * *

"Here's another one," Daly said. "'Saint Nazaire. A War Office communique issued this afternoon states that a combined operation was carried out in the early hours of this morning. Units of the three services were involved in a minor raid.'"

"Minor?" Smith pulled a face. "I'd 'ardly call it that."

"And where do they get their 'three services' from?" Gibson demanded.

"There was supposed to be an air raid," Pickering said, "just as we was going in."

The crew of *194* were quartered in a dormitory that was also home to ratings from the scuttled craft. Most of these were agreeable types, simply pleased to be back; some to the extent that they took to their beds and refused to get up. But others behaved as if still in combat, the slightest sound being enough to set them jumping and, when an enamel mug slipped from Pickering's hands, there was nearly a riot.

Consequently, the gunboat's crew had gravitated to the NAAFI which, though busy, was large enough to provide a private corner with a selection of old newspapers.

"Heard them going over right enough, but didn't see no bombs," Gibson said, "so I don't see how the Air Force can be called part of the raid."

Daly looked up from his paper. "Maybe it was a diversion?"

"Diversion?" Gibson grunted. "More like they warned the

Hun we was coming."

"There's more." Daly was back with the newspaper. "'A further communique will be issued once our forces return but heavy casualties are believed to have been inflicted, and prisoners brought back.'"

"If that's the case I'd like to meet them," Pickering said.

"And here's another, 'The German News Agency reports a force made up of minor Royal Naval units, backed by aircraft from the RAF, have attempted to penetrate a port on the French Atlantic coast. Nearly every British vessel was sunk, and those troops able to land were quickly rounded up.'"

Gibson sighed. "Why does Jerry always say more'n our lot?"

"'Cause we don't say nuffin' till we knows it to be true," Smith replied.

"But we didn't bring back no prisoners," Pickering pointed out.

"This one says 'the British force suffered 'eavy losses from German naval and anti-aircraft artillery,'" Smith said. "'German troops took rapid action in which they surrounded the enemy forces. Most of the British Naval units were sunk, and the remainder fled' – I suppose they means us."

Pickering scratched at his chin. None of them had shaved for several days and, until someone noticed, none of them would. "We can nae be the only ones," he said.

"We weren't, there were two other launches an' a gunboat." Daly spoke from behind his newspaper. "Them what were scuttled."

"If they were scuttled, they didn't make it back." Pickering again.

"Yeah, but the Germans don't know that." Gibson had collected another newspaper and was flattening it out on the table. "Here, look at this; 'British Destroyer part of heroic raid on major port'."

"That's more like it," Smith said.

"'It is believed a Royal Navy warship has been sacrificed in an attempt to destroy the lock gates at the St Nazaire dry dock. Full story page four.'"

They waited while Gibson leafed through the newspaper.

"Only there ain't no page four..."

"Well at least one of them's on the right lines." Smith had picked up another newspaper but that was also incomplete. "And I suppose one day someone'll think about telling us."

"If we were allowed off base we might get a few papers of our own." Smith looked around. "Anyone seen Newman and Godliman?"

"Gone to see the MO," Gibson told them. "Medical check, we're all getting them."

"Mine's at 08.00 tomorrow," Pickering said. "Someone hold me a breckie."

"Wonder what the sawbones'll make of poor old Lenny." Daly had found the sports section and was analysing the racing results.

"Why should he make anything of him?" Smith asked and Daly shrugged.

"You know what the young fellow's like, tight as a clam most of the time. Even when you speak direct, he don't always give an answer."

"Not now." There was an element of pride in Smith's tone. "Not since we got back."

Pickering nodded. "That's right, we was sharing the PO's mess on the way home, and he were gannin' on at nineteen to the dozen."

"We're talking about the same Godliman?" Gibson checked.

"There's only one," Smith said.

"So, what caused the change?" Daly asked and Smith shrugged.

"Blowed if I knows," he said. "But can't say I'm sorry."

* * *

194's steering gear would be an easy fix. Three of the unions were bent out of shape and one had snapped but they were common parts with replacements readily available. Carter and his team were working on it and, providing the linkages could be straightened sufficiently, believed the boat would be serviceable by the following day. Then there would be the short trip back to

Falmouth and the promised de-briefing.

Harris was keen to hear the exact details and Anderson had gone off base for a paper although news about the dock gates' destruction was already circulating with all the energy of a scandal. And though much must be hearsay and rumour there seemed little doubt Operation Chariot's main aim had been achieved. It was something Harris never dared expect, and, secretly, he was proud to have taken even a minor part in such an accomplishment. Yet there were still aspects of the raid that concerned him.

For a start, it had been rushed, there was never any doubt of that. Corners were cut and chances taken that even the pressures of warfare should never have allowed. Yet time was an important factor; little good would have been done if more exercises and changes to the schedule produced a better plan that proved unworkable due to a lack of water over the shoals. And however careful the preparation, an assault of that nature would always rely on the initiative and resourcefulness of those on the spot.

There had also been a high casualty rate; Harris lacked the exact figures but his being the only small craft to return to England must be an indication, while there were a darned sight fewer commandos walking around Plymouth than had left Falmouth. With luck some would have been captured, though with so many Fairmiles coming to a sticky end, even that did not seem likely; exploding motor launches did not make for prisoners of war.

Yet Operation Chariot's importance was already starting to fade; Harris was beginning to think of other things and, specifically, the future. They would shortly be back in Falmouth and then, afterwards, Dover. So much had happened since, it was hard to believe it was less than two weeks since first leaving their old base. *194* would need further repairs but the yard at *Wasp* was capable enough, and it would give the lads a chance to rest a while; they'd earned it.

And as for himself, he could do with a break and possibly some social life. This was a new concept for Harris; previously leave had been spent with his parents, but this time would be different. This time there would be Laura.

With moving to Falmouth, then the build-up to the raid itself, he had only thought of her occasionally though this was not due to any reticence on his part. Harris was simply unaccustomed to having someone else in his life; someone to worry over, someone who may be worrying about him. He considered phoning a couple of times and might still, yet there was little point as not much could be told over an open line. No; better to wait, get back to Dover and speak face to face. Then the two of them could pick up exactly where they left off.

Chapter Twenty-Four

They raised Falmouth at 19.00 the following evening and were greeted by good news. As *194* rounded Pendennis Point and the dock proper came into view, four Fairmile Bs were moored at the quay. Engine trouble had forced one to turn back before the raid but the other three must have been at St Nazaire.

"I can see *443*," Anderson said as he surveyed the craft through his binoculars. And that looks like *307*. From memory, they were both in the port column."

"But that's *160*." Harris pointed at another vessel. "She was with the starboard lot and had a different objective."

"So, when did they get out of St Nazaire – and how?"

Harris shrugged, "They must have come along later."

"Or earlier?"

"Whatever, they missed the rendezvous with the escort party."

Anderson lowered his glasses. "In which case they probably made it back on their own; I guess there's a story to be told there..."

"Which we'll doubtless hear at Commander Ryder's debriefing tomorrow."

"Are you sure we're invited?"

Harris raised an eyebrow. "We do have a habit of being left out," he said.

"It's odd, when you think about it," Anderson was glancing about the bay. "Less than a week ago, this was a busy base."

"And now a good many are in enemy hands," Harris agreed. "Or dead."

"Well, let's hope Ryder tells all tomorrow. Ten o'clock aboard the *Princess Josephine Charlotte*."

"*Charlotte the Harlot*." Phillips spoke from the helm then, feeling the eyes of the two officers on him, added, "Beggin' your pardon, gentlemen, but it's what they calls the commando ship."

Harris and Anderson exchanged looks. The past few days had been hard for them all, but it seemed at least one of their number was showing signs of recovery.

* * *

And Phillips was not alone; most of the gunboat's ratings had been quick to recover from the trauma of St Nazaire, while Godliman may even have benefitted from it. But sharing their accommodation with other veterans of the raid had not been easy and they were glad to get away from Plymouth.

Not that they resented a bit of strangeness in the Fairmiles' crews. Most were more used to coastal trips and might not have seen enemy territory before, yet they had crossed many miles of blue water and then entered a hostile and well-protected harbour. And neither would they be accustomed to the shot and shell of close combat, or seeing their shipmates fall. For those, St Nazaire would have been a baptism of fire and they were probably entitled to a few nightmares.

Being faced with this, and the realisation they had got off relatively lightly made *194*'s crew keen to be gone. They might have lost one man, but Jenkins was only a temporary hand and barely known to them, while their boat required relatively minor repair and would be back in combat before long.

Besides, Falmouth was almost their second home and, once on the familiar road that led to The Rose, it was as if they had never been away. More than that, they could place the horrors of St Nazaire firmly in the past, which was a concept approved of by all.

It was early morning, and the streets were still empty, yet there was a welcome in the air that had little to do with the town itself.

"Old Mona'll be pleased as punch to see us lot!" Smith grinned. With the boat's late arrival, they had not been given liberty until that morning, but breakfast at The Rose was infinitely preferable to the NAAFI version.

"Pleased or not, I'll be happier with some of her sausages down me gob," Pickering said.

"And bacon," Smith added. "Don't forget the bacon!"

"First thing I'm doing is takin' a bath." Gibson stretched in expectation. "And they can stuff their five inches, this one's going to be long and deep."

"Providing Mona can take us," Daly said. "Couldn't she have let our rooms out to someone else?"

"Someone else?" Godliman repeated in disgust. "When we said we'd be coming back?"

"Sure, but not everyone did," Daly reminded him, "and we're still missing Jelly."

"Aye, no one's seen Wobbler since Guzz," Smith again. "Maybe he's had a better offer?"

"Wouldn't surprise me." Godliman had truly become more talkative. "He came back in a destroyer and probably saw the chuckin' about we got under tow."

"Well one less means more for us," Gibson said as they rounded the corner, and the full splendour of The Rose was revealed to them.

"What d'you say, lads?" Pickering was suddenly unsure. "Think we'll still be welcome?"

"We only been away a few nights," Godliman said.

"To be sure," Daly agreed. "Mona won't have forgotten her boys."

But even he slowed his pace as they approached the red front door, and there was a moment's hesitation before one of them dared to knock.

* * *

Gentlemen, I will keep this brief," Ryder announced when they had assembled aboard the *Princess Josephine Charlotte*.

The wardroom was a dance hall when the ship carried passengers, so the handful of officers looked particularly paltry, especially when not so long ago the room had been full. Harris and Anderson were sitting close to the back, which felt appropriate considering their role in the raid, and both were conscious of an air of mild despondency.

"I expect most of you'll have read something about Chariot in the press, and there might not be much I can add," he began. "Though if you hear it from me, you'll know what to believe and what to doubt." Ryder paused and appeared to take stock. "Let's start with some good news; three more Fairmile Bs have made it

240

back." He indicated the group of six Naval officers to his right. "It seems our rendezvous arrangements did not appeal, and they preferred to make their own way home."

There was a brief rumble of laughter, but the atmosphere remained tense.

"And I understand they accounted for at least one enemy aircraft on the journey, so really they are to be congratulated."

This was greeted with a smattering of applause that finished almost as soon as it began. Then Ryder started again.

"Now down to business; first off, a few figures. Slightly over six hundred went across, and only a little more than a third returned. We have yet to hear from the German authorities but suspect roughly the same number were taken prisoner. And the rest, I'm sad to say, must be considered lost.

"I should also add we were hoping to see Ian Henderson here today as *306* was reported leaving the port, but she is another casualty. Apparently, Ian ran into a German Type 24 and fought an heroic battle." Ryder paused for no more than a second; all could imagine the outcome when a wooden motor launch engages a steel warship eight times her size. "I regret to inform you that Ian, along with his officers and a good proportion of the commandos they were carrying, was killed."

All murmuring stopped and a deathly hush descended.

"That, if you like, is the debit side of the account and not one we anticipated, at least to that extent. But to balance there is more good news.

"Micky Wynn was a later addition to our force; many of you'll have met him or at least been aware of his vessel. After *Campbeltown* was successfully beached I directed him to target the gates to the main basin which he did with his characteristic enthusiasm. The charges have yet to detonate but were on especially long timers; we have every reason to expect at least one of them will, meaning the main basin should only be usable at certain points in the tide."

A mixture of relief and appreciation swept the room although Ryder remained deadly serious.

"When last seen, Micky's boat was sound and heading for home, but I'm afraid we've heard nothing of him since."

Once more they became still.

"Moving on to *Campbeltown*, most of you'll have heard her

charges exploded as intended. Judging from evidence received from the Photographic Reconnaissance Unit, both cassions are damaged beyond repair meaning the graving dock will be out of use for many years to come."

Now there was a brief murmur of comment. To receive confirmation that their ultimate objective had been met brought an immediate lightening in the mood.

"Without a dock that can cater for her, *Tirpitz* is unlikely to be deployed in the North Atlantic. The pressure this takes off our convoys, and those in the business of escorting them, is enormous, while we can now use the home fleet more effectively. In short, though the losses at St Nazaire may have been great, I think we can say with some certainty that the end of the war has been brought a good deal closer."

There was no argument from the audience; even those still raw from the loss of friends could appreciate what had been achieved.

"And there's another benefit," Ryder continued, "although one I hesitate to mention to a room full of seasoned men such as this. Some of you may regard public morale as an unnecessary consideration, believing what counts in a war is the ability to strike hard and strike often. And there is some truth in that, but we mustn't forget why we are fighting and who we are fighting for."

Again, they were silent and, in some cases, curious as to where their impulsive leader would take them.

"Never forget the morale of our nation is central to what we do; without the support of civilians, there'd be no point in continuing and even an outright victory could have little value. Those of you who've seen the press reports or listened to the wireless will know information about the raid has been sparse and, in some cases, misleading, but you can expect that to improve: improve and continue. To do what we did took guts and a lot of brave men died; it's right that the civilian population know of it. And it is right also that they take pride in our accomplishments.

"In the past few months there have been several incursions onto enemy soil with considerable damage caused, and this less than two years after Dunkirk. I trust such exercises will continue and, for as long as they do, it's clear which way this war will go. And now that we have America alongside, I think there is room for a little optimism."

It was hype, hoop-la, puffery, but of the highest order and totally justified; Ryder's audience would allow it.

"Those of the military that returned will be rejoining their regiments for redeployment elsewhere and any salty types lucky enough to keep hold of their boats can look forward to a brief spell of rest. Those that find themselves temporarily homeless are sure to be afloat again shortly and we that are left can look forward to a return to normality. But I ask you all to remember this.

"When speaking of St Nazaire, you may be challenged; there will be those of your own service and others who mention the loss of life and equipment. They might also believe a story already put about by the Hun that our true mission was the destruction of the U-boat pens, which were unharmed, while there'll probably be some who suspect we were trying to open up a second front on specific instructions from the Bolsheviks..."

There was a pause for muted laughter.

"And even if they do know exactly why we were there, they might wonder if the destruction of a single dry dock could be worth such expense. Exactly how you reply is your choice, but please remember the lives saved as much as those that were lost.

"Remember the merchant shipping that would have been sunk were *Tirpitz* allowed free rein over our convoys, the escorts and capital ships required to deal with such a menace, the depleted rations our civilians would have needed to survive on as well as the attitude on both sides when the balance tipped nearer to Nazi domination. As it is, our new allies will hear of this raid and realise we do not intend waiting for them before making a decisive move, and neither are we afraid to risk our men and machinery. And, lastly, don't forget the French."

There was a rumble of comment which Ryder dispelled with a faintly accusatory look.

"We might think of them as anything from gallant allies to despicable conspirators, but the average French man or woman has equally varied opinions about us. Some understand we are fighting this war together, and a major aim is to rid their country of German occupation, while others see only an Air Force that left them in their time of need, a Navy that sank many of their finest warships, and an Army that promised much, then ran when the invaders arrived. To those we have sent out a strong and unequivocal message that they are not alone, and we are still very much involved.

"Invasion, and their eventual liberation, may still be some way off, but it will come, and the promise has been written in the stone of St Nazaire."

* * *

"Boys?" she enquired cautiously from behind the half-closed door.

"Open up, Mona love," Smith told her, "you got a load of hungry mouths to feed."

The door opened a little wider revealing the woman's shocked face. "But I thought you were gone."

"We was," Godliman grinned. "We go, and now we come back!"

The door swung back fully, and Mona stood to one side.

"So, what's with shutting up shop?" Gibson demanded as he and his shipmates flowed in. There it was just as they remembered, although some of the tables had yet to be cleared from the night before.

"Oh, we had to." Her tone was soft, and she still appeared slightly stunned. "Place got too popular. We only open in the evenings now, and that's becoming a trial I can tell you."

"Your fault, Mona," Smith said. "You shouldn't cook such lovely grub."

"I don't know about that," Mona glanced around the dishevelled room, then back at the group of men and finally smiled. "But we missed you – with the serving I mean. My ladies get quite rushed off their feet. Vera an' Marge are washing up at the moment, then we got to cook an' lay up. We open at six, that only gives us eight hours."

"Maybe we'll lend an 'and," Smith said. "But before that, any chance of 'aving our old rooms back?"

"Of course, they're just as you left them. I haven't changed a thing."

"Kind of you, Mona," Daly said. "Specially as you couldn't be sure you'd ever see us again."

"I thought I wouldn't, not when I read the papers." She had gone behind the bar and was reaching for a kettle. "So, I locked them up and no one's been allowed near since. Tea, is it?"

For a moment the men were silent, and then Pickering

spoke. "Tea would be grand."

"Do you still have them papers?" Newman asked.

"Oh, you can take a look, she pointed vaguely at a pile on one of the tables. "I ain't seen one today, but what they said before were bad enough. 'Daring raid on French port and ever so many killed...'"

She seemed to cough but quickly turned away so they couldn't be sure.

"How did you know it were us?" Daly asked.

"Didn't take a lot of working out." Still with her back to them, Mona started laying out cups and when one fell to the floor, she left it there. "They said our forces came from a West Country port," she continued, her voice now oddly strained, "and we ain't as daft as people think; everyone knew about them boats in the harbour..."

"We don't die that easily," Newman assured her.

"Well, there's no doubting that!" It was almost a snap.

And then Mona turned, finally they could see her face and the men gave a collective gasp.

"I suppose you'd all like a spot of breakfast?" she said.

* * *

"So that's that, then," Harris told Anderson when they were heading back to their hotel. "We patch *194* up a bit more, then set a course for Dover; after what everyone's been through, Hellfire Corner and serving under Johnston will feel like a holiday."

Anderson scratched at his chin. "I guess so, though can't help feeling something of an anti-climax."

"Oh, undoubtedly," Harris agreed. "Apart from those we rescued, nearly every other commando landed was either captured or killed. Most stayed aboard the launches, and a good number of those ended up as casualties."

"It hardly speaks well for the Naval side of things."

"It hardly speaks well for whoever planned the whole damned charade!" Harris' tone was louder than he intended and drew the attention of a passing CPO.

"I'm not talking about anyone actually on the spot," he continued more softly. "And certainly have no beef with men who sail several hundred miles in harbour defence vessels to take on the might of an enemy port. But who decided they should?"

Anderson shrugged. "Someone must have."

"Aye, someone, or a team of someones; probably in a dry and detached Admiralty office. And the same someones decided to use lightly armed and totally unprotected Fairmile Bs, expecting them to remain afloat and immune to enemy fire for up to two hours."

"Was there an alternative?"

"I'd say so. If we could adapt and equip one destroyer there could have been more. *Campbeltown* was carrying eighty commandos, not all made it ashore, I'm certain, but enough to hold the area next to the dry dock for quite some time. Even one more destroyer landing a similar force at the Old Mole would have held that as well, while a few four-point-sevens and some armoured steel would have been far more use against searchlights and gun emplacements than Oerlikons and laminated mahogany."

"I suppose so."

"Or did the Army have to go at all?"

Anderson blinked; it was not something he had considered.

"By far the main casualties were the Fairmile Bs, and the commandos they had on board. Had this been a totally Naval operation two or three properly adapted destroyers could have handled it; they'd only need a small number of military to see the steaming party off the ram ship. The result would have been broadly similar, with fewer lives lost."

"But surely the aim was to totally devastate the docks," Anderson said.

"That was never going to happen." Again, Harris realised he had spoken too loudly, although they were well on their way now and the street was empty. "I was speaking to one of the army types at Plymouth," he said. "Their total force was considerably less than three hundred men. Do you know what they faced in opposition?"

"Only vaguely."

"Over six thousand crack troops; I'm not counting the mechanics and dockyard workers. And the enemy were dug in!" he exclaimed. "I'm a long way from being a tactical genius but know enough about displacing an existing force; you can't do it with a tiny fraction and inferior weaponry."

Anderson supposed Harris was right, but whether due to exhaustion or something more permanent, he simply could not summon the strength to continue the conversation. There was no doubting firepower, ammunition supply and troop numbers had been against them, while the attention paid to organising a safer withdrawal did rather suggest the commandos, and those delivering them, were considered expendable. But what was the use of going over old ground, or fighting past battles? Were that deemed necessary it could be done later, although Anderson hoped not; far better to remember a bold venture and the brave men who tried to see it through.

Besides, he had other matters to consider. There'd been a letter waiting for him on his return. It was from Eve and its contents were enough to wipe all thoughts of St Nazaire clean from his mind.

* * *

Simmons looked again at his notes regarding the young leading telegraphist. There was nothing wrong with what he had written, all his observations were correctly recorded and would stand inspection by any recognised medical body. It was just the conclusion, and his final recommendations that were causing him concern.

Before committing himself, Simmons had spoken to a colleague serving with the Territorials who had also been drafted in to help. His patients were members of 2 Commando and, though many had witnessed terrible sights, few exhibited any of the psychological effects noticed in Jelly.

Simmons was only a Naval officer through necessity; he remained a physician at heart and knew considerably less about the Service than a regular RN Commander. Yet the disparity between soldiers and seamen involved in the raid was readily apparent. The majority of those Simmons examined had been forcibly enlisted, which meant their training was brief and centred on the current conflict. In contrast, those making up 2 Commando were predominately professional soldiers, with many having volunteered before the war. Their preparations for the raid were the culmination of constant exercises and drills that, in some cases, went back years. Of course, they had also come face to face with the enemy, while the Navy's task was simply to deliver them, yet still the inequity was obvious.

So, what was he to do about Jelly? A note from him would refer the lad for psychiatric assessment, which was probably the correct course. Simply speaking with a specialist would not automatically divert the young man to a succession of therapies Simmons knew little about and trusted even less, although the chances were high. And apart from a single strange obsession with a girlfriend's letter, Jelly appeared totally normal; given the chance to reunite with the young lady, the condition would probably disappear.

Simmons hoped so, just as he hoped that, if not, no great harm would have been done by the delay, and Jelly might still receive the medical attention he needed. The war had several years to run, but already many had been affected in ways that were not obvious. Some, the majority he hoped, should come through with only marginal changes to their personalities, but others might already be suppressing symptoms that would only come to light a good while later. Such were the legacies of every conflict and, in time, they might be taken as seriously as more obvious physical injuries, although he remained doubtful.

Simmons looked again at his notes. Jelly was a bright young lad with a good career ahead of him; with luck, and the support of a loyal woman, he should survive. And it was with that hope in mind that he signed him off as medically fit.

Chapter Twenty-Five

"Hello, Laura."

There was a pause; Harris guessed she was thinking. Then, finally: "Frank? Is that you?"

"No." Harris tried to keep the disappointment from his voice. "It's Bob. Bob Harris."

"Well, hello stranger." She sounded reserved but at least he thought she might be smiling. "Where've you been hiding?"

"We were seconded," he said. He was using a lobby 'phone at The Grand, which was about as private as a bookie on Derby day and her's was probably some wall-mounted affair in a corridor so it wouldn't do to say too much. "West Country," he added. "Combined Operations."

"I say, you weren't mixed up in that Chariot caper, were you?"

Harris winced. "Something along those lines," he said.

"In that case, it's remarkable you came out alive."

Remarkable; was that the best she could do?

"Look," he said, "I wondered if we could meet up sometime."

"Meet up?"

He stiffened. Surely it wasn't such a strange request; he'd been away less than a fortnight.

"Yes, the boat'll be in the yard for some time so I'm pretty much at a loose end. How about lunch?"

"Today?"

This was getting foolish. "Unless you've something planned," he said. "With Frank."

"Oh, Frank." She paused as if deciding whether to say more and Harris' suspicions rose. "It's nothing to do with Frank, I'm on duty in an hour."

"I see. So, how about this evening?"

"This evening's out as well. But I might be able to make Thursday."

"Thursday? Why not tomorrow?"

There was a pause. "I suppose I could do tomorrow," she said at last. "If it's really important."

"Not important as such, but I'd like to see you."

"Well, that's good to know. Only you haven't been particularly attentive."

"Attentive? I was on secondment. You do know where I've been?"

"I discovered – eventually. Falmouth, wasn't it?"

Harris paused. "That's right."

"And they don't have telephones in the West Country?"

"Look, Laura, I'm sorry. Really. But it was quite a job."

"Yes, I'm sure," she said. "And I know it wasn't just Falmouth; I'm glad you're back safe. Look I'd better be going, I'm still in my nightdress."

An image flashed into Harris' mind that he quickly dispelled. "Tomorrow then," he said. "Shall we say nine? I'll pick you up at *Lynx*."

"No, I'll meet you there; I assume we're going to The Grand."

"We always seem to," he said.

"Yes, we do, don't we? Okay, nine o'clock it is. TTFN."

Harris opened his mouth to say more but there was a click, followed by the dialling tone. He replaced the receiver and looked about. The lobby was deserted, yet still he felt the need to put on a smile. Tomorrow night was not so very far off; the time would soon pass.

* * *

Anderson had also been making a telephone call although he ensured himself a little privacy. But as he walked away from the derelict 'phone box he was hardly reassured.

Eve's letter mentioned she was to be transferred although censorship rules prevented her from saying where or when. It included a Guildford 'phone number, along with the best times to catch her, and he had been lucky at the first try. It wasn't even a trunk call, and his pockets were now considerably lighter, yet he remained in the dark.

An elderly lady answered although Eve came on almost immediately. And as soon as he heard her voice Anderson knew nothing was different between them. But she remained just as cagey about the transfer, which had already been made, it seemed. Not only was it a completely different department, there was also more training – quite a bit, by the sound of it – and a move; she was staying with an aunt who lived nearby.

The lack of any real information was understandable – or so he told himself. Even if not officially monitored, long-distance calls were regularly checked on by the operator and whatever Eve had agreed to was definitely top secret. But there was good news as well; her next leave would be up in two weeks, and she intended to spend it in Dover.

The timing was a shame; *194* would be back on the water by then and on active service, yet it must still be possible to meet during the day and maybe the occasional evening. Then they could talk without the restrictions of blue pencils or suspect 'phone lines. Anderson could not begin to guess what Eve had let herself in for, although he doubted it would be trivial. And she was a grown woman who knew her own mind, so really he shouldn't be worried. Still, it would be nice to know what he shouldn't be worried about.

* * *

It was a crowded compartment, but Jelly found a space in the middle and stowed his duffel bag on the luggage rack overhead. After finally being released by the medical unit he had returned to the Plymouth barracks to find his boat, and shipmates, were already bound for Falmouth. The transport CPO gave him a travel warrant to join them. It was almost twelve; if all went well, he would arrive before three, or so he hoped.

The train he had run so hard to catch was showing no signs of moving off and as he sat there, still panting, he inspected his fellow passengers. Some were in uniform with two Naval ratings similar to himself, but opposite was a young mother who had taken her child onto her lap to make space for him, as well as a couple of older ladies, one of whom appeared to be asleep. It was a single compartment with no corridor and both windows were shut; already it was stuffy, and Jelly felt a wave of panic oddly similar to that experienced a few nights before in St Nazaire. Of course, there was no comparing the two situations, although he would be trapped in this small space for some time and suddenly the idea appalled him.

There was a jolt, and the train began to move off. It gathered speed steadily and, as Jelly's back faced the engine, he was forced to brace himself to avoid falling forward. Eventually, it settled to a regular pace, and he could rest, yet not relax. The compartment was no less airless and, though the panting subsided, he could not draw a full breath.

Everyone else was behaving normally however, even the child – no more than a toddler – had settled and was sucking wetly on a dummy. He looked away and tried to focus on the window, through which he could see Devonport dockyard. They were making progress, but the journey would be so much easier if he could calm down.

Easier, but impossible. The crowded space was closing in on him; breath came in snatches and his heart began to race. Perhaps this was a shared experience? Others could be affected as well; there might be gas entering the compartment or something else as yet unknown though equally general. But his fellow travellers appeared depressingly normal; whatever he felt was peculiar to him.

He glanced at his watch; they'd been travelling for no more than ten minutes; the journey had hardly begun and already he was longing for the end. Maybe the train would break down, with its passengers released into that clear free world that lay beyond the grimy windows? He needed to change at St Austell, which could not be far. The next train would be less crowded and might have a corridor; he'd like that. They passed through a station without slowing; this was a fast train: it would be ignoring most of the smaller stops. He was effectively trapped.

His breathing remained irregular. He closed his eyes, willing himself to relax while still aware of his racing heart and an incredibly dry mouth. Sweat was gathering on his forehead and under his arms, even though he felt cold. On opening his eyes, nothing had changed, he remained stuck in the grip of crowded normality.

Then, suddenly, Jelly knew he was going to be sick. That or defecate, or maybe just die, but his body was in the midst of significant change. Time spent in Coastal Forces had forced him to come to terms with seasickness although in the privacy of his W/T office, not a space crowded with people and without his trusty bucket. He glanced about and caught the eye of the mother, now considering him with obvious concern. He swallowed. Something would happen shortly, and he was not sure what, but he needed a bathroom and privacy. He needed to be alone. To be free. And then, mercifully, the train began to slow.

The train began to slow and soon it would stop; a station was imminent and Jelly caught a brief look at a sign that told him it would be Keyham. He stood, then staggered as a wave of giddiness overwhelmed him yet, so urgent was the need to be gone, he still reached for his duffel bag. It was a small station, the train might move off at any moment: he must get out.

Dragging the small bag down, he disturbed a larger suitcase leaving it hanging precariously over its owner's head. The man, some sort of soldier, objected loudly, but Jelly had no time for that, or even to apologise; he must be off the train before it started again.

He made for the door: there were feet in the way. He trod on one, causing the old lady to wake noisily. Another made him trip, though by then he was at the door and desperately snatching at the handle. There was a steep step down; he took it in one, stumbling as his boot hit the hard platform, but the air came cold and fresh, and the giddiness began to subside.

Behind him, the door was slammed shut by an angry hand, and there were harsh words which he had no mind for. Being free of that terrible compartment was the only thing that mattered. The train pulled out amid a cloud of steam and grit; good riddance to it; he would take another, one not so crowded. He collected his bag. A uniformed porter, old enough to have retired long since, was changing the indicator board. Jelly approached.

"When's the next to St Austell?"

The old man was taken aback. "Why, you just got off it," he said. "Won't be another till later."

"What time?"

"Ten past seven; gets in around half eight."

Jelly looked away. His breathing was back to normal and there was no longer the need to find a cloakroom.

"You alright, son?"

"I'm fine," Jelly said, and it was almost true. By the time he got to Falmouth – *if* he got to Falmouth – the others would have turned in.

The porter regarded him with concern. "If I were going for that service, I'd get myself here early," he said. "Only it's a worker's special and bound to be packed."

* * *

"It's like we was never away." Pickering launched himself onto his bed, lay back, and let out a deep, satisfied sigh.

"Apart from no Wobbler," Smith added.

"An' there was a packet of Weights in here before we left." Gibson was going through his locker.

"None of us would have taken them," Pickering told him.

"Damn right," Gibson agreed. "None of you would have dared."

"And what does that mean?" Pickering enquired. Gibson fixed him with a glare.

"I mean, them what pinches from me knows what they'll get."

"After what we've been through, haven't you had enough of fighting?" Newman was leafing through a book abandoned before they set out for Falmouth.

Gibson pulled a face. "I ain't fussy who I hurts."

There was an uneasy silence. After an early start, *194* put in to Dover that afternoon and was immediately taken in hand by the Wellington Dock, *Wasp*'s own repair yard. She was to be inspected at first light, but all knew the gunboat would not return to active service for at least a week. With the draughts from numerous bullet and shell holes and the stink of fish and injury permeating her living spaces, it had not been the most comfortable of trips. Soon they should be filing down to the NAAFI for their main meal, which would be nothing like as large, sustaining, or enjoyable, as Mona's cooking. So why Gibson wanted to cause trouble was anyone's guess.

"Who fancies hitting the Lion later?" Godliman was now one of the most garrulous members of *194*'s crew.

"We've not been paid," Smith reminded.

"That should come tomorrow," Godliman said. "Our fortnightly insult's well overdue."

254

"S'right," Pickering agreed. "Didn't get a sniff all the time we was away. Good job The Rose weren't a proper boozer."

"Okay, how about tomorrow?" Godliman suggested.

"Wobbler might be back by then," Smith said.

"Aye, tomorrow, or the day after," Newman added. "I called Soph earlier, she's on lates all week."

"So how is yer lass?" Daly asked.

"Fine, though still a bit wary after what happened at her old digs."

"Terrible thing," the Irishman shook his head.

"Terrible?" Godliman enquired.

"Her friend being attacked like that," Daly explained.

"I have to collect Sophie from the Wrennery now," Newman said, "and see her back after. It ain't the same."

"What about the other one?" Pickering this time.

"You mean Wobbler's bit?"

"Na, the one what got bothered."

"No one knows," Newman said. "They took her away right after and she ain't been seen since."

"That'll be procedure I'm thinking." Daly spoke with apparent knowledge. "Questioning her and things; it's what they do."

"Should a caught the bugger weeks since," Pickering said.

"Sure, an' what kind of animal would do such a thing?" Daly added.

"A right bastard, I've no doubt," Smith replied.

"Well, it's changed her life, and that of the other Wrens," Newman said.

"Most must be nere more'n bairns." Pickering sighed. "It's a wonder he can live with hisself."

"Hey," Smith said. "I don't suppose Wobbler's bint knows anything about him."

"What, the attacker?" Godliman asked and Smith shook his head.

"I were thinkin' of Jelly. There's been no sight nor sound since he were sent to the sawbones."

"I'll ask when I call tomorrow."

"He might be back by then," Daly said.

"Fingers crossed like." Pickering again. "Then we can really get back to normal."

"So," Godliman persisted. "Is it the Red Lion tomorrow?"

"We ain't been given liberty." Daly had picked up his racing paper and spoke over it.

"We'll get it," Newman said.

"I'm not goin' to no Lion." Gibson's voice sounded unnecessarily loud.

"That right, Gibbo?" Pickering was only vaguely interested. "Thought you'd be up for a wet."

"Then you thought wrong, see?" There was definitely something in the gunner's insistence and several of his shipmates began to take notice.

"To be sure, there're other pubs," Daly supposed.

"But we know Alf," Smith said. "He's almost a mate."

"I said no to the Lion!" Now Gibson was almost shouting.

"Pressed the wrong button, did we?" Pickering enquired.

"Press all you want, I ain't going an' no one's gonna make me."

"He's right there," Daly was back in his paper.

"Shame, though," Godliman added. "Lion's still got that dartboard..."

* * *

Possibly it was to do with them dining in the evening, but The Grand felt different. There were obvious changes, of course; the restaurant seemed busier, and darker; blackout curtains being closed while the management appeared to be economising on light bulbs. There were different waiting staff on duty as well and Harris was unable to get their favourite table, the corner one that looked out onto the road. He tried asking more forcefully; he was a resident after all, and they were regular customers, while the table itself was empty and might not have been requested specifically. But the waiter pointed out that being near a window held little benefit during the blackout.

Laura found this amusing, so Harris allowed them to be guided to a table on the other side of the room. There was more space although a party of ten were having some sort of celebration nearby and Harris was not sure if he liked the look of them.

"So, tell me about Chariot," she said when they were finally seated.

"Not much to say, other than what you'll have read in the papers."

"Yes, wasn't there something in today's?" She unfolded her napkin and collected the menu. "A torpedo exploding, or something?"

That was true; Harris was informed the day before. One of Micky Wynn's 'toys' had finally done its business and partially wrecked the gates to the main basin. Which was good news on several levels, but mainly because the U-boats would be forced to match their future movements with the tides. And there was a more subtle benefit; after *Campbeltown*'s original delayed detonation, the Germans must now be wondering what other surprises awaited them; when the second torpedo decided to blow, a state of paranoia was almost guaranteed. He'd discussed the implications at length with Anderson yet strangely didn't wish to share any of this with Laura.

"They say the boat that fired it was later sunk," she added.

"That's right, her captain and chief motor mechanic were saved," Harris said.

"Well, that's alright then," she was looking at the menu, although Harris' mind remained with the past.

Micky Wynn wasn't the only one to have fallen into German hands. News had come through that Sam Beattie, who captained *Campbeltown* on her final voyage, was also a prisoner, along with the pipe-smoking Colonel Charles. It was hard to believe it all happened so recently.

"The cod looks nice. At least it'll be fresh, and you can't do much wrong with fish."

"I'm sure The Grand will try," Harris said, and she smiled politely. "Actually, I've something to show you," he added. She looked up, interested, but not greatly so. Harris reached into his pocket.

It was a small blue box, the kind a shop would use for pieces of jewellery; maybe a broach, a bracelet... Or even a ring. He passed it across the table, and she looked at it – then him – in horror.

Harris noticed the expression. "It's not for you," he said. "Something that's been given to me, actually."

She opened it carefully and smiled. "Oak leaves! Why Bob, you've been Mentioned in Despatches!"

"That's right."

"A few of the chaps in Ops have them," she continued. "It's about the only award they can expect."

"I'd never thought of that."

She shrugged. "Hard for pen pushers to win an actual medal, yet neither are they in the front line. But surely this is early for St Nazaire?"

"Indeed. Before we left my boat rescued another, and the base captain included it in his report."

"Good old Brookie!"

Harris smiled; this was going better.

"I'll have the cod." Laura's back was to the wall, so the waiter had crept up on them without Harris seeing.

"And me," he said. "And a pot of tea for two."

"Tea, sir? We do have a small selection of wine..."

"Tea." Harris replaced the menu. "And keep the pot topped up."

For a moment they smiled together, and it was like old times but then she was looking over his shoulder and her expression changed to one of disbelief. It would be that damn party, Harris decided, and he turned in his seat only to see Lieutenant Commander Johnston approaching.

"Bobbo!" Johnston exclaimed, clapping him soundly on the shoulder. "Never thought I'd see you in a dive like this. And definitely not with such a lovely companion; how are you, Laura?"

"Fine thank you, Buster."

She was smiling, but out of politeness, Harris decided, while he was equally sure Johnston must be at least three sheets to the wind.

"I say, do you mind if I join you, old boy? Only my date's failed to show." Johnston's look of incredulity would have been amusing, were it not for the circumstances. "I'd booked a table by the window," he said. "but spent the last hour in the bar waiting, and you've plenty of room."

Harris went to reply, but Johnston was already pulling back one of the empty chairs.

"So, what's The Grand got to offer," he said, settling and reaching for the menu. "Don't be fooled by the cod, that's down to us." He gave Laura a wink. "Happy Hopgood let off a depth charge on the way back from our last job. Bagged more fish than we could

258

handle, so we sold most to Carlos in the kitchen. I suppose some might've been cod…"

"When were you last out?" Harris asked, and Johnston closed his eyes. "Let's see, weather's been bad for a while, I suppose that would have been Saturday night; I hope old Carlo's fridge's up to scratch."

"And you're not out tonight?"

"Weren't rostered, old boy, though we should be down for the next three. It's a shame you can't join us, but I suppose after St Nazaire you need your rest."

"The boat was badly shot up," Harris began, but something else caught Johnston's attention.

"I say, what's with the jewellery?" He leant forward and collected the box, then treated Laura to a generous leer. "Not interrupting a significant occasion, I hope?"

"It's Bob's," she said. "He's had a mention in despatches."

"Well about time too!" Johnston opened the box and actually touched the treasured oakleaves; it was all Harris could do not to snatch the thing from his grasp.

"Mind, I got mine a few months back." Johnston nodded down at his own award. "And would have several, but you can only get them once, you do know that, I suppose?"

"I have heard," Harris said. The evening was starting to go downhill, and his mind searched for some way to save it.

"So, why d'you get it?" Johnston demanded. "What incredible act of heroism did you perform?"

In Johnston's current state, admitting it was for rescuing Joseph's torpedo boat would not go down well, and the last thing Harris wanted was to argue with a drunk.

"Look, I think you should call it an evening," he said. "You're on duty tomorrow night, get some sleep and you'll feel a lot better."

"Sleep you say?" Johnston blinked, then seemed to remember something. "But I'd been looking forward to tonight."

"There'll be others," Harris assured him.

"Booked the window seat and everything…"

"I'm sure you did." Harris glanced at Laura, who was trying to suppress her giggles.

"No. No, I need food," Johnston said, returning to the menu. "There must be something in this damn place worth eating."

"Miss Morris and I wish to dine together," Harris stated firmly. "Alone. You are not welcome and should go."

Johnston stared at Harris for several seconds.

"Not welcome, old boy?" he said at last. "But I'm your senior officer!"

"Out in the Channel maybe. This is a hotel dining room, and we're of the same rank. Now take yourself back to wherever you berth and leave us in peace."

"It's all the same with you straight stripers." Johnston's voice had risen to the extent that the party several tables away were aware. "Career Officers who think the Royal Navy's their personal property!"

"There's no need for that, and I'm not discussing the matter further. You'll leave, or I'll make you, is that understood?"

Laura cleared her throat and Harris wondered if he'd gone too far, but the man was an embarrassment, and looked set to ruin the entire evening.

"Oh, I'm going, don't you worry." As Johnston stood, the menu dropped onto his plate with a clatter. "And we'll certainly talk of this later." He lowered himself to speak straight into Harris' face. "And I hope your boat will be fixed shortly, because I simply can't wait to have you back under my command!"

Harris met the stare. "I'm looking forward to it," he said.

Johnston straightened up and turned to Laura. "Nice to see you, though why anyone would waste their time with this puffed-up has-been is beyond me." He gave a mock salute and turned to go when something made him stop. "I say," he said, looking back at Laura. "I'll be meeting up with Frank tomorrow; shall I send him your love?"

Chapter Twenty-Six

"Hey up, it's Wobbler!" Pickering announced and Jelly gave a wave to the corner table before making for the bar. The Red Lion was busy, and it took a while to be served so when he finally joined his shipmates they had their questions ready.

"So, where you been?" Smith asked.

"Last we heard you was Temporarily Medically Unfit," Pickering added.

"An' how d'you know we'd be here?" This was from Godliman; Jelly was surprised he should speak at all.

"No one was in the billet, so where else would you be?" he asked.

"No one?" Newman questioned. "But we left Gibbo there."

"Well, he wasn't when I dropped my clobber off."

"We brought the rest of your stuff," Smith said.

"I wondered where it'd gone; thanks, matie. So what's been happening?"

"That's what we're wondering," Daly said. "TMU they told us; did you get yourself wounded?"

"Aye, you was in the lead boat," Godliman added. "Must have been hell."

"It weren't pleasant," Jelly admitted. "But I was below much of the time."

"So why the TMU?"

Jelly shrugged. "Blowed if I knows, the quack examining me thought there was something wrong, then changed his mind. Meantime you lot had legged it to Falmouth and, when I got there, moved on to Dover. I've spent the last three days jumping from train to train."

"Ah to be sure, and aren't we so terribly sad to hear it?" Daly's tone lacked compassion.

"But three days to get from Plymouth to Dover?" Smith seemed doubtful.

"You know what trains can be like," Godliman said.

"Too right." Jelly, who knew exactly what trains could be

like, reached for his pint.

"Have you met up with your lass?" Pickering asked.

"Annie? Not yet, but I called her on my way back." He had, several times, and she was wonderful. "I'm seeing her Saturday, if there's liberty."

"Reckon that's a certainty," Newman said. "Though they seem to have forgotten all about survivor leave."

"Our fault for not losing the boat," Godliman said.

"So why's Gibson not with you?" Jelly asked.

"No one knows," Smith said.

"And neither do we care," Godliman added.

"We'd be the last he'd tell," Pickering agreed. "Lad's been behaving queer for some time."

"I reckon St Nazaire's changed quite a few," Jelly said. "You should have seen some of them I had to bunk with in sickers."

"It started before then," Daly said. "Before we left Dover. I reckon he's got something on his mind."

"Gibbos' mind ain't big enough," Newman said, but Jelly shook his head.

"I'm not so sure, he's no fool."

"Just a bully," Godliman added.

"Maybe so, though ask me there's more going on." Smith had drained his pint and was looking about.

"But enough about him, we got some celebrating to do," Newman announced. "Sink that, Wobbler, we'll get another round in."

Jelly obediently emptied his glass.

"We got time?" Godliman asked.

"Should 'ave." Smith glanced at his watch as Alf gave the bell over the bar three stout rings. The sound echoed painfully around the crowded room.

"Last orders!"

Alf's call was almost as loud and instigated a minor riot. Men rose from every table; soon the bar was rocking to the noise of shouted orders and the tapping of coins.

"We'll have to be quick," Smith said. "Alf don't give more'n ten minutes drinking up time." Then, after looking back at his shipmates, he added, "Anyone know what's happened to Wobbler?"

* * *

"I'm sorry about Johnston."

Their food had arrived, and the cod did look relatively edible, although neither felt that inclined to eat.

"I think he's been under a lot of pressure," Laura said.

"Indeed." Harris was more interested in finding the vinegar than Johnston's welfare.

"A lot of reservists don't find it easy," she added.

"Oh, I don't know." At least the chips looked decent enough and Harris liked chips. "On the whole, the RNVR are doing alright." He glanced up. "Those that are good are very good indeed, but the bad ones can be perfectly dreadful. I say, you're not a reservist, are you?"

She shook her head. "Joined as an ordinary Wren at the end of 'thirty-eight but wouldn't have been commissioned so quickly if the war hadn't come along."

"In which case you chose the Navy or, in some respects, the Navy chose you. And not out of necessity."

She began to play with her food. "Really, Bob, I don't think it's very different. Big or small, war changes everything. Do you think you'd have two-and-a-half stripes if it weren't for Hitler?"

"I've no idea, and neither do I care. Hitler or not, I'd have been in the Navy, while Johnston and his lot were too busy making a mint in totally different professions."

"Why condemn them for that?"

"I don't, not the average reservist anyway. As I've said, most do a splendid job and I take my hat off to them. However, with Johnston I'm prepared to make an exception." He tried a smile, but she was not responsive.

"Because he's in charge of you?" she persisted. "Even though everyone knows it's only temporary, and you'll have a brand new flotilla before long?"

"I wouldn't say I was quite such a shoo-in."

"Well, you are," she said. "Come on, Brookie's a man of his word and has you down as the next flotilla SO. All you need do is keep your head down and not make too much of a fuss. Yet it seems that's hard, even for a professional officer such as yourself."

Harris wondered how much of that she really meant, but her expression looked sincere.

263

"A bit harsh, don't you think?"

"Maybe so, but it needed to be said." She picked up a chip with her fork and considered it. "Of the two of you I'd say Johnston's in the worse position. Should the situation be reversed, and you suddenly found yourself in his line of work, how would you fare?"

"I think I'd survive," Harris said. "With sufficient training."

"But that's just it, you know the sort of preparation most RNVRs get. Some might have experience of the sea, but not all, definitely not all. Much of what they learn they pick up from others, mainly old salt horses like you. Yet rather than help, you look for ways to undermine his position or complain because he doesn't fit your idea of the perfect Naval officer."

"That's not fair, I'll go out of my way to help anyone, whatever their rank or branch; they only have to ask."

"And do you think that's likely? A man who's been running a flotilla successfully for some time finds he has a straight striper under his command. And this one's a real stickler; so stuffed full of Naval etiquette he might have served with Jellicoe. Poor guy can't make a move without upsetting the old codger – you think he's going to ask him for help?"

Harris shrugged. "I hadn't seen things quite like that, though it hardly makes any difference. Anyway, I was prepared to follow his rules – providing they made sense."

"Oh, wonderful! How'd you like a subordinate who'll obey orders as long as he agrees with them?

"Can we leave it?"

"I beg your pardon?"

"For tonight, can we just leave it?"

She put down her fork. "You mean you want to go?"

He shook his head. "No, of course not. I just don't wish to spend the rest of the evening talking about Johnston."

"I'm sorry," she said. "Look maybe we should call it a day; I'm tired and I'm sure you are also. Let's pretend tonight didn't happen."

"Do you think that's possible?"

She smiled. "I'll try if you will."

"I'll see you home."

"There's no need, it's not far; I can walk." She was standing now, and Harris knew himself incapable of retrieving the situation.

"Am I allowed a question?" he asked as she collected her hat.

"Of course." She waited.

"Who is Frank?"

* * *

The lure of a final pint had obviously proved too much for his shipmates and Jelly was forced to wait outside the pub for quite some time. Yet he was glad none of them followed him out. It gave him time to think and maybe concoct a story, although why the simple act of a bell ringing had affected him so would take some explaining. He was in for a ribbing, that was obvious.

Of course, he needn't have waited at all; nothing was stopping him from heading back to *Wasp*; he could have been in bed by the time they returned and dodged their questions, and jibes, easily enough. But Jelly was not one to avoid unpleasant situations and preferred to face his mates there and then. So, when The Lion's customers finally started to leave, he was ready for them.

Godliman was the first to appear and made his way over. "What's going on, Wobbs? he asked. "Didn't you fancy another?"

Jelly shook his head. "Been a long day," he said. "I weren't feeling too chipper."

"But you're alright now?"

"I'm fine."

"Probably a bit run down." Godliman took a place next to him on the wall and Jelly thought it strange that, of them all, he seemed to understand.

"Just needed some air," he said.

"It can get you like that, when you been in action," the youngster agreed. "Can't think straight; like your whole life's goin' down the drain."

"I been in the thick of it often enough before," Jelly said. "St Nazaire weren't the first time things went bad."

"Maybe." Pickering had joined them now and also settled himself on the wall. "Though you got to admit, St Naz. were different."

"The worst, I suppose," Jelly agreed.

265

"Was for us," Godliman said. "And we weren't in as deep as you."

"Aye, must have been hell," Pickering added, "leading boat an' all. Not surprising you felt a bit dicky."

It was not the reaction Jelly expected but, though he appreciated his shipmates' understanding, bolting from a pub once could probably be excused. There'd been many similar instances over the past few days; how would they react if they knew about them?

Newman had also left the pub, along with Smith, though neither paid him any attention. Then Daly appeared but the streets were wet from the rain that had only just stopped and he and Smith took to kicking puddle water at each other. The three sitting on the wall stood and, once more a group, they started the slow trip back to *Wasp*.

Reaching a road, Daly glanced left to see if it was clear when suddenly he stopped. "Well, will you look at that?"

"What's up, Paddy?" Newman asked.

"It's y'r man, Gibson," Daly said, pointing down the side street.

"Whatcha, Gibbo!" Smith called, as the seaman drew nearer.

"Evenin' lads," he said. "Good oiling, was it?"

"You should've come," Smith spoke without enthusiasm. "We've met up with Wobbler an' all."

Gibson nodded towards Jelly but said nothing. All could see the newcomer was flushed and slightly out of breath while his uniform appeared damp, presumably from the earlier rain.

"Howay man, what you been doin', like?" Pickering asked.

"Aye, what was better than a night in The Lion?" Godliman added.

Gibson scratched at his nose. "Oh, you know, this and that." He gave a crafty smile. "There's always something going on if you knows where to look."

* * *

"I say, sir, terrible news about Laura."

194 should be fit for active service by the weekend so Harris had attended the weekly intelligence briefing. Still, why this

266

RNVR lieutenant had singled him out was beyond him; the face was both distinctive and vaguely familiar, although he could not place him.

"Ives," the officer said, extending a hand and presenting a dazzling smile. "Frank Ives; we met briefly when you dropped in at Ops just after Christmas."

Harris took the hand and was surprised to find it oddly delicate. "So, you're Frank?"

"Yes, I suppose Laura's mentioned me, sir." Ives was completely unabashed.

"What news?" Harris demanded.

"She was attacked, night before last. It was just outside *Lynx* – poor girl was almost at the gate."

"Really? Is she alright?"

"I'd say. Gave the fellow what for, by all accounts, even chased the blighter for a while and made a deal of noise." He grinned. "You know what she can be like."

Harris made no comment.

"But it's really not good," Ives continued. "This is the second assault on a Wren in the last month and it was a sailor both times."

"What are the Regulating Branch doing?" Harris had already decided Ives presented no threat.

"Mainly the usual. From what I gather they're checking who had liberty though, with no boats out that night due to the storm, they'll have their work cut out. That said, they're playing it down; don't want to start a panic amongst the girls, or something."

Harris regarded the man more carefully. He was well groomed, as might be expected of a shore-based officer, but Ives' uniform was especially smart and probably tailored. His skin could never have felt the bite of a Channel wind while high cheekbones and a pale complexion made him look quite feminine.

"I need to talk to her," he said.

"Of course," Ives agreed. "You'll probably catch her at the Wrenery, I understand she's been given forty-eight hours' leave."

"Thank you, Ives," Harris said, and the lieutenant showed his teeth once more.

"Oh, do call me Frank, sir."

* * *

267

"Why didn't you tell me?" Harris demanded when Laura let him into her room. Rather than uniform, she wore blue slacks and a grey jumper that was showing signs of moth.

"I suppose you've been talking to Frank," she said. "Can I make you tea?"

"If it's no trouble. Yes, I ran into Ives at this morning's briefing," Harris said.

"Sweet boy," she smiled. "He's been terribly nice." She pointed to a vase filled with spring flowers. "Brought me those."

Harris, who had come empty handed, gave a nod. "If he hadn't sought me out, I'd never have known."

"You weren't supposed to," she said. "The Crushers want it kept quiet, which suits me; I've no wish to shout my mouth off."

The room was small but comfortable with a pair of single beds and a wardrobe. There were also two wooden chairs, one of which was covered in clothing, and a small sink. Laura collected a kettle which she filled before placing it on a single gas ring.

"Are you supposed to have that in here?" Harris asked as she lit the ring with a match.

"Not really." Laura was unconcerned. "Jen's boyfriend's a fitter; he's set one up in several rooms."

"You were going to tell me what happened."

She shrugged. "I wasn't actually; there's nothing to say. This matelot jumped out of the bushes and put his hand over my mouth."

"He didn't..."

"He didn't do anything." She spoke quickly and avoided looking him in the eye. "We were taught the basics of self-defence in the first week," she added.

"What did you do?"

"Do? Why, I bit him!"

Harris' grin was automatic.

"I'll tell you, he let go pretty damn quick, and then I made all the noise I could." She finally flashed a look in his direction. "The biting wasn't part of the training, by the way: I improvised."

"Glad to hear it."

"After that he made a run for it, and I started after him, but those damn shoes are awful. Anyway, I was almost outside this place so reported it and then all hell broke loose. Got me two days leave but frankly I've been going spare. Back to work tomorrow

268

and it can't come fast enough."

"There aren't any clues, he didn't leave his hat behind or anything?"

"Wasn't wearing one," she said.

"Then he'd have got into trouble if the shore patrol caught him. You're sure he was a sailor?"

"Oh yes, full monkey suit."

"It would have been raining," Harris pondered. "He must have been wet."

"Look, what's with all the questions, Bob? Don't you think I've been through all this already?"

Harris sighed. "I suppose so, I just feel responsible."

"Well, you're not. It was my choice to leave the restaurant early, and my choice not to have you see me home." The kettle began to whistle; she switched the gas off before turning back to him. "But I do appreciate your concern, even if you do show it in a strange way." Then she smiled. "And I must say, it's good to see you."

Chapter Twenty-Seven

The yard proved as good as their word. Eight days after they had taken her in, *194* was ready to be signed off and, as the Wellington Dock was a stone's throw from *Wasp*, they could begin working up immediately.

But before then there was much to do. The gunboat was in a serviceable condition with yet more tingles covering minor areas of damage, and a fresh coat of Admiralty Grey now hid the Plymouth Pink. Yet she still needed a compete sweep and swab out internally, and there were several areas of the living spaces that Anderson wanted painted while the boat was relatively empty. Ordnance were due to visit in two days' time, although their new guns could not be sighted in until they put to sea, and before then a multitude of stores must be taken on. In addition to major consumables like fuel, oil and ammunition, there were smaller items ranging from charts and pilots to medical supplies, while most of the lines needed replacing, and Anderson also needed to put in for fresh ground tackle and safety equipment. But when all was taken into consideration, he was as confident as any first officer could be that the empty hulk would soon become a viable warship once more.

He looked about the bridge, oddly quiet in the spring sunshine, and remembered occasions when it was otherwise. And it felt equally strange to be there alone; Harris was at *Wasp* attending one of the SO's regular briefings. They were still several days from returning to active service, so he had no need to be there and normally would have used any excuse to miss a lecture from Johnston. But that morning even the prospect of inspecting a repaired *194* was no distraction; Harris had bustled off and even appeared keen at the prospect. All of which only confirmed Anderson's belief that he would never truly know, or understand, his captain.

Yet in some ways he was pleased to work unsupervised. A line of figures was making its way towards the boat; ratings he would shortly organise into working parties. Carter was already below with his precious engines and soon the entire boat would be alive with activity. He glanced down and noticed Jelly on the quay surrounded by a mess of packing cases and shavings.

"New toys, Tel'?" he shouted, leaning over the side.

Jelly looked round and then up, squinting slightly at the bright sunshine.

"Yes, sir. Came in first thing so I thought I'd make an early start."

"Does you credit; are they what you expected?"

"Pretty much; I know the model of receiver well." He indicated the smaller unit with his boot. "It's the naval version of the 1155; this one's made by Plessy but looks the same as what I had last time. And the transmitter's an Admiralty Type 8D, which is just a modified 1154."

Anderson nodded as if he understood. "You'll be alright fitting them yourself?"

Jelly grinned. "I'd prefer to, sir."

"They seem to have made a good job of the W/T office." It was one of the first places Anderson inspected and, though much had been made good, with a new door and fresh paint, the horror discovered on his last visit remained on his mind.

"I've not checked that out yet." Jelly looked mildly uncomfortable, although the conversation was taking place over a long distance, and Anderson supposed he would be distracted by the new equipment.

"Give a shout if you need a hand getting anything on board."

"Thank you, sir. I'll clear up this mess shortly, there's still a bit more to unpack."

Anderson gave a wave before turning his attention back to his own work. The previous anchor had been a CQR and he saw no reason to change; likewise, he would be more than happy with the standard issue life raft. However, their galley equipment might need looking at: if they were to undertake any more deepwater cruising, they definitely needed a larger stove.

And so he gradually immersed himself into the life of the boat; something he found relatively easy as it was known to him and, to some extent, under his control. Only later, much later, did his mind wander and he began to think of Eve once more.

271

Yet again, Gibson would get away with it, and the knowledge made him swagger slightly as he made his way along the hard. He was amongst the group now heading for *194*, and each had been questioned about the attack outside *Lynx*. The interviews were separate and in private, however, so it was a simple matter to claim he'd spent the evening with his shipmates at the Lion. With no reason to suspect otherwise, the Crushers proved as gullible as any regular police force and lapped it up like the saps they were.

Which was encouraging, he supposed; not that his confidence ever needed boosting. However, Gibson's ambitions had expanded significantly of late so it was interesting to discover what could be done with a confident manner and a few well-told lies. And though he had not exactly profited by his more recent activities – at one point he thought that Wren officer was going to do for him – Gibson had never felt so sure of himself or his abilities. This injection of faith was opening up fresh avenues for future ventures and his mind felt positively alive with ideas for the next project.

The first was one he had considered in the past. War attracted vast sums of money and equipment that was positively screaming to be diverted by someone with a bit of nous and the front to carry it off. His rough costings for the flotilla's equipment came back to him, although there were bound to be other, more lucrative, channels should he care to look for them.

Of course, some might need the help of an accomplice; if it came to it, he would find someone on the inside to give him the necessary gen. A goon later to be silenced, either by intimidation or something more permanent.

But he now knew his activities could also contain an element of personal gratification. Though not financially rewarding, the later crimes were profitable in a different way and definitely worthy of repetition. Even with the last, there'd been a certain satisfaction in manhandling that commissioned lovely.

"Right, Oerlikon gunners will be detailed first." They had arrived and were being formed up on the hard and Anderson, the Jimmy, was addressing them from the boat's prow. "Hog out the mess deck and work your way aft through all the living spaces. Vickers gunners can do the same topside, then we'll see where paint is needed."

That sounded easy enough; Gibson much preferred working with his guns but waving a brush about was no hardship. Besides, he would shortly be getting a new pair of Vickers to play with. And they might be a later model, which should include a modicum of instruction although, even if not, he intended to be around when they were fitted. That way he would get a chance to speak to the armourers and possibly sound out a likely cohort.

He collected a brush from the bin and followed Daly onto the boat. Being a successful criminal required the intelligence to spot opportunities such as this, and sufficient spunk to exploit them to the full. Gibson was fortunate in having a surplus of both.

* * *

Two days saw *194* brought back into shape; on the third Anderson's carefully drawn-up requisitions bore fruit and the first of the stores and replacement equipment arrived. On the Thursday afternoon, *194* was taken to the oiler so by that Friday morning she was ready to begin working up.

Which initially was only intended to check the boat itself although, as their guns were now installed and with armourers available to sight the beasts in, it would have been foolish to miss the opportunity.

Carter and his team had worked hard on the engines, but nothing could replicate running them under pressure and for an extended period, while there were also the new steering linkages to test. Jelly needed to be sure his new wireless sets worked as well at sea as in harbour and other minor snags, such as the port wheelhouse door that proved difficult to open, were identified. In the end *194* spent several hours in the Channel and, when she finally returned, all aboard were tired and, in some cases, mildly seasick. But it was clear the gunboat would soon be a going concern once more.

On the bridge, spirits were especially high; according to Phillips, *194*'s handling was better than ever, and Harris was due to meet up with Laura that night. So when he noticed Brooks, the base captain, waiting for them on the quay as they came in, he

273

naturally assumed it to be good news.

"Boat's looking excellent, Bob," Brooks told him when Harris stepped ashore. "I'd say you've done a marvellous job."

"We have to go out again tomorrow for the final run, though the armourers are happy and there are only minimal adjustments to be made."

"Glad to hear it, and then you'll be ready to rejoin Johnston?"

Harris paused. "For now, though I rather hoped you'd have different news for me," he said.

Brooks shook his head. "I'm afraid not, Bob. But your presence at the morning meetings have been noticed; Johnston says you've attended every one, despite not being rostered. It seems you're finally settling in the flotilla."

"That's what I wanted to talk to you about, sir," Harris said. "I understand two more British Powerboat MGBs are pencilled in for delivery."

Brooks grinned. "Not much gets past you, does it?"

"Johnston seemed to think they would be spare boats for his lot, yet with the two already promised, that makes four by the end of April."

They had reached the hard, and Brooks stopped. "And your point is?"

Harris shrugged. "With *194* that'll make five boats, which is surely the basis for a new flotilla..."

The base captain sighed and began to walk again, although his pace was slower and Harris easily caught up. "It doesn't work like that, Bob, as you well know. Johnston's craft have been taking a hell of a battering recently, and frankly it didn't help you swanning off to Falmouth, then coming back with a partly wrecked boat."

"I'm sorry about that, sir..."

"Now there's no need to be like that. You know as well as I do eight is the minimum for a workable flotilla which is where Johnston is at the moment. Take your boat away and he's running short; even with the yard working flat out he'd be lucky to field a reasonable number while a flotilla of five would have no chance at all. We'd be back to where we were at the end of last year, and I really thought we'd moved on from there."

"So had I, sir."

"And might I remind you, builders' estimates aren't always kept? We're at war; anything can go wrong, from parts out to the yard itself being targeted in an air raid. My promise remains the same; once we've a good number of boats here, physically, in Dover, you'll have your flotilla; until then we have to maintain the status quo."

"I see, sir."

"But your change of attitude is definitely encouraging," he paused again. "Tell me, what brought it on?"

"I suppose it was something someone said." Harris shrugged, and Brooks smiled.

"Well, whoever it was, I'd say they deserve a medal."

* * *

Jelly couldn't get out of the W/T office fast enough. The installation had gone perfectly; both sets were on the top line, with every test transmission sent and received without difficulty. The new receiver was even clearer than his previous unit and the bridge repeater also worked well but being in the enclosed space had been hell.

The last time he'd worked in *194*'s wireless room was on the way down to St Nazaire; it had been wrecked since, although that made no difference, and neither did the fact that some poor sop was killed while sitting in his seat. What truly upset him was the similarity to the W/T office aboard *314*, the gunboat he was transferred to, although even that wasn't the entire problem.

Jelly now hated being cooped up in any way – small spaces, packed train compartments, or even crowded rooms – like the pub that night the bell sounded. He simply couldn't take being in the tiny compartment for more than a few minutes while any loud noise was liable to send him into a frenzy. And the sad thing was, cramped spaces and loud noises were common aboard a gunboat.

Having the armourers on board hardly helped. The sighting process meant every gun was well used and, being stationed below, he received no warning. At virtually any moment he might be interrupted by the stark rattle of either Vickers, with one mounted barely inches above his head, while the steady pom-

pom of the Oerlikon brought back memories he would rather forget.

At one point he took refuge in the wheelhouse. It was no safer, but the extra space at least allowed him to breathe, and no one was there to witness the shivering, gasping fool he had become.

There was a positive angle though; at least his personal terrors kept the seasickness at bay. Others could have suffered but, for the first time in ages, his bucket remained empty and he wondered if this signalled a permanent cure. By the time they were rostered for active duty the periods of anxiety may have passed, and he might never be seasick again.

And this wasn't just youthful optimism; Jelly had every reason to believe whatever troubled him would soon be forgotten. For he may even have found a cure, an unconventional one perhaps, but one that worked for him.

He and Annie had met four times since his return from St Nazaire. On the first occasion they walked about the town and Jelly felt immediately safe, despite the risk of air raids and unannounced shelling from the French coast. He found the wide and often deserted streets comforting, although it was her presence that made the greatest difference.

With Annie around it was easy to keep the nervous child that was his other self at bay. Even when they were caught out and forced to spend half the night in a shelter packed with strangers, he survived. Then later, on one of their cliff walks, they watched German bombers dropping their terrible loads on the town below, and he was almost dispassionate.

Of course, they never discussed his problem directly; there was no point – it was starting to fade – *she* was making it go, yet Annie never took credit or revealed she knew. It was a shame he'd let himself down on the first day back at sea, but it was only a minor setback, and as all were concerned with their particular responsibilities, no one noticed.

Tonight, they were due to meet again; she was working an early and would be off at four. Having the armourers on board delayed their return but there should still be time to collect her from the Wrennery after which he intended treating Annie to a proper restaurant meal. He still had much of his unpaid wages from Falmouth and was quite prepared to blow the lot; she was definitely worth it. Of course, the thought of being cooped up so still did not appeal, but with Annie around, Jelly knew he could cope. More than that, they would enjoy themselves and it should mean another barrier broken; one step closer to being normal again.

At least he hoped so.

* * *

Gibson had drawn a blank. The rating who showed him round his new weapons proved far too stupid for anything he had in mind while the officer, a wrinkly old fool, was more interested in retaining their spent cartridges and looked too much like one of the screws in Pentonville for him to approach. Yet he was not downhearted. They were due liberty that night, and he would have several hours to himself. Exactly what kind of mischief could be conjured up on a damp April evening in Dover remained a mystery, although Gibson was catholic in his tastes and always up for a challenge. But of one thing he was certain, he would not be bored.

* * *

"There are a few things in your story we'd like to check," the Regulating Petty Officer announced as he opened the door to the interview room. Jelly was stopped by the Crushers on his way to pick up Annie and they insisted he went with them in their van. That was some time ago and he was already late collecting her.

When questioned before it had been at *Wasp*; this time they took him to another part of town. The building smelled like some sort of hospital, and he'd seen enough of them recently, while the room itself felt far too small and enclosed. The door shut with a solid click that brought a touch of finality.

"Nothing to worry about," the RPO told him. "We're going over every statement and need to speak to those what stand out."

"Stand out?"

"Let's start at the beginning, shall we?"

The last interview was conducted by a rating roughly Jelly's own age; this was a far older man and a warrant officer to boot. He also had an air that almost induced a feeling of guilt.

"So, you were drinking in a pub with your mates. Then felt a bit queer, an' left early." he checked.

"That's right. I needed some fresh air."

The officer licked his pencil before making a note and Jelly moved uncomfortably on one of the iron chairs. Apart from them, and the table that held several files of papers, it was a bare room while the peeling lino did nothing to make it feel homely.

"Look what's all this about? I haven't done anything."

The petty officer was probably a veteran of a previous war and in no hurry. "That's for me to decide," he said. "And what time did you leave?"

Jelly thought. Until then, his chief memory of that evening was being spooked by the unexpectedly loud bell, though that could hardly be of interest to the Crushers.

"Alf had just called last orders," he said.

"He would be the landlord, I'm thinking." The man wrote slowly. "Therefore it must have been approaching ten-thirty."

"Yes."

"And your lot had been in the pub," he looked at his notes. "The Red Lion, since when?"

"Most were there all evening, but I'd only just arrived."

"That's what we thought and why we called you in a second time." The older man gave a knowing smile and wrote again. "Only. Just. Arrived."

"I'd been travelling from Falmouth." Jelly was starting to feel the first signs of an attack. His breathing became shallow and there was sweat on his palms. "I came in on the London train, from there I reported to *Wasp* and dumped my stuff then went to the Lion."

"We can check what time you reported in," the man reminded him.

Jelly drew a quick breath. "Fine."

"And once you met up with your pals, what then?"

"I had a pint, and then didn't feel so well." Again, he shifted in his seat and the petty officer made another note.

"In what way?" he asked, and Jelly fidgeted some more.

"It was when the bell rang, it... it made me jump."

"Made you jump?" The man was staring at him now and Jelly shook his head.

"I know how this sounds, but it happens sometimes." It

was close to happening then, though this old man would never understand. "The room was crowded; I'd been travelling all day and the bell just caught me unawares."

"I see." More notes were added, and a faint smile appeared on the petty officer's face. "And do loud noises often catch you like that?"

Jelly stared at the table. "Only since St Nazaire," he said.

The man had been writing but stopped, mid-sentence, and looked up. "You were there?" he asked.

"I was a telegraphist in Commander Ryder's boat."

"Must have been rough." There was a hint of understanding now.

"It's not something I'd like to repeat."

"Shake you up, did it?"

Jelly raised his eyes. "Yes," he said. "It did."

The petty officer was watching carefully, and there may have been a measure of empathy in the elderly eyes.

"Nothing to be ashamed about, son," he said. "Nothing at all." He finished writing. "And after the pub you headed back to *Wasp*?"

"Yes."

"All of you?"

"Yes – no; Gibson was missing." Jelly paused. "He wasn't there the entire time, actually. We only met him on our way back."

"I see." The petty officer reached for one of the files and began to leaf through it while Jelly tried hard to think of open spaces and Annie's face. Eventually the old man looked up.

"You're quite sure this Gibson had not gone to The Red Lion at all that evening?"

"I can't be certain," Jelly said. "I only arrived at the end, but he wasn't there then, and neither was he at the dorm when I called there."

"But you met up afterwards?"

"Yes, we ran into him on our way home. And he was wet."

"Wet?"

"It had been raining earlier."

"I remember; quite a storm. And do you know what this Gibson had been up to while your lot were in the pub?"

Jelly shook his head.

"Was he wearing a hat?"

279

"I'm not sure." He paused. "No, that's right he wasn't; we ribbed him about it."

The symptoms were starting to pass now, Jelly was becoming accustomed to the pattern. But they would be back, and stronger – he knew that as well.

"And you've no idea what he'd been doing?"

"No, you'll have to ask him," Jelly said.

Once more the petty officer fixed him with his eyes, and this time the expression lacked compassion. "Oh, don't you worry, son, we will."

Chapter Twenty-Eight

Eve was expected on the 20.28 from London Victoria, but it was gone nine and still no sign of a train. Anderson silently paced the platform. The rain was easing though it remained uncommonly cold, but at least the earlier bad weather meant they were unlikely to have a raid that night. He inadvertently caught the eye of the porter who gave a wry smile; Anderson had already asked the man twice: there would be no more news.

Then the tracks began to sing, and he grew more hopeful. A train was on its way though whether it would be Eve's was another matter. The sound grew and what had once seemed like a normal cloud turned out to be smoke as the engine drew nearer, finally coming to a halt in a clatter of machinery and hissing steam. The station came alive with heavy doors slamming, shouted greetings, and calls for a porter while the engine muttered and gave out copious quantities of smoke. Anderson looked around in increasing desperation; it must surely be the London train, yet where was Eve? And then, struggling with hat, case, and gas mask, he saw her.

Really there was little difference; if anything, she looked younger, although also more confident. Her lipstick was definitely a shade darker and the longer hair unrestrained. And she was not in uniform which was mildly intriguing; instead, she wore a smart tweed suit under a plain raincoat. But it was the same smile, the same welcoming look in her eyes and, as he held her tight for the first time in ages, the same glorious body.

"You were late," he said. "I was worried."

"I know, and I'm sorry, the train kept stopping and they wouldn't let me drive."

He smiled and took her suitcase and then they were walking arm in arm, shoulder to shoulder, towards the wrought iron gates. An elderly man was taking tickets and Anderson explained he had been meeting a friend.

"Should've had a platform ticket," the attendant told him gruffly, but he glanced at the Naval uniform and nodded Anderson through.

"Grand was full," he told her. "Americans are making it their base it seems, so I've booked you in at the Sea View."

"I'm sure that'll be fine," she said. "But will you be able to visit?"

"I doubt it, the place is run by nuns and they're mostly armed." They'd drawn away from the station entrance now and the street was agreeably quiet. "So come on," he urged. "What's the news?"

"Oh, I see; no 'how are you?', or 'where've you been?'"

"That as well," he said. "Especially the last bit – but you mentioned a transfer..."

"That's right, Y station's been put on hold, I've been recruited somewhere else."

"Recruited?" It was an ominous term. "Where to?"

She paused and turned to him and, even in the poor light, he could see she was smiling. More than that, her eyes were oddly alight.

"SOE," she said. "Only you mustn't say a word – it's all terribly hush-hush."

* * *

Even without a raid the blackout remained as tightly enforced so their table by the window had lost much of its charm. But Laura was definitely in a brighter mood and Harris, buoyed by a successful first sea trial, felt uncommonly genial.

"So, will you have to go out again?" she asked when he had related the day's events.

"We've still a few loose ends to tie up," he told her. "But it could have been so much worse. I reckon this time tomorrow *194*'ll be fit to be rostered."

"And you'll be back under Johnston's thumb?" She smiled and he knew she was teasing.

"Did I make it sound that bad?"

"Pretty much."

"Well, it won't be for much longer."

"You've spoken to Brooks then?"

"Let's just say we've come to an understanding."

Someone else was entering the dining room and Harris

282

looked up in mild interest. And then he froze.

"Bob, whatever is it?"

He glanced away. "Nothing, nothing really."

"But you're behaving like someone's trodden on your grave, I say, it isn't Bubbles again?"

"No, nothing like." He gave a sheepish smile. "A crew member, actually, and one of the best. Only I hadn't expected to see him in a place like this."

* * *

Jelly was equally surprised. The Grand might not have a top-class restaurant – such things being rare outside of London – even the few that remained lacked their pre-war glory. However, it was the most expensive place to dine out in Dover, and Jelly had so wanted to give Annie a treat. Even ignoring the letter that kept him sane, her constant support made such a difference to him. And selfishly he had thought the hotel's exclusivity would guarantee a quiet meal, although that was not to be.

Apart from the smoke coming from cigars, rather than Woodbines, the scene might have been from any one of several Dover eateries. And though the combined talk from maybe a dozen full tables was slightly more refined, the room was as loud as any NAAFI. He glanced at Annie.

"I think this might have been a mistake," he said.

"A mistake?" She seemed surprised, and then her look changed to one of concern. "You're alright, Dave?"

"I'm fine," he said. The waiter was making for a table. One appeared free next to a curtained window which looked quiet enough; with his back to the wall Jelly could face the room – something he'd learned was a definite advantage. And then he noticed his captain, Lieutenant Commander Harris, sitting about ten feet away.

Annie only realised he was no longer following after several steps. She turned and was about to go back when Harris himself caught Jelly's eye and, of all things, smiled.

Suddenly the skipper was walking towards him, his hand held out in welcome.

283

"Hello Tel'," he said. "Didn't expect to see you here; are you on your own?"

Jelly clumsily indicated Annie, who had abandoned the waiter.

"This is Ann," he said.

Harris turned, smiled, and then held out the hand once more. "And I'm Bob, Bob Harris; delighted to meet you." Jelly noticed Annie blush slightly. "I'd ask you to join us, but we have just the small table – as do you, I see!"

The waiter was actually standing by Jelly's with a look of mild annoyance.

"Yes, sir." He was feeling the first signs of another attack. The room was starting to spin and his palms were becoming wet.

"Well, it's good to see you both," Harris said. "Enjoy your meal."

Jelly made his way through the mist and found his chair then, when properly seated, began to feel better.

"You're really alright?" Annie checked.

"Yes, yes, I'm fine," he said. "Just a surprise that's all." Glancing across he could see the skipper was back at his own table and talking animatedly to a Wren officer.

"Was that your captain?" she asked.

He blushed. "Yes, I'm sorry I should have introduced you properly."

"That's fine, I think he gathered you were embarrassed." She smiled and rested a hand on his arm. "And who wouldn't be in your place? But I reckon he's a nice man, and understood."

Jelly was about to reply when the sound of a bell broke into the hubbub of diners. "Ladies and gentlemen, if I could just have your attention." The hotel manager had entered and was holding a small sheet of paper. "There's been a message from the Naval Base, HMS *Wasp*. All seagoing personnel are to report without delay."

The silence continued for several seconds, then the first man rose, and soon he and three more were heading for the door. Jelly looked at Annie with an expression void of hope.

"I'm so sorry," he said.

"That's alright, you go – I'll be fine."

"Tel'?" Now the skipper was standing over their table. "Looks like we're needed at the boat; shall we share a cab?"

"V-very good, sir." He stood, then noticed the Wren officer had also joined them.

"But there's no need for us to miss out on a meal," she told Annie. "What say we keep each other company. Ann, isn't it?"

* * *

"SOE? That's Special Operations Executive?" Anderson checked. "Dalton's bunny."

"Got it in one: 'Set Europe Ablaze' and all that."

Eve began to walk again and, after a moment he followed.

"But it's secret agent stuff," he said, catching up, "spying and sabotage…"

"So I've been led to believe…" She seemed to be taking this very lightly and Anderson was mildly horrified.

"But that's not like you," he began. "I mean, what happened to your pacifist stance?"

"Ian, I've been in the Wrens for over a year!"

"Yes, but on the welfare side. And Y Station; that would hardly have been combat."

"It was vaguely connected," she said. "Besides, SOE isn't all espionage and bombing, least, not where I'll be going."

"You mean you're not being sent abroad – to enemy territory?"

She laughed. "Not at all. At least, not for a very long time, though they are starting to send women agents now."

They were nearing her hotel and, despite its relaxed policy, gentlemen callers would hardly be welcomed at this hour. Yet Anderson was desperate for the conversation to continue.

"So, it's a possibility?"

"I'm being trained for the London office," she said. "It's complicated stuff but so necessary, and perfectly safe I assure you."

"It doesn't sound it," he said. "Safe, I mean."

"Well, it is – initially, and probably forever. It's mostly clerical anyway. Oh, and I'm learning French, to go with my German."

"And then what? You'll be looking after agents?"

"Something like that," she said.

"And staying in England?"

"Usually, though a few of us are embedded abroad."

Embedded. It was not a word he liked.

"Look, Ian, nothing's going to happen for a while. I've got a heck of a lot more training to do. Besides, they've started me off in F-Section; there're plenty there who know a darn sight more about France than I do."

"I'm sure. It's just not what I thought."

"I'm very glad to hear it," she said. "The last thing I need is anyone suspecting I'm mixed up with such a crowd. Actually, you're the only one on the outside that knows. Not even my family – not even my brother, Billy."

"I'll keep my mouth shut, but wish you'd said something before..."

"So you could have talked me out of it?"

"Yes – No!" He shook his head. "Oh, I don't know what to think, it's all so sudden."

"We have five days," she said. "Plenty of time for walks, and talks, and explanations. Maybe after that you'll feel better?"

"Maybe," he said and was about to add more when he heard the sound of running footsteps. The blackout encouraged petty crime and, remembering the recent spate of attacks, Anderson wrapped a protective arm about Eve as two men approached.

"Number One, is that you?" Though breathless, it was a voice he knew well. "There's a general call, we're needed at the boat."

"The boat?" Anderson noticed the second man was Jelly. Why *194*'s telegraphist should be with the captain at this time of night was a mystery and, on top of Eve's news, his brain felt close to capacity.

"Yes, the boat. There isn't a cab to be had, we have to move."

Anderson looked to Eve. "I'm sorry," he said, and she smiled.

"That's fine, I can see my way from here. But are you going into action?"

"I should think so."

And then the smile turned into a grin. "Well just make sure you stay safe," she said.

* * *

"It would be nice to know what's going on," Harris grumbled.

On reaching *Wasp*, Jelly had been sent straight to the boat while he and Anderson were directed to the briefing room. There they met with other officers from their flotilla as well as some Harris only vaguely recognised. Most were in uniform although Hopgood wore a sports coat and another, one of those unknown to him, was resplendent in white trousers and a cricketing jumper.

"All set, Bob?"

He turned to see Johnston behind him.

"Fine, but what's all this about?"

Johnston gave a quick smile. "You'll know all shortly, but Brookie says *194*'s ready for sea – is that correct?"

"Pretty much."

"Excellent, then she'll be included. Hold on, I think I'm wanted."

While they were talking Commander Brooks, the base captain, had entered along with an unknown lieutenant. Johnston joined them at the back of the room.

"Gentlemen, gentlemen please." Brooks tapped at the table with his knuckles. "If you would kindly take seats, we'll get this over as soon as possible."

"Due back at the club, sir," the cricketer called out. "We've an important match Sunday."

"You'll have to practise later, Belcher," the lieutenant told him. "We've a job on – an important one."

The words were quickly absorbed and suddenly there was silence. Brooks cleared his throat.

"I'm sorry to drag you away like this," he said. "First of all, I'd better introduce Sam Rooke to those who don't know him. Sam's just taken over Cooper's MTBs. We had thought the only activity tonight would be a spot of minelayer protection that Buster Johnston's lot are taking care of. I believe your lads have been stood down; is that right, Sam?"

Rooke nodded. "I wasn't supposed to assume command until the day after tomorrow, sir, but this came up and I said we'd do it."

"Well, let's get on," Brooks said. "The sooner we're out, the sooner we get back." He turned to the large scale map of the

Eastern Channel that was a permanent fixture on the briefing room's wall.

"We've just heard a relatively large convoy has left France and is heading north. Right now we expect them to be about here." He tapped the board with a wooden pointer. "No idea why Jerry's left it so late, one of their number might have problems, or they could simply be hoping to catch us unawares. Weather's clear at the moment, though it's expected to deteriorate again later; which might also be on their mind. But whatever the reason, we want to nab them."

There was a murmur from the collected officers, although Brooks did not linger.

"Providing we leave without delay that should be possible, though it'll mean a high-speed run out and we might end up only catching their tails. In which case you could be recalled," he continued. "But a four-merchant convoy's a prime target, and I think we should have a bash – don't you?"

There was more general agreement, and then Johnston spoke.

"Three of my lads are still out on minelayer escort, which is why I've called the rest of you here," he said, nodding towards Harris and his other commanding officers. "Providing everyone lights up successfully we'll be fielding five gunboats, which is a reasonable number in the circumstances. Those ratings given liberty have been recalled; with luck, they'll have been in the building, or Dover itself. If there're any major deficiencies we can jiggle a few about, but let's hope not."

Hopgood had his hand raised and Johnston turned to him. "What is it, Happy?"

"You say it's a four-merchant convoy, sir; what do we know of the escorts?"

"Very little I'm afraid. We weren't aware any ships were due to sail; our last aerial reconnaissance only showed two colliers in Boulogne. But the RDF's definitely picking up four vessels and, from their speed and placement, they do appear to be merchants. Escorts are ten in number and grouped to cover all angles, though naturally biased towards the west. If we move quick, it might be possible to sneak ahead and position our MTBs between them and the enemy coast."

"Which makes it important that everyone heads straight

for the Camber and assembles their crews without delay." Brooks had taken over again. "Report any deficiencies as soon as they become apparent. I'm banking on all putting out within forty-five minutes, which doesn't leave much time." He glanced around the room. "Very well gentlemen, you are dismissed."

Chapter Twenty-Nine

They were particularly lucky, or so it seemed. Most of *194*'s ratings had been watching a show at the Hippodrome when the knife-throwing act was interrupted by the order to return. With much of the audience comprising Coastal Forces personnel, a general exodus ensued leaving confused performers facing an all-but-empty auditorium.

Phillips and Carter were drinking in the Red Lion when a shore patrol found them, and Newman was planning an early night with a booklet on the Dumbflow silencer. Gibson was the last to arrive, but the general call even interrupted his evening and he came swaggering down to the boat then launched himself aboard amid a chorus of ironic cheers.

Once her engines were warm, and after Jelly reported *194*'s readiness, there followed several minutes of waiting while others finished their preparations. And when the signal to leave finally came not everyone was ready. The torpedo boats fired up successfully as did Hopgood's and Brentwood's MGBs, but Johnston's starboard wing engine proved difficult to start while Bell's gunboat had a faulty transmitter and lacked her Oerlikon crew.

"You're going to have to lead, Bobbo!"

Harris grinned when Johnston's words came over the bridge repeater; never had he minded less about the nickname.

"My CMM thinks the problems'll be solved shortly," Johnston continued, "so I'll be right behind. But for now, you're the flotilla SO and have charge of the op."

Johnston had been speaking over R/T, meaning all in the flotilla would hear, and sparing Harris the need to announce his authority. He turned to Anderson.

"Very good, Number One, take us out."

194 was already singled down to two wires, these were cast off and she led the small yet deadly force to sea. Even at such an hour there were onlookers on the harbour wall and Anderson gave a hearty wave. A little over an hour before he had left Eve outside

290

her hotel and, as he realised this, he also remembered her news.

It would take him some time to accept such a bombshell, although they had five days to fully discuss matters; five days for her to explain exactly what her transfer entailed and, he hoped, five days for him to persuade her otherwise. But what seemed more important, they would spend the time together, which was what Anderson focused on as *194* broached the open sea. And for that reason alone, he could not wait to return.

* * *

They were still far enough from any enemy for the radio telephone to be relatively safe though, even if not, Harris felt it important to address his force. He leant towards the W/T office speaking tube.

"Patch me through to the others on R/T, will you Tel'?"

Jelly's acknowledgement was lost but a loud click came from the bridge repeater and Harris picked up the handset.

"Good evening, gentlemen; it seems I'm your senior officer for the night." He flashed a quick smile at Anderson.

"I probably won't deviate too much from flotilla standing orders, but frankly won't mind if you do. We'll be intercepting a large convoy that's well escorted, and few rules cover such a situation. The gunboats' aim should be to separate escorts from their charges, so allowing the torpedo boys to do their work. Once we get a better idea of where Jerry's hiding, I'll ask Lieutenant Rooke to take his MTBs off independently. But even if not, you are all experienced and don't need a nursemaid. Good luck to us all, and anyone sinking a German buys a round."

He replaced the receiver and glanced at Anderson again.

"How did I do, Number One?"

"I'd say that was pretty near perfect, sir."

"Glad to hear it," Harris said. "I must be learning."

* * *

Jelly turned off the bridge repeater. With luck, and his captain in charge of the flotilla, the R/T would not be needed again for some while. The deck beneath him vibrated; Carter and his men must be increasing revolutions, which was usual after leaving harbour. But this was no gentle rise to a brisk cruising speed, *194* was hammering through what must be a sizeable chop at close to maximum revs. He had already messaged Dover Command with their departure time and course; until anything else happened there was little for him to do. He glanced at his watch; not long ago he had been horrified to see the skipper dining at the same restaurant. But the old man proved a perfect gent and later they'd run through Dover's damp streets together like a couple of lads.

Jelly smiled at the memory. In fact, as he sat back in his chair, he was feeling altogether more comfortable. The horrors of St Nazaire were finally starting to fade; replaced – permanently he hoped – by far more pleasant images of a loving partner and supportive shipmates.

The boat began to buck wildly; he may need his bucket before long. But that was usual, expected, and nothing like the terrors of the nightmare train journey or what had come after. With Annie by his side and a well-led, well-crewed boat to be a part of, he might do anything and, as a message came through from Dover Command – one probably containing the latest position of that night's target – he was ready for it.

* * *

"I said, were you dining with Jelly?"

Phillips was close by at the helm, but *194* must have been travelling at over thirty-five knots and if Harris could barely hear, Anderson didn't think the coxswain would.

"He was at another table." Harris' teeth showed white in the poor light. "With a charming girl."

Anderson nodded; this might not be the time or place for a conversation, but it was good to see his captain so relaxed. Not long ago Harris would have been incensed to discover a general rating with the temerity to book the same restaurant.

There was a faint whistle from a speaking tube and Anderson bent forward to answer it.

"Tel' reports Johnston's finally left harbour," he said.

"Very good." Harris' reply was automatic. "That'd make him some way behind us," he added.

"A good twenty minutes."

"And when will we be running in with Jerry?"

Anderson pointed over their starboard bow. "They should be about a mile over the horizon."

The French coast was coming into sight; whoever had charge of the convoy must be hugging it tight.

"This is where Johnston's radar would be useful."

That was certainly the case; even one RDF set amongst the eight boats would have been a godsend.

Anderson looked to where the MTBs were keeping tight station on their port beam. Each carried two, twenty-one-inch MkVIII torpedoes. With Harris in command, Anderson reckoned at least one of the merchants would be sunk. He knew all about Brooks' promises, as he did the new boats due to be delivered. Yes, Johnston needed additional craft, but the supply of MGBs was increasing all the time. Even ignoring what they'd been through at St Nazaire, a successful operation tonight should see Harris resuming his rightful place as a flotilla SO.

And the next intake was likely to include new models; great things were being said about British Powerboat's new MkVs – over seventy feet in length and with a decent forward-facing gun. A flotilla of such craft with Harris at the head would be truly formidable.

He glanced across to where the MTBs were travelling just as fast. Anderson knew little about the new man that led them. Though a straight striper, and presumably experienced, this was Lieutenant Rooke's first operation from *Wasp*. But whether he turned out good or bad, Harris outranked him; *194* would be the lead boat for as long as Johnston remained out of the picture.

Harris should soon be able to order Rooke to position his MTBs between the convoy's projected course and the enemy coast. This would enable an attack from the east, which was always the favoured option. Before then, *194* and her fellow gunboats must draw the enemy escort's fire for long enough to allow the torpedo boys room. After St Nazaire, such a duty seemed almost pedestrian. They would be facing a superior force, one that was better armed, better crewed and, in some cases, faster, but *194* had been built with just such an enemy in mind. And there would be the chance to hit back, and hit back properly, which is more than could be said about their last operation.

The moon, still relatively new, was starting to rise above

the dark shadow of oncoming land. And the rain had returned which was not ideal, though they were used to worse. Eve should be safe in her hotel room; tomorrow they could talk, tomorrow she could tell him all about her new venture. But tonight, Anderson had only one aim, and that was for *194* to really prove her worth.

* * *

Jelly finished sending the captain's orders to Lieutenant Rooke and returned the set to standby. The message went by Morse on the W/T – a method he thoroughly approved of and, depending on the conditions up top, probably more secret than an Aldis.

He turned to the receiver and brought up the volume. There had been no reporting of the target that he was aware of, but the previous signal from Dover Command put the enemy convoy nearby; at their current speed they should be in contact within a matter of minutes.

Meanwhile, in *194*'s turrets, Daly and Gibson were scanning the horizon for the first sign of the enemy. Daly had served with Harris when he led his own flotilla. That his captain was back in overall charge now – albeit temporarily – was a good thing to his mind and privately he was looking forward to the night's activities.

And Gibson was equally eager, even though being summoned back to base disrupted a lucrative evening. The frustration of getting nowhere with the armourers, along with his personal need for action, had made him slightly rash. After surveying several areas of Dover, the house he eventually burgled turned out to be on the same road as the one where the young girl surprised him and, though there were no additional benefits this time, he'd come out over forty pounds the richer. And it was in banknotes, stashed amateurishly between bed and mattress.

The money was with him at that moment, there being no time to hide it. On leaving the house he ran straight into a shore patrol and anything other than obeying their instructions would have been suspicious. He pressed at the tight wad resting between his vest and the canvas of his Ursula. Tonight's mission was only a convoy interception. Chances were they would come out in one piece, and there was no reason why he shouldn't start making plans now.

294

For such a pile must be treated with care; it would buy him a great deal although any sudden riches could equally bring unwanted attention; perhaps a more subtle use was in order? The prospect of pulling off a truly major job on Government goods was still very much on his mind, and forty quid would turn more than a few heads as well as shutting a lot of mouths.

And before then he could expect a modicum of excitement. He and Daly had new weapons and were eager to use them although, in Gibson's case, the actual target hardly mattered. Killing was killing as far as he was concerned; should the enemy come his way they would be dealt with, but he could gain as much satisfaction from shooting up a flock of seagulls.

* * *

"Shouldn't be long now..."

Anderson spoke slowly and mainly to himself; Harris had ordered a slight reduction in speed several minutes before, yet the engines were still running in the low twenty hundreds and conversation soon became tiring. But Harris heard and gave a nod of agreement.

The French coast lay close by; either the enemy would appear shortly, or they had turned back, and Dover Command would have advised were that the case. There was now no sign of Rooke and his torpedo boats; presumably they were somewhere off *194*'s port bow and it was significant that they hadn't reported running into the convoy. The slight moon was almost clear of land, but it was raining more heavily, and Anderson donned his steel helmet purely for its weather-keeping qualities. He wondered vaguely what conditions would be like for Eve, in Dover.

"Well, would you be looking at that?"

Anderson jerked himself back to the present; it was Daly in the starboard turret, and immediately the Irishman corrected himself.

"Vessels in sight bearing green fifteen."

Anderson turned in that direction and Harris raised his glasses. Nothing. And then slowly, as if revealed by some stage magician's trick, a line of shipping could be made out making silent progress off their starboard bow. A couple of small vessels lay close to, and would probably turn out to be escorts, but further back, and barely visible through the rain, were four well-laden merchants.

"That's them," Harris said.

"And they appear to be colliers," Anderson added. It was not unknown for a squadron of warships to limit their speed in an attempt to pass off as freighters.

"Report them, Number One; I'll see the rest of our lads know by Aldis."

Dover Command would require an accurate position as well as an approximation of the enemy's speed and course; Anderson turned to go. Then, just as he was about to lower himself down the bridge ladder, he stopped. "What about the MTBs?" he asked.

Harris considered for a moment. "They'll pick up on our W/T to base."

Yes, that made sense, and Anderson continued to the wheelhouse.

* * *

Which was dark, all shutters being firmly closed; only the lamp from his chart table gave the place an eery red glow. He headed straight for the plot; their position had been calculated fifteen minutes before, it took no time to allow for the reduction in speed and make a likely estimate for the enemy. A quick note on his pad, then he tore off the sheet and headed for the W/T office.

As he went, Anderson couldn't help remembering a similar trip to the wireless room when he'd encountered a scene worthy of Dante. The door had been shut then as well and he paused for a moment before opening it. But this time there was no bloodstained body or smouldering wireless sets, although what he did see shocked him almost as much.

Jelly was slumped on the deck and for a moment Anderson thought he might be seasick. But the bucket was nowhere in sight, while the man himself lay crouched like a ball half under the desk. Both hands were wrapped tightly about his legs, and he was pressing his face down on the raised knees.

"Tel'? Whatever's the matter?"

There was no answer, though Anderson hardly expected

296

one. He had no idea what unearthly power controlled the young man, but it was too strong to allow speech – he'd be surprised if Jelly could even breathe.

Anderson placed a hand on the telegraphist's shoulder; it was rigid, yet also shaking slightly; the boy was crying.

"Tel', we have to send a message to Dover Command," he said. "And we have to send it now. Come on, man, pull yourself together; this is important. You can't let us down."

Chapter Thirty

Harris was content. They'd made excellent speed on the way out – so much so that, rather than having to play catch-up, the convoy was perfectly located off their starboard bow. And if the new fellow, Rooke, was any good, the MTBs should be in an equally prime position. The next step was for his own force – and for the time being it really *was* his own force – to create a diversion off the western flank. A concerted attack by three well-handled gunboats would put the shakes on any enemy, especially one hoping to get by scot-free. Drawing their attention and fire need not be arduous and once Rooke's torpedo boys did their stuff they could all hightail it for home.

He had no idea what was taking Anderson so long below; surely reporting a contact and passing on its location was a simple matter? For a moment he considered raising the W/T office on the blower, but Anderson and Jelly were sound men. Nothing he said would make them work faster, or harder, and may slow them down. He smiled to himself; at the start of the war he would never have thought in that way, but then much of his upbringing and training ignored factors like expecting initiative in others; trusting junior men to work without supervision was very much against the grain. A lot had happened since, and he'd learned a good deal along the way.

If this operation was successful, it could not be long before he was back in permanent charge of a flotilla. And this time he'd make a better fist of it.

* * *

Anderson was having problems; he could not heave Jelly's dead weight from under the desk. He considered calling for help; Gibson or Daly could be summoned quickly enough although an extra pair of hands would have been all but useless in the cramped space. Besides, Anderson had no wish for others to see their shipmate in his current state.

"Come on, man; get yourself up!"

His back ached, but Jelly's body might have been glued down. He stood up, then slapped the back of the rating's head. The blow was light and driven by frustration; Anderson regretted it immediately, although there was some effect. A deep guttural moan came from the hunched figure and then, miraculously, Jelly turned towards him.

Anderson watched in horror. The face was flushed and swollen; dark holes peered unseeing amid a sea of tears and the mouth, though barely open, gave that same low and regular groan.

"Tel' – you must listen to me!"

The head turned further and Anderson sensed Jelly's pain.

"We have to signal Dover Command," he persisted. "Tell them, and Rooke's lot, the enemy's location, course, and speed. And we have to do it now!"

"Signal?"

It was a word at least, and Anderson seized upon it.

"Yes, signal, Tel'. Make a signal. Dover Command – 'enemy convoy in sight' – you know the score."

The moaning stopped and there was no further verbal response, but Jelly did at least begin to rise. Anderson reached for the piece of paper, and it was all he could do to stop himself from thrusting it under the rating's nose.

Finally Jelly perched himself on the end of the seat, before reaching for his headphones and turning to the transmitter. And then the movements became more fluid; a steadier hand clicked at a switch while the other felt for the Morse key. Anderson gently laid the paper down and Jelly looked at it for no more than a second. And then his finger began to tap.

It was fast, though measured. At one point Jelly paused, and seemed to be listening, then tapped some more. Finally, it must have been done, and he leaned back on his chair.

"I'm sorry, sir, truly sorry."

Anderson could think of nothing to say.

"It's the space, you see; being cooped up so." Jelly paused and considered this. "And crowds. And noise." He shook his head. "I'm finished, I just can't handle them no more."

"Very well, we'll see you get help." The boy was sobbing quietly now but Anderson felt he could be left. "I'll try and check back later."

There was a nod, and Anderson was about to go when he saw Jelly turn.

"Could you leave the door open?" he asked.

* * *

Daly was proud to have been first to sight the convoy and sensed the faint mass to starboard, also just reported, would be an enemy VP. The skipper was yet to increase speed; as soon as he did it should attract more escorts and then they would really see some action.

He swung his Vickers back and forth in anticipation. New guns on a new mount, and all as smooth as silk. Being to starboard meant he might not have much of a target at first, but he knew Harris of old; the skipper was not one for a hit and run and always gave his gunners a good go.

* * *

"About time, Number One." Though pleased to see Anderson, Harris was still too old school to recognise the fact. "Did you get an acknowledgement?"

"From Dover," Anderson said.

"Well, I wouldn't expect Rooke to reply," Harris snapped. "Daly thinks he can make out further escorts to starboard, so it looks like we've got the head."

Which was good news, so it was strange that Anderson did not respond.

"Jerry's made no movement, and we've not been seen, so I'm keeping the speed down."

Still no answer from Anderson.

"Give it a while longer; if we remain unnoticed I'll lead the lads to starboard, and we can make a fuss along their western column."

"Very good, sir."

"I don't suppose there's been further news from Johnston?" If the man was close by it would be nice to know.

"Nothing, sir."

300

Harris considered his second in command a little more carefully and then drew breath. "Whatever's happened, Number One?" he asked. "You look like you've seen a ghost."

* * *

Ten minutes later and Daly could no longer see the convoy, although that would not last; things were definitely hotting up. The skipper had made the expected turn to starboard some while before and then stepped up to full throttle. Now *194* led a broken line of fast-moving gunboats as they bore down on the enemy. The increased speed created a towering wake behind each boat; if the Germans missed that, along with the scream of nine supercharged Packards, they really shouldn't be fighting a war.

In the opposite turret, Gibson would be in a far better position to see. Daly glanced across and noticed his oppo's guns were already level as he waited for his chance. That would come soon enough although the Irishman doubted much would be made of it. All mouth, that one, and too inclined to take the lead without the sense to carry it off. His thoughts ran back to the first time they served together when Gibson almost ruined everything by opening up on that E-boat. Shipmate or not, Daly had never taken to the man and neither did he trust him.

Looking aft he could see Smith and Godliman. They were far more businesslike and, considering the acute angle at which *194* was closing, should get a crack at the enemy. Exactly what they would all be facing was another matter, though. German escorts also carried Oerlikons, as well as other, heavier weapons, yet the larger pieces did not worry the Irishman unduly. He was an experienced gunner and had long since proved what a pair of half-inch Vickers could do. Besides, pretty much anything the Germans mounted could sink *194* but only if they caught her, and Daly was quietly confident they would not.

* * *

Anderson felt the first escort was almost in range and, as if to prove the point, several streams of green began flowing towards them. The enemy was a VP, and her shots fell short of their port beam, or appeared to; tracer was not always a perfect indicator.

But no hits registered aboard *194*, and neither did she reply, although Harris' hand was ever hovering over the firing gongs.

He knew exactly what his captain was doing and equally that he was doing it well. When three gunboats attacked a convoy protected by ten escorts, all of which were likely to be better armed and better protected, there was little point in wasting ammunition. Any advantage gained from a lucky hit would be more than outweighed by their own tracer making themselves an easier target. If Harris could distract the escorts long enough to let the torpedo boats have their say, they would still end victorious.

"Another coming up," Anderson warned. "Almost straight ahead."

"Starboard ten."

"Starboard ten, sir!"

"Meet her, midships."

"Midships, sir!"

The oncoming vessel was another armed trawler, but this time the range was shorter and, despite their recent change of course, it would be less easy to dodge. Harris must decide whether to steer further to starboard and maybe entice the escort from the barely visible merchants or turn across her bows. Anderson could not tell what his captain intended and wondered if even he knew.

194 was heading marginally away from the convoy now. He glanced back; Hopgood, in the following boat, had mirrored their course so far, but their temporary SO's liking for initiative was firmly established. Sure enough, on coming across the second escort, Hopgood steered to port, clearly intending to head the enemy off.

"Port fifteen," Harris ordered.

"Port fifteen, sir!"

"Midships."

"Midships, sir."

Now *194* was heading back for the same enemy just as Hopgood's boat slipped in front of her prow, delivering a barrage of red tracer as she went. There was return fire, but the gunboat was fast and *194* would soon provide a further distraction.

Harris finally hit the firing gongs; bells began to ring throughout the boat and a barrage from Gibson's Vickers quickly followed. With Hopgood still firing on the enemy's starboard bow, the threat to her stern must have come as a shock and one that quickly increased when Smith opened up with the Oerlikon.

The gunners were given their heads for less than ten seconds, then Harris ordered them still and *194* to starboard once more. They may have caused damage, although VPs were notoriously well protected. But if the escort, and maybe some of her sisters, could be enticed away from the merchants it would be enough.

"Bring her back to eighteen hundred."

"Eighteen hundred, sir!"

Again, Anderson fully approved. The change was not great; *194* would still be travelling fast but a slight reduction in speed might induce the enemy to follow. It was not to be, however, even as they raced away from the convoy a new shape appeared almost directly ahead.

"Enemy fine on the port bow!" Gibson's voice rose above that of the engines although all on the bridge had already noticed the E-boat.

"Port ten, increase to maximum revs."

Anderson continued to analyse the situation. This must be an outlying escort they'd missed when closing with the convoy. Now very much in touch and heading to cut them off, it also effectively blocked their means of escape.

Faced with an opponent so placed, a less experienced captain might have turned further to starboard and tried for safety. Doing so would bring them across the enemy's bows; usually a prime position in any close action. However, it would also take them dangerously near to the faster craft; even at her maximum speed, *194* would be caught in no time and destroyed for sure. By turning to port, Harris was choosing a reciprocal course; to give chase the E-boat must make a full one-eighty turn, which would buy them a considerable amount of time.

Again, the firing gongs, and this time Daly's Vickers spoke first, sweeping the German craft with a generous dose of tracer. Several streams of green came in return, although all fell wide. Then, once more, Smith was able to bring his Oerlikon into play.

By that point the danger was almost passed. The E-boat had not deviated from her course and the two vessels separated quickly; within a minute she was fading into the night.

"Hard port rudder!"

Anderson knew Harris had no intention of closing further

with that particular opponent, but neither did he wish to leave the convoy behind, which was becoming a definite possibility. *194* heeled to starboard as she was thrown into the turn and, caught unawares, Anderson fell sideways, smacking his right arm against the side of the bridge. Despite her apparent mishandling, the gunboat recovered quickly. Righting himself, and rubbing vigorously at the sore spot, Anderson looked forward once more.

The E-boat had apparently vanished but that was no surprise. Despite a rising moon, the night remained dark; both vessels had also been travelling at speed while the rain was continuing to fall in sheets. The two VPs must remain in the area though, as well as Hopgood's and Brentwood's boats.

"Midships. And reduce to twelve hundred."

Now *194* was heading for the centre of the convoy and, though barely on the plane, still moving relatively fast. A merchant came into sight and Anderson decided this must be the back marker – certainly no other vessels were visible astern of her. And then a bright light erupted off their port bow, spewing flames and debris into the night sky. All on the bridge knew the sight well, and that the explosion had been petrol fuelled.

"Hopgood," Harris grunted, and Anderson could only agree. After leaving *194* in her wake, the E-boat must have fallen on the second gunboat; that or Hopgood had been foolish enough to make a run for home. But he was gone now, and it seemed likely the German lay between them and Brentwood's boat. Anderson had no idea how Harris would play this but was eager to find out.

"Bring her back up, 'Swain."

Once more *194* leapt forward to the sound of her straining engines and soon encountered the sorry wreck of Hopgood's burning craft. Anderson glanced at it briefly; the explosion would probably have killed all below. Some on deck may have been thrown clear though there was no chance of stopping for survivors.

"There's the E!"

It was Gibson, in the port turret. Despite abandoning protocol, he was right: the E-boat's stern lay off their port bow.

At that moment Anderson would have paid handsomely for a decent forward-facing gun, but the only weapon that could reach was their half-inch Vickers. At least *194* was approaching unnoticed and the enemy's aft armament – usually a pair of 37mm flak cannon – remained silent. Once more, Harris' hand was close to the gun control but went no further; for as long as they were being ignored it would be a mistake to open fire and invite trouble.

The E-boat was travelling fast, though not at her top speed and *194* continued to gain. To starboard, Anderson could see they were closing on the sternmost merchant and still there was no evidence of Rooke's boats making an attack. No sign of Brentwood's gunboat either. And then he spotted another VP.

"Enemy trawler on the starboard bow!"

It was Daly, but he had only anticipated Anderson by a split second. At their current speed, the German would soon be on their beam and must be one they engaged earlier. Once more Anderson looked to Harris.

"Starboard twenty."

Another sharp turn; they would be heading for the convoy's centre but further from the E-boat; Rooke's torpedoes must surely start striking soon.

"Midships."

Now they were crossing the stern of the VP which proved more alert. Tracer was already reaching out for them, and Anderson silently cursed as several shells dug deep into *194*'s foredeck. The firing gongs rang out; Gibson and Smith set to work and soon the Oerlikon began scoring hits on the enemy's superstructure.

He looked forward and towards the nearest merchant; she mounted a cannon aft that began peppering the dark waters with random shots. The next trader was keeping station about half a mile ahead; Anderson could just make her out. Beyond that he could see nothing, although a torpedo strike on any vessel would surely have been noticed; exactly what was Rooke playing at?

* * *

Gibson had only a vague interest in the British torpedo boats and what they might achieve; he was far too engrossed in his own private war. The new Vickers were proving to be excellent guns; far smoother than his old pair and a darned sight easier to load. Currently, he had a prime target in his sights, and it was relatively simple to keep a steady bead while the weapons did their work. And the VP was a spunky little beast, even as he fired, a part of his mind kept track of the green fizzing shells passing overhead and occasionally creeping too close.

It was hard – impossible – to tell what damage his own guns were doing but there was evidence of something larger also striking the enemy and starting what might be a small fire. That would be from Laurel and Hardy aft, and good luck to them; bigger guns fired heavier shells; Gibson was content with what he'd been given. Deep inside his Ursula he could feel the wad of notes; useful fodder for what he had in mind, but that was in the future. For now, he was being paid to fire at distant enemies; folk he'd never met nor ever would. But satisfying targets, nonetheless.

* * *

Smith and Godliman were also working hard. This was the first time they had been in action since St Nazaire and, though the gun was a new one, recently installed, and only fired for the first time that morning, all was going swimmingly. Godliman was just as reliable with the fresh magazines so Smith no longer worried when they were coming to the end of a drum. And even though the armourer had wanted to fine-tune the sights, it was clear they were getting results.

Mixing it with the E-boat earlier had been disquieting, but that danger was being left in their wake. Now there was just the trawler to deal with and Smith found it hard to take any enemy looking so much like a child's toy seriously.

They might not sink her, but he and Lenny were making the Germans keep their heads down, as was shown by the standard of return fire. He ducked only slightly as a further barrage passed nearby, then sent a firm rat-tat-tat of shells directly at the gun position responsible. That would give them something to think about. If they wanted to silence him, they'd have to try a lot harder.

* * *

Deeper inside *194*, Jelly was less assured. The W/T had remained silent for some time, as had R/T; it was as if no one was communicating anymore – or at least not communicating with him.

Jelly only vaguely recalled the earlier incident and could not begin to guess how he came to be on the deck where the first

306

officer found him. Yet, though he must have let everyone down, he felt no guilt, just an odd and pleasing calm.

194 had been in action a fair time, with him being thrown about like a pea in a whistle while the sound of their own gunfire was pretty constant. And they had taken hits in return; several enemy shells had struck them forward, or so he thought. He really should check the boat remained sound with no fire started. But Jelly had not moved, and neither did he intend to. It was as if his final combat – as this must be – had rendered him numb.

He remembered Bishop, a previous shipmate, reacting similarly and had heard about others from different flotillas. One day they were there, the next they weren't, and, despite speculation, no one really knew where they went. But Jelly sensed he would soon discover, along with what measures the Navy held in place for just such an eventuality.

The skipper would send in a report that set the wheels in motion. It almost happened with the old doctor in Plymouth, when Jelly was clever enough to disguise his condition; he wondered now if that really had been sensible after all. Whatever, he would be taken away; away from the boat, from the flotilla – from *Wasp*; away from everything. But, most of all, away from Annie. And that would be the part that hurt the most.

Chapter Thirty-One

The first torpedo struck when *194* was finally free of the VP's clutches. Anderson noticed it immediately; a billowing cloud of water and steam erupting on the starboard side of the nearest merchant. The stern gun fell silent and she veered off course, her bows turning for France as if in some wild attempt to gain safety. Then a second, internal, explosion followed, the collier slowed visibly, and her ultimate destination became clear.

"Port ten!"

There was no time for comment, Harris had to take evasive action; *194* was in danger of ploughing straight into the doomed hull.

Which, Anderson knew, was just one of several factors he must consider. Though they were clear of the VP, the sudden sinking would act as a rallying cry for nearby escorts while it also meant at least one of Rooke's boats was in the area. Harris should make sure they made a clean getaway, whilst also checking the other MTBs were equally safe. And then a further torpedo hit the next merchant in line.

"Meet her, midships."

Now the cat was definitely amongst the pigeons, although Harris' voice remained as strong and steady as ever. But Anderson was far less comfortable; this second strike meant every warship in the convoy would be heading in their direction. Surely they must now disregard the torpedo boats; *194* would be lucky to save herself.

For a while all went well; the VP was lost in their wash, and they could pass the sinking hulk of the first collier without attracting further attention. With the weather deteriorating by the second there would be shelter in the nearby squalls. Then, and from just such a hiding place, the E-boat reappeared.

She was close enough to their port beam for them all to see and, without waiting for permission or even announcing the enemy's presence, Gibson opened up, sending a stream of tracer towards her.

"What the hell?" Harris began, then, "Hard starboard rudder; maximum revs!"

It was a brutal turn but necessary. Even in the current conditions their presence should have been noticed, yet Gibson's actions had removed all doubt.

The E-boat was not travelling fast; *194* quickly straightened, then extended her lead, and might yet gain safety. A barrage of green landed off her port quarter, but the enemy was being left in her wake. Ahead, the second stricken collier was beginning her final voyage, although enough of the hull remained to act as a screen. Harris made for it and, only when they were close to colliding, did he correct the turn, allowing them to scrape past the sinking vessel.

But the E-boat was in pursuit and picking up speed; soon she began to gain. Her streamlined prow gave a minimum of spray and was the perfect target for Smith's Oerlikon. Yet despite a succession of shots sweeping her foredeck, she did not slow, while the forward-facing gun proved equally immune and, as she crept up on *194*'s port quarter, began to speak in return.

Seeing this, Harris ordered a tight turn to starboard that continued until his command was approaching the second stricken coaster once more. The E-boat's longer hull was less manoeuvrable and, when the chase resumed, she had fallen back considerably. *194* remained in range, however, and the German's shells soon began to bite.

The first destroyed her CSA gear, although the British gunboat's speed remained unaltered. At the Oerlikon, Smith knew he was fighting for his life and held a steady bead on the ever-approaching enemy, while Godliman was equally solid and changed magazines with his customary efficiency.

For upwards of a minute it was almost an equal contest, with both sides exchanging fire and causing minor damage. One of the gunboat's engine room ventilators was sent spinning while she, in turn, raised visible sparks from her enemy's armoured plating. Then the E-boat struck lucky; a series of lower blows entered *194*'s hull and her starboard wing engine fell silent.

The sudden loss of power caused her to slow and veer dangerously towards the sinking collier, forcing Phillips at the helm to correct, and throwing Smith's aim. Red tracer flew wildly but the E-boat continued her relentless fire while the lead gained

309

from their recent turn was quickly swallowed.

Back in control, Smith sent a stream of shells directly at the enemy's forward gun which immediately fell silent. Several seconds passed without return fire and he was able to exchange a quick grin with Godliman. Then the E-boat fell away to port, her heavier aft ordnance came into play, and *194*'s stern received a thorough pounding.

Smith and Godliman were quick to fall. Their gun, several hundredweight of machined metal, was struck by a barrage of shells that made equally short work of their tender bodies. Further shots were taken lower down with several more entering the gunboat's cramped engine room where her centre Packard was also struck.

Robbed of both speed and hydraulic power, and with the one remaining engine struggling to keep her on the plane, *194* was in serious trouble. The E-boat promptly straightened to resume the chase and, though Smith and Godliman's final act had robbed her of forward fire, she could more than double the gunboat's now pedestrian pace. On closing to less than five hundred yards she turned once more, allowing her aft 37mm cannon a second chance and this time the damage was more concentrated.

Watching from the bridge, Anderson sensed this was the end. The E-boat quickly turned back to resume her pursuit but it could not be long before she closed again. And when she did, and her aft cannon was given free rein once more, *194* would be finished.

* * *

In the W/T office, Jelly was almost in a trance, yet losing control earlier had left him with a feeling of release that was welcome, if mildly disconcerting.

The boat was under fire; he knew that. Shots were striking her hull – her deck – her superstructure. *194* would soon be destroyed; indeed, she might blow at any moment, like so many he had known, yet it did not trouble him. And neither was he concerned when the first engine failed. It was as if his previous fears were worse in thought than reality, which made no sense at all.

A whistle from the bridge voice pipe brought him back to

the real world. It was the captain wanting him to alert other vessels. Switching to R/T, Jelly quickly announced their situation to any nearby British boats. He only had a rough position, but it would be enough. As he finished, Johnston, the SO, came on and Jelly patched him through to the bridge, though continued to monitor the call.

"Okay, Bobbo, I hear you and am close by."

Jelly winced as the boat took more hits. The desk light dimmed, then died, and for several seconds he was in darkness before power returned with a surge, causing the transmitter to blow.

Instinctively he grabbed for his box of small spares. It took less than thirty seconds to replace the burnt-out fuse, but by then they had received further hits to the stern and lost another engine. And then more shots landed almost immediately above Jelly's head, and he knew the bridge had been struck.

The receiver soon warmed, and Johnston was still talking but there was no response from either of *194*'s officers. Jelly blew down the speaking tube but either the captain had forgotten to close the flap, or the pipe itself was ruptured, and he thought he knew which. He broke into Johnston's call.

"Telegraphist here, sir. I've lost contact with the bridge."

Johnston was unfazed. "Very well," he said. "I see an E by a sinking ship; I'm guessing you're with that little lot and am heading your way. Be a good chap and tell the captain."

Jelly swallowed; it was a direct order and one he would have liked to obey. Yet though he was feeling better, the thought of going on deck – and especially the bridge – felt like a step too far.

"Do you read me, *194*?"

"Yes, sir. I'll advise the captain."

"Very good. And tell him to watch out, we're closing fast."

Jelly ended the call and drew breath. He could tell they were no longer running under one engine; another was back online although it appeared to be spluttering. The boat was also beginning to weave; whether that was intentional or not was hard to tell.

Then he raised himself and started for the bridge. And whatever he might find there.

311

* * *

Gibson usually enjoyed sparring with the enemy. Firing two powerful machine guns at the government's expense was invigorating in the extreme and brought a feeling closer to satisfaction than was usually found elsewhere. Consequently, he felt no guilt at his unauthorised attack on the E-boat, indeed that particular emotion had always been a stranger. However, the silencing of their centre engine did trouble him. The subsequent loss of hydraulic power caused his Vickers' mounts to seize leaving the weapons almost useless and the sudden switch from hunter to hunted was not to his liking.

The enemy was closing off their starboard quarter so, being in the port turret gave him a measure of protection. And, when in an outright chase, the Germans were unable to fire forward. But everything changed when the E-boat fell away, and that terrible rear cannon came to life. Laurel and Hardy had already fallen; he and Daly would probably be next.

In a seventy-foot wooden boat stuck several miles out at sea there was nowhere to hide, while knowing the main fuel store lay beneath his feet gave little comfort; he knew only too well that gunboats blew up with depressing regularity.

He considered jumping overboard; it might save him from an explosion, but on such a night there would be little chance of rescue. So what? Wait for the next shell, the one that either found him, or several hundred gallons of high-octane petrol?

Gibson dithered; his cork life jacket should keep him afloat, but it would be a slow death and probably painful; not his cup of tea at all. But neither was being blown to pieces – or worse, a simple fire. He'd seen enough poor blighters burn alive and had no wish to become one.

In most predicaments he could usually find a measure of control and often an advantage. Even his spell in clink had been put to good use; he'd learned much and made useful acquaintances while being drafted into the Navy opened up no end of fresh opportunities. Yet Gibson was finally out of options.

He felt helpless and at the mercy of something far larger, far more deadly; something determined to have its way: something he could not fight. He remembered the satisfaction of placing others in similar positions and, though there was no

312

regret, did feel a measure of empathy. Another shell struck, this time further aft where a few remnants of Smith and Godliman still clung to the deck. For them it was over, but his great adventure was yet to begin and, for probably the first time in his life, Gibson knew what it was to be afraid.

* * *

Phillips was dead, struck by one of several shells that also made a mess of the bridge fittings though miraculously missed Anderson. Harris had been hit, however, and now leant against a bulkhead, one hand thrust into his torn clothing to stop the bleeding from his chest. The coxswain's broken body lay in an untidy pile beneath the wheel, forcing Anderson to ease it to one side with his foot before taking control.

"Set her weaving, Number One," Harris said. "It's our only chance."

They were back under two engines; Carter and his lot must have worked miracles below. But both were wings; *194* still lacked hydraulics, and strong arms were needed just to keep her on course. Yet she could also be manoeuvred, provided he had the strength. Anderson took a firmer grip on the wheel and, closing his mind to its slippery dampness, eased it firmly to port.

"Is this as fast as we can go?" Harris asked.

Anderson hauled the boat back to starboard. "We only have the wing engines," he said, "and one keeps cutting out."

There were no gauges on the Elco's upper steering position. Instead, a small screen gave sight of the oversized instruments mounted in the wheelhouse below. But the glass was now a mass of tiny cracks and Anderson's only measure of engine speed was what he could hear above the sound of driving rain.

"What of the enemy?" His arms ached and sweat was gathering on his forehead.

Harris looked back. "Still gaining – no wait, I think she's about to veer once more."

Anderson heaved the wheel again as a shower of green tracer passed overhead.

Another turn, this time catching Harris by surprise, forcing him to step on the remains of their coxswain as he steadied himself. Anderson gritted his teeth; his shoulders throbbed, and the rain was increasing; surely this could not last much longer.

"Take her to starboard next time!" Harris had pushed himself alongside and was shouting directly into his ear.

Anderson looked around. "Not too predictable?"

"We must keep heading away from the convoy."

Yes, that made sense. Anderson strained at the wheel again. With a couple of merchants already hit, the E-boat's captain would not wish to stray too far from his remaining charges. The convoy must already be a considerable distance behind and heading in the opposite direction.

"Now to port."

Anderson obediently turned the boat and was rewarded by a flurry of tracer landing off their starboard beam. Their only hope was to reach the point where danger to the German convoy outweighed the destruction of one minor British warship.

Yet the E-boat was proving determined, and *194*'s remaining Packards were starting to struggle. Anderson braced himself before swinging the helm once more, then over corrected and threw the boat in the opposite direction. He snatched a quick look aft.

The E-boat was closer than ever and would have been well within the reach of Gibson and Daly's redundant Vickers. He turned back and wrenched at the wheel again, just as another wave of tracer passed overhead; it only needed a slight reduction in elevation and *194* would be sharing Hopgood's fate.

Yet this time Anderson thought he saw red trails amongst the green. The captain also noticed and was looking back.

"It's a gunboat, Number One!" Harris gasped. "And British by the looks of her!"

Anderson chanced a glance himself, but nothing had changed; if anything, the E-boat was closer. Then something beyond the German caught his eye.

"Looks like Johnston." It was Harris again. "And one more, probably the other MGB that was delayed."

"Bell," Anderson said.

"That's right, Dinger Bell."

Harris' use of the nickname was so out of character that, despite the situation, Anderson grinned. And then, with horrible insight, he sensed hysteria lay dangerously close. He forced the helm to port.

"Yes, that's Johnston!" Harris said as Anderson strained to correct the turn.

Quite what the new arrivals could do was another matter. Both lacked decent forward-facing weapons although their turret gunners were already sweeping the German with tracer. Anderson heaved the helm to starboard. Johnston and Bell had shown the sense to separate and so divide the enemy's aft firepower. But now it was more important than ever to maintain this erratic course while every foot took them further from the convoy. Another turn, then another after that...

Eventually, it proved too much; the E-boat fell away to port and, in a flurry of spray and foam, turned back for the convoy. Anderson watched her go and drew a deep sigh. They were not out of the mire by a long way, *194* could still sink while the damage already received might yet trigger an explosion.

"Looks like they've saved our bacon," he said, and Harris nodded sagely.

"Must say, I never thought I'd be glad to see Buster Johnston."

* * *

Jelly's eyes were accustomed to the light below so he could see little in the gloom of night. Something at the top of the bridge ladder was blocking his way, but he had already climbed high enough to make out the captain. Encouraged by this, he roughly pushed the thing to one side before clambering further up and onto the duckboards.

His eyesight was adjusting, and he paused for a moment to take in the damage. Nearly all the fittings and fixtures were wrecked and every surface was littered with shards of metal and slivers of glass. Both officers were alive, however; the captain half stood, half leant against the aft bulkhead while Anderson was at the wheel; where Phillips, the coxswain, had got to was anyone's guess. At that moment the boat gave a lurch as one of their engines stuttered then died.

"May as well shut down the other, Number One," the captain said, before turning to Jelly. "Is there a problem, Tel'?"

"Message from the SO, sir," Jelly said. "He's sighted us and is closing fast."

315

"Already here, Tel'," Anderson told him.

"And just in the nick of time," the captain agreed. "But why the personal visit?"

"Speaking tube's fractured, sir, and the repeater's US."

"Aldis is gone as well." The captain was clearly injured and in pain; Jelly's heart went out to him. "Do you have R/T?"

"Yes, sir."

"Then tell the SO we're unable to proceed under our own power: if he could provide a tow it would be appreciated."

"A tow, sir. Very good."

Jelly instinctively touched his forehead as he turned to go, and it was then that he saw the horribly disfigured body of Phillips, their late coxswain. It must have been in the way before and now barred his return to the W/T office. For a moment he hesitated, then a stronger impulse took control and he moved it to one side before squeezing past and continuing down to the wheelhouse.

* * *

Anderson was once more on the bridge. *194* had been taken under tow, though at a slower pace than last time; Johnston's boat may have been fast but even three supercharged Packards lacked the raw power of a destroyer. Of the convoy there was no sign and, with her own engines silent, the gunboat felt oddly peaceful. But he could not rest; *194* was still in a bad way, as were many of her crew.

After summoning support from the SO, Jelly had returned and together they helped the captain down to the wheelhouse. There he was laid out on a makeshift bed of oilskins and Anderson injected a syrette of morphine. The drug brought instant torpor allowing them to cut away his torn goon suit.

It was a shallow injury but widespread, covering much of the chest and, once exposed, bled profusely. But two packs of field dressings stemmed the flow and, when enough strapping was added, Anderson felt he could be left.

The first place he needed to visit was the engine room and, as he clambered into the cramped space, Anderson was immediately struck by the changes. Only a rumble from their generator broke the silence while wide and savage gashes to deckhead and hull added cool air and refreshing rain to what was

316

usually a hot and hostile environment.

And Carter was not there to meet him; instead, his body had been placed neatly to one side by the need for space. Anderson glanced at it, noting the man must have died instantly, then turned to Pickering, calmly addressing a fuel leak on the centre engine.

"We was struck a number of times." The mechanic spoke slowly as if mildly stunned, although he obviously had his wits about him. "First didn't do much damage, just winged Billy here." He nodded to Newman, currently adjusting the generator's carburettor with one hand while the other was stuffed into his overall as an improvised sling. "Then they hit us square on and I thought that were it. We lost the starboard wing and some of the electrics, but Mr Carter were at the switchboard and got the lights back."

Pickering paused and seemed to be taking stock before continuing. "Then the centre mill were hit, though we'd sorted the starboard wing by then and were thinking of ways to power the hydraulics through it when they got us the third time. And that's what killed Mr Carter."

"You couldn't have done more," Anderson said.

"Maybe you're right." The mechanic nodded silently. "Though it'll be strange without the governor."

Moving forward, Anderson next inspected the living spaces. Shells had entered in several places and, had *194*'s structure been stronger, more would probably have detonated. As it was, several unexploded rounds rolled about his feet as he made his way to the mess deck. That was also wrecked, but generally safe. A quick look aft told him nothing more; much of the damage had been visible from the bridge or below, only the Oerlikon, standing defiant though misshapen, stood out. Bandstand and depression rail were missing as was every piece of splinter matting, and the rain had finally washed away all trace of Smith or Godliman.

Then, after checking on Harris – still unconscious and being cared for by Jelly – he returned to the bridge. Even in a boat powered by another, and despite the presence of their late coxswain on the duckboards, it seemed the logical place to be. And it was from there that he finally caught sight of the entrance to Dover Harbour.

317

Chapter Thirty-Two

The lights came on to a chorus of curses and groans.

"Alright my lads, no cause for alarm. Everyone stays in their beds!"

Pickering was the first to surface. "Haddaway man, we were only just getting down to kip!"

"Sure." Daly also raised himself from his pillow. "And haven't we been out half the night battling with the Hun?"

The Regulating Petty Officer was now fully in the room, with two younger patrolmen by his side while a pair of blue-raincoated civil policemen stood self-consciously by the door. "We just come for the one of you," he announced. "Rest can stay where they are. Which is Gibson?"

"You're standing by him," Pickering said, and the elderly officer looked to the nearest bunk.

"Reginald Arthur Gibson?" he asked. Gibson was awake but half hidden by his bed sheet.

"I might be."

"Gather your things, you're coming with us."

He raised himself onto one arm but didn't attempt to leave the bed. "What's this about?"

"This is about your activities of late, sunshine," the petty officer told him. "Some of which 'as broken military law, and some civil. We're going to find out which is which and decide who hands out the punishment."

"You're kidding." Gibson looked around for support. "Like Paddy says, we're just back from a shout; half our lot were killed last night; ain't you got no respect?"

"Are you coming, or do we have to carry you?"

Both patrolmen were a good sixteen stone and clearly able to handle themselves. Gibson swore once, then thrust back the covers and swung his legs out. "I calls it a bleedin' liberty."

"Calls it what you like, we ain't leavin' without you."

The petty officer glanced about the half-empty room. Both Daly and Pickering looked back, although Jelly remained under the covers and did not meet his eye. The other beds were empty and the old man's attention returned to Gibson.

"May as well take all your clobber, you'll be gone a while."

Gibson paused in the act of collecting his duffel bag. "You think so?"

"Son, I'm certain."

The exchange of looks lasted no time at all; Gibson knew himself beaten. Soon he was slipping on trousers and tunic then lacing up his boots. Finally, he picked up his hat and bag.

"Well, I guess I'll be seeing you, maties," he said.

There was no response from his shipmates. The two patrolmen stepped forward and took an arm each, one hand grasping Gibson below the shoulder, the other his wrist.

"Where's the rest of your lot, then?" the petty officer asked as his prisoner was led away.

"One's injured, the rest didn't make it," Pickering replied.

"I'm sorry to hear it." Once more the elderly eyes surveyed the room, barely hesitating as they encountered Jelly. Gibson was almost gone now, and the old man turned to follow. "But glad we got this one," he added.

"And welcome to him, so you are," the Irishman said.

The lights went out, the door closed and for a moment there was silence. And then Daly spoke again.

"Good riddance to bad rubbish."

* * *

"Better tell me all about it, Number One," Harris said when Anderson was finally admitted.

"They said you weren't to be excited. Isn't there something about an operation shortly?"

"Seems I'm carrying shrapnel the Germans might want back," Harris agreed. "I didn't get a thing to eat for all of yesterday and must say I'm starving."

The ward was filled to capacity and its other patients were being served breakfast; the scent of fresh toast was overpowering, and Anderson decided his duty was to distract Harris.

"I couldn't get to you until today," he said. "There was a lot to see to with the boat; Wellington Dock were reluctant to take her."

"It'll be a big job; do you think they'll cope?"

Anderson shrugged. "At least they can make her seaworthy enough to transfer to a larger yard."

Harris nodded. "She'll be gone some time."

"Undoubtedly." The captain looked better than when Anderson last saw him yet was clearly far from well. "And so will you, by the looks of things," he said.

"That's what they say," Harris agreed. "And what about yourself?"

"Me?"

"While I'm getting fit, you may as well carry on."

Anderson collected a nearby chair and sat down. "The base captain did mention something about a spell at *St Christopher*'s..."

Harris sighed. "Brookie tries that on everyone. But training's not for you, not yet." He paused. "It might be the time to consider a command of your own. You should apply – I'd back you."

"You're forgetting the mess I made bringing *194* in after Christmas."

"I remember you seeing a poorly armed and under-fuelled boat back in the middle of winter," Harris said. "Just as I remember you spotting those E-boats, then signalling their location to Dover Command before tailing them for several miles. And then there was that wounded gunner you pulled from the water. To my mind you've the makings of a first-rate captain."

"Even without a captain's 'presence'?" Anderson grinned.

"A captain's presence, as you call it, did little to stop Gibson letting off and alerting that E-boat."

"I guess not," Anderson admitted. "But command's hardly something I'd considered."

"Well do. Not that I wouldn't have you straight back as my number one." He raised one eyebrow. "Brooks can't hold out on the offer of a flotilla forever..."

"And by the time you're back, it should be waiting."

Harris gave a weak smile. "I'd like to think so. But if not, I wouldn't mind staying a little longer under Johnston."

"Really?"

"It's down to him that we made it back at all." Harris was starting to sound more tired now, but Anderson was loath to interrupt. "And you have to admit, the old boy's come round quite a bit since we joined his mob."

To Anderson's mind, Johnston wasn't the only one to have made changes. "I suppose you'll be going back to your parents," he said. "To convalesce, I mean. Midhurst, wasn't it?"

"They'll have to wait; I intend staying in Dover. There's someone here who'll do me a lot more good."

"Someone?"

"I might not have mentioned her," Harris looked away. "A Wren," he added, his voice now definitely fading, "though it's nothing serious."

Anderson was only mildly surprised; for Harris to have found a mate explained a lot.

"Jelly did well," he muttered.

"Jelly?" Anderson repeated, and now he was definitely on the back foot. Their telegraphist was one of several problems still to be addressed; in fact, he was already late for the appointment.

"Yes, kept us in touch, despite the circumstances." It was now more of a mumble. "And I hear he looked out for me on the way back."

"We're ready for you, Lieutenant Commander."

The arrival of the nursing sister saved Anderson from having to reply.

"We shouldn't keep him long," she added as a porter appeared and made the bed ready to be moved. "You'll be able to visit later this evening."

"Don't you bloody dare," Harris said, rallying suddenly. Then, turning to the nurse. "He's a girl in Dover who'll make far more attractive company."

"I'll see you later – tomorrow perhaps," Anderson said.

"Do that, Number One." Harris' bed was being wheeled through the double doors. "But think about what I said. A training spot would be a waste, you should be out there doing it for real."

* * *

Spring was firmly in place. The trees were properly green and there was blossom on many while birds competed noisily for nesting material and mates. But Anderson had stayed too long at the hospital and was late.

They were to meet in the park; a neutral spot. It was Jelly's

321

idea, and he would be bringing his young lady with him. Anderson had no objection to either; as far as he was concerned the rating had more than made up for any momentary lapse in his duty. But in Harris' absence it would be down to him to write the sitrep; a record of the previous night's events that would be countersigned by the flotilla SO and Commander Brooks. One whiff of whatever seized Jelly would see him sent straight to the PMO for examination, something Anderson had no wish to be responsible for.

The park's tea garden appeared ready for the coming season, yet the small building had remained shuttered since its owner fled to the West Country at the start of hostilities. Some outside tables remained, however, and Jelly and a Wren driver were seated at one.

Anderson approached and took a bench facing them.

"I'm sorry to be late, there was a hold up at the hospital."

"Would that be the captain?" Jelly asked and Anderson nodded. "They're operating at the moment."

"Will he be okay?"

"They think so, but you know how these things can go. And Bill Newman's got a broken arm."

"I'd heard," Jelly said.

"So, how's it with you, Tel'?" Anderson asked.

"I seem to be okay, thank you, sir. Slept like a baby most of yesterday, which were a surprise; first decent kip for a while."

"Are you going to report him?" the girl, who had not been introduced, demanded. Anderson considered her.

There was no trace of friendliness in her eyes though it was clear she was there with, and intended to speak for, Jelly. But this was much more than a prisoner's friend; Anderson sensed they were holding hands under the table.

"With the captain injured and *194* needing to be slipped there was a lot of important stuff to do," he said. "I've not had chance to even start on the action report."

"And what happened to Dave isn't important?"

"I didn't say that." Anderson spoke more coldly. "He probably should be referred for a full medical assessment."

"Do you know what that means?"

"Not in detail, but he'll be cared for."

"Well, that's kind, I'm sure."

Anderson sighed; yesterday truly was a blur; in Harris' absence it seemed as if he had twice as much to do, while Eve spent most of the day with her wounded brother. They'd managed a couple of hours together later, but he'd missed breakfast that morning. "Look, I don't know if you realise it, but your young man could be up on a charge."

She stiffened and Jelly gave a faint groan.

"For what?" The girl was first to recover. "For almost getting himself killed?"

"For not carrying out his duty when ordered." Anderson had been about to say something else but changed his mind at the last minute. "We were depending on that signal getting through to Dover Command," he added. "Without it, there'd have been no attack on the enemy convoy."

"From what I gather he had every intention of sending your precious message," she said. "And did – it were just a bit delayed."

"A delay that could have cost lives."

"Maybe, but it were done. And, from what Dave tells me, he did well afterwards."

"Oh yes," Anderson agreed. "He did very well indeed."

"Then you needn't say anything." The tone was definite, although he could now see a measure of appeal in those eyes.

"I haven't decided yet," he said. "Has such a thing happened before?"

"A couple of times," Jelly said. "Maybe more, though not so bad. It all started after St Nazaire; Commander Ryder's boat was right in the middle of things; I didn't find it easy."

"I see," Anderson said, and to some extent he did.

"I've been alright since the other night, though," he added. "And I know it sounds strange after so short a time, but somehow I don't think it'll happen again."

"I'm no expert, but this sort of thing doesn't just disappear."

Jelly shrugged. "Maybe not." He rested lightly against the girl. "But being with Annie helps."

"I'm sure it does," Anderson said. "So, what do you intend?"

"That depends on you," the girl reminded him. "Report Dave and he goes away – we all know that. And he'll be gone a long time," she added. "Even if I ever get to see him again, it'll never be the same – *he* won't be the same."

"I can't lie," Anderson said.

"You won't have to, just don't tell all the truth."

"And what if I say nothing? Then David goes back to sea, and it happens again?"

"I'm not going back," Jelly sounded definite.

"You're not?" Anderson was surprised. "You mean you'll be putting in for a transfer?"

"I can," Jelly said. "I've served in Coastal Forces a fair while and my skills are readily transferable."

That was certainly the case; *194* had been blessed with a fine telegraphist who was also a first-rate technician, but such riches could not last forever.

"There's a course, training to work with RDF," the girl said. "We've been considering it a while; it's right up his street."

"And shore based," Jelly added. "In Portsmouth but at the Signal School – a non-combatant role."

"From what you say these attacks can occur on land."

Jelly went to reply but the girl was ahead of him. "In which case he'll deal with them," she said. "Do you realise all the time Dave's served with your lot he's been seasick?"

"That's not unusual."

"Maybe, but he never let it affect his work. I'd say that takes a special kind of bravery, not one they gives out medals for, p'raps, but bravery nonetheless."

Anderson nodded; she had a point.

"And now he's done his bit there's no shame in stepping back; some might say he deserves that." Suddenly her eyes came alight. "Some might say it's being one of your so-called Glory Boys that caused his problems in the first place."

"Do you think you'll be alright?" Anderson was now speaking directly to Jelly.

"I think I'll be fine, sir," he said. "And'll have more chance of getting back to normal on land, than at sea. Or in one of them institutions."

Anderson was not going to argue that one. "I suppose it's the right time," he said, "what with the boat being out of commission. Though there's no certainty you'll be accepted."

"It'd be more likely with your recommendation," the girl said.

Anderson sat back. "I'm not sure and frankly can't decide now. I might have to talk this over."

"Don't mention it to his captain," she insisted. "Once he knows, Dave'll be straight off to the funny farm."

"I wasn't thinking of the captain," Anderson said. "Let me discuss it with someone else. Someone who'll probably be on your side."

"Very well." She seemed resigned now, although Anderson could still see the worry in her eyes. "Only remember this, Dave's given a lot for your precious set up – not as much as some p'raps but, to my mind, more'n enough."

"What are you saying?" Anderson asked.

"I'm saying you can't have him no more," she said, before turning to look at Jelly and there was a faint smile. "From now on, he's mine."

Author's Notes

Apart from there being no seventy-foot Elco gunboat at St Nazaire, the attack took place very much as I have described. My interest was from the naval angle, however, so it was depicted from that point of view. Many of the incidents portrayed, such as the shortage of Oerlikon shells, Pike accompanying Ryder ashore armed with a broken bayonet, the lone gunner aboard *Campbeltown*, and Ryder's distress signal failing, did take place. Several of the characters were also drawn from history and deserve further mention.

In the same year as the raid on St Nazaire, **Commander Robert 'Red' Ryder** went on to take part in an attack on the port of Dieppe. Though largely unsuccessful, the operation proved useful when planning the D-Day landings. He was promoted to post captain after the war and appointed Naval attaché in Oslo. After leaving the Navy he served as a Member of Parliament for five years. He died in 1986. For his actions at St Nazaire, he was awarded the Victoria Cross.

After being unable to find a homeward-bound launch, **Lieutenant Colonel Augustus Charles Newman, 'Colonel Charles'**, fought a gallant rear-guard action before his eventual capture. After the war, he continued in the Territorial Army, subsequently commanding 21st (Artists) Special Air Service Regiment and serving as Deputy Lieutenant of Essex. In 1959 he was appointed Major in the Engineer and Railway Staff Corps. He died in 1972. For his actions at St Nazaire, he was awarded the Victoria Cross.

Lieutenant Commander Sam Beattie, *Campbeltown*'s final captain, was captured when Rodier's launch, ML*170*, was sunk. At the moment his late ship exploded he was being interrogated by a German officer who assured him the damage he had caused was minor and would be swiftly repaired. He spent the remainder of the war in various prison camps and was made post on his return, spending the rest of his professional life as a Royal Naval officer. He died in 1975. For his actions at St Nazaire, he was awarded the Victoria Cross.

Able Seaman William 'Bill' Savage, gunner aboard MGB*314*, became another recipient of the Victoria Cross. The official citation noted the award was made in recognition 'not only of his gallantry and devotion to duty but also of the valour shown by many others, unnamed, in Motor Launches, Motor Gun Boats and Motor Torpedo Boats, who carried out their duty in entirely exposed positions against enemy fire at very close range.' In 1990 his widow was forced to sell his awards; the Coastal Forces Veterans Association helped to raise part of the £55,000 needed to purchase them for the National Maritime Museum at Greenwich. They have since been moved and are now displayed in his home town of Smethwick.

After losing an eye, **Sub-Lieutenant Robert 'Micky' Wynn** was taken to Marlag Nord POW camp near Bremen from where he attempted to escape. Subsequently he was moved to Colditz before being repatriated on medical grounds. Hearing that Bill Lovegrove, his former chief motor mechanic, was still held captive, Wynn joined the relieving force and was reunited with the man who had saved his life. At the end of hostilities, he returned to farming, later becoming High Sheriff of Merionethshire, and succeeding his father as Lord Newborough. He died in 1998. For his actions at St Nazaire, he was awarded the Distinguished Service Cross.

Lieutenant Dunstan Curtis went on to serve with the 30AU (assault unit) led by Commander Ian Fleming. Fleming later credited him as a partial inspiration for his fictional character James Bond. After training as a lawyer, Curtis later stood for election as a Member of Parliament. He died in 1983. For his actions at St Nazaire, he was awarded the Distinguished Service Cross.

Not mentioned in this book, but worthy of note, was **Sergeant Thomas Durrant** of the Royal Engineers. Durrant manned a Lewis gun aboard ML306 (Lieutenant Ian Henderson RNVR) during the unequal fight with the German warship *Jaguar* (Kapitänleutnant Friedrich-Karl Paul). On two occasions he ignored Paul's call to surrender and later died of his wounds. Kapitänleutnant Paul singled him out for his bravery, and Durrant remains one of the few to have received the Victoria Cross on the recommendation of an enemy officer.

Les Fenton, who captained ML156, acted in over sixty films. After convalescing from injuries sustained at St Nazaire he retired from active service. After the war, he took to directing and died in 1978. War correspondent **Gordon Holman** became known for placing himself in situations of extreme danger in the interest of a story. He later published several books based on his exploits.

612 officers and men from both Services took part in **Operation Chariot**, with only 228 returning to England. Of the 169 killed 105 were from the Royal Navy. 205 were held as prisoners of war and 5 commandos managed to escape to Spain, then sailed to England from Gibraltar. The explosive charges carried by HMS *Campbeltown* disabled the *Normande* dry dock for the remainder of the war, effectively preventing *Tirpitz* from entering the North Atlantic. The warship was eventually sunk by RAF Lancasters from 617 (Dambuster) Squadron.

Both of **Micky Wynn's** torpedoes eventually exploded, destroying the lock gates to the main basin and causing alarm amongst the German army. A group of labourers employed in clearing up the debris were mistaken for British commandos and shot, while several civilians were also killed in the subsequent house-to-house search of the town.

The **Special Operations Executive** was formed in the June of 1940 to carry out clandestine operations on enemy territory independent of the War Office. From April 1942, and in direct violation of the Geneva Convention, women officially began to be employed as field agents.

A brief mention of HMT *Lancastria* is made; readers wishing to learn more about her tragic loss may care to read *Lancastria* (Oldbourne, London), by my late father, Geoffrey Bond.

As a final, ironic twist, HMS *Tynedale*, the *Hunt* class escort sent to investigate U-593, sighted on the way to St Nazaire, was sunk the following year. It was in a different sea, and under a different captain but her attacker was the same submarine.

Selected Glossary

Abbots Cliff:	The nearest Y Station to HMS *Wasp* and one that directly served Dover Command. Such sites were used to monitor enemy wireless traffic. Those sent in plain language were analysed locally while coded messages were forwarded to the Admiralty and then on to the Government Code and Cypher School at Bletchley Park.
Aldis:	A form of signalling lamp.
Amatol:	A high explosive mixture of TNT and ammonium nitrate.
Anderson shelter:	A mass-produced air-raid shelter made mainly from corrugated iron. It was provided free to those with an income of less than £250 pa.
Andrew:	*(Slang)* The Navy.
BEF:	The British Expeditionary Force; part of the British Army sent to France after war had been declared on Germany.
Bob:	*(Slang)* A shilling (twelve pennies). A tanner was sixpence, florin two shillings and a quid was (and still is) one pound.
Bint:	*(Slang)* A female.
Buzz:	*(Slang)* Rumour or gossip.
Camber:	An area of Dover's eastern docks where the launches were berthed.
Carley float:	An inflatable life raft issued mainly to warships. Designed by American inventor Horace Carley (1838-1918).
Char:	*(Slang)* Tea. From the Chinese tcha.
Caisson:	A form of lock gate.
China (plate):	*(Rhyming Slang)* Mate.

Chine:	The change in angle on a hull. A 'hard' chine hull has sharp steep sides. A vessel so designed has a flat underside that creates hydrodynamic lift allowing it to rise up onto the plane at speed.
Clink:	*(Slang)* Prison. From The Clink Prison (Southwark) that closed in 1780.
Clobber:	*(Slang)* Belongings.
CMM:	Chief Motor Mechanic.
CO:	Commanding officer.
Codger:	*(Slang)* An elderly, or old fashioned, man.
Commissioned lovely:	*(Slang)* A Wren officer.
CPO:	Chief Petty Officer.
CQR:	Clyde Quick Release. An anchor designed by Geoffrey Taylor in 1933.
Crusher:	*(Slang)* A member of the Regulating Branch; the RN police force.
CSA:	Chlorosulphuric acid produces a smoke screen that can be released from the craft itself, or via a smoke float, which would 'burn' for approximately ten minutes.
Defence area:	An area designated especially at risk of invasion. Anti-tank, minefields and other defensive measures were increased and casual visitors banned.
Dobbin:	*(Slang)* Horse.
East Grinstead:	Home of the Queen Victoria Hospital which, under the directorship of Sir Archibald McIndoe, pioneered plastic and reconstructive surgery. It remains a centre of excellence in the field. During WW2 the inhabitants were so supportive of those undergoing treatment that it became known as 'the town that didn't stare'.
Five inches:	The recommended depth for baths taken in wartime England.
Geordie:	*(Slang)* One from Tyneside, North East England.
Glory boys:	*(Slang)* Common term for those serving with Coastal Forces.

Goon suit:	*(Slang)* A kapok-lined one-piece suit similar to a boiler or flying suit. See Ursula.
Guzz:	*(Slang)* Seaman's name for Plymouth, supposedly due to it being the Hindi unit of measurement equating to 36 inches (Plymouth's previous name being 'The Yard'). Occasionally Guz.
HMS *Beehive*:	Coastal Forces base in Felixstowe, Suffolk.
HMS *King Alfred*:	Initial training base for RNVR officers at Hove, Sussex.
HMS *St Christopher*:	Coastal Forces training base at Fort William Scotland.
Heads:	Toilets.
Hog Out:	*(Slang)* Clean up.
Holman projector:	A weapon using pneumatic power to fire an explosive charge. Mainly intended for anti-aircraft use, it proved ineffective and was eventually withdrawn.
Hostiles:	*(Slang)* 'Hostilities Only'; ratings called up for the duration of the war.
Insult:	*(Slang)* Seaman's name for wages.
Jakes:	*(Slang)* A toilet or W.C., usually outside and often without conventional plumbing.
Jankers:	*(Slang)* Military punishment.
Jig:	*(Slang)* The mark of a vessel or object on a radar, or RDF, screen.
Jimmy (the One):	*(Slang)* The first lieutenant.
Kip:	*(Slang)* Sleep.
Kye:	*(Slang)* A drink made from shavings of chocolate mixed with boiling water and usually heavily sweetened.
Lyons:	In 1894 Jo Lyons established one of the first chains of teashops.
MGB:	Motor Gun Boat.
ML:	Motor Launch.
Mole:	A heavy structure usually made of stone that acts as a pier.
MO:	Medical Officer.
MTB:	Motor Torpedo Boat.

NAAFI:	(pronounced naffi) The acronym for Navy, Army and Air Force Institutes, an organisation set up in 1920 to cater for servicemen and their families.
Nissen hut:	A prefabricated hut made from corrugated iron with a concrete floor.
Nous:	*(Slang)* Knowledge or common sense.
Nutty:	*(Slang)* Seaman's term for chocolate (whether it contained nuts or not).
Pentonville:	A prison in North London.
PMO:	Principal Medical Officer.
PO:	Petty officer.
Pompey:	*(Slang)* Seaman's term for Portsmouth.
Pongo:	*(Slang)* Soldier.
Prisoner's friend:	An officer that supports a defendant at court-martial.
Q-ship:	A merchant ship carrying concealed weapons to combat raiders.
Quack:	*(Slang)* Officially a fake doctor but used indiscriminately.
Rozzers:	*(Slang)* Civil police.
RNVR:	Royal Naval Volunteer Reserve, formed from the Royal Naval Volunteer Supplementary Reserve.
R/T:	Radio Telegraphy (voice).
Rubber:	*(Slang)* A loan.
Rymill:	John Rymill (1905 – 1968) Australian polar explorer.
Salt horse:	*(Slang)* A regular sea officer without specific training in a technical field, and often taken to mean one with an old-fashioned (usually pre-WW1) approach.
Saucepan (lid):	*(Rhyming Slang)* Kid.
Scot-free:	*(Slang)* To avoid punishment. (Old English; originally from the Scandinavian, 'Skat,' meaning tax.)
Sitrep:	*(Slang)* Situation report, a brief record of events.

SOE:	Special Operations Executive. Formed by Hugh Dalton in 1940, SOE was responsible for organising sabotage, espionage, and reconnaissance in occupied Europe.
SO:	Senior officer.
Straight striper:	*(Slang)* A regular RN officer. Due to the stripes denoting rank being straight (rather than 'wavy' for RNVR officers).
Syrette:	Single-use syringe usually containing a strong analgesic.
Togs:	*(Slang)* Clothes.
Trick:	*(Slang)* A watch or period of duty.
Trunk call:	A long-distance telephone call made in the same county.
TTFN:	*(Slang)* Ta Ta For Now – a catchphrase from *ITMA* (*It's That Man Again*) a BBC wireless comedy programme popular during WW2. In many ways *ITMA*'s mixture of satire and social comment paved the way for the *Goon Show*, and similar later productions. It was also one of the first to use catchphrases – which it did to great abundance. Many became adopted into everyday speech, and several feature in *Glory Boys*.
Tingle:	A wooden or metal patch used to repair the hull or deck.
Ursula:	Heavy, waxed cotton clothing derived originally from motorcycle racing wear.
US:	*(Slang/acronym)* Unserviceable.
VP:	*Vorpostenboote*. German patrol boats usually converted from fishery, or similar, vessels. Heavily armed with medium to light calibre weapons (usually 88, 40 and 20mm) which could be used against aircraft or shipping. Crewed by up to seventy men and with gun emplacements often reinforced with concrete, they were a

	formidable, if slow, opponent to Coastal Forces' craft.
Vosper:	A prominent maker of high-speed launches that was also responsible for Malcolm Campbell's record breaking *Bluebird K4*.
Wavy (Wavy Navy):	RNVR officers' stripes denoting rank were wavy, (rather than straight for regular officers).
Weights:	A popular brand of cigarette. Some maintained the title was a prophetic acronym for 'When England Invaded Germany Hitler's Troops Surrendered'.
Whaleback:	Distinctive feature in the lines of Vosper high-speed launches.
W/T:	Wireless telegraphy (Morse).
WVS:	Women's Voluntary Services; founded in 1938 the WVS recruited women to assist in air raid precautions and with general civilian support. It was noted for having no hierarchy; all members being considered of equal rank and value.
Y Station:	Dedicated monitoring sites that analysed enemy wireless traffic. Coded signals were forwarded to the Admiralty and then on to the Government Code and Cypher School at Bletchley Park.

About the Author

Alaric Bond has written for various markets including television, radio and the stage but currently focuses on historical nautical fiction with nineteen published novels, fifteen of which being in his acclaimed 'Fighting Sail' series. *Glory Boys* is the second instalment in the 'Coastal Forces' series that centres around the small ship navy of high-speed launches used during ww2.

He lives in Sussex, is married, and has two far taller sons. Apart from researching nautical history he enjoys cycling (in gumboots, rather than lycra), sailing and carpentry as well as jazz, blues, swing, and dance band music from the thirties onwards. He also plays a variety of musical instruments and collects 78 rpm records.

www.alaricbond.com

About Old Salt Press

Old Salt Press is an independent press catering to those who love books about ships and the sea. We are an association of writers working together to produce the very best of nautical and maritime fiction and non-fiction. We invite you to join us as we go down to the sea in books.

www.oldsaltpress.com

The Latest Great Reading
from Old Salt Press

Rick Spilman
Evening Gray Morning Red
A young American sailor must escape his past and the clutches of the Royal Navy, in the turbulent years just before the American Revolutionary War. In the spring of 1768, Thom Larkin, a 17-year-old sailor newly arrived in Boston, is caught by Royal Navy press gang and dragged off to HMS *Romney*, where he runs afoul of the cruel and corrupt First Lieutenant. Years later, after escaping the Romney, Thom again crosses paths with his old foe, now in command HMS *Gaspee*, cruising in Narragansett Bay. Thom must finally face his nemesis and the guns of the *Gaspee*, armed only with his wits, an unarmed packet boat, and a sand bar.

Joan Druett
Tupaia, Captain Cook's Polynesian Navigator
Tupaia sailed with Captain Cook from Tahiti, piloted the *Endeavour* about the South Pacific, and was the ship's translator. Lauded by Europeans as "an extraordinary genius", he was also a master navigator, a brilliant orator, an artist and mapmaker, and a devious politician. Winner of the New Zealand Post General Non-Fiction Prize.

V E Ulett
Blackwell's Homecoming
In a multigenerational saga of love, war and betrayal, Captain Blackwell and Mercedes continue their voyage in Volume III of Blackwell's Adventures. The Blackwell family's eventful journey from England to Hawaii, by way of the new and tempestuous nations of Brazil and Chile, provides an intimate portrait of family conflicts and loyalties in the late Georgian Age. Blackwell's Homecoming is an evocation of the dangers and rewards of desire.

Seymour Hamilton
Ellie: A Story from the World of The Astreya Trilogy

Ellie is a story about losing your way and finding it again. Ellie, the youngest navigator in the fleet, challenges the authority of her uncle Astreya, the Grand Commander. Only hours later, cannon shots cripple her boat, she falls overboard and is lost ashore. Ellie tries to return home to Matris, but unexpected friends and threatening foes intervene. As her uncle, sister, and cousins search for her, Ellie is forced to travel by foot, horseback, and land crawler to the Castle, where the Governor is fomenting war.

Ellie is the sixth book set in the world of The Astreya Trilogy.

Antoine Vanner
Britannia's Morass: The Dawlish Chronicles September - December 1884

1884: Florence Dawlish remains in Britain when her husband, Captain Nicholas Dawlish, leaves for service in the Sudan. She faces months of worry about him but she'll cope by immersing herself in welfare work for Royal Navy seamen's families at Portsmouth. It'll be a dull but worthy time . . .

. . . until the suicide of a middle-aged widow whom Florence respects. Left wealthy by her husband, this lady died a pauper, beggared within a few months, how and by whom, is not known. The widow's legal executor isn't interested and the police have other concerns. Lacking close family, she'll be soon forgotten. But not by Florence. Someone was responsible and there must be retribution. And getting justice will demand impersonation, guile and courage.

Linda Collison
Water Ghosts

Fifteen-year-old James McCafferty is an unwilling sailor aboard a traditional Chinese junk, operated as adventure-therapy for troubled teens. Once at sea, the ship is gradually taken over by the spirits of courtiers who fled the Imperial court during the Ming Dynasty, more than 600 years ago. One particular ghost wants what James has and is intent on trading places with him. But the teens themselves are their own worst enemies in the struggle for life in the middle of the Pacific Ocean. A psychological story set at sea, with historical and paranormal elements.

337

Alaric Bond
On the Barbary Coast
(The Fighting Sail Series)

Spring 1814 and, after four exhausting years on the North American Station, HMS *Tenacious* is finally heading home. With the war in Europe drawing to a close, it is even doubtful whether she will be needed again while her captain has his own reasons to reach England.

But their journey is broken by a strange encounter, and many are soon robbed of the peace they have earned as a new and particularly wicked enemy emerges, one that threatens far more than their personal safety.

With engrossing naval action and intense personal dynamics, *On the Barbary Coast* is a thriller in the best tradition of Historical Nautical Fiction.